UNTOUCHABLE

A BULLY ROMANCE

SAM MARIANO

This is a work of fiction. Names, characters, businesses, places, events and incidents are either the products of the author's imagination, or used fictitiously. Any resemblance to actual persons, living or dead, or actual events is purely coincidental.

Untouchable © 2018 by Sam Mariano

All rights reserved.

———

"I believe that love is the greatest thing in the world; that it alone can overcome hate..."

– John D. Rockefeller, Jr.

To Jen,
Thanks for being my cheerleader.

AUTHOR'S NOTE

Please, please take me seriously when I say this is a **BULLY** romance. This book contains some dark shit, and if you have sexual violence/abuse triggers, this may not be a good fit for you. I know where the *characters'* limits are, but you know your own sensitivities much better than I do.

Carter Mahoney is not a comfortable hero, and this is not always a comfortable love story. If you need safe, good-guy heroes in every romance you read, this is not the story for you. These characters have their own unique damage, needs, desires, and proficiencies, and they are seeking out partners who fit them as they are, not partners who need them to change and be something they're not. I have very much enjoyed Carter and Zoey's story, so I hope you will too, but I want to make sure I've prepared/warned you adequately. ;) Carter Mahoney is not for the faint of heart.

CHAPTER 1

HIGH SCHOOLS and small towns have a lot in common. Groups of people in their own separate tribes, forced together arbitrarily, made to coexist in order to achieve optimal pleasantness. Not everybody actually likes everyone else, but most days, that doesn't matter. Most days, you might experience at worst a tightening smile, a twinge of annoyance when someone nudges your comfort zone, challenges you just enough to wake you up and make you notice.

Most people don't like to be challenged. Most people like to be comfortable. But that moment of accidental discomfort is usually fleeting, it can be glossed over and forgotten so you can go on to have another peaceful day alongside people you don't *actually* like, and another, and another after that.

Then there are the rarer times when something too eventful to ignore happens. The kind of thing we're forced to notice; it energizes us, interrupting the comfort of our everyday monotony; it separates us, inevitably pitting some of us against others, and that's when the ugliness comes seeping out of every previously unnoticed hole. Smiles are wiped from the faces of those who liked you well enough when you didn't cause trouble, but like you a lot less once you open your mouth and say something they don't like.

I am the thing that happened in this high school, in this small town. I am the person who made people uncomfortable. I am the catalyst that shook everyone's fake friendliness and brought out their ugly, and what did I do?

I dared to speak up for myself. I dared call out someone they liked more than me for doing something wrong.

When people told me I was overreacting, when they told me to sit down and stop causing a scene, I ignored them. I didn't shut my mouth until they were so desperate to shut me up, they finally imposed consequences for wrongdoing—like they should have done from the start.

It was not a popular thing to do, standing up for myself. That's all right. I don't need people to like me; I just need them to respect me as much as common decency warrants and leave me alone the rest of the time.

The problem is, after I demanded justice and it was finally served, the harassment intensified. Knowing I was right to stand up for myself and other girls who might not want to endure this whole ordeal is one thing, but being treated like a pariah, stared at with open hostility in public, talked about when I'm in the same room, called names and ostracized at the school where I'm trying to focus on my studies during senior year… after a while, it starts to get to you.

Today has been an especially bad day. I arrived this morning to catcalls and a "Zoey the ho" chant that turned my cheeks pink with anger, then opened my locker to find lube oozing down the inside of the metal door. The book I left in my locker yesterday was ruined and I had to go through the incredibly embarrassing ordeal of going to the office and asking them to send the janitor to my locker to clean up KY jelly. Worse, the receptionist— whose son is on the football team—barely tried to stifle her smirk, apparently finding it funny that someone would squirt lube inside the vents of my locker and ruin my personal belongings.

Since dealing with all that this morning, I've been walking around in a tired state of paranoia, holding my breath before entering a new classroom, wondering what kind of fun the rest of the day has in store for me. I want to go home, but it's only lunchtime. There's no way in hell I'll go to the cafeteria. I'm not sure where to hide, though. I don't want to eat lunch in the bathroom again.

Is this what it's going to be like for the rest of the school year?

Dread weighs down on me at the exhausting thought. I head back to my newly cleaned locker to get rid of my books and grab my sack of lunch. Holding up the paper bag, I eye it with distaste. Even though the locker was cleaned, it still smells faintly of lube. Do I really want to eat a peanut butter and jelly sandwich that has been sitting in this locker all morning? It's in a paper bag, and the sandwich itself is in a Ziploc bag inside, but still...

Sighing, I shut my locker and take my brown bag to the trash can down the hall. Maybe I'll go to the vending machine and get myself a bag of chips or something instead. I don't have cash on me, but I probably have enough change in my car for chips.

The halls are emptying out. I duck into the bathroom to pee, figuring by the time I'm done everyone will be in the cafeteria and I can hit the vending machine without encountering anyone.

After I've dawdled as long as possible, washed my hands, and paused to listen for footsteps, I finally go outside and walk the empty halls toward the vending machines outside the cafeteria.

I don't make it far before I hear someone call out behind me, "Hey, Ellis."

The blood running through my veins surges with a spike of adrenaline at the sound of his voice. I turn around, the movement slow with dread. Three football players stand at the end of the hall. Shayne Sutton, Carter Mahoney, and *Jake*.

Oh shit.

Jake is supposed to stay away from me. I even had to move out of the class we had together to enforce it, but right now, instead of staying back, they all start walking toward me.

Foreboding niggles at me. Logic tells me we're at school and they can't do anything to me here, but every instinct I have compels me to run. I turn back around, my steps slow and heavy at first, then I walk as fast as I can away from them without blatantly running. I don't want them to think I'm afraid of them, even though I am. Three to one odds aren't fair to begin with, but taking into account that I'm 120lbs soaking wet, and they're three well-built jocks who have regular weight training sessions for football, I wouldn't stand a chance fighting back against them.

My gaze darts around the hallway, but there's nowhere to go that's safe. Just empty classrooms—no students, no teachers.

"What's wrong, Zoey?" Carter calls out, clearly amused. "Why are you running?"

I guess I wasn't speed-walking subtly enough.

I want to believe they're just taunting me, but I've seen the way Jake has looked at me since Coach told him he couldn't play for the rest of the season. Hell, the way *everyone* has been looking at me—like I'm the bad guy.

You don't fuck with the football players in a football town. That's the number one rule, above absolutely everything else. They are gods here, and me? I'm no one. Who am I to police the behavior of deities?

I knew the risks when I reported Jake Parsons for harassing me; I just thought it was ass-backward bullshit. My mom begged me not to make a fuss, but I refused to be silenced.

Now I'm silenced by fear—paralyzing fear. I don't know what happens if they catch up to me. Maybe nothing. Maybe they are just trying to scare me, but maybe they aren't. I don't want to find out.

"Ain't so talkative now, are you, Zo?" Jake calls out, his voice closer.

Giving up any pretense that I'm not running from them, I sprint down the hall, my heart racing. They're athletes, so they're all in better shape, all faster than I am. I don't know what to do, so I grab the door jam and hurl myself inside a darkened classroom, grabbing the door and flinging it shut. I reach to engage the lock so they can't follow me inside my makeshift sanctuary, but my heart drops.

There isn't one. There are no locks on the doors.

I turn around, grabbing a chair and preparing to try to jam it under the handle to block it, but before I can even try, the handle turns and the door opens.

Oh, no. I thought I could lock them out, but all I did was cage myself in.

Jake saunters in first, a smirk on his handsome face, his blue eyes already shining with arrogant amusement. I remember the last time he cornered me, when he was behind me and I tried to get away from him. The way he held me in place and pushed his hand inside my shirt, grabbing my breast. I told him to let me go, and he chuckled, told me we were just getting started.

Now I hold up the chair, backing away like a cornered animal. "You stay away from me," I tell him, heart in my throat. "The principal said—"

"The principal?" he interrupts, stopping to cock an eyebrow. "Fuck the principal. You know what *Coach* said, Zoey?"

My face heats up at the reality of being confronted face-to-face like this. I was pleased that Coach imposed consequences and made Jake sit out the rest of the season. The coach has a daughter just a couple years younger than me, so he *should* take a stand against the willful sexual harassment his football players are guilty of. If he cares, if they suffer consequences for their misbehavior, then they'll stop doing it.

Jake starts talking, walking closer. He's trying to intimidate me, so his pace is slow and deliberately menacing. "Coach said because you're a stupid fuckin' tattletale whore, *I'm* suspended for the rest of the season. My *senior* year. I can't play, Zoey. This goes on my record. Colleges, scholarships—you're fuckin' with my *future*. All because I grabbed your tit. Is your tit that special, Zoey?"

"I think we should take that shirt off her and see what's so great about them," Carter proposes.

Coming from someone I don't even know, the taunt is jarring. My gaze slides to Carter Mahoney, easily the most popular and celebrated guy at this school. The guys love him because he's a hell of a quarterback—and, to an extent, probably because the girls love him, too. He has dark hair they dream about running their fingers through, dark eyes they want to get lost in. Maybe it's only because of my circumstances, because of what he just said, but looking at him now, I can't help seeing a void in those dark eyes that I never noticed from a safe distance.

My grip on the chair tightens and fear travels down my spine. Shayne slides a different chair under the door handle like I considered doing. "Zoey the ho and her special tits," he says, before snickering.

"Open that door right now," I demand, my gaze jumping from guy to guy. I don't know which one is the weakest link, which one I should appeal to. They *all* seem like assholes. "Y'all can't corner me and treat me like this. We're at *school*. You'll *all* get suspended—not just from the team, but from school altogether. Think a football suspension will look bad to colleges? Imagine how that's gonna look."

"You think so?" Jake asks casually. He has the confidence of an asshole people like, and it frustrates me to no end. "See, I think what would happen in that scenario is someone would burn down your fuckin' house with you inside. Imagine all three of us off the team," he says, glancing back at his buddies with a little smile.

"What team?" Carter asks dryly. "Wouldn't be anything left."

"Exactly," Jake says easily, taking a step toward me.

That's true enough of Carter, at least. Considering how much shit I've had to deal with, it's crazy to think I'm *lucky* Jake was the one I had to go after, but if it had been Carter Mahoney, my family would have had to move.

Despite the football-crazy town I live in, I don't have much interest in the game, myself. Still, in my four years going to high school here, it has been impossible to miss the praise and wonder the mere mention of Carter evokes in people—the excitement in their voices and the stars in their eyes when they talk about the starting quarterback and his promising football career. Everyone says he has a golden arm, the form and instincts of a natural athlete. The whole team is built around him. We don't win games because we have an amazing football team; we win because we have Carter Mahoney.

Personally, I would rather be able to sleep at night knowing the girls in town are safe from assholes forcing unwanted attention on them, but the most vocal people in this town seem to prefer winning football games.

I jab the chair at Jake as he moves closer to me. I don't like violence, I have no desire to fight with any of them, but I'll bash him right in the face with the chair legs if he tries to touch me again.

"Here's what I think," Jake says, reaching forward and grabbing the chair right out of my hand. It's so easy for him to disarm me; clearly, I need to work on my upper body strength. I stumble forward trying to hold onto it, then lurch back quickly, trying to put more space between myself and them. "I think you're gonna tell everyone you lied," Jake states. "That you were pissed off at me and you overreacted."

"I'm not going to do that," I tell him. "I didn't lie. You touched me, I asked you to stop, and you wouldn't. You laughed. I was deeply uncomfortable, and you thought it was funny. You behaved like a douchebag, and you deserved to be punished."

Irritation flashes in his turbulent blue eyes. "You act like I fuckin' *raped you*, Ellis. All I did was feel you up."

"I didn't *want* you to. I said *no*, I told you to stop, and you didn't listen," I tell him, my eyes widening.

He tosses the chair aside and it skids across the dingy linoleum floor. "Yeah, well, I don't think the punishment quite fit the crime. I think if you're gonna ruin my motherfuckin' life, I should get a little more out of it."

With every step he takes forward, I've taken one back. Now I bump up against the window. There's nowhere else to go, and he's right on top of me. I look behind him at the other two guys, searching for some sign of uncertainty on either of their faces, some glint of guilt or sympathy, anything I can appeal to in order to maybe get some help.

There's nothing. The guys stick together. In their delusional minds, I've betrayed *them* by speaking up for myself.

In the whole town's eyes, I'm the asshole for not wanting Jake Parsons to touch me. For making a big deal about him ignoring my rejection and doing it anyway.

What a prude.

Suck it up, princess.

Jake Parsons wanted you? You should have been flattered.

Now Jake Parsons reaches out his hand, braces it on my chest, and shoves me back against the wall between the window panes. He makes sure to touch as much of my breast as he can while he does, then he fists his hand in my shirt and meets my gaze, a hint of challenge dancing in his eyes. I know he's either going to tear my shirt or rip it off over my head, I just don't know what he's going to do after that.

CHAPTER 2

"WAIT," I say, grabbing his hand, trying to stop this before it can go any further. "Listen, I won't take back what I said, but I'll— I'll talk to the coach. I'll ask him to cut your suspension in half. Okay? Then you'll still get to play this year."

"Half the fuckin' season," Jake says, shaking his head. "Nuh uh. You're gonna take it back. You're going to tell them you were confused, upset, you made a mistake. Tell them you were on your period and PMS got the best of you—I don't give a fuck what you tell them, but you tell them something to make this stop."

"I won't let you bully me into lying," I tell him, tilting my chin up. "You messed up. You wouldn't stop, you wouldn't apologize, and now you're payin' for your mistake. That's how life works when you're not an untouchable, Jake. That's how mere mortals live."

"That right?" he asks, yanking me forward by my shirt, then pushing me back against the wall so hard, it rattles my teeth and makes my stomach rock with fear.

The other two guys close in now, their eyes narrowed on me with contempt.

Bringing my gaze back to the asshole jock in front of me, I swallow down my fear. "Do you really want to make this worse, Jake? You're supposed to stay away from me. This is definitely not stayin' away from me."

"You've already ruined my fuckin' life, Zo. What's gonna happen to me now?"

The sullen way he says it irritates me—like this really is my fault instead of his. "I have not ruined your life. They won't let you play football—that's it. A game."

He shakes his head. "You don't get it, do you? My whole future hinged on playin' this year, Zoey. It's not just a game to me, it's a ticket out of here I can't afford any other way."

The honest vulnerability in his words plant hooks in me like nothing else he has said or done. Wanting to get out of this town is something I can relate to, and if I had a chance and lost it, I would be rocked with regret, too. Casting my gaze down, momentarily finding myself feeling bad for this jerk, I repeat my previous offer. "I told you, I'm willing to talk to Coach and try to get your suspension reduced so you can still play this year. If you walk away now, I will still do that."

Shayne snickers. "Do you hear this little bitch? If you walk away now."

"I'm bein' more than fair," I tell Jake, ignoring Shayne. "Your behavior was out of line. Someone had to show you that your actions have consequences. I did you a favor in the long run; you won't live in the football bubble forever. Pull that shit after high school, and you're goin' to jail."

Jake shakes his head at me, like he can't figure out who the hell I think I am. "And I told you, that wasn't good enough. I don't want a reduced sentence, I want the accusation retracted. I want this bullshit off my record."

"And I wanted you to stop touchin' me. Looks like neither one of us will get everything we wanted out of this exchange. Why don't we just stop escalating it and get out while we can with the least amount of damage," I suggest.

"I think it's time I show *you* the consequences of *your* actions, nerd. What do you think about that?" He watches me for a reaction as he presses his body firmly against mine, a move intended to remind me of my place.

Everything he does pisses me off. I give him an out, and he throws it away. He's such a fucking jerk. I struggle to keep my attitude in check though, knowing no good can possibly come from making him feel small in front of his friends. People are more dangerous in groups with other like-minded individuals, and the two guys he brought with him are clearly on his side.

I turn my face so I don't have to look at him and swallow. "Please just walk away, Jake. For both our sakes. Don't make things worse."

He ignores me, yanking my shirt up to my waist, exposing my pale midriff. I try to fight him, grabbing the shirt and shoving it back down. He grabs my wrists, shoves them over my head, and pins them against the brick pillar.

"No!" I cry, my heart somersaulting. My mind races for the next idea as his hands graze my midriff, but I can't come up with anything. Things are happening too fast, and I'm getting scared.

He lifts my shirt again. I fight, but his arm locks around me. He's too strong, and he gets the shirt off, flinging it behind me. I can scarcely breathe as he locks me against his chest with one hand and uses the other to unhook my bra clasp.

"Jake, please." My voice is muffled against his chest. I despise him, but his chest is the only shelter I have to keep Carter and Shayne from seeing me, too. "Please, don't do this."

"Tell everyone you lied," he orders.

"I *didn't!*"

He yanks my bra off, pushing me away from his chest and locking his arm around my neck. Before I have time to process what he's doing, he turns me around so I'm on display for his friends. "See anything you like, gentlemen?"

A burst of heat engulfs my whole body like I've just been dropped into a pit of flames. Shame burns through me as their interested eyes rake over my exposed body, as they smirk and make fun of me.

"They don't look so fuckin' special to me," Shayne remarks.

"Yeah, I wouldn't let those little things ruin my life, either," Carter chimes in, chuckling.

Tears of rage and humiliation leak out of the corners of my eyes. I want to lash out. I want to punish Jake more, not less. He can fuck off if he thinks I'll talk to the coach on his behalf after this.

"Stupid little hoity-toity bitch. Thinks she's too good for us, doesn't she?" Shayne mutters.

"Zoey thinks she's too good for everyone," Jake sneers.

No, just you, I want to say. Stupid fucking asshole. Not wanting to escalate things, I keep my words locked inside my mouth, but holding onto my cool is getting harder. It feels like someone put my nerve endings on a hot skillet, and it heats up a few more degrees with every passing second. My self-control is slipping. All I want to do is snap and rage, to fight and scream and rip them all apart.

Shayne walks closer, his hungry eyes on the breasts he supposedly finds so unimpressive. "Hold her arms, Parsons. I want a feel."

Jake locks my arms, using his chest to push against my back, keeping me still. "Be my guest. I think I'm paying enough for all three of us. Carter, you want in on this?"

"No," I cry out, shaking my head in angry denial. "No, you can't do this. You can't *do* this!"

Directly disproving my words, Shayne's big hands close around my breasts and he squeezes them like he has a right to.

I'm spiraling down a sinkhole of shame, never wanting to come back out. I told myself for as long as I could they were only trying to scare me, but this is more than that. This is too far. I don't want to be present for this.

"Take your hands off her, Sutton."

My heart stalls. Carter's deep voice pulls my head above water. Perhaps foolishly, I resist the pull of emotionally detaching from this moment to save myself, and instead grasp onto a flimsy thread of hope that he'll finally put a stop to what's happening.

He sees it, too. I don't know how the glint in his eyes speaks to me, but it does. He knows he holds my hope in his hands, and he likes the feel of it.

"You don't want Sutton's hands on you, do you, princess?" he asks.

I shake my head no, but there's something I don't trust in his tone—something too light. I know there's a catch, but I also know out of everyone in this room, Carter has the most power.

Social power and actual power—he's the alpha in this room, so he can hit the brakes on this train wreck, if he chooses to.

You don't pick a fight with the alpha unless you want him for an opponent, and I sure don't need another opponent. Tapping down the rage burning inside me, I offer up something softer, something that might appeal to any protective instinct he might possess.

"Thank you," I say, softly.

He cocks his head curiously, but doesn't speak.

I swallow, not confident in my next step. I don't *know* Carter Mahoney on a personal level, so I don't know how best to appeal to him. I don't even know if I need to. He spoke up on his own, so maybe he doesn't need me to pull him in the right direction. In any case, while Jake is still holding onto me from behind, Shayne is no longer groping me, so that's an improvement.

Carter takes a slow step forward, his dark eyes traveling over every exposed inch of my body. Foreboding snakes through me and a chill runs down my spine, my body responding more like he's the predator I should fear than any potential saving grace. I wish I could see his eyes, see the look in them—at least, until it happens. When our eyes lock, I see dark amusement, not sympathy, not protectiveness over some girl he doesn't even know. The strings tethered to my hope start to snap. My stomach sinks, and my heart along with it.

"Oh, Zoey," he begins, reaching out and touching my face. The feigned sympathy dripping from each syllable is so condescending, it makes my gut wrench, but I can't look away from him. "If you're looking for Prince Charming and *I'm* your best shot, you are in a truly dire situation."

Since my stomach can't drop any lower and hope can't save me, my fight-or-flight instincts start to overtake everything else. My body works overtime, realizing we're in danger and we need to get out, fast. I hate the way my chest heaves with each new breath, drawing more attention to my naked breasts. I hate the way my voice shakes, but I can't control it. "So, you didn't stop him to help me. He was just, what, in your way? Are you gonna grope me now, too?"

"I'm not really a tit man," Carter murmurs casually, looking me over again like a potential purchase he thinks might be over-priced. "I wouldn't say no to getting my dick sucked, though."

My eyes widen as his gaze drifts back to mine to see my reaction. For a stunned moment, the whole room falls quiet.

"What? No!" I shake my head, new horror exploding inside me like a triggered landmine. Surely, they won't escalate things that far, right? I already reported Jake for groping me—do they really think I'll keep my mouth shut after a group sexual assault?

Shayne's dark eyebrows rise and he looks at Carter like he's crazy. "You're gonna stick your dick in her mouth? Man, you got me fucked up, ain't no way I'd do that shit." Smacking Jake on the arm and grinning like this is funny, he says, "Mahoney's got balls of fuckin' steel. Don't know how much good they'll do him after she bites his dick off, though."

Carter meets my gaze and smiles at me—it's a mean smile, though. His next words sound like a command from him to me, even though he's supposedly addressing Shayne. "Nah, she's not going to bite me. You're gonna be a team player, aren't you, Zoey?"

"No," I say, astounded by his absolute fucking gall.

Carter shrugs like it doesn't matter. "All right. I'll stick it in her cunt instead, if she can't play nice."

His words are bad enough, but the accompanying glint in his eyes wreaks havoc on my nerves. I can't believe he would actually do it, but at the same time, I can't say with any confidence I'm sure he's bluffing. I think I might throw up.

"Please…" I hate this. I can't believe they're making me beg —beg not to be abused any more than I already have been. It's almost laughable that I looked at Carter hoping he would temper Jake's belligerence, and instead he's the one making the torment worse.

"Now, hang on. If anyone gets her pussy, it's gonna be me," Jake objects. "I'm the one payin' for her bullshit."

"We can all have fun with her," Carter assures him, his gaze raking over me again. "She has three holes, doesn't she? Plenty to go around."

Fear has such a tight grip on me, I think I might pass out. The possibility sends a new strain of terror shooting down my spine. If I lose consciousness, they can do anything they want to me, and I won't even know. "Please don't do this," I say, not even sure who I'm appealing to anymore. "Please just walk away. I won't tell anyone this happened if you walk away now, I swear to God."

"Have you taken a dick before, Zoey the ho? What am I sayin'? Of course you have," Shayne says. "How many?"

"I haven't," I say, heart leaping. It's embarrassing to share such personal information with these assholes, but maybe they'll have at least a remnant of common decency and realize they don't want to take it this far. "I'm a virgin."

Instead of shaming them into releasing me, Carter's dark eyes light up with interest. I get the immediate sense that sharing that information with him was a massive misstep. "Oh, even fucking better," Carter drawls. "I'm going first."

Jake's arm tightens around me and he takes a subtle step back, bringing me with him. I think he's realizing this is supposed to be his show, but Carter is strolling casually toward center stage. "Now, hang the fuck on. I said you two greedy bastards could cop a feel, not fuck her."

I cannot believe I'm in the astounding position of hoping and praying they *only* grope my naked breasts.

Carter shakes his head, stepping a little closer and stroking my breast anyway, despite apparently not being a "tit man." His eyes lock onto my anxious face as he tweaks my nipple. "I want the little virgin. I say we fuck her right here, right now. We show her who she fucked with and make her our little whore."

"No," I cry, tears burning behind my eyes. "Please. Please don't hurt me."

My words are a plea for whoever will listen, and for a heart-stopping moment, I think it might be Jake. He pulls me closer almost protectively, like Carter is pushing too hard. I'm not sure I can envision Jake standing up to Carter, but this *is* Jake's thing. Jake has the ability to stop it, too. His resistance is subtle, just a whisper right now, but if I can grow it, make it stronger, maybe I *can* stop this.

My opponent must notice too, though. Before I can try to reach Jake, Carter pounces on his weaknesses.

"She's a lot nicer when you're mean to her, you notice that, Jake? *You* merely touch her and she runs and tattles on you. *I* toy with her, and she manages a 'please' and 'thank you' for me. Makes you wonder what the difference is, doesn't it?"

"I do notice that," Jake grumbles, wrapping his stupid mouth around Carter's bait. "She must like bein' toyed with like a little fuckin' slut."

His words make feel cold all over. Carter is appealing to the worst parts of Jake, subtly trying to make him angry at me again, since the possibility of sharing me with Carter suddenly incited a flash of protectiveness. He knows Jake has it in him to be petty and jealous, and now he's manipulating him with it so Jake will do his bidding.

That could work on Jake. I feel like I'm going to vomit. I almost hope I do. Surely they won't want to touch me anymore if I throw up all over myself.

Since the bile remains lodged stubbornly in my throat, I have to resort to other means of saving my own ass. "Please don't let him do this, Jake," I add, subtly shifting the blame off him and onto Carter, giving *him* the chance to play Prince Charming, since Carter turned down the role. Keeping my tone soft, I tell him, "I'll ask Coach to let you play. I'll tell him I made a mistake. I'll tell him you shouldn't be punished. That I don't *want* you to be punished."

Everything stops for a moment. Carter glances at Jake behind me, and Shayne looks up, too. Carter has a nice hold on the worst parts of Jake, and now here I am, interrupting to appeal to his better side.

"She's lying," Carter states, immovably. Like he has an exclusive window into my mind, and he alone has this insight. "She thinks she can play you for a fool, Jake. She thinks you like her so much, you'll believe all her bullshit. Think about her actions, not her words. When you touched her before, it was because you liked her, you were attracted to her. You *wanted* her. Your motives were pure, Jake, and she hung you out to dry anyway."

"Stop it," I say, appalled at the way Carter is warping the events to make me the bad guy.

Ignoring me, Carter continues his appeal, gesturing around

the room. "But this? We had bad intentions. We wanted to scare her, and do you really think someone like Zoey is going to back down after that? Do you really think she felt so strongly that you needed to be punished for touching her, but *now*, after *this*, she doesn't want you to be punished?" Carter shakes his head, almost sympathetically. "She's playing you, man. Manipulating you. Don't let her get away with that."

"He is the one manipulating you, not me," I snap, outraged. I can't see Jake's face and he isn't saying anything, so I can't tell if Carter's bullshit is working.

Carter cocks a skeptical eyebrow. "What reason could I possibly have for manipulating my friend?" He asks me the question, but doesn't wait for an answer. "You think I'm that desperate for a blow job, Ellis? I could leave this room now and have three girls fighting each other for the honor in under five minutes." Cutting a disbelieving look at Jake, he takes yet another run at his insecurities. "Man, she really is full of herself, isn't she?"

That's exactly the right note to hit. My rejection clearly still stings Jake, so more than anything Carter has said before, that hits home.

"Yeah, she is," Jake murmurs.

"I'm not," I declare, trying to maintain my slippery grasp on Jake's good will. "I'm sorry if I come off that way, I really don't mean to. My offer is real, Jake. I'm not lying."

Carter's commentary continues. "Of course not. Zoey would never lie—except when she's telling the whole town you sexually harassed her, of course."

That Carter can say that with a straight face amid the events currently unfolding blows my mind, but that Jake can make himself believe it is even worse. Reality has no value here, because the facts don't cast Jake in a flattering light.

Gritting my teeth, I pray for the strength to keep my cool. Anger will turn Jake off. Everything I do has to convince him to choose my side over Carter's, and Carter is an unexpectedly diabolical opponent.

"Tell me why he's wrong, Zo," Jake says, running the back of his hand along my jaw in a gesture that whispers of tenderness he still has for me. "Tell me why you don't want me to be punished anymore."

His mind is so easily bent, I could puke. Carter may be the literal worst, but at least he's consistently terrible. Jake is like a loose cannon, shooting off destruction in whichever direction anyone points him.

Jake is weak. I doubt he'll ever be strong because he is clearly too fragile to be wrong, too insecure to learn from his mistakes instead of blaming them on other people. I hate him so much, I want to set him on fire.

But I also don't want to be raped. My problem is an astounding one: I think what Jake wants me to say is that I like him, and I don't. I tell myself to force that lie past my lips, to tell this stupid asshole that I don't want to get him in trouble because I have discovered a secret soft spot for him, because the thought of being the thing that tanks his future is too much. Because, hell, I want to sit in the bleachers and cheer him on every Friday night, and then give him a kiss after his big win.

Yuck.

I'm not that girl, I don't want to be that girl, and it's one of the reasons I rejected him in the first place. We are not right for one another. We have absolutely nothing in common—he only likes my physical appearance, and he's mistaken in thinking that's enough.

Regardless of my genuine disinterest in him, I know I could probably outsmart Jake Parsons and gain his protection. The problem is, it would only be a temporary fix to a long-term problem. If I lead Jake on now, he'll pursue it later, and I'll be right back where I started—only this time, I'll have incited his attention.

Settling on something I can stomach, I tell him, "Because I just want all this to be over. I don't want to fight with you. I just… I just want it over. For you and for me. Let's put an end to the fightin' and move on."

"Move on to what?"

"To… gettin' along? Not bein' at war? You'll get to play again, Jake. That's what matters to you, right?"

None of that is what he wants to hear, but it's something. It's all I have to offer him.

I can't see Jake so I look at Carter, hoping to read into his reaction, but Carter isn't looking at Jake—he's watching me. His brown eyes are narrowed in consideration and he looks like he's trying to work something out.

In the silence of his disappointment, Jake apparently gets stuck inside his own head, twisted up in a web of delusions and imagined slights, because his next words are faintly hostile. "All right. Fine. You'll tell everyone what a lyin' little whore you are, and I'll get my life back. I want an apology, too. I think I deserve an apology for all the shit you've put me through."

He's getting so tangled up in his own warped perspective, I'm not entirely sure he knows how unreasonable he's being. "You and I both know I didn't lie, Jake," I murmur. "I'll talk to Coach and bail you out anyway. Just accept your win and let it go."

"I don't win until you tell *everyone* you lied, Zoey, not just Coach. Some girls look at me like I'm a fuckin' creep now."

"Smart girls," I mutter, unable to help myself.

He shifts his hold on me, pinning my arm under his and reaching across my chest so he can play with my nipples the way Carter was a minute ago. My skin crawls and I twist, trying to get away from him, but I can't.

"Stop touching me," I demand, my chest heaving with the strain of not exploding.

Instead, he rolls my nipple between his thumb and index finger. "Nah. I'm a creep, remember?"

"I want a taste," Shayne says, seeing his opening to get back in on the action. "Hold onto her good, Parsons."

"No," I snap, before he can come closer. "My offer only stands if this shit stops right now. If it goes any further, I rescind my offer. No matter what you fucking do to me, I will never take back what I said. I will never appeal to anyone on your behalf. Never."

Shayne looks at Jake, but Carter jumps back in now, too.

"You know what, Jake?" Carter says, meeting my gaze instead of Jake's. His voice carries the unmistakable tone of authority, as if he has some deeper understanding of the situation than he does. "I still think she's lying. Zoey doesn't want you, but she doesn't want you to have anyone else, either, so she won't clear your name."

"That's legitimately insane," I tell Carter.

Again, he ignores me. "I think if you let her walk out of this room today without enforcing any consequences, she'll come after you even harder. I think if you let her off the hook, it will embolden her to keep doing all the shit she's been doing to you."

I gape at Carter, absolutely astounded. He held my gaze shamelessly while he sold every line of that bullshit, and the twisted hilarity of it all is he's using *my* logic to convince Jake to hurt me. I wanted Jake to face consequences so he would think twice before mistreating the next girl, and here Carter is painting me as the bad guy and feeding Jake's delusion.

"You just wanna use her pussy," Shayne says to Carter, amused.

"He might be right, though," Jake murmurs, somehow swayed by Carter's baseless bullshit. "I certainly didn't think she'd run and tell on me last time, and she fuckin' did. Why should I trust her now?"

"I don't want to be raped," I cry, my voice shaking with anger. It's infuriating enough to feel, but that they're making me *say it* to them is almost unbearable. "I'm not folding because I care about you; I'm folding because I don't want to endure any more of this bullshit. Believe me, I have a healthy sense of self-preservation. What would lying get me? Out of this moment, sure, but tomorrow? The next day? Next week? Next month? You win, okay? Just get your hands off me and give me back my clothes."

I don't think he hears anything past my declaration of indifference—I feel it in the way his body stiffens against my back. I didn't *mean* to say it, it just slipped out. It's one thing not to say I like him; it's another thing entirely to state in front of his friends that I don't.

He lets go, all right—but not of his anger and resentment, not of his intense case of Nice Guy Syndrome. He lets go of *me* and pushes me right into Carter's waiting arms.

"Take her," Jake says, his tone dead. "Do whatever you want with her."

CHAPTER 3

TERROR CLAWS at my insides as Carter catches me in his arms. I tried to stop myself, but momentum propelled me right into him. Now I shove against his muscular chest, struggling to get away, but he locks his left arm around my waist and keeps me trapped against him as he looks me over.

"Mm, what a thoughtful present," Carter remarks.

"Get your hands off me, Carter," I demand, my voice breaking with desperation.

"No," he replies calmly, then nods at Jake. "Didn't you hear? Parsons said I can do whatever I want to you."

That's a terrifying thought. My breath hitches as Carter's amused brown eyes lock on mine, then he slowly reaches down between our bodies and unbuttons the top button of my corduroy wrap skirt.

"Please," I say, trying to shove his hand away. "Carter, please don't."

Clicking at me in disapproval, Carter says, "Now, now, don't try manipulating me, princess. I just watched you do it to him, and I'm a fast learner; it won't work on me."

"I wasn't manipulatin' anyone," I say, the accusation making me uncomfortable.

"Mm-hmm," Carter murmurs, savoring the violation as he unbuttons the rest of my skirt, then lets the fabric fall to the floor.

Now I'm standing here, heart pounding, stripped down to a pair of thin black panties in front of these three assholes. I'm sick. Literally sick. Bile rises and I feel myself wanting to heave, but nothing comes up.

"Stop this now," I say, trying to grasp some kind of authority. "If you stop now, I still won't say anything. That window is about to close, though. Y'all are taking this too far."

"Listen to her, getting mouthy," Carter says, caressing my jaw with his free hand.

"I didn't even do anything to you," I snap at him. "What's your excuse? Why do you want to hurt me?"

"I don't have one," Carter says, his tone indifferent, almost bored. "I just like seeing you helpless and scared. It gets me hard. Want to feel?"

So much of that sounds like the truth, I can only stare at him, wide-eyed. "You're a psycho."

Flashing me a predatory smile, he says, "Maybe."

"How 'bout all them holes you were talking about, Mahoney? Let's see 'em, man," Shayne encourages, nodding at my panties.

My heart thuds in my chest as I consider Carter stripping me of the last scrap of fabric offering me even minimal coverage. At least on this, I get a diminutive measure of relief. "Sorry, Shayne, you're guarding the door," Carter tells his teammate.

"What?" Shayne says, disappointed. "Man, seriously? Why do *I* have to do it?"

Carter ignores Shayne, as if that question is too stupid even to answer, and turns his attention to Jake. My stomach pitches, thinking he's going to invite Jake to join in, but now that he doesn't *have* to share to have me, his interest in double-teaming me seems to dissipate.

"Her pussy is mine," Carter states, then his gaze drifts back to my face. I squirm against him, trying to pull away again, but his hold on me is too effective and it's a waste of my energy. "I want it first. I want her innocence. I want to be the one to make her bleed."

Carter's chilling words even make Jake a little uncomfortable, I can see it on his face. Not uncomfortable enough to back down, though. "I should get to fuck her, too. It's my life she ruined," Jake complains.

"Fine, then fuck her after me. Wear a rubber."

"You're not going to?" Jake asks, his gaze snapping to his teammate.

"Oh, no. Her blood will be the only lube when I take her. You'll probably have to cover her mouth while I fuck her so no one hears her scream."

Oh, my God, he cannot be serious. As hard as I try to keep it at bay, fear paralyzes me as a vision of Carter's scenario plays out in my mind. My body trapped beneath him, Jake covering my mouth and helping hold me down while Carter violates me.

I look at Jake to see what he'll do, hoping against hope he'll stand up to Carter. I know he's been reluctant up to now, but he has to realize *this* is definitely too far.

Again, Jake looks uncomfortable, but for whatever reason, he nods like he'll follow Carter's orders. Unbelievable.

Carter looks down at me, captive in his arms. My heart is pounding violently and since he has my chest pulled against his, I bet he can feel my fear. I bet he likes it. "Want to beg me one more time, princess?"

"No," I tell him, hating my voice for continuing to shake. "I hope it's worth it to you, because if you do this to me, I'll ruin your life, too."

Carter smiles, a smile that would be overwhelmingly attractive if he weren't such a monster. "Oh, you won't ruin my life, Zoey. It's fucking adorable that you think there's even a shot in hell you could get *me* kicked off the team, but football's not my end game. We both know I could shoot someone in the middle of a crowded stadium at halftime, and they'd rush to clean up the blood so I didn't slip and fall while I finished up the game. Even if you *could* get me kicked off the team though, princess, it wouldn't matter." Reaching down and caressing my breast again, he murmurs, "Football's just a pit stop for me, nothing more."

"You're 18." My voice shakes again as I shove his hand away, but it doesn't make my words any less true. "When I report you for rape, it's gonna be much worse than a football suspension."

Carter doesn't appear to be intimidated, but he does appear

to be amused. "Oh, you won't report me, Zoey. You're not that stupid. I think you know if you fuck with *me*, my retribution will be much worse than cornering you and fucking you in an abandoned classroom."

I swallow, my chest working. I *don't* know that, but my stomach sinks because I can't help believing him. "Raping me, you mean. This isn't fucking. If you do this, this is rape. It's a violation, it's a crime. You'll have to live with that for the rest of your life."

"Let me count all the fucks I give," he says, so cavalier.

"Hey, maybe we're takin' this a little too far," Jake finally realizes.

Fucking finally!

"Maybe we're not taking it far enough," Carter counters. "She just threatened me, and you know what, Parsons? I don't like being threatened."

"If you stop now, I promise not to report anybody. I won't say a word," I offer, only because I'm starting to suspect Carter might be a full-blown psychopath. I'm beginning to worry how far *he* might take this if I keep pushing back. It started at groping and intimidation, some humiliation, threats, and bullying; very quickly, it's progressing to full-on gang-rape with Carter egging Jake on.

What's the next escalation? Murder? Carter will convince Jake the only way to ensure my silence is to snap my neck and toss my body into a river?

I'll be the girl on the news.

The town will light candles and hold a vigil, girls who hate me will muster tears when they tell news anchors what great friends we were, and my sobbing mother will stammer about how she can't imagine who would do such a thing to me, how I was such a nice girl, how everyone loved me. In a few months, the town will forget me, my family will have to leave to escape the pain and try to start over, and the only lives ruined will be ours. Carter will be crowned prom king, Jake will play college ball, and I'll get a full-page memorial spread in the senior yearbook.

Cold fear slices through me. I don't want to be treated like this, but I don't want to lose my life to these entitled scumbags either, and I know enough about psychology to understand Carter could convince Jake and Shayne to do something they would never do on their own. He's appealing to their group mentality, making it them vs. me, and painting me as the bad guy. The logic doesn't have to hold up; it only has to make sense long enough for them to act rashly, and at the rate he moves, that wouldn't take long at all.

They could literally kill me, and I would be just another easily forgotten statistic. My life lost, all so these assholes can play a damn sport despite their horrible behavior.

Carter watches me as these thoughts flit through my mind. He's dangerous. These other two, they're nothing sinister, harmless assholes left to their own devices, but not with him leading them like stupid horses to a poisoned well. I never saw it in him before, but then I've never spent any time with Carter Mahoney. I see the same superficial side of him everyone else sees—the wealthy, privileged quarterback with a golden arm. I've never looked twice at him, so how would I have noticed a monster lurking beneath the surface?

I try to take a more conciliatory tone when I address him. He's like a rabid junkyard dog with a bone, and I need him to unclench his jaws so I can run away. "Look, I don't want to go to war with you, Carter. I don't even have a problem with you. This is supposed to be between me and Jake."

Carter ignores my attempt to make peace and glances at Jake.

"She's a stickler for consequences, this one," Carter muses aloud, like he can read my mind. Like he knows why all of a sudden I'm trying to backpedal with him. "I'm wondering if it's safe for any of us to let her go, Parsons."

"It is," I offer quickly. "If you let me go now, we can act like this never happened. Just stay away from me and I'll stay away from you."

"Yeah?" Carter asks calmly, flicking his thumb across my nipple and watching my face as I gasp at the sensation. "You'll sit in history class with me tomorrow and keep your pretty little mouth shut if I let you go?"

My heart thuds in protest, but I ignore it. The time for

protest has passed. It's degrading to nod when he worded it that way, but that's why he did it. He wants to humiliate me. I don't care anymore. I just want to get the hell out of here. I need this whole awful experience to be over.

The thing that scares me is Jake wants to punish me and Shayne is just a joiner, but Carter? Carter *wants* to rape me. He doesn't care about Jake's thing, he's just here for the fun. This is *fun* to him.

Carter walks me forward, finally releasing me long enough to push my back against the pillar Jake had me against to begin with. Then he bends his head and takes the nipple he's been playing with into his mouth and sucks it. I gasp, closing my eyes and stiffening my body, pushing my head back against the brick pillar as this near stranger sucks on my breast. Revulsion swims through my gut, crawls up my spine, and sends chills down my legs.

I shouldn't have told him I'm a virgin. I thought it would appeal to their humanity, that they wouldn't want to cross that line, but I think it made Carter want me more. He doesn't want *me*—he wants to steal my innocence, like he said.

Carter grabs my body and tugs me closer to his, releasing that nipple and moving his mouth to the other. I push against him, trying to get free, but he doesn't budge. His muscular arms don't even strain. He can hold on to me and keep his mouth on me at the same time, that's how easy it is for him to overpower me.

His tongue swirls around the peak of my breast, then he bites. Not hard, just enough to make me jump and give another futile push against his broad shoulders. This is the strangest sensation. My breasts have never been in anyone's mouth before; I never thought the first time would be against my will—and I damn sure didn't think the mouth suckling my breast would be Carter Mahoney's.

Jake looks away from this torrid display, I think finally realizing he unleashed a beast on me, but unwilling to help chain it back up.

I swore to myself I wouldn't beg anymore, but as Carter's big hand slips down inside the front of my panties, I can't keep the words from spilling from my lips. "Carter, please don't do this." I say, squeezing my legs together.

"Beg more," he murmurs, his hand still casually inside my panties. He drags his lips along my neck, his mouth shockingly ravenous, like a hungry beast about to feast on my flesh. Given the context of what I know he wants from me, it's absolutely terrifying, and everything within me quakes.

He's probably just fucking with me, but on the off chance I can stop him, I give him what he demands. "Please. Please, Carter. Please let me go."

"Tell me you'll be a good little whore and keep your mouth shut," he says, biting my neck.

I let out a sharp cry of surprise, then start crying, not even attempting a brave face any longer. "I'll be a good little…" I can't get it out. His finger slips inside me and I sob harder, closing my eyes.

"Say it," he says sharply.

My stomach sinks as I cry, "I'll be a good little whore. Please stop. Please."

"You won't say anything," he repeats, as if bored, even while his thumb presses against my clitoris.

"Please," I beg, my broken cry humiliating me. "I won't say anything."

Withdrawing his hand from between my legs, Carter grabs a fistful of my hair and pushes me down to my knees. "Open your mouth, princess. You're going to suck my dick. You do a good job and I won't stick it in your cunt next."

Jake shifts from foot to foot, then finally walks over to the door like he just wants to check out the window, but I think he can't watch this. How things got from him pushing me up against the wall and intimidating me out of anger to Carter pushing my mostly naked body to the floor and unzipping his pants is probably a bit beyond him.

Grabbing my jaw, Carter warns me, "If you bite me, I'll knock your fucking teeth out."

I hate meeting his gaze, especially because I know expecting him to be decent is expecting too much, but I look up at him and beg one more time. "Please don't make me do this."

"Try not to throw up," he advises me. "I like to go deep."

He doesn't let go of my hair. He keeps one hand there to keep me down, I guess, and uses the other to pull his dick out of his pants. I can't believe this is happening. Tears stream down my cheeks as his cock comes at my face. I lean back, trying to get away from it, but when my head hits the wall, there's nowhere else to go.

"Open your mouth," he demands.

I keep my lips sealed shut, shaking my head, looking up at him with wordless pleas in my eyes.

"Now, or I take your virginity instead," he says simply. "Your choice."

My heart drops and my mind races, but there's nowhere for it to go. Carter isn't bluffing, and I don't want to lose my virginity this way, to this asshole. I don't want to give him head either, but if I have to do one or the other, there's only one choice to make. Although it's a struggle to wrap my head around the action, I take a deep, hitching breath and open my mouth.

"Good girl," he says almost soothingly, grasping his cock and guiding it into my mouth. I squeeze my eyes shut, unable to look, but Carter doesn't allow me even that much escape. "Open your eyes and watch your teeth. I'm not kidding about knocking them out. I don't want to, but I will if you piss me off. Now, you take good care of me, all right, princess?"

I don't even know how to do this. I've never let a guy do this before, and now the first time has to be him. When a moment passes and I do nothing, he punishes me, shoving his cock so deep in my throat, I can't breathe. I panic, grabbing his hips, trying to pull him out of my airway, but he forces my face even closer to his pelvis. My eyes burn and I can't breathe. He's literally choking me on his dick, and now my gag reflex is working, trying to make me throw up, but I can't even get anything up because his dick is lodged so deep in my throat.

My vision starts to go gray as panic seizes me, and I realize this might be it. I'm going to die here of asphyxiation with Carter Mahoney's cock in my throat. And then, because he's a fucking psycho, he'll probably fuck my corpse.

Black starts to eat away at my line of sight and I weaken.

Suddenly, Carter yanks me back by the hair and I gasp dramatically, trying to suck as much air as I can into my deprived lungs. I sob, curling in on myself and nearly collapsing on the dingy linoleum floor.

"This is disappointing, princess. I thought there'd be more foreplay before I took your cunt."

"Please don't," I say, but I sound tired even to my own ears. Tired of making pleas I know he will ignore anyway, tired of hanging onto hope that I can stop him when I know I can't.

"This is your last fucking chance. You wanna suck me?"

I nod my head, swallowing and pushing to my knees with a shuddering breath. "Please don't do that to me again," I say quietly. "I'll suck you."

"Good girl," he murmurs, caressing my cheek, then grabbing my hair. "I'm going to keep a hold of you, just in case you get ornery."

I crawl forward on my knees, eyeing up his cock as I do. It's so hard, maybe even harder after what he just did to me. I know he'll hurt me worse if I don't do as he says, so I take his cock in my hand and slowly start pumping it. He's thick, that's the most relevant thought that springs to mind. If he pushes that thing inside my unwilling body, it's going to hurt like hell. I don't know how long it would take for him to get off, but every thrust would be torture physically, in addition to the mental wounds he would be inflicting.

No, I can't let it get that far. Swallowing, I take one last look at the smooth tip that was just lodged in my throat. It's glistening from my saliva. I push down my dread, lean forward and take it in my mouth again, then I start to suck.

Carter hisses and I look up to make sure it's with pleasure. His head is thrown back and his long fingers caress my head almost affectionately, rewarding me rather than punishing me. That must mean I'm doing something right down here. I keep sucking, figuring it's the suction that feels good. The faster he comes, the faster I can put my clothes back on and get the hell out of here.

"Oh, princess, I like your mouth," he murmurs, caressing my

head like a gentle reward in the midst of his brutality. "Keep doing what you're doing."

I want to bite the fucking thing off, but I believe him when he says he'll knock my teeth out. Instead of hurting the monster, I do my best to pleasure him. I have to break the suction, so I try to do something else that will feel good, but I don't know what. He said he likes to go deep, so I lean forward and take more of him into my mouth, running my tongue along the underside of his dick. My teeth scrape him when I pull back and his hand fists in my hair again.

I pull back quickly. "I'm sorry. It was an accident, I didn't mean to."

He nods, pushing my face back onto his cock and pushing until he hits the back of my throat. I start to panic again but he doesn't make me stay there this time, he lets me go back to the shallow end. I want to stay here, so I pump my hand faster and suck on his head while I do.

"You like having a cock in your mouth, princess? This is where you belong, isn't it?"

My stomach sinks, but I do my best to ignore his words. I just have to get him off, then this will be over. It's not that hard. Other girls do this all the time, so surely I can get through it once.

"How come you've never let anyone fuck you yet, Zoey? Is your pussy special, too?" he inquires.

My whole body heats with humiliation, but I ignore his words and labor over his cock, sucking it, licking the tip, trying everything that might feel good. My jaw is already starting to ache, and I haven't even been sucking him for that long, but he's so freaking thick.

"And your mouth," he continues, his tone conversational as I suck him off. "How the fuck do you make it to senior year without sucking a single dick? Don't you date?"

I don't know if he *needs* to put me down to get off or he's just doing it for fun, but I ignore his comments and keep working.

Finally, he stops running his fucking mouth and starts caressing my head again. "That's good. Suck harder, Zoey. If you want to be my little whore, you're gonna have to earn it."

I don't want to be his little anything, and he knows it. This is so humiliating. That I *am* going to have to sit in the same class-room as him tomorrow is completely horrifying. Maybe I could transfer to a different history class. Maybe I can convince my mom the torment over the Jake situation is so bad, I need to switch schools.

He groans and pushes my face closer to his pelvis, lodging more of his cock deeper in my throat as a hot jet of salty release spills into my mouth and I gag. I'm one part mortified, one part disgusted, and one part relieved.

It's finally over.

"Open your mouth," he demands. "I wanna see it."

I look up at him, confused, but I open my mouth so he can see his cum inside.

"Mm, good little princess," he murmurs, caressing my cheek approvingly. "Now swallow."

I swallow twice to get every last bit of his release off my tongue and down my throat.

"Fuck," he murmurs, looking down at me again. He looks like he wants to say more, maybe do more, but Jake has now reached hyper levels of freaked out.

"We need to get the fuck out of here, man," Jake says.

Carter nods, but his dark eyes remain locked on me. I'm hunched on the floor, my palms pressed against the linoleum, still on my knees. I feel like a trained pet appealing to an abusive master for a little mercy. Looking up at him like this, he looks even more untouchable than he usually does, prowling through the halls in his letter jacket, surrounded by fans.

"Now, you're going to keep your mouth shut about this, right, Zoey?" he asks calmly. He already knows the answer, he's just reminding me—like I need a reminder after that.

I nod wordlessly, breaking his gaze and looking down at the floor.

"Good. If you start thinking about this later and feel I need to share Jake's lesson about consequences, let me promise you, it will be your last crusade—and it won't be worth it."

I don't say anything more. He's already touched me, used me, and humiliated me. I know he wants to do more, and as much as

I want to stand up for myself, I want to survive much more. Taking on Jake was one thing, but Carter? No way.

There's no remorse in him for what he just made me do, so I know that whatever is rotten inside him, whichever wires are crossed in his brain to make him capable of such atrocities, he could do much worse to me without batting an eye.

Submission is so much more than he deserves, but it's the only way I know to keep myself even a little bit safe, so as he stands over me, looking down at me, I stay on the floor and keep my head bowed like his well-trained pet.

"Until tomorrow, princess."

And with those last parting words, the door opens, and they all slip out into the hall, leaving me here to cry by myself.

CHAPTER 4

I DON'T SLEEP MUCH all night, and when morning comes, I don't even consider going to school. I've been so strong throughout this entire ordeal with Jake, I've never let them chase me into hiding, but yesterday was too much. Today, I will hide out at home, because the alternative of facing Carter and his minions at school is something I just can't handle right now.

Every time I close my eyes, I see Carter or Jake or Shayne—in the worst moments, I see all three of them. I relive Jake dragging me around so they could gawk at my naked breasts, Carter's mouth sucking on my nipples, Shayne's smirk as he pawed at my breasts.

Carter is the most traumatizing, obviously. I remember the way he made me suck him off, the way he shoved his dick so far into my throat, I thought I would lose consciousness. The filthiness of him making me show him his cum in my mouth afterward, before swallowing the evidence of his assault.

I've tried to study so I don't fall behind, but I can't concentrate long enough to read all the words on a single page, let alone a whole chapter. I can't outrun my own memories, so I lose the afternoon mindlessly perusing apps on my phone to distract myself.

By the time evening rolls around, I am beyond frustrated with myself for letting this get to me so much. I don't want Carter

Mahoney in my head. I want to forget all about what happened yesterday, and never see any of their stupid faces again. They don't deserve to make me listless and scatterbrained.

I tell myself I have a two-day limit. For two days, I can get stuck in my feelings if I need to, but after that, I have to pull it together, get back to school, and go on like Carter Mahoney never happened.

Come evening, my mom calls me down to help with dinner. I don't have energy to do that either, but arguing about it would be too taxing, so I make the mashed potatoes and keep my mouth shut.

"You're still in pajamas?" my mom asks when she notices, her gaze raking over my sweats and baggy T-shirt.

"I'm still not feeling well," I tell her.

"Well, it's too early in the school year to be missing classes, honey. Didn't you say you have a test this week?"

Ugh, yes. In *history*, of all classes.

How am I supposed to sit in the same classroom with that psychopath? Is he done with me now? Will he leave me alone, or is he just waiting for another chance to pounce? He's probably bored with me already, but I feel like I need to watch over my shoulder even more now than I did before, when Jake was my biggest problem.

How many more problems am I going to have to juggle? It's getting out of hand.

"I think I just need one more day," I tell her, nodding confidently. "I'll get lots of sleep tonight, do some yoga to get my head straight... I'll be better after tomorrow."

The doorbell rings and my little brother calls out, "I'll get it!"

I frown, glancing at the clock on the wall as I grab a serving spoon for the potatoes. My step-dad should be home any minute, but he wouldn't ring the doorbell. Grace wouldn't stop by unannounced. Hopefully, it's not another jerk playing a prank.

Last week, someone rang the doorbell and when I answered it, there were a pair of Longhorn blue panties on the ground with a note card reading "slut" stapled to the flimsy fabric. Probably from one of Jake's admirers who have the audacity to be offended that he showed me unwanted attention. It could have been someone on the football team, but the handwriting seemed girly. Probably a desperate rally girl or one of the meaner cheerleaders.

Just when I'm about to head to the door to make sure it's nothing like that, my younger brother pops into the kitchen just long enough to say, "She's in here," then he heads back to the table to obsessively line up butter knives. He's in fourth grade, and they just finished learning how to set the table, so now every night he's double checking that spoons are in the right spot and butter knives are facing the right direction.

Behind me, my mother offers a halting, confused, "H ––Hello."

I turn to look and suddenly feel as if I've swallowed my whole heart. I can't explain why, but Carter Mahoney is standing in my kitchen—all 6 feet 3 inches of him. He's wearing gray sweats and a white T-shirt with his letter jacket over it, to subtly remind us all who he is.

I feel like a monster snuck into the house, like I should grab a wooden stake and drive it through his black heart. My kitchen is the last place in the world he should be.

"Ma'am," he says respectfully, flashing my mom an admittedly charming smile. "I'm sorry if I'm interrupting your dinner. I heard Zoey wasn't feeling well today, so I wanted to bring her something." Now he holds up a clear container of what appears to be chicken noodle soup.

My mother recovers from her confusion quickly. Rather than being remotely cautious of him, she sinks into a relieved sort of admiration, like she's a damsel in distress and he's the gallant knight who just showed up to save her.

"Oh, isn't that so thoughtful? Zoey, look," she says excitedly, as if I don't have eyes or ears, and I must be missing this, because Carter Mahoney is in my kitchen bringing me feel-better soup, and I don't look happy to see him. "Wasn't that so nice? What a sweet boy."

Carter smiles at me, and I glare back at him.

It is so outrageous that he is here; I have no idea how to respond to his presence in my house, let alone in front of my mother. Swallowing, I put down the serving spoon with some effort. My hands are trembling and my insides feel hollow, like they've been scooped right out of me. I can't find my voice. That must have been scooped out, too. I want to demand he get the hell out of my house, but my mother has stars in her eyes, and I don't know what to do.

Carter doesn't wait for an invitation to approach me. Now that my mom is adequately impressed, he comes right over, puts the soup on the counter, and wraps a strong arm around me. Ignoring the way my body stiffens when he touches me, he pulls me in for an uncomfortable hug. "How ya feeling, babe?"

Babe?

I am not his *babe.*

What the actual fuck is he doing?

I look beyond his stupid broad shoulder and see my mom. Her eyes are wide, her cheeks flushed with pleasure, and I can practically see visions of wealthy, secretly psychopathic grandbabies dancing in her eyes.

Glaring up at Carter, I try to keep my voice steady. "What are you doin' at my house?"

"Told ya, I wanted to bring you soup. You also missed history today and we have a test tomorrow. I made you a copy of my notes."

He pulls back and fishes a piece of notebook paper out of his gym bag.

"Sorry I couldn't come earlier; I just got out of practice."

Ha, practice. Nice touch, psychopath.

His brown eyes glitter with pleasure as he hands me the folded-up sheet of notebook paper. My brain tells me I should, but I can't even bring myself to say an insincere 'thanks' for my mom's sake.

"How thoughtful! Do you want to stay for dinner?" my mom asks eagerly.

"No. No, he can't stay."

Carter's tone is apologetic. "Yeah, I've gotta get home and help my dad with some yard work."

"Aren't you sweet? I wish I had a son like you," my mom gushes.

Ugh, vomit! If only she knew.

Carter laughs, saying lightly, "Hey, maybe someday."

Oh, my God, that's enough of this. I don't understand what he's playing at, but it's time for this game to come to an end.

I feel bad when my gaze drifts back to my mom, and for all my confused anger, she is bursting with joy. Of course she's charmed by him, and even more by his family's wealth and reputation, no doubt. After I made our whole family look bad by telling on Jake Parsons, now the star quarterback is showing up to check on me and calling me babe.

To her, Carter Mahoney must look like my redemption wrapped up in an already-appealing package.

I can't even believe this shit.

At least I'm feeling things, I guess. I've been completely numb since he left me alone in that classroom yesterday, but now I'm feeling anger. So much anger, my skin is hot with it.

"Anyway, I hope you're feeling better soon, princess," he tells me, making me cringe with his use of the nickname he dropped when he was degrading me in that empty classroom. "I want to take you to Porter's downtown this weekend."

What the hell is he talking about?

"Porter's?" my mom asks, before I can respond. "Oh, I've heard that's a really nice restaurant."

Carter looks back at her and nods, his smile charming. "My sister and her husband actually own the place, so it's nice to stop in and see family, plus get good food. Win-win."

Can she seriously not see how full of shit he is? Apparently not, but then why would she? What normal, properly functioning human being would do what Carter is currently doing? None of them. Zero.

Carter looks back at me, like he's serious. I can't *believe* he is serious, but the mocking vibe of a private joke only he gets to enjoy has passed, and his facial cues seem to indicate the forthcoming invitation is sincere. "What do you say? Saturday night?"

I know this word doesn't mean much to him, but I toss it out, anyway. "No."

"Sunday, then," he counters, his tone slightly less friendly.

I shake my head. "No, thank you. I'm busy all weekend." And forever, if going somewhere alone with him is the alternative. What the hell is he thinking? I'm so baffled by his presence in my house, by the soup, by this bizarre dinner invitation… My head is spinning. What kind of game is he playing?

"Zoey, don't be rude," my mother admonishes, frowning mildly at me.

I feel my face flush, wondering how rude she'd think *he* was if she knew he sexually assaulted me yesterday and has the nerve to barge into my home—a place I should be able to feel safe—today. Looking up at Carter, I say calmly, "You should go."

"All right," Carter says, nodding, holding my gaze. "Walk me out to my car?"

I open my mouth to say no, but my mother is already rushing forward, glaring at me in confused disapproval. "Of course she'll walk you to your car. She's not normally like this, she really must not be feelin' good," she adds, bringing the back of her hand to rest against my forehead.

"Mom, stop," I mutter, swatting her hand away.

Carter smirks faintly, but catches himself, since he's pretending to be charming right now. "I won't keep her long," he promises.

"You take as long as you want," my mom says, shooting me another look of admonishment.

I'm so angry, I could explode. I definitely don't want to be alone with him, but I don't think he'll do anything horrible to me in the driveway with my family waiting inside. Just in case, as I resentfully walk toward the front door, I warn him, "My stepfather will be pulling in any minute, so yeah, you probably want to leave before you get trapped in the driveway."

"Yeah. Being trapped is no fun, is it, princess?" he murmurs, following behind me.

Unease creeps down my spine. "Stop calling me that."

"I'll get right on that, princess," he mocks.

"Was that fun for you?" I demand, wanting to know what possible reason he could have for whatever that was.

Shrugging, he says, "Kinda. I like playing with you."

My jaw locks and I try to breathe without expelling fire. "Why did you come here?" I ask, pulling the front door closed behind us.

Since we're alone now, he doesn't bother feigning his golden boy bullshit. "I brought you soup," he says, amusement clear in his tone.

"Is it roofie soup?"

"Of course not," he says dismissively. "I wouldn't roofie you. You're no good to me unconscious. I like mentally and physically stripping away your will. A pill is cheating."

"You're sick," I inform him.

He shrugs, apparently unconcerned. "Why don't you want to go to dinner with me?"

Eyes wide, I stare at him. "Is that a serious question? Did you hear all the words that just came out of your mouth? Also: you sexually assaulted me yesterday."

Hissing apologetically through his teeth, he says, "Hope you're not planning to tell anyone about that. I mean, you just accused Jake of the same thing, and your mom even knows we're a thing now. Seems like you just like throwing around accusations, doesn't it? Maybe you like the attention."

If he thinks I'm interested in playing this game with him when we don't have an audience, he is seriously mistaken. "Whatever, Carter."

I stop in front of his car—a pricey, deep red Mustang with two black stripes running down the center. It looks like something a spoiled asshole would drive, so of course this is his car.

"Here's the thing," he tells me, opening his driver's side door and tossing his gym bag inside. Then he closes the door and leans against it, shoving his hands into the pockets of his gray sweats. "Remember yesterday I said I'm not a tit man? I'm not, but I can't stop thinking about yours."

Shaking my head as I look off at the street to avoid looking at him, I say, "That's… I honestly don't even know how to respond to that."

"I suggest lifting your shirt and giving me a peek," he offers.

"Suggestion denied."

He shrugs. "It was worth a shot. So, dinner."

Is he for real right now? "You can't seriously think there is even a *sliver* of a chance I'm gonna willingly take my clothes off for you, ever. After what you did to me yesterday, you should spend the football season wearin' an orange jumpsuit and afraid to bend over in the shower to pick up the soap. I told you I wouldn't tell anyone, and I won't, but I thought it went without saying that I wanted you to leave me alone going forward. You are legitimately insane if you are *seriously* askin' me on a date. Not if you were the last man on Earth. There's no way you thought this would work."

"I'm giving you an opportunity to say yes this time," he informs me, like it's quite the boon.

"An opportunity. How considerate of you," I deadpan. "And I'm saying no," I add, immovably.

"I can work with that, too." Pushing off the car, he grabs my arm and yanks me against him.

My heart stalls, then hammers hard in my chest. I try to pull back, but he gets his arms locked around me, trapping me against his hard body like he did yesterday. "Get off me," I tell him lowly, struggling to get free, but he's too strong.

"You don't have to fight tooth and nail, you know," he tells me casually, moving my arms behind my back so he can keep me restrained and free up his other hand. "I like a little struggle, but you can take it down a notch."

He is so infuriating. I struggle harder, looking out at the road for potential help. There's no one outside across the street, no one driving by, so I cast a desperate glance back at my house. Right now would be a convenient time for my mother to be spying on me through a window, so of course she isn't. "Carter, seriously. Forget me telling on you, this is a good way to get caught red-handed."

"Stop fighting me and you'll get me out of here faster." His free hand moves to my chest now, groping my right breast. He palms it, his dark eyes locked on my face.

For a sliver of a moment, there's a break in my focus on getting away from him. Curiosity tugs at me. He's searching my gaze for something, but I don't know what. He knows I don't want to be touched—he's admitted as much. It's part of the fun for him. So, why does it feel like he's looking for interest? He can't *honestly* think he's going to find any, can he?

Knowing my step-dad will be pulling in any minute, I

swallow down my feelings and curiosities. Meeting Carter's gaze as if his actions don't rattle me, I ask, "Are you done?"

His hand leaves my breast, but only to slide up under my T-shirt so he can touch me without the fabric barrier between us. "Not just yet."

Over the shirt, I thought I could deal with, but under the shirt is a different story. My arms are still locked behind my back, though, so I can't fight him off physically. "Carter... please stop touching me."

"I like when you say please," he tells me, smiling faintly while he ignores my request. "It's cute."

"Then I'll never say it again."

He shakes his head as he catches the weight of my breast in his palm, running his thumb over my pebbled nipple. "That's the wrong tack, Ellis. I don't find it cute when you're petulant."

"I don't want you to find me cute. I want you to leave me alone."

He nods his head toward the car. "Then take a ride with me. I'll fuck you now and get you out of my system."

"Go to hell," I tell him, shifting to try to dislodge his hand. I gasp as he squeezes my nipple. There's a bite of pain, but a strange sort of tension lying just beneath it. It feels weird, but I actually don't completely hate it.

I hate him, though.

"I don't know why I like these so much," he murmurs, playing with my breast. I seethe as he brushes his thumb across the nipple, caresses my flesh, gives it a squeeze. As if we're friends and he's sharing something in confidence, he tells me, "I'm normally an ass man. Haven't even touched yours yet."

"There is no *yet*," I say, trying again to pull back, but his arm just locks around me tighter. "Look, I am *really* tryin' not to make trouble with you, Carter, but you're makin' it impossible. What is wrong with you assholes? When you get in trouble for something, you're supposed to stop doing it, not come back for more and make it worse."

His explanation is simple and crushing at the same time. "You have no power over us, Zoey. I know you fucked up Jake's year, maybe you feel all proud of yourself, but we both know you can't fuck up mine. You can't touch me. You can try, if you want to. I'll bury you if you do. I wouldn't advise it, but hell, if your honor is so damned important to you, go ahead and take me on, princess. Let's see who emerges the ultimate victor."

I know he's right, but that injustice is difficult to swallow.

"*Or,*" he says, releasing my breast and cutting his gaze toward the road as a car slows to a stop in front of my house, "you can roll with it. Reap the benefits. You've already sucked my dick, so I owe you a dinner, don't I?" he almost teases, smoothing his hand down the outside of my arm for the benefit of our approaching audience. "Just say yes."

"No."

"Suit yourself," he murmurs, releasing me and taking a step back. "I'll see you tomorrow. Make sure you study those notes. You might learn something," he says with a wink, before dropping into the driver's seat and pulling his door shut.

I wrap my arms around myself as he fires up the engine, but I don't wait around to watch him back out of the driveway. Instead, I head inside the house to retrieve those notes. Now that he said that, I'm worried he wrote something my mom shouldn't see, and I left them out on the kitchen counter.

I barely make it inside the door and she comes at me, her eyes wide with excitement. "You didn't tell me you were seein' Carter Mahoney. How in the world did that happen? Especially with all this Jake business. They're teammates."

"I know what they are," I mutter. "I really don't want to talk about it, Mom. Carter and I are *not* a thing. He's an asshole."

"Now, Zoey, that boy just brought you soup because you were home sick," she says, her tone skeptical, verging on lecturing. "He doesn't seem like an asshole to me. I think maybe you're bein' a touch judgmental. It certainly wouldn't be the first time."

Of course she does. Because why ask if I have a legitimate reason for feeling this way about him when she can just hope and pray I'm dating him instead? My mother is the physical embodiment of blissful ignorance, and while usually I can handle it, right now it's too much.

"It doesn't matter," I say, heading into the kitchen and grabbing my notes. I glance at them, seeing lines of words, but I fold the paper and shove it in my pocket without so much as skimming them.

Mom is right on my heels. "I think you should give him a chance, Zoey. Not all boys are bad. And he wants to take you out to Porter's. Wouldn't that be so nice? Just imagine the look on Betsy's face after all those snide comments she made about you and Jake."

"I'm not interested in him, all right? Let's drop it."

"But why?" she asks, following me. "He's handsome and popular, he comes from a great family, and he seems to really like you. Maybe if people see he's takin' your side, they'll stop givin' us all such a hard time about your dust-up with Jake."

She is so transparent. I hate that she cares so much what other people think that she's willing to turn a blind eye to my problems if Carter can make them all go away. As a kid, I followed in her footsteps and worried endlessly over what other people thought of me, too. As I've grown up, I realized that putting the opinions of others in such high regard is a shortcut to misery, and I don't want to take that path. My mom never found her way to that conclusion.

If she's going to campaign for him all night, I'm not going to sit here and listen to it. Instead of going in to the table to eat now that Hank's home and dinner is ready, I head for the stairs.

"Where are you goin'?" my mom calls after me.

"To my room. I'm not hungry. I'm gonna take a nap."

Since I've been "sick" she lets me go without argument, but I suspect this will come up again. It's so uncomfortable to even think about what happened yesterday, so I really don't want to have to tell her, but I might have to if she keeps pushing me at Carter.

He's a peculiar guy, and his abnormality does stir an academic interest within me, but he's also at such a clear social advantage that he's legitimately dangerous. Carter thinks he's above the law. He has money, talent, popularity, and the carefully constructed façade of an all-American golden boy. He has it all, so he can do as he pleases. Case in point, I haven't done a damn thing wrong, yet I've been targeted, bullied, and abused three times now—and that was for messing with Carter's best wide receiver, not Carter himself.

When I get to my room, I close my door and curl up in bed. I dig Carter's notes out of my pocket and read them. The first line is, "Of course I'm not really going to take notes for you, but while Mr. Hassenfeld is yammering on and you're hiding out at home like a coward, I thought I'd share with you the dream I had last night."

Oh, boy.

I shouldn't keep reading. It's going to be stressful, but it might also be evidence. Is he so cocky he would leave me a handwritten page full of threats? If so, I'm definitely hanging onto this. This could be gold.

Of course, that's not what it is, but it *is* filthy. It's not the confession I hoped for, it's not even a depiction of the rape he suggested interest in yesterday, it's just pure filth. He talks about nibbling on my breasts and eating me out until I come, crying out his name. He talks about me touching him and tasting him again (as if I did it willingly the first time). He talks about fucking me, but he makes no mention of force—nothing that would stick, anyway. Nothing some people wouldn't be into, anyway.

There's heat beneath my skin and an uncomfortable sexual stirring inside me as I read his filthy words. They're explicit, so I guess that's not insane, but they come from him. They depict sex between the two of us, and after what he did, that makes it so much more perverse.

I definitely can't keep this to use against him. The way he talks, anyone reading this would think we're involved in a consensual sexual relationship. It would hurt my case more than help it —especially his slick mention of me tasting him again. No sane, guilty person would refer to what he made me do in a love letter. It's a he-said she-said situation, and without Shayne or Jake attesting to my unwillingness—which they never would—it just sounds like I willingly blew Carter. If anything, if I tried to speak out against the asshole, this letter would probably make *me* look more like a liar than him.

I want to throw it out, but I tell myself there's a reason to keep it. A logical reason, not a shameful one. Maybe there is some scenario where it could prove useful, and I just haven't thought of it yet. Just in case, I fold the sheet of lined paper and shove it under my mattress.

Then I curl up in bed and try not to think about tomorrow, and what it might bring.

CHAPTER 5

JUST PULLING into the parking lot of my high school is daunting today.

I sit in the car for several minutes, trying to gear up to show my face. It kills me. I haven't done a damn thing wrong, and I'm the one who has to hide.

They should be hiding.

They're not. I never used to pay them much attention, but now as I clutch my books to my chest and keep my eyes straight ahead, I see the jocks in their letter jackets, sitting on and around the stone half-wall in front of the entrance doors.

I feel eyes on me, but I refuse to look and see if it's Jake or Carter. They can both fuck off, as far as I'm concerned. Shayne Sutton, too. They can all go rot in Hell together.

"Zoey!"

Even though that's not one of them, my heart freezes and I look over my shoulder as my friend Grace grins at me and hurries to catch up. The last thing I needed was her to call out my name like that right in front of them and draw even more attention to me, but I know she didn't do it on purpose. I love Grace, I love her bumbling obliviousness—she's one of the few people willing to be seen with me right now—but she doesn't understand what I'm up against. My fault, because I haven't told her everything, but I didn't want to stress her out with more of my mess.

As she approaches, she pulls her phone out of her pocket, beaming at me. "Wait up. I have to show you something!"

"Can we go inside first?" I ask, taking a step forward.

"It's so beautiful out this morning. What's your rush?" she asks cheerfully.

I don't want to, but as I adjust my backpack strap on my shoulder, I glance over at the horde of jocks. As expected, I meet Carter's gaze immediately. His lips curve up and he winks at me, so I promptly look away.

"Come on, Grace, you can show me inside."

"Wait." She holds her phone up in my face. I rear back slightly, then focus on the photo she's showing me. It's a picture of an adorable puppy in her backyard, its tiny puppy mouth closed around her thumb as he gnaws on her. "Is this not the most precious fur baby you have ever seen in your life?"

"Aww." I flash her a smile. "He's adorable. Is it a he?"

Nodding her head, she rubs her thumb over the screen. "His name is Scout. Isn't he just the sweetest thing? Mom surprised me with him last night. I posted a picture online, but you must not have seen it. How come you weren't at school yesterday?"

I head for the entry doors, expecting her to follow. "Bad cramps."

"Oh, those are the worst. Last week—"

Before she can finish, one of the other guys from the football team calls out, "Hey Zo, why don't you come on over here for a minute?"

I speed up instead. I can't imagine Carter shared the truth about what he did to me, but having witnessed him in action the past couple days, I wouldn't put it past him to tell a different version of the story and get ahead of it, just in case I did decide to talk. Tell them all some fallacy about how I went down on him because I like him, or because I was desperate to find some favor with everyone hating me for Jake, to turn me into a pathetic punch line—and a potential target to the other guys, who would think I'm easy if Jake and Carter have both had a go at me.

I hate Carter Mahoney even more than Jake Parsons.

Grace slows down behind me, looking back at the assembled group, then she hustles inside, pushing a chunk of wavy brunette hair behind her ear.

"Are they still bothering you?" she asks, her voice low.

"Something like that," I mutter vaguely.

"Well, you just keep your head up and don't let them get you down. No one can dull your light unless you let them."

Rather than respond to her unsolicited platitude, I glance back at the doors to make sure Carter didn't follow me inside to terrorize me some more. He didn't, so I push out a breath of relief.

"We should have a coffee date after school," Grace suggests, already onto the next thing. "When forces of evil are trying to get you down, focus on the things you love—liked iced coffee, and me."

I do love Grace, but I don't have the emotional capacity to deal with her right now. Sometimes she is so unwaveringly optimistic, I want to shake her. Luckily, she doesn't require much in return to keep the chatter going. A nod and murmur here and there, and she can talk for days without end. It's probably the main reason we're friends.

My first classes of the day pass uneventfully, but when it comes time for history class, my stomach knots up until I think I might actually be sick. Will he try to talk to me? Make fun of me with his friends? How will I even be able to concentrate on this test?

I'm a few minutes early, so I head to the bathroom before class begins. I stop before I get there when I see Carter walk out of the boy's bathroom.

Without time to think, I pivot and race back to the classroom. I don't want to be there with him, but I *definitely* don't want to get trapped alone with him in the hall or by the bathrooms. I don't think he would follow me inside the girl's bathroom, but who really knows? Clearly, I have his attention for the time being. I probably will, as long as he thinks he can corrupt me. I should hurry up and give my virginity to someone else so he'll lose interest in me. If only there were some contenders to choose from.

My heart races as I drop into my seat. I sigh with relief, putting my books down atop my desk. A moment later, Carter walks in. I have no idea what to expect. After last night, I shouldn't even be surprised when he approaches my desk, but I was hoping he wouldn't.

He doesn't linger, though. Just places his giant hand down on top of my books and says, "You should join the track team, Ellis."

"I'm not fast unless I'm runnin' from monsters," I inform him.

He flashes me a smile over his shoulder, his golden boy smile, the one he uses to charm everyone. I roll my eyes at him. I'm not fooled by that bullshit, and he knows it. I've seen who he really is, and I won't soon forget.

Unexpectedly, that small interaction does more to calm my nerves than unsettle me. Half of my anxiety today is the uncertainty, not knowing what to expect, what he will do or say, how he'll treat me. For the moment, I'm relatively safe, because I'm in a classroom full of other kids and a teacher. Carter may be ballsy, but he's not going to pounce on me in front of a teacher. He could still make me uncomfortable, though.

Despite my lack of concentration studying for it, I manage to finish the test. I can't help looking over at Carter once I'm done. He finished his test before I finished mine. Because he's sharp, or because he doesn't care? Now he's kicked back in his seat, playing on his cell phone. His attention isn't wavering and his thumbs are moving across the screen like he's texting someone. I wonder if it's a girl. I never paid much attention to Carter's love life before, as jocks have never been my cup of tea.

I am also not someone they usually notice. Now that a portion of the team has seen me naked, sure, I have their attention, but before Jake noticed me, there's no evidence the rest of them even knew I existed.

It makes me feel foolish now, how flattered I felt when Jake first noticed me over the summer. Carter wasn't on my radar then; he was so far out of my league, we didn't even exist on the same plane. We still don't. Now we're just bonded by a bizarre instance of abuse at his hands, by a dirty secret I have to keep.

I wonder how many other people have seen that side of Carter. Do all of his teammates know what he's really like, or just Jake and Shayne? What about girlfriends? Who has he even dated? I can only think of one ex-girlfriend of his in our grade—Erika Martin. She still associates with him since she's a cheerleader, but I don't know if she actually likes him. I'm tempted to pay closer attention, to see if she regards him more like an ex-boyfriend, or a former abuser. Was he like that with her? Does anything else get him off, or does he need to do what he did to me?

There's clearly something wrong with him, but why? Did something make him this way, or was he born with something off in his head? Is he pure evil, or is there anything more underneath?

I shouldn't even wonder. I shouldn't even care. I'm curious by nature, but whatever the reason, Carter is who he is, and that's someone dangerous. Someone to be avoided at all costs. Whether he doesn't *have* a conscience, or he can just ignore it more easily than most people, something makes him capable of hurting people. Capable of being amused by it.

Carter Mahoney thinks the rules don't apply to him, and the damndest thing is—at least for now—he's right. In this little town, football isn't a sport, it's a religion. Carter is the star quarterback, the handsome, shiny senior everyone expects to lead us to the state championships. His parents have also bought up half the town, so even if he did get in trouble, they can afford to bail him out of literally any situation.

I'd like to think someday he'll fall, but the ugly truth is, he probably won't. He has a dirty, rotten soul, but enough money and privilege that it will never matter. His victims will always be swept under the rug—and if one gets too noisy, I'm not positive there's a line he's afraid to cross. If he believes he's invincible, what does he have to be afraid of?

I'd love to be the one to show him he's not invincible, but how?

What *is* important to him? He says football doesn't matter to him, and that could be true. Football gives him more power and status, so that's probably what he likes about it, not necessarily playing the game.

Something has to matter to him. There must be *something* it would hurt him to lose. I don't know how I would find out what it is, though, without actually interacting with him.

Last night flashes to mind again, him actually having the gall to invite me out to dinner. What the hell was he thinking? He's so strange.

Now he puts his phone down and opens his notebook, grabbing a pencil and hunching over it, running the lead of his pencil across the paper in careful strokes. I crane my neck to try to get a peek, but I can't see what he's drawing.

A few minutes later, the bell rings. Carter flips his notebook shut, then grabs it and slides out of his seat. My gaze darts away before he notices me watching him. I shouldn't be, but something tickles at the back of my mind, the idea that maybe I can find out what does matter to him, then I won't be defenseless against him. I may not be able to bring him to justice, but it could benefit me to have some kind of ammunition to use against him. What if I could fight back in a less direct way, by costing him something that matters to him the way he took something that mattered from me?

Grace would tell me this is a bad idea. She would quote some Bible verse at me, or maybe that quote about digging two graves before you start on a journey of revenge. Grace would tell me to be the bigger person, to pray for him.

But Grace isn't here, and that's another reason I haven't told her about all this. Well-meaning as she is, she'll only piss me off with her unwanted advice. No one is going to tell me how to feel about my own experiences, how to feel toward the people who hurt me. Many have tried before it even got this bad, when Jake's grabby hands were the extent of the damage, and I didn't want to hear their bullshit, either.

The hell of it is, nobody would believe me a second time. A lot of people didn't even believe me the *first* time, and the ones who did? They didn't care.

I'm on my own now, and up against someone I stand no reasonable chance of defeating. Maybe no one else will defend my honor or stand up to the untouchables, but I'll figure out a way. It's not about hurting Carter because he hurt me, it's about ensuring that he doesn't do it to anybody else. I can't tell on him, but I don't want to keep my mouth shut and forever wonder if my silence endangered some other girl—maybe a bunch of them, littering the trail he blazes for the rest of his life.

I'm feeling stronger than I have since all this started, since even before Jake. I feel a little proud of myself, too. Carter may have knocked me down, but I didn't let him keep me there; I picked myself up and dusted myself off.

Of course, that is the moment Carter Mahoney walks up beside me and casually slings his arm around my shoulders. My whole body stiffens, but I'm infused with enough of my own protection that I'm able to look over at him and lift an eyebrow, as if unfazed.

"Can I help you?" I ask.

"How'd you do on the test?" he asks casually.

"I think I did all right. You?"

His eyebrows rise and fall briefly, like he only wanted to fuck with me and didn't expect a real response. "I'm a straight-A student," he assures me. "I'm sure I did just fine."

"Are you a straight-A student because you're smart, or because you play football and all the teachers pad your report card?" I inquire.

His lips curve up faintly. "The first one. Unless I'm hung over and I don't feel like giving a fuck, then sometimes it's the second one."

"I figured," I mutter.

"Speaking of being hung over, there's a party next weekend at Erika's house. You should come."

"Yeah, I don't think so." His arm is still draped around my shoulder as we walk, and given the halls are packed full of people, I can't help noticing people gawking at us. "You really shouldn't be seen with me, you know," I say, somewhat lightly, all things considered. "I'm not sure even your reputation can handle it after all the Jake stuff went down."

"Please," he says dismissively. "I could levitate a boulder with my reputation. Hell, Jake's not even playing this season; if I really felt like it, I could kick him out of everyone's good graces and put you on top."

"That sounds strangely like a proposition," I state.

He shrugs. "Just saying."

I fall silent for a moment, wondering how sincere he is. I would never actually consider selling myself out to save something as insignificant as my reputation in this ridiculous town, but if he's willing to turn his back on Jake for me, either he *really* wants my virginity any way he can get it, or…? Just or, I'm not sure what the "or" would be in this scenario. I would say, *or he likes me*, but that can't be the case. Before Jake made me notorious, Carter Mahoney didn't even know my name.

"I don't care about bein' popular," I inform him. "That doesn't matter to me."

"Above it all, huh?" He doesn't sound offended, more like he's taking stock of what he can offer me that will net him better results. "Okay, then. What matters to you?"

Like I'd tell him that. "What were you drawing?" I ask him.

Carter cocks a questioning eyebrow and looks over at me. "Excuse me?"

"In class. It looked like you were sketching something."

Amusement tugs at the corners of his lips. "Ellis, were you spying on me?"

My face flushes faintly, but I refuse to be cowed right now, in relative safety. "I keep an eye on the predators in my immediate vicinity," I inform him.

"Likely story," he replies with an effortless charm. "How'd you like the notes I took for you yesterday?"

"Those were not notes. That was written porn."

"Erotica, then. Don't be basic and pretend you don't know there's a difference."

I roll my eyes at him. "I work at a bookstore; I know what erotica is."

That catches his interest, but he keeps his tone conversational. "Yeah? Which bookstore?"

Shit, why did I say that? He already showed up at my house, I shouldn't tell him where he can get me alone on my way to my car. "You didn't answer my question, so why should I answer yours?"

"Why do you care what I was sketching? That's a better question."

Shaking my head, I say, "Never mind. Forget I asked."

A few seconds pass in silence. He still hasn't removed his arm from around me, and a cheerleader walking past stops dead and turns to stare, but Carter keeps moving. Finally, he says, "A bottle."

"You were drawin' a bottle?" I ask, skeptically.

He nods. "I was working on lighting and shading. Nothing significant, just practice."

"For class?"

"For someone who hates me, you sure have a lot of questions about me."

"You have to know your enemy to defeat them," I inform him with exaggerated haughtiness.

That only makes him grin. "Are you gonna defeat me, princess? I'd love to see you try." Tugging me close, he brings his other hand up to grab my jaw. "Remember that little chat we had, though? About you being a good little whore and keeping this pretty mouth shut, unless you're opening it to take my cock?"

My heart kicks up a couple speeds and I jerk my chin free. "I don't think we agreed to all that," I mutter, trying to pull away from him now. I've tried to play it cool with his touch, but now he's pushing farther, and my insides are starting to twist up. I don't want him to know that, so I try to maintain an even tone. "I haven't said anything. If I intended to, I probably wouldn't let you wrap your arm around me in the hallway."

"Let me, she says," he murmurs with amusement, like we're friends sharing a joke.

"Does it feel like I'm fightin' you, Carter?" I shoot back.

"Nope. Finally taking my advice?"

I shake my head, looking straight ahead. "Just trying to keep the peace, puppet master."

"Good." He says it calmly, like he lacks investment in whether or not I listen to his warning. "I'd hate to have to crush you publicly. You're so far beneath me, it just seems mean-spirited."

"Do you get off by mocking and threatening me?" I ask him.

"No, I get off when your eager little mouth works my cock," he informs me.

I look left, then right, then glare at him. "Could you not? I'm already referred to by the entire student populace as Zoey the ho. Ironically, for *not* wantin' sexual attention from a viable male, but they're not the brightest bulbs in the box; they'll probably forget the actual reason and turn me into the class whore."

"I can stop that, too," he informs me casually. "My friends set the tone around here. If I make them stop picking on you, everyone else will, too."

"I don't want your help. I can guess what kind of strings come along with it."

"I'm gonna fuck you eventually, Ellis. You should stop fighting it. Hell, maybe accept my help and get something out of it." Tapping his temple, he says, "Use your brain."

"You are delusional," I inform him.

Carter shakes his head. "Nah, I just know how to get what I want."

"It doesn't count as 'getting what you want' if you just take it," I tell him.

"Sure it does. I haven't exhausted all my efforts yet, though. I haven't resorted to taking yet, now, have I?"

Since his tone seems to convey I should be appreciative of his restraint, I can't help shaking my head at him. "You really are a spoiled little rich boy, aren't you? You should try actually workin' for something for once in your life. Not resolving to take it if your efforts aren't good enough, but open yourself up to actually failing. Give yourself some real stakes. You might find it strangely exciting."

Carter smiles at me like I've just tipped my hand. "You want me to find you exciting, Zoey Ellis?"

"I was not talking about me," I reply, rolling my eyes.

"Sure you were." He finally drops his arm from around my shoulder, just before backing away. "I'll think about it, how's that?"

I nod my head. "You do that. Consider bein' a decent person. See if you can figure out how to do it."

Flashing me a grin, he tells me, "I'm a straight-A student, remember? I think I can manage."

"We'll see," I reply, before he turns and disappears into the crowd.

CHAPTER 6

I END up going with Grace for a coffee date after school.

Iced coffee may not solve all of life's problems, but to be honest, after handling Carter so effectively in the hallway after history class, I'm feeling a little better about mine. I can't stand being bested by someone just because they have more money or more power than me. I hate being silenced by something like fear. But competing on even ground, that's fair. As long as I stand a chance of winning the game, I don't mind playing.

The problem, of course, is even if Carter pretends to play by the rules, he could stop at any time. He probably didn't even mean what he said in the hall, he was just running his mouth. Cheaters don't have to play by the rules, and he doesn't mind being a cheater.

Still, I'm feeling less like a victim and more like someone with a little control over her life, so I take advantage and try to be a normal teenager for the rest of the day.

Thursday doesn't feel as daunting. I'm not as afraid of seeing Carter (or any of the other guys) at school. In fact, I'm wondering if I'm the one giving them all their power. If I let them make me afraid, then yeah, their intimidation works. If I refuse to betray awkwardness or discomfort in their presence, I'm taking away the only power they have over me without committing a crime.

It was different when they had me cornered in a classroom on Monday, but now the halls are swimming with students and faculty. Honestly, it feels like another world. I don't like having a secret with those three assholes, but no one else knows about it. Maybe if no one else knows, it doesn't have to be real.

I made it real with Jake when I told on him, and boy, did that not go well. Since telling on Carter is off the table anyway, I'm going to control this as long as I possibly can.

Carter and I don't talk at all on Thursday. After class he heads out without looking at me, and I tell myself I've probably *already* lost his interest, just by implying he might stand a chance if he actually tried.

Well, good. I didn't mean it, anyway. Out of my league or not, Carter Mahoney is a predatory ass, and I don't want anything to do with him and his dark, messed up games.

After school, I head straight to work. Money is tight at my house, always has been, so I don't have anything like a college fund. My mom opened a savings account for me when I was 8, and it has $100 in it. Or, whatever $100 plus 10 years of interest on $100 is, which still isn't much. Saving for college became entirely my problem, so I took a part-time cashier job at a discount bookstore. I enjoy reading, so I'm tempted to spend all my paychecks there. To compromise, I allow myself two books per biweekly paycheck, then I give myself a small allowance, but I save most of my money for tuition and books next year.

Unless I'm able to get a free ride at one of the schools I'm looking at, my first stop will likely be community college. Since I'm paying for everything myself, I have to make my dollar stretch as far as it can, and that means forgoing the typical college experience and commuting to a nearby school for the first two years. Definitely not what I want, but I have to be realistic.

Whatever I end up doing, I eventually want to get out of this town. I love my family, I'm sure I'll miss them once I'm gone, but I've never lived outside of Texas, and I want to see what else is out there. When my mom and Hank first got married, we took annual vacations to Missouri for a week during the summer, but once they had my little brother, money got tighter. The vacations stopped since they had to buy things like diapers and formula, and we haven't had one since.

Someday I'm going to live somewhere with burnt orange foliage every fall, with snow every Christmas, and I'm going to be able to afford to go on vacation somewhere different every single summer.

"What's that dreamy look on your face for?"

My eyes widen and snap to the roguish smile of Carter Mahoney. "Seriously?" I ask. "What are you doing here?"

"There are three bookstores in the area. I'm almost disappointed by how easy it was to find you."

"Stalking is illegal, you know?" I tell him.

"But shopping isn't," he states, slapping a book down on the counter.

Before I look, I guess at what it will be. Maybe a well-worn copy of *Tales of Ordinary Madness*. Carter seems like a Bukowoski kind of guy. Not the kind who buys it just to put on their bookshelf so they'll seem edgy and interesting, but the kind who would actually consume every page and appreciate the madness, relate to the filth.

The first time I tried to read Bukowski, I ended up red-faced and grimy with such a thick coat of shame, I felt like people could see it on me. Carter doesn't know shame, though. He would be able to enjoy Bukowski the first time through.

I realize my own thoughts sound a lot like admiration. Like there's some part of me that revels in his brazen depravity. Come to think of it, my first bout with Bukowski made me feel a little like I did when I read the "notes" Carter wrote for me in class. They were more explicit, less openly twisted than Bukowski, but that's because we live in a more casually vulgar time than Bukowski wrote in, and Carter couldn't reference his actual crime. Besides, it wasn't the dirty words so much as the mind they came from that made Carter's note so depraved. Even though I knew it was sick and twisted, I felt that same faint stirring of curiosity, just like when I read Bukowski that first time.

Forcing myself to focus on the book he's actually buying instead of trying to guess at his literary tastes, or how his degree of madness relates to a controversial poet's, I take in the cover and immediately realize he must be fucking with me.

The book he placed on the counter is a kid's book with a glittery unicorn on the front cover.

My eyebrows rise and I pick up the book to show him, as if he somehow confused it for Kerouac. "In the mood for a little light reading tonight?"

Before he has a chance to answer, an adorable little girl with hair as dark as his comes running up and puts a mermaid plush with pink yarn hair on the counter. Her dark eyes match his, too, and she has his air of tacit authority as she turns to look up at him. "And this, too."

My eyes widen as I take in the mini-Carter. "There's a tiny, adorable version of you?"

"Baby sister," he explains, cracking a smile as he looks down at her.

"Wow. Big age gap," I remark. Leaning across the counter so I'm closer to her, I ask, "How old are you, cutie pie?"

"I'm five," she announces with pride, holding up five fingers to show me.

I pick up her mermaid and walk her along the edge of the counter. "What's her name? Did you pick one yet?"

"Not yet. What do you think I should name her?" she inquires, eyeing up the pink-haired mermaid.

"What about Ariel?" I suggest.

Wrinkling up her nose adorably, she shakes her head. "No, she doesn't have *red* hair."

Dramatically smacking my palm against my forehead, I tell her, "You're right, what was I thinking? You'll have to pick a name for her. I bet you're better at it than I am."

She eyes up the mermaid for two seconds, then brightens. "What about Seashell?"

"That's a great name for a mermaid. You must be so smart to think of such a good name. What's *your* name?"

"Chloe," she answers.

Carter must be tired of sharing the spotlight, because he hip bumps her out of the way. "All right, move it, squirt. I need to pay for your stuff."

She turns and makes her merry way to a display of coloring books set up near the register. She grabs one, sits down on the floor, and starts flipping through it.

"Your little sister is adorable," I inform him.

"She knows it, too," he tells me, pulling out his wallet.

I shake my head, grabbing my scan gun and ringing up his items. "Bringing a cute kid in was pretty low. I can't be mean to you in front of your baby sister."

"I mean, you could be," he reasons. "But yeah, I kinda figured you wouldn't. You're a sweetheart underneath it all, aren't you, princess?"

Sliding an unamused look his way, I remind him, "I told you not to call me that."

"And I told you to say please," he returns easily.

Flicking a glance at his sister to make sure she's still out of earshot, I murmur, "That only works when you have me half-naked and a little afraid."

"And you wonder why I like *having* you half-naked and a little afraid," he shoots back.

Depraved. Carter Mahoney is absolutely depraved.

I ignore his attempt to revisit that day and place his items into a bag. "Your total is $12.72."

His dark eyebrows rise. "Damn, really? This place is cheap."

"Correct. That's sort of the appeal," I tell him.

Glancing at the impulse buy Dr. Seuss pencils and the rack of assorted gift cards on the counter, he asks, "You like to read?"

"I do."

"What do you like to read?" he asks.

Sighing heavily, I glance behind him. I'm looking for an excuse to kick him out, but there are no waiting customers, so I don't really have a viable reason I could get by my manager.

As if he understands my mission, he grabs a *Cat in the Hat* pencil and puts it down on the counter. "Here, I'm buying this too. I'm not done shopping yet. This might take a while."

"Uh-huh. You can't just stand here and harass me, you know? This is my place of work. I can tell my manager and he'll make you leave."

I'm bluffing. My manager is easily overwrought and would

probably be too afraid of a lost sale, but Carter doesn't know that.

"You can tell your manager that I'm thinking too hard about my *Cat in the Hat* pencil purchase and get me kicked out?" he questions. "Wow, you're a real hardass."

I roll my eyes, but scan his pencil and drop it in the bag. "Anything else today, sir?" I ask with mocking sweetness.

"You can call me that again," he tells me, suggestive amusement flickering in his dark eyes.

"If there's nothing else, your total——"

"I'm not done," he insists, fingering the stacks of plastic gift cards. "In your professional opinion, if I wanted to buy a gift card, which design is best?"

"Literally any of them," I reply dryly, since he's just wasting my time. "They all serve the same purpose."

"I expect more guidance from a professional such as yourself," he states, shaking his head in mock disappointment.

I look over at his sister again, since he is clearly a terrible babysitter. She hasn't moved from her spot on the floor. She appears to be tempted to rip the crayons out of the front of the book and start coloring, though. Clearly, she has more self-control than her brother, because she hasn't done it yet.

"How old is your other sister?" I ask him.

"My other sister? What makes you think I have two?"

"Well, you told my mom your sister is married and owns a restaurant in Dallas. Assumin' the tiny one over there isn't a major overachiever, you must have at least one more."

Fingering through a row of gift cards, he says, "I do. She's twenty-seven. Why do you ask?"

"I'm just wildly confused about how your parents decide to have kids. Did they have her young or something?"

He nods his head, giving up his pretense of looking at gift cards and shoving his hands into his pockets. "Yeah. My mom was a freshman in college. Dad was a senior. She was definitely not planned."

I do the math in my head. "So... she had your sister in college, then you 9 years later, then decided not to have another child until she was 41? Another surprise baby?"

"You have a lot of questions about my life," he remarks.

His little sister gives up the good fight and rips open the crayons on the front cover so she can start coloring a picture. "There it is. Now you have to buy that coloring book," I inform him.

"Oh no, how will I ever afford the expense?" he jokes, without even bothering to look.

"How old were you the first time you had sex?" I ask.

He seems to know exactly where my mind is wandering. He doesn't answer me, but he does assure me, "She's not my kid, Zoey."

"I mean, I would hope not, because you would have been way too young to even have sex—"

"It's not too young. I *was* thirteen the first time I had sex."

That stuns me a little. "You were having sex when you were 13?"

His enlightening response is a shrug. "We don't all wait until we're growing gray hair, Ellis. That's just you."

I shake my head. "That honestly makes me sad for you. That had to have been truly terrible sex."

"All you have to compare it to is what happened in that classroom between us. You want to feel sad for someone, save your tears for yourself."

I frown because he sounds defensive, and people generally only become defensive when they're feeling attacked. He aims what happened in the classroom at me like it's a loaded weapon, like he *wants* to hurt me with the memory. I know it's absurd to worry that he feels judged, but a pinch of guilt bites me. I do judge Carter for what he did to me, but not for having sex at a young age. It's just unfathomable to me. I was still such a kid at 13, sex wasn't even on my radar yet.

"I wasn't—I just meant—"

Cutting me off, he looks over his shoulder at his little sister. "Squirt, bring that over here."

"Coming!" She closes the book and pops up off the ground, bringing her coloring book and opened crayons over to the counter.

"You're not supposed to open stuff when we're still at the store," he tells her.

"Sorry," she says, sounding not at all sorry.

I crack a smile and scan her coloring book, carefully putting the crayons back in their packaging and putting it all in the bag. "Wow, you sure cleaned up today, didn't you?"

Chloe looks back at the spot she was sitting in, confused, then back at me. "I didn't make a mess."

"Oh, no, that's not—I meant, you sure got a lot of stuff. Carter must be a pretty nice big brother to buy all this stuff for you."

She nods her agreement and hugs his leg. "Yeah, I love him. He's my favorite."

She's so adorable. Even though he's the devil, seeing her hug his leg like that tugs on my heartstrings.

Carter grabs one of the gift cards he was playing with and tosses it on the counter. "Load 50 bucks on that, too."

I scan the card, load it with $50, and read him his new total. He pulls out a credit card and pays the bill like it's nothing, but it's more than I will make working here this week. He doesn't even *have* a job; he just plays football and goes to school. His parents will undoubtedly foot the bill for whatever he wants now, and then they'll pay for him to go off to some fancy four year college. I can't imagine what that must be like.

The printer spits out a receipt and I slip it in the bag, gathering the handles and holding it over the counter. "There you go."

Carter takes the plastic bag, holding my gaze. "You should come to the game tomorrow night. We're all going out for food after—a whole group, so you won't be alone with me," he adds, as if anticipating that's a deal-breaker.

"Yeah, I wasn't alone with you the other day, either," I remind him. "An audience doesn't seem to put you off."

Instead of looking remotely ashamed, he cracks a faint smile. "That's fair. This is different, though. My ex-girlfriend will be there, and I assure you she would not be down to watch. I'll behave myself, I promise."

I shake my head. "No. Thanks for asking this time, I guess, but... no."

"You're making this harder than it has to be, Ellis," he tells me, lowering the bag to his side.

Chloe wastes no time, spreading the bag open so she can reach in and grab her mermaid doll out of it.

I'd like to tell him I don't like him and I don't like his friends, so it's unreasonable to expect I would want to go out with any of them after a football game I frankly don't care about, but I can't, because he brought a tiny, adorable, raven-haired buffer.

He doesn't seem to expect a reply. "Think about it," he tells me, before turning and heading toward the door with the little girl.

Just as he's opening the door to leave, I notice he left his gift card on the counter. "Carter, wait! You forgot your gift card."

"No, I didn't," he calls back, just before the door closes.

I frown at the door, then hesitantly pick up the gift card. It takes a few seconds before I take his meaning.

He bought the gift card for me?

CHAPTER 7

PAYDAY IS THE BEST DAY, but it's even sweeter this week. Instead of hoping against hope there'll be something I'll want to read in the clearance section, I browse the full-price aisles. This week, I get books from the very top of my to-read list, and when I hit the clearance section just to make sure I'm not missing anything, I have the extra funds to pick up a book for my younger brother. It's satisfying when my manager rings up my selections and instead of paying with a portion of my hard-earned income, it's as easy as swiping a gift card.

I did briefly consider the moral ramifications of using a gift card Carter Mahoney bought for me. On one hand, it could probably be looked at as selling myself out for $50 worth of books. But I haven't sold myself out at all. I don't like him any more for leaving the gift card behind; I just figured since he did, I might as well put it to good use.

I meet Grace for iced coffee after I pick up my check. She shows me more pictures of her new puppy, shares snippets of Bible study at me, and takes a two second video of us drinking iced coffee and flashing peace signs. It's a thing Grace does—she takes a quick two seconds out of every day and records it, then at the end of the month, she reviews them and tells everyone in her youth group about all the blessings she has experienced.

As she reviews today's clip, she shakes her head and tells me, "I've already experienced so many blessings this month. Mama giving me Scout, coffee dates with my best friend. I wonder what else the month has in store for me."

"All good things, I hope."

Beaming up at me, she puts down her phone. "Have you had many blessings this week?"

Have I? If I didn't have to explain, I would probably count my bookstore gift card a random blessing that I appreciate, but the deliverer poses a moral dilemma, and I don't want to lie.

"Here's a quandary for you," I tell her. "Hypothetically, say the devil sent me a blessing. Would that still count? Would I be ethically compelled to forfeit said blessing?"

Frowning, Grace sits back, sips her drink, and mulls it over. "Well, are you sure the devil sent the blessing? Some blessings come in disguise."

"I'm fairly certain. In this scenario, let's say the blessing came from a very bad person. A gift from someone who wronged you."

Her tone is immediately more dismissive. "Oh, well, I wouldn't say that's from the devil at all. I'd say that sounds more like…" She pauses, trying to find a way to word her thoughts. "Sometimes good things come from unexpected places. Sometimes a blessing might be rooted in evil intent, but there might be an opportunity to reclaim grace and glory, to lead someone onto the right path." Barely missing a beat, she leans forward and meets my gaze. "Is Jake tryin' to make amends for what he did?"

Shaking my head, I watch the trail of condensation on my cup rather than look at her. "No, it's not about Jake. It was just a hypothetical."

"Well, it sounds to me like maybe you have a chance to act with love and make a difference," she states stubbornly. "There's nothing wrong with standing up for yourself, Zoey, but sometimes forgiveness does more good for everyone. I know he behaved so inappropriately, but maybe this is his chance to learn something, to start on a path toward being a better person. You should invite him to church. I know he already goes to one, but… well, that didn't stop him from groping you, so maybe it's not such a good fit for him. Maybe he'd like ours better. Pastor James is younger, more relatable. Maybe he'd get more out of our services than the one he goes to now."

"Again, this is not about Jake," I tell her.

Grace frowns. "Well, who else has wronged you?"

I shake my head, grabbing my iced coffee and taking a sip. "Like I said, it was just a hypothetical. A situation from a book I'm reading, not about me. I just like to dig in and think about what I'm reading, you know?"

Grace doesn't know, because if it's not assigned by a teacher, about Jesus, or a devotional in her journal, Grace isn't reading it. That's why it's the right excuse, though. She immediately loses interest, nodding at my silly reading hobby and jumping topics, telling me all about these new canvas paintings she's thinking about buying to hang up in her bedroom.

AFTER I GET HOME and changed into some comfy pajamas, I do maybe the least productive thing I could do—I quietly stalk Carter Mahoney's social media.

It starts out as mild curiosity, the thought that maybe I could find out more about what kind of person he actually is by looking at what he takes pictures of and shares with the world, but it's just more bullshit. From the looks of Carter's profile, he's a typical golden boy. I almost choke on some of the bullshit captions, envisioning him choking on laughter as he types them out.

"Such a privilege to have the governor show up for my team tonight. #GoLonghorns #Longhornlife #blessed"

"Oh, my God, you are *so* full of it," I say to no one, shaking my head. I'm lying tummy down on my bed with my feet in the air, perusing this stream of lies.

A picture of him eating fries with Jake, Shayne, Erika, and some other girl whose name I can't recall is captioned "Good food, good friends, good times."

"How long did it take you to come up with that one, Kerouac?" I mutter.

His latest post is a shaky ten second video of the football field, then he turns it around and flashes it his practiced trouble-making grin. Despite being posted only an hour ago, it already has nearly two hundred loves and 42 comments from lovesick girls who go to our school. Like me a few weeks ago, Carter probably knows none of their names.

Before that picture, he posted a moody black and white shot of him on the field in his letter jacket, just his back and stony profile visible. That one looks the most real, like maybe someone caught him off guard and he wasn't performing for his audience when the shot was taken.

Why are you always performing, Carter Mahoney?

I hate that question because it has to have an answer. Even if it's a shitty answer, there must be one.

Unless he really is just a monster. I suppose some people are born broken, with brains that work differently, with impaired empathy and a literal inability to function the way most of us do without even thinking about it.

I remember a saying I heard once, some trite, throwaway phrase: Hurt people hurt people. Did someone hurt Carter Mahoney? What is his home life actually like? I suppose I don't know. He has one of those families where everyone knows *of* them, but who actually *knows* them? Do the people in Carter's life see beneath the bullshit façade he puts out in the world, or does he keep that side of himself hidden even from those closest to him?

Perhaps most curiously, why show it to *me*? If he doesn't have a trail of victims behind him, why make me his first? Was it just an opportunity he couldn't pass up? I'd like to believe the situation spun out of control and he just got carried away, but I know that isn't true. I think that's exactly what happened to Jake, but not Carter. Carter knew exactly what he was doing, and he didn't so much as hesitate. He struck me down without consideration, without care, and I have to wonder why?

Normal, healthy people don't have impulses like that, do they?

Rather than listen to the echo chamber in my mind, I steer away from Carter's pictures and open my Internet app, attempting to ferret out answers that way. I get lost down a rabbit hole, researching fantasies common to both men and women, speculation as to why some people have such fantasies, conjecture that perhaps it's related to a wider sexual repertoire—more sexually open-minded people may be more inclined toward a greater variety of fantasies. History of abuse, gender roles, luck of the draw—lots of theories, but no solid explanations.

None of these are helpful in understanding what he did though, they're mostly about rape fantasy. A common fantasy, apparently. Huh.

This isn't the way I saw my Friday night going, but hell, I like to learn new things.

I research outright rape next. The reasons people might do it. There are a lot of stances and theories. Could he, in some way, for some reason, be "getting back" at women? That seems unlikely, given that he's popular and girls love him, but I don't know about his home life. He's far from the ugly guy in the back of class, watching the other guys clean up and feeling left out. The power motive seems feasible. Carter admitted he liked having me vulnerable and afraid, begging him. I don't know if he's ever committed that crime, though. I know he forced himself on me in the classroom, but has he hurt other girls? If not, why now? I try to research that, too, but it's murky and difficult to wade through all the information, then pick out relevant pieces without even knowing much about him.

I lose the whole night that way, traversing rabbit holes about a decidedly unpleasant topic. I feel so desensitized, so academically removed from the situation by the time I stop researching, that I'm able to relive that experience in the classroom in a detached way, without feeling as uncomfortable as I usually do when it crosses my mind. The one article was quite thorough, and it suggested that men who do these sorts of things generally start right around this age—high school or college. Some may commit the crime once or twice, while others are serial offenders.

But why? What makes the difference?

I could probably spend years studying this and not know the simple answer, but to be honest, right now, I only want to know the answer in regards to Carter Mahoney. I don't like to let Grace's words hang around in my head, and I'm by no means some angel of outreach, trying to save every soul I come across. That's more Grace's arena than mine, but knowing what I know about Carter, I can't deny feeling a certain level of culpability. A responsibility for his behavior, because I know about it, and maybe no one else does. I've already sworn I wouldn't tell anyone what happened in that classroom, and I meant it, mostly because I'm afraid of him. But I need to know some other innocent girl isn't going to be hurt because of my silence. I *want* to know why Carter wants to hurt me, but I *need* know he won't hurt someone else.

The problem being, of course, that's not the kind of information I can collect in a group-hang or from dissecting his social media posts. To keep myself safe, I can't be alone with Carter, but I don't know how else I can communicate with him. I don't think he's dumb enough to discuss any of this via text, because then I would have evidence to use against him.

I wish I could just divorce myself from this whole situation, but I can't. It'll drive me crazy wondering. I'll lose sleep every night worrying about every other girl who ever crosses Carter's path. What if he has the taste for it now? What if his inability to further abuse me only frustrates him, and he find someone easier to victimize? I'm not one of them, but there *were* 42 eager girls commenting all over his shit. It wasn't because they found the football field so compelling.

Carter is perhaps the most dangerous predator around because he can attract prey so easily. How many girls might be uncomfortable by things he wants to do sexually, but rather than voice that, they would feel pressured to go along with it and keep their mouths shut because he's Carter Mahoney?

My imagination is running away with me and by the end of my pondering session, I'm so hyped up, I feel like I need to tie a cape around my neck and go protect every woman in town from the presumed predilections of the damned quarterback.

Why does *he* think it's okay that he did what he did? Nobody thinks they're the bad guy, right? In his mind, he must have some justification for his behavior. When I asked him what I ever did to him, asked what his excuse was in the classroom that day, he was blasé, told me didn't need one, but he was bullshitting me.

There is a reason, there has to be, and I won't find peace until I know what it is.

CHAPTER 8

WEEKEND SLIPS AWAY and before I know it, it's Monday morning. Time to start a whole new week.

I worked both days of the weekend, but when I wasn't studying for school, I was studying for my pet project—my Carter Mahoney project. I did more and more research online, trying to peg him. It's useless to try to understand his actions separate from him, so I've made understanding him my mission. A tricky project with perilous research that I can't conduct easily, but at least research is something I'm comfortable with.

Given a sense of purpose, I find it much easier to get through the days. No longer a numb bundle of feelings wrapped up in a blanket without the ability to feel safe anymore, now I am a woman on a mission. Now, I have an objective. Once I have achieved that objective, I can let this whole thing go and move on with my life.

I don't even see Carter until history class today, and he doesn't get to class until seconds before the bell, so there's no chance for interaction until afterward.

And of course, because I'm curious, he pays no attention to me whatsoever and leaves class talking to his friends instead of harassing me.

Tuesday morning, I show up to a renewed chorus of "Zoey the ho" chants, and Carter is right there at the center of the asshats doing the chanting. He doesn't add to the noise, but he leans against the wall, arms crossed, watching me hear it. He looks like a king holding court, and his subjects are all assholes.

Definitely not going to approach him when he has an audience to perform in front of. I might be curious about Carter, but I'm still sensible enough to be wary of him. Whatever he's like with me when we're alone, I know he won't be the same person in front of them, and I have no interest whatsoever in *their* Carter.

Since I caught his attention on the way in the building today, after history class, Carter falls into step beside me as I'm leaving.

"Missed you at the game," he remarks, like we've lost no time.

Glancing over at him as I hug my books against my chest, I remind him, "I told you I wouldn't be there."

He shrugs casually. "Could have changed your mind."

"No offense, but I honestly could not care less about football. I know that's a sacrilege in this town, but it's not my thing."

"Your friend Grace was there," he states.

I didn't even think he knew Grace's name, and the way he says that, like he knows it will unsettle me… well, it *does* unsettle me. It sends chills of caution dancing across the nape of my neck.

He probably wants a reaction, so I don't give him one. "I don't go everywhere my friends go; I'm not *you*."

His tone is amused, and as he speaks, he reaches his arm out and drapes it around my shoulder. "Yeah, you have a mind of your own, don't you, princess?"

It shouldn't be an accusation, but I know it keeps me from fitting in with my peers, even some family members, so it feels a little like one. "Yes, as a matter of fact, I do."

"I like that," he tells me casually enough, but it feels real. "I like smart girls who navigate their own paths instead of following everyone else's. You strike me as that sort of girl."

Excitement shouldn't jump within me, but he just gave me a free puzzle piece, and I grab it up with greedy hands. "Yeah?" I ask, with genuine curiosity. "Do you know many women like that?"

He nods his head, and I begin making mental notes. *Doesn't look down on/disdain all women.* "My older sister is sharp as a tack. You'd like her."

"What about your mom?"

His lips curve up faintly, but he doesn't respond. "I just answered a question, didn't I? Your turn. Give me something about you."

"I don't know what you're lookin' for. What I like in a woman?" I ask lightly.

"Hey, if you roll that way, I am all ears."

I know he's joking, but I answer him anyway. "I don't. I mean, girls are pretty, but I seldom have to resist the urge to corner them in classrooms and grope them against their will, so... I'm probably not that into them."

"Is that the barometer?" he asks, amused.

"Seems to be." My heart speeds up, but this is such a perfect opening to ask the one question I *need* an answer to, I don't see how I can resist. Shoving down my doubts, I ask, "Have you... have you ever done that before? To anyone else, I mean? Before me?"

Predictably, he falls silent. His arm feels heavier around my shoulder, but he doesn't move it. When he doesn't want to answer a question, I notice he ignores it. I expect him to change the subject altogether, but instead he asks, "Why do you want to know?"

My pounding heart tells me I should stop, that I should break away, cut my losses, and flee his company. My gut tells me maybe giving him something real is the way to go. I go with my gut. "I... I can't help wondering if my silence is endangering other girls. Telling isn't just about consequences for the sake of myself, for some sense of justice, it's about correcting the behavior. I assumed when I told on Jake, he would be punished, then if he ever thought about behaving that way again, he would remember the consequences he faced and choose differently. Obviously, it didn't work out that way, but it wasn't all about satisfying my own ego. It wasn't just that someone dared wrong me, and my fury had to be sated. It was about more than that. It was about making sure someone more vulnerable than me wasn't hurt. Maybe someone who… who wouldn't be able to handle it the way I did."

I feel stripped bare, having said that to him. My insides are shaking with the vulnerability of exposing myself to a known predator, my gut roiling with dread as I wait for him to strike me when he knows he can land a good hit.

The moment stretches on forever, bile rising in my throat as I wait. When he continues to hold his silence, I finally work up my nerve to look at him, half-expecting him to look amused at my little speech. He doesn't, though. A small measure of relief courses through me because he looks pensive, the way I must have looked when I was perusing article after article, trying to understand him and his behavior.

"Yo, Mahoney!"

The shout breaks the spell. Carter's arm falls from my shoulders. We both look up as one of his teammates stalks toward us, nodding at Carter, then looking over at me. His smirk grows when his gaze lands on me.

"Careful, man, you don't wanna mess around with Zoey the ho. She'll run and tell her mommy on you for lookin' at her wrong."

I stiffen, but tilt my chin up stubbornly. "No, you can look all you want, just don't touch unless you want a criminal record." My tone is deceptively sweet, but my eyes are two orbs of blue ice.

He shakes his head at me, his gaze dropping to the most inappropriate parts of my body. "It's a damn shame someone so fine has to be such a prude."

"I prefer selective. Tossin' a ball around with your buddies doesn't really go the distance in impressing me. Sorry."

Scoffing, he says, "Tossin' the ball around with our buddies? We don't play ball in someone's backyard, darlin'; we're champions."

God, who cares? I've talked to jocks enough for one day, and I'm definitely not going to get any more insight into Carter with his bonehead friend here, so it's time to wrap it up.

"Great. Well, if you're so impressive, surely there are girls who *want* your attention, so there's no need to force it on the ones who don't," I point out.

"No one buys your bullshit, Zoey," he tells me, his blue eyes glowing with contempt. "Parsons has never struggled with the ladies, and frankly, I don't see anything so special about you to make him lose his damn mind." Advancing a step closer, his voice drops with menace. "We all know you're just a stuck-up, lyin' little bitch."

I swallow, resisting the urge to take a step back. It's easy to run off at the mouth with these meatheads, but when they bring physicality into the arena, I can no longer compete.

"That's enough," Carter says, surprising both of us.

My gaze darts to him, and his friend's eyebrows rise, but he takes a slow step back. Despite his obedience, he regards Carter with the confusion of a junkyard dog whose owner just commanded he let a thief escape unscathed.

Carter doesn't explain himself. He moves away from me and nods at his friend as he walks ahead of him, clearly expecting him to fall in line and follow his lead. "Come on, I'm starving. What'd your mom make good for me today, Cartwright?"

His friend smiles, shaking his head. "You're such an asshole."

As unimpressed as I am when other girls are struck stupid by the sight of Carter Mahoney, I find myself watching him disappear down the hall, wondering endlessly about why he does everything he does. Why did he let me mouth off like that without joining Cartwright's side. Why stop Cartwright when he got mean? What just happened doesn't jive with Carter's all-important image. I'm the enemy, and Carter let them chant at me just this morning.

I'm so distracted that I don't even realize Grace sidles up beside me until I hear her voice. "Why were you walkin' with Carter Mahoney?"

Finally tearing my eyes away from his disappearing figure, I force my feet into motion. "I wasn't walking *with* him. We were both leaving class at the same time, that's all. He's in my history class."

"I'm aware of that. But it definitely looked like you two were talking until his friend broke up the party."

I shrug. "Sometimes when he leaves class and doesn't have anyone else to talk to, he talks to me."

"Now that I think about it, I haven't heard him joinin' in lately when people are talking crap about you with that lame nickname the jocks used absolutely no brain power to dream up," she says.

"Right? Zoey the ho is so easy. They could have at least gone with something fun, like harlot or trollop."

"Harlot is such a fun word," Grace agrees. "Ho is unimaginative."

"Yeah, well, they're not popular for their cunning wit," I point out.

Glancing over at me, Grace decides to go fishing. "Carter Mahoney is kind of gorgeous. Don't pretend you haven't noticed."

"Ugh." I roll my eyes, shaking my head. "Don't do this. Not today, Satan."

Shrugging innocently, she says, "I'm just saying, he doesn't follow me out of classrooms talkin' *my* ear off. Do you like him?"

"Definitely not. No. He's… bad news."

"I can't disagree with that," Grace says, hugging her own books as we walk. "I don't like to gossip, but considering the women he's known to spend his time with, I'm sure he's way too fast for you, anyway. Romantically, I mean. If you're just reaching out in a casual, Christian way, then no big deal, but he's definitely not waiting for marriage, I'll just say that."

I nearly stop in my tracks, staring with new eyes at my best friend and possible fountain of information. "You know things about Carter's sex life?"

Heat blossoms on Grace's cheeks. "It's not nice to gossip."

My mind shoots off so many questions, I don't even know what to ask first. "No, I know. It's not gossip. I won't tell anyone else, I promise. Tell me everything you know. Everything. Leave nothin' out."

Grace fidgets. "Well, I don't know *all* the details. I try to close my ears to that sort of talk."

Dammit, Grace! Don't be a goody two shoes right now!

"I do know he generally sleeps with women a lot older than

us, though. For the most part, he acts like high school girls are beneath him—not like he hasn't slept with any, but the only one he kept around for a while was Erika Martin, and that's probably just because he's stuck with her in his friend circle so he got pushed into dating her."

I suppose that sounds feasible. Carter guards his image, and Erika is popular, too. I'm not familiar enough with their dynamics to know how her social power stacks up to his.

"I heard the reason they broke up was because Carter slept with a teacher, and Erika caught them red-handed, makin' out in her classroom. Remember last year when that pretty redheaded art teacher just disappeared halfway through the term? Rumor was, that's what happened. Once their affair was found out, she had to resign and leave town quietly before it all blew up into a big legal hoopla. It was crazy too, because she was married, and she and her husband had bought a house from Barbara Lane from church." Grace shakes her head. "It was a terrible situation."

"What?" I demand, wide-eyed. "How do I not know these things?"

Grace shrugs. "You've never cared about Carter. Why do you think I was so surprised to see you talkin' to him? Not to make you sound like a snob, but I always thought you were too swept up in your own world to even notice the jocks until this Jake thing happened."

Why does everyone keep saying that? When the jocks suggest I'm a stuck-up bitch, I'm not surprised, but my own best friend? Grace wouldn't be mean to me on purpose, so she must really think that.

"Yeah, well, it's kind of hard not to notice a guy grabbing your breasts," I mutter.

"I heard Carter dated a stripper once. I bet *she* wouldn't have noticed," Grace jokes.

CHAPTER 9

EVERYTHING GRACE TOLD me about Carter Mahoney *should* have diluted my interest in him. While I don't have a clear picture of who he is, one thing is abundantly clear—whatever he is, for whatever reason, that guy is every variety of bad news.

I tried to fact-check Grace's story about the art teacher, but there's no record of it. Of course, there wouldn't be. I may not pay attention to the goings on around school, but Carter would have been 17 a year ago, and if a scandal involving a minor and a teacher had made the news, I would have noticed that.

I try to distract myself with things that actually matter—homework, a four-hour shift at the bookstore, and the $1 clear-anced paperback I couldn't resist bringing home with me since I don't have to pay actual money to buy books right now.

Around bedtime, my mind drifts back to Carter. I decide to check on his social media again, and the newest picture causes my stomach to sink and my face to curl up with distaste.

It's his rally girl, mooning at him as she leans in the window of his car. His number is painted on her cheek, her top is cut so low she might as well be wearing a Band-aid for a shirt, and she's holding up a tray of carefully detailed chocolate-covered straw-berries, decorated to look like footballs.

"Post-practice treat. Best rally girl ever," he commented, with his stupid Longhorn hashtags.

As I'm giving my phone dirty looks, I shift my body, suddenly uncomfortable for reasons I don't even understand. Then I pick the phone back up, my thumb slips, and the worst possible thing happens—I accidentally 'like' the photo.

Gasping, I stare, horrified, at the little red heart. "No! No, no, no, no." I quickly click the button again to unlike it, then I drop the phone like it turned into a tarantula, afraid to even touch the damn thing.

It takes a moment for the screen to go dark, but I stare at it the whole time, as if it's a bomb that might detonate. The panic begins to subside, and my desperate hope is that he'll never know. I may have unliked it fast enough and he'll never get the notification. As much action as his profile gets, it's not at all unreasonable to think he would never even notice a single like. Unless he's literally looking at his phone right now, surely by the time he checks, a dozen more people will have interacted with the post and our names will all be grouped together. Surely as many people as like his posts, he must not even read all the names—

My hopes die as my screen lights up with a notification that he just sent me a message. Motherfucker!

"Shit," I hiss, grabbing the phone and sliding the message open.

"That's shady," he says simply.

My face flushes, even though he can't see me. I can't even think of a way to defend myself—I am outright stalking his profile like a creep. Telling him I can't seem to sate my curiosity about him would be even worse than letting him think I'm a psycho stalker, so I figure I'll just let him think that and ignore his message.

Only he doesn't wait for me to respond; he sends another message. "Was that a passive aggressive like because I posted a picture of a girl, or an accidental like because you're keeping tabs on me?"

All I can do at this point is roll with it, so I send back, "Neither. It was an intentional like, but it was all for the strawberries, not you OR the rally girl."

"Uh-huh," he sends back, clearly unconvinced. "Strange how you saw my picture, but you're not following me…"

"Your profile is public," I tell him. "People on my feed follow you, and I saw that they liked that picture. Purely accidental. I didn't even realize it was your profile, I just thought the football strawberries were super cute, so I gave them a like. I thought I was liking that girl's picture, not yours. Once I realized it was your account, I unliked it."

This is a feasible explanation. It's total bullshit, but it sounds enough like the truth that I will cling to it with my dying breath.

"I see," he answers. "Well, if you like the strawberries so much, I'm happy to share."

"I'm good," I assure him. Then, before I can even stop myself, I type out, "Did you date a teacher last year?"

"Date? No." A moment later, he follows up with, "Asking around about me, huh?"

"No, my friend saw me talking to you and she thought I should know that you usually date teachers and strippers, so we're not in the same league."

"Didn't date the stripper, either. You have bad information."

"I may be using overly polite terminology," I admit.

"Fuck is the word you're looking for."

I roll my eyes. "Gross. A teacher?"

"She was in her mid-twenties, definitely not gross."

"And married?" I demand.

"I forgot to ask," he sends back glibly. "Ordinarily I would never sin, being the good Christian boy I am."

"I'm legitimately stunned you didn't burst into flames just typing that," I reply.

He doesn't reply. I wait, wondering if he's sending a long message. Maybe he stepped away. Finally, I close the app, figuring he abandoned the conversation.

I should probably get to sleep, anyway. It's late, and I'm already dreading the sound of my alarm in the morning. I climb off my bed and head to the bathroom to brush my teeth. As I'm swishing the water in my mouth, another notification pops up.

It reads, "Were you convinced?"

I frown, typing back, "Convinced about what?"

"That I had burst into flames."

I cock my head, momentarily confused, then I scroll back up

to read the conversation. Once it hits me why he stopped responding, a short laugh of surprise bursts out of me. "It didn't feel like the world had suddenly become a better place, so no," I send back.

"All that sass," he types. "You need another lesson about manners, princess."

"My manners are just fine," I assure him.

"Come get some of these strawberries and we can have some fun."

Shaking my head that he would even try, I shoot back, "I'm sure your rally girl is up for all sorts of fun."

"She is," he replies, not even denying it. "But I'm inviting you."

"Should I feel special?" I ask, hoping my sarcasm translates.

"You can feel special if you want to. I'd rather make you feel dirty. I'd rather see all your feelings in your eyes when you hear the cold bite of my voice telling you how to please me. I'd rather you half-naked, on your knees, waiting for permission to suck my cock like a good little whore."

His words steal the breath right out of my lungs. I don't have a snappy comeback for that. The agonizing part is his words take me so completely off guard, they cause a pleasant stirring between my legs.

It's a wicked scene he describes, but as I read his words, the scene unfolds inside my mind. I can see it. Half-naked and a little afraid, just the way he likes me. He doesn't hurt me, though, not in my mind. We both know he could, but we both also know he won't.

I try to shake off the image he planted in my mind. I'm sure that's not what the scene looks like in his, so I can't afford to let myself get carried away.

For a moment, I'm almost ashamed to feel a pang of arousal, but I immediately walk myself back out of that trap. Hell no. I'm not going to feel bad about that. It was my body's natural reaction, and the words are written on a screen. If I just happened across naughty words like those unexpectedly online, of course my body would react to them.

It's not because they're from him.

I should probably try to use this to my advantage, try to get him to admit to what he did to me last time he had me on my knees. The way he worded it in this message, just like in the "notes" he wrote me in history class, it all sounds consensual. Naughty talk between lovers, not communication between a psycho and his victim.

Then again, it might be hard to sell that I would even be responding to his messages, if I wanted people to believe that. Maybe if I turned the tides right now, said something about what he did in that classroom to try and trick him into admitting to his crimes, but I'm tired, I don't feel like potentially provoking his mean side, and I don't think he'd fall for that, anyway.

Instead of trying to trick him, instead of responding at all to his highly inappropriate message, I close out of the app, set my alarm clock, and climb into bed. I know I'll have to see him at school in the morning, I just hope that visual he planted doesn't get stuck in my head. The last thing I need is the inability to escape Carter Mahoney even in my dreams.

I'M RUNNING LATE on Wednesday, so by the time I make my way into the school, there are no longer kids assembled outside in their various groups: mere mortals sitting on the black metal benches, the jocks assembled around Carter in front of the wall. I make my way inside with no nasty looks, no whispers, no "Zoey the ho" nonsense. It's lovely.

Being late to school seems to set me on a path to rushing all day long, though. I barely make it to history before the bell rings, and when I fall into my desk with a huff, I don't even have time to glance in Carter's direction before Mr. Hassenfeld begins his lecture.

Once class is over, I gather my things and head straight out the door, lamenting the rumbling of my stomach. Since I got so far behind this morning, I didn't have time for breakfast, and I didn't pack myself a lunch. I could buy food in the cafeteria, but that would require *going* to the cafeteria, and I won't do that.

Once we are out in the hall, Carter falls into step beside me. "What's up, Ellis?"

"Nothin' new," I tell him.

"Did you fall asleep on me last night?"

I flash him a smile. "Nope, I just stopped responding."

He feigns a puppy dog pout. "Meanie."

"I'm sure you didn't lose too much sleep over it," I say casually. "You could have always hit up your rally girl; I'm sure she's always around, ready to dirty talk with you to keep up your team spirit. Best rally girl ever and all that."

Carter grins over at me. "Man, you are insanely jealous of my rally girl."

My gaze snaps to his and narrows. "I am *not* jealous. That's absurd. Do I find the whole concept of a girl literally assigned to cater to you, give you presents, and fawn all over you just because you know how to throw a football a little archaic? Yes. But it's not jealousy, and it has nothing to do with you."

"Hey, rally girls boost our morale and give us encouragement. Our own personal cheerleaders."

"Right," I say dryly. "And I'm sure none of you ever take advantage of the stars in their eyes to have sex with them."

"Is it really taking advantage if they want it?" he questions.

"It's icky," I inform him.

He shakes his head, rejecting my explanation. "You're jealous. Are you territorial, Ellis? Now that you've sucked my dick, you don't want anyone else to? You're gonna have to be more diligent, if that's the case. My dick requires a lot more attention than you're giving it."

Swallowing down a ball of embarrassment, I snap, "I didn't willingly show your dick *any* attention."

"No?" he asks, lifting an eyebrow. "I seem to remember you saying you wanted it."

"You *made* me say that," I remind him, wide-eyed.

"Nah, I gave you options, and you made your choice."

"You're insane," I inform him, aghast.

Not sounding all that concerned, he says, "Maybe." Then, barely missing a beat, he changes the subject. "So, where do you sit for lunch? I noticed yesterday I never see you. Not that I expect you'd be sitting with the cheerleaders, but I took a quick look around the cafeteria and didn't see you anywhere else, either."

"I don't eat in the cafeteria. Not since all this... stupid Jake stuff started. People stare and make disparaging comments. Your cheerleader friends can be real bitches, and I don't even know why *they* care. They should be offended on my behalf, not taking his side. They need their girl cards suspended until they take a remedial class on girl power or something, I swear."

"Birds of a feather," he says simply. "Jake is one of theirs, you're not."

"Yeah, I noticed."

"You could be," he says, giving me a once-over. "You're attractive enough, and even though you keep to yourself, you're clearly not shy or you wouldn't be able to spar with me the way you do. Get yourself some Longhorn gear, one of those sparkly ponytail holders, and slap a smile on that pretty face, I'm sure you could find a spot at their table."

"I'll pass," I tell him. "I used to sit with Grace and the youth group kids from our church, but they became quickly offended by the 'ho' coughs your jock buddies would walk by and deliver. I didn't want to make Grace uncomfortable anymore, so until it all blows over, no cafeteria for me."

"Well, you've gotta eat."

"Last time I tried to sneak off somewhere solitary to eat, I got cornered by three jock assholes and—wait, I think you know the rest of this story," I say sarcastically. My tone dropping to its normal decibel, I conclude, "Now I eat in my car with the doors locked."

"That's sad, Ellis."

"It isn't sad. Well, today it is, because I didn't have a chance to pack my lunch, but most days it's actually quite peaceful. A little bit of quiet time in the middle of the day, I can read a couple of chapters of whichever book I'm reading. It's like a little midday break from people. I enjoy spendin' time by myself. I don't need company all the time."

Carter nods his head. "Well, today you're gonna have company."

"No, today I'm gonna read the whole time, not even interrupted by the sound of my own chewing."

"Nope. You like wings?"

"Wings?" I question, glancing over at him.

"Chicken wings. You're not some kind of vegan, are you?"

I shake my head. "No, I like wings."

"Great. Let's go get some."

My eyes widen and I slow down. "What? No. It's—We're—The school day isn't over, for one thing, and if you think I'm goin' anywhere alone with you—"

Holding up a hand to halt me, he says, "Relax, Ellis. I'm not going to fuck you at Wingstop, I'm only going to feed you. You just said you didn't bring your lunch, and as I mentioned before, I feel like I owe you a meal."

"I am not getting in a car alone with you," I inform him.

Unconcerned, he shrugs. "Drive yourself, then. I mean, it's literally a one-minute drive so I think driving separately is pretty stupid, but if that makes you feel safer, knock yourself out."

I shouldn't even consider going anywhere with someone who has to add "if that makes you feel safer" to an invitation to hang out with him. The thought of wings does make my mouth water, though. It's been ages since I've had them. We used to order wings on a Friday night once every month or so for a treat, but then Hank had to get his car fixed, it was an expensive repair, and my parents haven't caught up enough to be able to afford even the occasional wing night at home.

"You promise this isn't a trick?" I ask, that icky vulnerable feeling hitting me again.

Carter offers a reassuring nod. "Temporary truce."

This is probably a terrible idea, but as if on cue, my stomach rumbles, begging me to let the nice man buy it some chicken wings. I tell my stomach he's not a nice man at all, but my stomach decidedly doesn't care what kind of man he is, so long as he's buying it some chicken wings.

Sighing, I clutch my books tighter. "Fine."

CHAPTER 10

I DON'T KNOW why I told him the story of my parents no longer being able to afford wing nights. I don't know why I let him drive, or why I even agreed to come, but by the time I'm polishing off my paper-lined tray of boneless BBQ wings, I'm sort of glad I did.

If you ignore the things that make him repugnant—like his whole rapey jock thing, for example—Carter is actually pretty all right to hang out with. The 95 seconds of exposed vulnerability I felt when I slid into the passenger side of his Mustang and wondered if he might pounce on me were stressful, but he kept to the driver's seat just like he said he would, and he has behaved himself ever since.

Instead of torturing me or trying to make me uncomfortable, he has behaved like a respectable human being. We've talked about Mr. Hassenfeld's uncanny resemblance to the host from that restaurant rescue show on the Food Network, my love for iced coffee (he doesn't get it), his love for hot wings (I don't get it), our mutual preference for orange Popsicles (why do they even make any other flavor?), and the new comedy we both want to see, currently playing at the local movie theater.

I'm wary of admitting to the last one, because it seems like the next step from "You want to see that, too?" could very easily be, "Well, we should go together," and I would prefer not to be put into another situation where I have to shoot him down.

As nice as this lunch is, I can't bring myself to agree to go on a date with him. How can I? It would be so twisted. Literally the first time he ever spoke to me, he made me go down on him. He showed up at my house with soup when he knew I wasn't sick. He showed up where I work with his sister, so I couldn't be mean to him. He's manipulative and potentially dangerous, and I can't let myself lose sight of that.

Even coming to lunch with him today, I worried I was putting myself in a dangerous situation. A date would give him the wrong idea. A date would make him think I'm open to maybe possibly sleeping with him someday, and I'm not trying to mislead him. Not least of all because, knowing what I know about him, I can't be sure he wouldn't take what he wants from me if he thinks it's owed to him.

Damn entitled assholes.

My fear proves valid when the next thing out of his mouth is, "Well, I've got practice tonight, but if you're not working tomorrow, we could go see it."

I shake my head. "Can't."

"Because you work?"

I sigh, feeling mean, and then get angry at myself for feeling mean, because he certainly deserves it. "Please stop makin' me tell you no, Carter."

"I'm not making you say no," he says easily. "You could start saying yes. It would be much more fun."

"I disagree. I was stressed out about spending two minutes in a car with you. If I agreed to sit in a dark theater with you, I would have gray hair by the time the movie ended."

"I'm not gonna pounce on you in public, Zoey. I do have an image to maintain, you know. I've pushed the limits, definitely, but even I can't get away with that level of misbehavior out in the open. A movie theater is crowded. Lots of people around. You could call for help if you felt the need to. I would behave myself. I want to see the movie. I'd invite you to my house if I just wanted to fuck you."

"No."

"How about we take someone else with us? I can bring a couple people so you won't be alone with me."

"Again, you brought people last time."

"Fine, then you can bring people," he offers. "Does Grace have a boyfriend? Bring them. I might want to shoot myself in the face if she likes the kind of guy I think she probably likes, but hell, I can survive alongside them for a few hours."

"Grace doesn't have a boyfriend anymore, and yes, you would have hated her last one. He's a goody two shoes. He even got on my nerves, and I'm friends with *Grace*." Looking at him as I grab my drink cup and take a sip, I add, "But the answer is still no. In fact, if 'bring Grace' is your suggestion, my answer is an even more vehement no. She was already scandalized that she saw me talking to you in the hallway, so something that looks like a date is out of the question."

"It would look like a date because it would *be* a date," he informs me.

"I'm not going on a date with you, Carter," I tell him, plainly.

"Why not?"

I stare at him for a long moment, then sigh and shake my head. "You are relentless."

"Yep," he agrees, before popping a salty French fry into his mouth.

"You know why I won't go out with you," I tell him. "You can ask 20 more times, the answer isn't going to change. If you wanted to date me, you should have started there, not... where you started."

"Well, I didn't *know* I wanted to date you then," he states, somehow reasonably. "I just thought you were some shy, boring nerd who grossly overreacted to Jake wanting to bang you. It took a couple interactions before I noticed what he must have noticed first. Now I see it. Now *I* want you. I'm much more persistent than Jake Parsons, I'll tell you that now."

"See, that sounds like a warning," I point out. "I don't go out on dates with guys who exude such willingness to do harm. My type is 'not a dangerous sociopath' and I'm not convinced you fit the bill."

Carter smiles like that amuses rather than offends him. "I'm not a sociopath."

I press my lips together with exaggerated firmness. "That's just what a sociopath would say."

"I'm aggressive when I'm going after something I want, that's all. That doesn't make me a sociopath."

I tick off fingers. "Superficial charm, intelligence, grandiose sense of self, ability to harm others without any apparent remorse, relentless pursuit of your own desires at the expense of others, liar liar pants on fire…"

Before I can continue my list, Carter laughs. "Was that last one a technical term, Dr. Ellis?"

"It was," I say with a nod.

"I haven't lied to you," he says.

"You lie to everyone," I state. "From what I can tell, your whole entire life is a lie."

"I didn't say I don't lie to anyone, I said I haven't lied to *you*," he repeats meaningfully.

My stomach bottoms out and I break his gaze, grabbing a French fry to distract myself. I'm not sure what to say to that.

On one hand, it could be a manipulation. He must know I have some kind of soft spot for him, because by all rights, I should be seething with anger and discomfort every time I see his face, not skipping out on lunch to go get boneless wings with him.

On the other hand, it could be true. If he's actually being sincere, I don't want to be mean and shut him down. If he's actually trying to reach out, I don't want to swat his hand away.

But I also don't want to be one more dumbass who has fallen for his act, and for all I know, that's all this is. For all I know, he knows exactly what he's doing, exactly how conflicted he's making me feel, and this is all intentional, just the best way he could figure to get what he wants.

His horrible words from that classroom float back to me, reminding me that this person acting like he's opening up to me in a way he doesn't with other people is the same asshole who told Jake Parsons to hold me down so he could rape me, the same asshole whose interest was only stirred by the knowledge that I'm a virgin, and who said he wanted to hurt me, that he wanted my virgin blood to be the only lube when he stole my innocence.

Regardless of the words out of Carter's mouth, I've seen him weave a web before I was emotionally involved, and he could easily be doing the same exact thing to me now, only I can't see it. My judgment is cloudy because deep down I want to believe he's not as bad as he proved he was that day, and when you want to see something so badly, sometimes you invent evidence to support that belief.

Carter's mind moves fast even when he hasn't had time to prepare—I saw that in the empty classroom, when he turned a routine bullying into sexual assault with a hint of potential murder if I didn't keep my mouth shut, when he hijacked Jake's crusade because he discovered I appealed to his particular appetites. That all happened in the space of a few minutes; Carter had no idea what he was walking into or that any of that would happen, and he still directed it like a fucking maestro.

He has had much more time to figure out how to play me. He's not winging it; he has had time to study me like I've studied him, time to gauge my reactions, time to learn how to get what he wants—which is possibly still me alone somewhere so he can hurt me.

That reminder is like a bucket of cold water dumped over my head. I toss the rest of my French fry into the empty wing boat and grab my phone, checking the time.

"We should head back. Lunch is going to be over soon, and I can't be late to my next class."

He regards me studiously, like he's trying to pinpoint where he went wrong. At least, that's how his gaze feels. Maybe now I'm being paranoid, seeing calculation where none exists, but I can't be sure and I'd rather be safe than sorry.

"All right," he says, easily enough. Looking at my mouth, he points to the corner of his. "You have a little sauce right there. Might wanna go fix it in the bathroom first, or everyone will know you had BBQ wings for lunch."

I cover my mouth, jumping up and running to the bathroom.

There's no sauce on my face. I see that immediately when I

get in front of the mirror. It also occurs to me the bathroom is down a hallway, more removed from the dining room. Isolated.

I swallow, looking at the door, half-expecting for it to swing open and Carter to bust in, smirking victoriously at how easy it was to get me alone. Visions of being attacked in this bathroom flood my mind and the walls start to close in on me.

Rather than stand here and work myself into a panic, I pull the restroom door open, braced to see Carter on the other side, waiting in the hall.

He isn't. The hall is empty, so I quickly escape it and head back to the relative safety of the dining room. Carter is lingering by the door, behaving himself. He threw out our trash and the table we sat at is empty now.

"Ready?" he asks me.

I nod my head and walk toward him, my stomach still rocking from the stress. He opens the door for me, and I murmur a distracted thank you. If he didn't send me to the bathroom to wipe away phantom wing sauce so he could corner me alone, then why?

Carter opens the passenger side door for me, too. I'm surprised, and even more guarded by his gentlemanly behavior. Carter Mahoney is not a gentleman, I know that to be true. Pouncing on me in this driveway would also be ill-advised; we are out in the open here. Even the high school parking lot would be a better spot, though given there are security cameras on the outside of the school (just not the inside, where they could have helped me) even that would be ill-advised. The football team would probably get him out of that one, though. My under-standing is Carter's position on the team is crucial to their success, so if I turned *another* football player in for their foul play, the tapes proving me right would probably mysteriously turn up missing. They already lost Jake Parsons for the season for the sake of my honor; they're not going to lose Carter Mahoney, too.

Plus, if I legitimately tried to get Carter in trouble, the whole town would turn on me in such a way that their response to my problem with Jake Parsons would look like a welcome wagon. Just like Carter told me the cheerleaders sided with Jake over me even though they're girls, and as vulnerable to sexual harassment as I am, it all comes down to who they like more. It will never be me. Grace is probably the only person in town who would stand beside me if I stood against Carter, and even she might struggle. We're good friends, but she has many more, and most of them would turn on me. Remaining loyal to me in that scenario would be stressful for Grace, and I'm not sure I could ask her to do it.

I'm not cut from the right cloth to fit in, while Carter Mahoney seems to be a chameleon. I don't know if I've actually seen the real him, or if this is just some other facet of The Carter Mahoney Show, but I do know he has a ready supply of charm and amiability, and I lack both. No one sides with the unlikable loner over the town's golden boy. Hell, my own mother struggles to support my defense of myself, and she should be my champion. She should be in my corner, no matter what everyone else thinks.

Carter pulls me right out of my thoughts when he drops something into my lap. I blink at the piece of plastic, the size of a credit card. Another gift card? I cast him a questioning look as I pick it up. "What's this for?"

"One of those family wing nights you told me about. Give it to your mom, she can use it to pay for dinner one night."

"Why?" I demand, frowning at him. "Why do you keep buying me gift cards?"

His lips curve up in amusement. "I've bought you two, Ellis. It's not exactly a habit."

"Why?" I ask again.

Carter shrugs. "Why not? I have money and you don't. Can't I just do something nice for you? It costs me nothing."

I lift my eyebrows, turning the card over and seeing $50 written in permanent marker on the back. "It costs you something. Between the two cards, you have given me $100. I'm startin' to feel like a low-class hooker."

"Except I'm not sleeping with you, so that doesn't make much sense," he points out. "I'm just doing something nice for you, that's all. Relax."

"Or you're grooming me."

He glances in my direction before turning his eyes back to the road. "Grooming you?"

I nod my head, clinging to my objections. "Sometimes when a predator has prey in his sights, he'll give them gifts to soften them up, to endear himself to them or make himself appear harmless, like a friend. But it's a trick. He's lulling them into a false sense of safety so they start trusting the predator, that way the predator can take advantage of that trust and pounce on them when he's ready."

"You already know I'm not harmless, Zoey. I don't think a few books and a belly full of chicken wings is gonna make you forget."

"It won't," I assure him.

"All right," he says, glancing at me as if to see if he's supposed to care. "Then we're in agreement. What's the problem?"

I can't put my finger on the problem, exactly. The first gift card had me questioning whether or not it was even okay to use it, but now that he's given me a second one, I can't shake the feeling that he's trying to make me feel like I owe him something. That he's building goodwill with the sole intent of exploiting it later.

I don't know if these concerns about him are all in my head, or these are instincts about him I should listen to. I hate how unsure of his motives I am. I hate how this constant swirl of questions about him gives him a permanent place in my mind. Every single day now, I live my life with questions about Carter Mahoney as constant background noise.

"You never answered me yesterday," I tell him.

"About what?"

"Before Cartwright interrupted, I asked if you had ever…" I pause, trying to figure out how to refer to what he did without making it even more awkward.

He doesn't make me say it. "Ah, that. No, I haven't. Never had an opportunity present itself to me the way you did."

"That's all that's stopping you? Lack of opportunity?"

He glances over at me. "That's not what I said. I said the opportunity with you was too good to pass up. That's not the same thing."

"How is that not the exact same thing? Same words, different order."

"I'm not running around victimizing other girls, if that's what you're asking," he states. "Believe it or not, I have an endless stream of willing women, all a phone call away. I don't have to try this hard, and I don't have to force myself on scandalized innocents to get off."

"Then why do it to me?"

He shrugs, more cavalier than I appreciate. "Variety is the spice of life."

"Bullshit." I don't even know why I'm so confident this is bullshit. He could mean that, I just don't buy it. He looks over at me wordlessly, so I keep going. "I deserve the truth," I tell him. "If I don't get justice, if I don't get to defend myself, I at least deserve to understand why it happened."

The last thing I expect is for my words to harden him, but that's what happens. As decent as he has been throughout lunch, now he turns it off. It appears to be as easy as flipping a switch, like he did at the bookstore when he thought I was judging him, but less fleeting this time.

"You want to know something, Ellis? I've got bad news for you, so listen up. Sometimes people do bad shit to you, and they don't get punished; they get away with it. Hell, sometimes they get rewarded for it. If all this shit with Jake didn't show you that, if all this shit with *me* hasn't shown you that, maybe you're not as smart as you think you are."

I don't even know how to respond to that, but we're at the school now, so I don't have to. Carter parks aggressively, slamming the car in park and killing the engine. Without another word, he shoves his car door open and climbs out.

I follow him silently, unable to find words to respond. I'm not sure I would, anyway. Whatever nerve I just hit, it was a real one, and I'm wary of tangling with him when he's mad. I shouldn't even care if he's mad, or what I said to upset him. I certainly shouldn't feel compelled to lessen the blow or make peace, but I wasn't raised to make waves. I'm teaching myself to do that on my own, but every bit of my upbringing tells me the right thing to do, the thing I'm *supposed* to do, is smooth over the feathers I just ruffled. My mother's voice echoes in my head.

Don't be rude, Zoey.

I shake it off. I love my mother, but that's bad advice. I'm not morally required to be polite to my abuser, and the conversation that pissed Carter off was one where I brought up what he did to me. If it touched a nerve, maybe it should have. It if made him feel badly, maybe it's because he should.

But then Grace buzzes around in my head, telling me it's perfectly fine to defend myself, but sometimes the better thing for everyone is to act with love.

There are too many people in my head pushing me in too many different directions. I take a breath and do my best to silence them, focusing on my own inner voice. My own instincts. Not the defensive ones I've had to adopt to combat the well-meaning guidance of my mother, but what's in my own heart. It's not purely anger or resentment. I would never be interacting with Carter this much if that's all that was there, and I refuse to entertain the notion that it could possibly be his extreme physical attractiveness that keeps my interest on him. I am not that shallow. It's not that. It's something more.

Putting my own ego aside and running through what Carter just said to me, I realize those words may not have been about me at all. Maybe he told me something personal, something real, without even meaning to.

"Carter," I call out, as he prepares to enter the school.

He pauses with his hand on the door and turns back to look at me, but his expression is still dark and stormy. He actually *looks* dangerous now, so it's probably lunacy that pulls me closer to him. Nonetheless, I ride out the crazy and take a few tentative steps closer until I'm maybe a foot away.

"We aren't what is done to us," I tell him. "People are going to hurt us, and it's going to be hard, and sometimes we might never get closure. We might never understand why. But that's the reason I asked. Maybe *deserve* isn't the right word. People don't get what they deserve, people just get what they get, and then they have to make the best of it."

He's still standing there, watching me, but there's a little less malice painted across his handsome features.

"But I *want* that closure, and you could give it to me. I don't need it from Jake, so I don't know why I need it from you. I guess Jake just feels simple and generic, and I can't help—I can't help feeling like there's more to you."

He stares at me for a long moment, and I'm struck by the thought that his mind is like an exclusive, secret club I desperately want access to. I want to know who he is, how he thinks. Maybe he's simpler than I want him to be, and I would be disappointed, but one way or the other, I could stop wondering. One way or the other, I would have my answers.

Instead of giving me any, Carter turns back around, pulls open the entry door, and says a little mockingly, "Come on, Ellis. Can't be late to that next class."

CHAPTER 11

THURSDAY AFTER SCHOOL, Carter messages me with a link to a trailer for the movie we both wanted to see. I actually *am* working, so I couldn't go even if I wanted to, but I don't bother offering up that explanation. He would probably just counter with a later showing, and I'm not going to a late showing with him. Alone with Carter Mahoney driving me home late at night? I'll pass.

I also don't want to tell him I'm at work because then he might pay me a visit, and I don't want to see him. It's hard enough to keep him out of my mind, and I already had to see him at school.

Friday as soon as history class lets out, I feel Carter's eyes on me, so I don't turn to look at him. He follows me out into the hall, falling into step beside me.

"You again?" I ask, somewhat lightly.

"Your favorite stalker," he returns.

"That's a factual statement," I mutter.

"Aw, I'm your favorite? I'm gonna tell Parsons. He's gonna be so jealous."

I roll my eyes. "I meant the stalker part."

"Says the girl who stalks my Instagram like a clingy ex," he volleys back.

Meeting his gaze as we walk, I ask, "Did you need something, Carter?"

Nodding once, he says, "Yes, actually. We have our first away game tonight. You gonna wish me luck?"

Sarcastically chambering my arm, then thrusting it in the air in a faux cheer, I say, "Go Longhorns!"

Carter smirks. "That's more like it."

"What, your rally girl isn't giving you enough attention? I thought she was the best," I remark innocently.

Carter nods. "It's all right. I find moderate jealousy cute in a girl. Keep it up."

"I don't want you to find me cute."

"Then don't wear skirts to school," he says, nodding to the suede button skirt I wore today. "Is that the one I took off you?"

Shooting him a warning look and glancing around to make sure no one heard, I hiss, "No, it is not. That one was corduroy."

"Looks the same."

I look down at my skirt, appraising it. "Nuh uh. This one flares more, the other one is straighter." Shaking my head, I look ahead and keep walking. "This is an absurd conversation to be having. Don't you have plays to study or cheerleaders to screw? Go away."

"I was paying you a compliment," he informs me. Then, just to annoy me, he reaches over and fingers the laced-up area around the bust of my black top. "I like this, too. Just a peek of cleavage, all restrained, just like you. You're a little tease, aren't you, Zoey?"

Swatting his hand away, I shoot him a dirty look. "Don't touch me."

"I touched your shirt, not you."

"Unless the alternative is tumbling off a cliff, don't touch me or anything attached to me. If I am about to plummet to my death and only you are around to save me, *then* you have my permission to reach out and grab me. That is the only scenario— and frankly, if I find myself alone on a cliff with you, you're probably the one pushing me, so I don't see much chance of it happening."

"That'd be a grisly way to go, wouldn't it?" he remarks,

shaking his head. "Free fall, then splat." Missing a beat, he says, "Anyway, while your overwhelming team spirit is a nice pick-me-up, that's not what I wanted from you. After the game, we're all getting together for a party at Erika's house. I want you to come."

"I think you already invited me to this," I tell him. "In any case, the answer was 'no thanks.'"

Nodding once, he says, "Yeah, I remember, I just figured I'd give you a chance to make a better decision."

"Oh, I've made the better decision," I assure him.

"Do you know where Erika lives?"

"I do, but I have no interest in going to her parties. Not to mention, if the whole team is going to be there, that means Jake would be there, and you must be out of your ever-loving mind if you think I'm going to put myself in that situation. Me at a football party with you, Jake, and Shayne, not to mention the whole rest of the team. I've seen *Carrie*, okay? I know how that story ends."

"With you exhibiting telekinetic powers?"

I nod my head. "Exactly. And I've gotta tell you, pig's blood is not a good look for me."

He takes an extra-long time looking me over, then says, "I don't know, you might be able to pull it off."

"Zero percent chance. That party has trap written all over it. You'd have to literally lobotomize me before you'd get a version of me who would agree to come to your jock get-together. Sorry. It's a hard pass."

"I'm not gonna let Jake hurt you, Zoey," he says, more seriously than I expect. "I don't think he would, anyway. Honestly, I don't think the guy has the stomach for it. He's the one who wanted to rough you up, and he couldn't even finish the job."

I shoot him a wary look and inch away from him. "You don't have to say that like it's a bad thing."

"I'm just saying, Parsons is nothing to be afraid of. All bark, no bite."

"Every single syllable from your lips right now helps make the case for why I won't be coming to the party," I tell him.

"You're coming to the party," he says, simply.

"I'm absolutely not. Now, if you'll excuse me, I have to go have lunch. Good luck at the game tonight."

I go to walk away from him, assuming he'll let it drop, but Carter surprises me by calling out, "I'm trying to be nice to you, Zoey."

I keep my gaze trained on the ground, shake my head, and keep walking.

THANKS TO CARTER, we get wings for dinner.

It's a little thing, but it puts everyone in a good mood. My mom doesn't have to cook, Hank has never encountered a chicken wing he didn't like, and my brother and I certainly aren't complaining, either.

It's the little luxuries you don't think about until you can't afford them anymore. I never realized I enjoyed the occasional wing night at home until they were no longer an option. Since we got this treat that we used to have when we had just a little more wiggle room in our dinner budget, it seems to make my parents feel like they're in a better place than they are. Normally, stress is present at the dinner table like a fifth mouth to feed, but tonight everyone is in better spirits.

Mom wants to continue the good night, so we do another thing we haven't done in a while—break out the board games. I lose all track of time until my phone lights up, alerting me to a message from Carter.

"Party starts in a half hour."

"Have fun," I type back.

"You coming?"

"I've told you 'no' 547 times," I tell him.

"All right," he sends back.

I frown, not sure if he's saying all right, like he gives up, or all right, like I'll hear from him again in an hour.

Ten minutes later, my phone starts vibrating. It's Grace's number flashing across the screen, so I go ahead and answer it.

"What's up, Grace?"

The volume of her voice, apparently. I flinch, dragging the phone from my ear as she squeals incoherently into the phone.

"Whoa, whoa, slow down," I say. "I didn't catch a word of that."

"We just got invited to a party at Erika Martin's house!"

Dread slithers through me. Seriously, Carter? Trying to use Grace to force me into going to that party? "Who invited you?"

"Shauna from church, she's on the cheer team. She just texted me and said they're having a party tonight and we should come. Both of us—she invited you, too."

"She didn't invite us, Grace. Carter did. He's been trying to get me to come to this party—" I stop, seeing my mom's ears perk up at the sound of Carter's name. Sighing heavily, I cover the mic on my phone and tell her, "Give me a minute."

"Honey, if you have a social gathering to go to with your friends—"

"I don't," I say firmly, walking into the other room and turning my attention back to Grace. "Listen, I know you're excited, but we can't go to that party. God knows what they'll be up to. It's not going to be like youth group parties. They'll probably be drinking and hooking up and—it's not a place for us."

"But I've never been invited to one of their parties before," she complains. "Aren't you the least bit curious?"

"You know what? I'm curious what would happen if I reached my hand down that little garbage disposal hole in the sink to retrieve a lost spoon, but not curious enough to try it. Jake is at that party, Grace."

"I *know* he is, but Carter will be there, too."

Eyes widening, I tell her, "That's the problem! You're literally describing the problem. They aren't good guys, Grace. They're not *safe* guys. You're right when you say they're faster than us. We're in bumper cars on a metal track, and they're off-roading somewhere in… whatever the fastest car you can think of is. Resist temptation."

"This isn't temptation, it's just a party," she insists. "We don't have to do anything we don't wanna do. We can still be us and go to a party with the popular kids."

"No," I say, shaking my head even though she can't see me.

"It's not safe. I'm sorry to be a buzz kill, but no. I won't go there."

"But I *want* to," she complains. "What if we just went for an hour? One hour. What could happen in one hour? We won't drink or do anything we shouldn't."

"No. Carter is trying too hard to get me there, Grace. It's not because he's up to anything good. No way. I'm sorry."

"I think you're bein' a little paranoid, Zoey," Grace snaps. "Not every guy wants to assault you. It's not even Carter that issued this invite, it was Shauna."

"Because he messaged me *ten minutes ago* askin' me to come and I told him no for the *third* time. This was just his plan B."

"You know what? You're bein' so self-obsessed right now, you can't even consider that maybe Shauna likes me, that maybe she wants me to come hang out with them. Maybe it's not all about you, Zoey."

I sigh, letting my head fall back against the wall. "That is not how I meant it, Grace. It's just… you don't understand because I haven't told you everything, but please trust me on this. I'm not bein' self-obsessed. I'm not bein' paranoid. This has Carter's fingerprints all over it. I promise you, he is the one behind this invitation."

Her tone is low and disappointed. "Whatever. I'm sorry I wanted us to actually go out and try something new and maybe have some fun with our peers."

Before I can reply, she hangs up on me. Glaring at my screen, I open Instagram and go to my messages, telling Carter, "Thanks a lot, asshole. Now Grace is mad at me and I'm STILL not coming to the party."

"Remember what I told you about how you don't always have to fight tooth and nail?" he replies.

"When you were holding me against my will and touching me without my consent in my own driveway? Yes, Carter, I do remember that."

Since he's not an idiot, he doesn't respond to that angrily laid trap.

I'm too mad after all that to even focus on the game, plus now that Carter has come up, my mother is bleeding curiosity and asking me a million questions about the party and why I don't want to go. It really should be enough that Jake is there. No one should expect me to want to go to a party he's at—Jake, who cornered me and touched me inappropriately when there *wasn't* alcohol involved—but everyone sucks, and I'm so pissed off, I just want to go to bed.

CHAPTER 12

I'M CURLED up in bed with my light still on, trying to get lost in a fictional world. I tried to fall asleep and couldn't, so I'm trying one more time to make myself love *The Great Gatsby*. I had to read it for English lit last year and do a paper on it, but every chapter felt like a chore. I want to give it another chance this year—another year older and wiser, maybe.

Maybe not, since I did go get wings with stupid Carter Mahoney and his stupid jerkbag face. Ugh, I'm so mad at him.

I shake it off, rolling out my shoulders and trying to refocus on Gatsby, but my mind keeps drifting back to Grace. She's almost never mad at anyone, so that she's mad at me makes me feel terrible, but I feel even worse that she thought I was being self-obsessed. She even made me doubt myself for a minute—maybe I *am* being paranoid. I really don't think I am, all my experience with Carter considered, but I guess he never actually admitted to being the one who told Shauna to invite Grace. It seems a bit far-fetched to me, but I guess it's not impossible he wasn't involved. I guess it's not *impossible* that Shauna decided for the first time ever, completely out of the blue, she would invite me and Grace to one of the parties they have all the time.

No, that's absurd. It was Carter's doing. I'm not being paranoid, I am right, and everyone else is wrong because they believe the bullshit façade Carter shows them. They all think of him as some golden boy, as the hot, wealthy football star—none of them know what he is. Hell, *I* don't even know what he is, but I've seen more of a glimpse than Grace has, that's for sure. Plus, Grace is always looking for the best in everyone, so even if she saw that there was something off about him, she'd probably try to save his ass rather than stay away from him.

God, Grace, I love you, but you need to get your shit together.

My phone vibrates on the bed beside me. It's like she can hear me thinking about her. Her name flashes across the screen —a video call. A smidgen of relief hits me. It must be bothering her that we ended our last call on such a sour note, too.

I stick my bookmark in Gatsby and put the paperback down, grabbing my phone and sliding my finger across the screen. Grace's face fills the screen and I offer up a smile.

"Hey."

I can barely hear her, but she's smiling. "Zoey!"

Something is majorly off here. Why is it loud? Is that music? "Where are you?"

"At the party! That's why I'm calling. You were totally wrong. I'm havin' a blast. You need to come have fun with me."

My smile falls right off my face and alarm wraps around me like a blanket. "What? You went to the party without me?"

Grace nods, but it's a loopy nod, and she's only half paying attention to me. Looking just out of sight, she grins and takes a red Solo cup. "Thank you. You're so nice."

My heart stalls. "Grace, focus. Are you *drinking?*"

She shakes her head dismissively. "Not alcohol. It's just punch. They do have spiked punch, but I don't drink, so Carter's been gettin' me some of the fruit punch out of the—the non-alcoholic bowl. Come have fun with me!"

It feels like my rib cage is shrinking, crushing my lungs and stealing my ability to breathe. "*Carter* is getting you drinks? Grace, put that cup down. Don't you dare drink that. Don't drink anything he touches." Throwing the blankets back, I spring out of bed and pace the floor, but I'm not sure what to do. If I go pick her up myself, Carter will get me inside that house. If I tell her mom, her mom will see that Grace has been drinking—non-alcoholic punch, my ass—and she'll have a conniption. Grace will be grounded forever, and then she'll *really* be pissed at me.

I could call the police with a noise complaint, but Grace is there, so she'd get in trouble for underage drinking, too. I could take *my* mom with me to get Grace, but she's being ridiculous about Carter, so if he comes out, she's going to switch sides and not be on mine anymore.

As I'm trying to figure out what I should do, I see an arm slide around Grace's waist. My blood turns to freezing water in my veins as she turns her face toward him, and then I see Carter Mahoney on my phone with his arm around my best friend.

"Hey, Ellis," he says casually, smirking like he's already won this round.

"Stop touching her," I snap. "Did you do anything to her drink? I swear to God, Carter—"

Grace has the absolute gall to shake her finger at me. "Zoey, you shouldn't swear to God."

My eyes bug out. "And you shouldn't take drinks from rapey jocks! But here we are."

"Stop being such a drag, Ellis. Come party with us," Carter says.

Grace nods vehemently. All I can focus on is his arm still wrapped around her, his hand resting on her hip. I want to burst through the phone and rip her away from him.

"Don't drink that, Grace. Not a single sip. I'm coming to pick you up. I am not coming inside the house; I will call you when I'm in the driveway."

Carter glances at his watch. "You're probably gonna have to come inside. See, as much fun as we're having here, Grace wants to talk to me about Jesus. We're going to go upstairs in a few minutes so we have a little privacy."

Hot fury hits me with a fear chaser. "Don't you dare take her upstairs, Carter. Grace, do not go anywhere alone with him."

Smirking, Carter cocks his head. "I bet she's a virgin, too. You know how much I like those good girls, princess."

I'm going to vomit. My hands shake with helpless rage as I grab the outfit I wore today and push down my pajama pants, since Carter can't see below my shirt on the phone. "I swear to

God, Carter, if you lay a finger on my friend, I will destroy you. I don't know how, I know you'll strike back harder, but I don't care. I will decimate you, and I will not rest until I do."

"Like I said, you can try," he replies easily, taking Grace's phone out of her hand and turning away from her. "Here's the deal, Zoey. Erika lives over on Meadow Ridge. That's about a 5 minute drive from your house, but I'm gonna be nice and give you 10 minutes to get here." He taps the watch on his wrist, lifting an eyebrow. His finger moves down just slightly. "Now, it gets to be 15 minutes and I take Grace upstairs."

My body is so amped up, I can scarcely breathe. "Carter, this is not funny. You leave Grace alone."

He taps the watch again. "It's in your hands now, Ellis." Pointing a little lower, he says, "I wouldn't let it get to this 20-minute mark, because if it gets to this 20-minute mark and you're still not here? Well, then good little Gracie's gonna lose hers before you lose yours."

My skin burns with rage. "Don't you touch her. I'm so serious about this, Carter. I'm not playing some stupid game with you—"

"Yes, you are, and the clock's running." With one last little smirk, he says, "Tick tock, princess."

Then he ends the call.

———

IT HAS BEEN 12 minutes by the time I pull onto Erika's road.

Dread moves through my body and my stomach aches, because I know this can't go well. I can't believe Grace came here without me. I can't believe Carter is being such an enormous shithead. I tried to call her four times on the way over and she didn't answer her phone. Why isn't she answering all of a sudden? Maybe she just doesn't hear it ringing over the music, but maybe Carter is doing something horrible and she can't.

I was a fool to believe him when he said he doesn't terrorize other girls. I can't even believe I fell into that trap—thinking I was some sort of exception. He's a psycho, and I want to rip his dick off and feed it to him.

Every step I take toward Erika's front door feels heavier than the last. This is the last place I want to be. These are the absolute last people I want to see.

I hesitate at the door, unsure what to do. Should I knock? Just open the door and barge in? There are six small windows on the front door, so I can see inside the house, right into the living room. I can see it packed full of people, jocks piled on the couch, a cheerleader sitting on the arm, grinning and drinking from a red Solo cup.

I decide to knock first, but if no one hears me, I'm busting in.

I grab my phone to check where I'm at on time. Fuck, 15 minutes. I look in the window again, searching for either Grace or Carter.

Instead, I see the blue eyes of Jake Parsons move directly into view on the other side of the window. The door drifts open, the noise growing louder, and Jake cocks an eyebrow at me.

"Fancy seein' you here, Ellis."

I glare at him. "Where is Carter?"

Now Jake rolls his eyes. "Tell me something, Zoey. How is it that *I* come onto you and get my ass handed to me, but after what me and Shayne saw him do to you, you're hangin' around the guy all the time? Is it because he's rich? I don't have enough money to impress you?"

"Carter doesn't impress me. He's terrorizing me. I do not have time for this—he has my friend somewhere *alone*. Alone, like he had me in that classroom. Where is he?"

Realization suddenly dawns on Jake's face. "Oh, shit." He turns and indicates the stairs. "He and Grace went up there a couple minutes ago. She seemed like she went willingly though…."

I don't waste time explaining, I just brush past him and jog up the stairs to go save Grace.

CHAPTER 13

OF COURSE, every single door upstairs is closed, so I have to open each one as I go. The last door on the left is the right one. I shove it open and there sits Grace on the edge of a bed, her hand on Carter's knee. The smallest tickle of relief moves through me when I see that they are both still fully clothed, and though she's touching him, Carter is not touching her.

Even drunk off her ass, Grace is proselytizing. Reaching out and trying to share with this asshole what helped her through her own struggles. Her voice is soft and dreamy as she tells him, "It's just the greatest joy you can fathom, Carter. I can't even explain it."

I don't know who to glare at first, but I go with Carter since he's the devil. His gaze drifts to me as soon as the door opens. Casually as can be, as if I didn't just interrupt, he says to Grace, "Is that right?"

She nods enthusiastically, visibly blissed out. "Open your heart to Jesus and you'll see. You'll receive His blessings, too."

I shake my head in disgust, walking over and grabbing the Solo cup out of Grace's hand. I peek at the red liquid inside, sniff it, but of course I can't tell if he did anything to it.

Placing a hand on Grace's shoulder, I tell her, "Come on, honey, up off the bed. Don't go into bedrooms with boys at parties, okay? Can we just make that a general rule?"

"Justice and I used to sneak off at parties all the time."

Since that was her boyfriend, I cock an eyebrow. "Oh. Okay, well... don't sneak off with boys who are not your boyfriend, and never Carter, Jake, or Shayne. Never ever. Even if they tell you there's a fire, and the only way to safety is into a room alone with them."

Grace widens her eyes at me. "Zoey, he's sitting right here."

"He knows my opinion of him," I answer, yanking on her arm. "Off the bed. Come on. How much of this punch did you have?"

"I'm not sure. It's not alcoholic, though!"

I glare at Carter. He smirks. I am not amused. "How much of this did she drink?" I demand.

"I wasn't keeping track," he tells me.

"Great. That's just great. You're unbelievable."

Leaning back on his elbows on the bed and eyeing me up like his next meal, he says, "Relax, Ellis. All that worrying's gonna give you an ulcer."

"I can't relax," I snap. "She's not supposed to have a lot of sugary drinks, and you've been dumping fruit punch down her throat. She's too drunk to keep track herself—this is all your fault."

"It's punch," he states, like I'm being ridiculous.

"She's diabetic!"

Now he sits up, a little less chill. "Oh. Shit, well, I didn't know that."

I shake my head, dragging Grace toward the door. "Of course you didn't. Not like you would have cared even if you did though, right? As long as you got your way, who cares who gets hurt along the way? That's the Carter Mahoney mission statement, isn't it?"

Grace chides me. "You're bein' so mean, Zoey."

"I don't really want to hear it from you, Grace. I told you it wasn't safe to come to this party, and you ignored me, and now we're both in a bad situation. Do you have your insulin? Do you *need* your insulin? Or a snack? I don't know how alcohol plays into this. You need to drink some water. You didn't have iced coffee today, did you?"

"I hate insulin," she mutters. "I want to be normal."

"You are normal," I murmur, leading her out into the hall and toward the stairs.

Before I make it to the landing, Carter grabs me from behind, shaking his head. "Nope. You're not going anywhere."

"Haven't you done enough? Get your hands off me," I snap.

Jake is right at the bottom of the stairs, like he was waiting for me. He glances up now and takes the first couple of steps. "Everything okay up here?"

Carter's grip on me tightens even as I try to wiggle out of his grip. He looks down the stairs at Jake. "Yeah, come get Grace. She needs water. Take her to the kitchen and get her a bottle."

Glaring back at Carter, I tell him, "Let go of me. I am going to get her a bottle of water, and then I am taking her home."

He couldn't be more dismissive. "After all I had to do to get you here? No, you're not." Meeting Jake's gaze as he reluctantly takes Grace's arm to guide her down the stairs, Carter tells him, "Don't get handsy, Parsons. Remember what happened last time. And keep a close eye on her. I didn't know, but she's diabetic. Don't let her have any more punch. If she starts acting weird, text me."

"I am not leaving Grace with *him*, and I'm not goin' anywhere with *you*. I have to keep an eye on her and make sure she's okay."

"Parsons is gonna do it," he tells me. "That's his job now."

"Carter, dammit," I object as he locks his arm around me and drags me back down the hall. "Let me go. Let me take care of my friend!"

"You're going to take care of me instead," he informs me.

Fury explodes in my veins. "No, I am not. Help! Somebody—"

His hand covers my mouth immediately. He sounds annoyed when he says, "That's a waste of fucking time, Ellis. Did anyone help you last time? People don't help. Try to keep up."

"I hate you," I cry out against his hand.

"Stop being so dramatic," he tells me, dragging me back inside the bedroom and closing the door. This time, he turns the lock. I struggle to get away from him, but he's too strong, his hold on me too tight. I thrash some more, but he holds me tightly against his body and drags me back toward the bed.

It's a strange thing to think in this moment, but it feels weird and wrong on even more than obvious levels that this has to be Erika's bedroom. There are trophies, sashes, ribbons, and pom-poms displayed all over, a lavender bedspread covering her mattress. They probably had sex on this bed when they were together.

I no more than think that, and Carter shifts my weight and shoves me down on the bed. Since he gave me a push, I hit the mattress hard. I immediately shove up to my hands and knees, trying to climb back off, but he's right there to stop me.

Fear explodes inside me as he comes down on top of me, flattening my body against the pillowy surface. I'm tummy down and he's straddling my ass, grabbing my arms, pinning them at my sides.

I shake my head in denial. Not like this. It can't happen like this. "Carter, please."

His voice is harder, more commanding than I expect. "Calm down." Then, instead of keeping me pinned here like this, he flips me over on my back. He still pins me before I can get away from him, but at least now he's looking at me. I can see his face. I don't have any more control than I had a moment ago, I guess, but it feels like I have more ground this way. I stand a better chance of appealing to him if he can see the emotions playing out on my face.

Actually, probably not. He's a fucking maniac.

Instead of feeding him more fear, which I know he likes, I do my best to clear that off my face. I shake my head and level my heaviest look of disappointment at him. "Was it all fake, then? Was every interaction since that classroom bullshit? This is all you wanted—why didn't you just take it at lunch Wednesday? You had me alone in your car."

"I told you, I was trying to be nice," he states. "And no, it was not all fake. None of it was fake. I made it clear I liked you. I must have asked you out half a dozen times. You said no every time."

My eyes bug out. "Yes, Carter. I said *no*."

He shrugs. "So, I had to get creative. You could've just gone to the movies with me last night and then Grace wouldn't be drunk right now, but you always have to fight tooth and nail."

Shaking my head, I tell him, "That's not trying, Carter. Are you really so spoiled that you consider that a great effort?"

"Doesn't matter," he says casually. "You're here now, little virgin."

I swallow, a feeling of foreboding sweeping over me as I look up at him. I'm full of anger because I *knew* this would happen if I came here tonight, but Grace gave me no other choice. I could let him hurt her or show up and risk him hurting me.

It's too late, so there's no point thinking about that anymore. I need to get out of this, and I don't know how. My skin is still hot from the surge of adrenaline, from the effort of fighting him off. It's hard to think with him on top of me like this, and then he makes matters worse, reaching down and casually slipping two buttons through their holes on my skirt.

"Carter, no." I shove his hand away and start to rebutton, but before I can get even the first one fixed, he shifts, grabs my wrists, and shoves them over my head on the mattress. The movement brings his body closer, brings his face close to mine.

My heart skips several beats at how easily he holds me down when I'm fighting against him with all my strength. His dark eyes hold mine captive. I can't look away. They don't betray even a shadow of conflict. Instead, they sparkle, like he couldn't be more pleased that this is happening.

It's terrifying, his disregard for right and wrong. The pleasure he gets out of making me powerless. He knows I am. I try to push his hands away with another burst of effort and his arms don't move an inch, even using all my strength to shove at him.

"You like having me at your mercy?" I demand, my tone scathing.

Without remorse, he says, "I do."

I try to free myself again, but it's like trying to push a truck off me—useless. I don't have the physical strength or stamina to match his. My body doesn't go through the same rigorous train-ing, so every burst of effort takes much more out of me than it does him. Cartwright's words ring out in my mind: *We're champions.*

I'm losing energy—and heart—with every failed attempt to get him off me. I'm breathing hard, flooded with so many different emotions; meanwhile, Carter hasn't broken a sweat. He's just waiting me out.

This is so unfair.

"Done fighting, princess?" he asks, casually, as if he could do this all day.

"What happened to you?" I demand. "What made you like this? Were you born this way, or did someone create this monster?"

Now he rolls his eyes, pulling my hands close enough together that he only needs to hold them with one, freeing his other hand up. "Let's not get into another counseling session, okay, Ellis? You're not getting paid by the hour."

"Don't do this," I implore him.

Ignoring me, he uses his free hand to resume unbuttoning my skirt. He pushes it open and smirks at the plain, white cotton panties beneath. "Of course. Virgin panties."

I flush with embarrassment, and that makes me even angrier. He slides his hand between my legs, cupping the last part of my body he should be touching. I draw in a few shallow breaths, drowning in humiliation. Tears sting my eyes, but I will them away. His knees are between my legs, so I can't even squeeze them shut. I can't stop him from touching me.

"Have you ever let a guy get you off?" he asks casually.

I refuse to dignify that question with an answer, glaring silently at the ceiling.

"Probably not, huh?" he replies, unbothered by my lack of participation. "You're a bit of an ice princess. Doesn't bother me, but... you are."

I almost manage to ignore him, but then he slides a finger up under the fabric and I panic, moving my hips to try to get his hand off me. "Carter, please."

He teases me, playing with the elastic, letting his finger brush the inside of my thigh. "Well, since you said please..."

I eye him warily, but he moves his hand away from my

panties and trails it up my abdomen. He runs the flat of his palm all the way up until he can cup my breast, then he caresses one in his hand.

"Mm, I've missed these," he tells me.

I'm still wearing a shirt, but it's the black one that laces up at the bust. Carter begins working the lace free from the top, and when he's done, the shirt gapes open all the way to my waist. He slides his hand inside and cups my left breast, palming it and sending a shard of ice straight through me.

I don't know whether to ask him to stop again or stop feeding him. Maybe I should just shut him out. He's probably going to do whatever he wants to me, anyway. This is out of my control now. There's nothing I can say or do—there hasn't been, since he got a taste for this in that damn empty classroom. He may as well have held me down and inflicted all the crude bullshit he desired that day, because now, on top of everything else, I feel like a fool. A fool for being intrigued by him, for letting myself feel even a sliver of sympathy for him, for letting myself wonder if there might be more to him, if maybe that day in the classroom, *he* got carried away, too.

He didn't. This is who he is, and I don't think he's sorry.

He releases my hands and despite all the doom and gloom of the moment, I'm hit by a swell of hope. Is he letting me go? Is he stopping?

Then I meet his gaze, and he smiles faintly. "Now, let's get this shirt all the way off."

CHAPTER 14

EVEN THOUGH I'M TIRED, even though I know I'll lose, I try my best to keep my shirt on. Carter seems to draw pleasure out of the struggle. Once he has my bra off, too, he shoves me back down on the bed in nothing more than my panties and removes the last of my doubts as to whether or not he enjoyed that; he grinds himself against me, and I can tell he's aroused by how hard he is.

I don't know how to get control of this thing, but force isn't working. Well, it's not working for me. It's clearly working just fine for him. Force only works if you're the stronger opponent. I don't have the physical strength, but maybe I can win using a different kind of weapon.

Even though I'm terrified I'm about to be violated, I force myself to go soft. I stop struggling against him, stop flinching when he runs his thumb over my nipple, stop wallowing in the humiliation of him looking at me mostly naked. I stop everything and do my best to switch gears, to fight his violence with the last thing I want to give him—submission.

My hands aren't pinned anymore. Tentatively, I lift a hand, reaching toward his face. As if on reflex, his fingers close around my wrist to stop me. He starts to move it like he has been, but when his hard eyes meet mine, I shake my head.

"I just want to touch you," I tell him gently.

My heart hammers in my chest as he regards me skeptically, but I suppose he decides if I'm lying and I slap him, it's nothing he can't handle. He releases my hand to see what I'll do with it.

My hand trembles slightly, but I bring it to his face, caressing his strong jaw. I bring my other hand up to the other side of his face and draw him closer. He lets me. I drag him closer until his forehead is resting against mine, then I kiss the corner of his mouth. He stiffens, but doesn't pull away. Understandably, he doesn't know what the hell is happening, but I keep at it. I keep touching his face, I kiss the other corner of his mouth.

His voice is low, more a grumble than anything. "What are you doing, Ellis?"

Ellis, not Zoey. He calls me Ellis when he's keeping me at a distance.

Instead of answering him with words, I kiss his upper lip, then his lower lip. Before I can decide whether or not I want to kiss him fully on the mouth, he takes the decision out of my hands, claiming my lips aggressively, pushing me into the mattress as his hand moves to cup my breast. He squeezes while he kisses me, harder, faster, much more powerfully than the tiny kisses I was giving him.

Something stirs inside me, and this time it's not fear. This time, it's something a little dizzying that knocks me off kilter. His tongue demands entrance to my mouth. I've never been kissed this way before, but I open my mouth on a gasp and he sweeps in, his tongue tangling with mine. I'm lost in a sea of sensation already, then his hand slips under the waistband of my panties.

"Wait," I cry, breaking the kiss. "Carter, please don't hurt me."

"Sh," he murmurs against my lips. "I won't. Just relax. I want to make you feel good."

I don't trust him, but I try not to let him feel that. I draw in a shaky breath and meet his gaze, searching for something to believe in. His big hand covers me again, this time without the thin barrier of my panties.

Not allowing me time to think or doubt, his lips claim mine again. This kiss is hard and hot—it's a brand and a drug all in one, marking me as ruined, then dragging me under so that I don't care. I struggle to hold on to sanity, but Carter pushes his finger inside me, gently caressing me, tempting me to follow him instead. I gasp against his mouth. He catches my bottom lip between his and bites—not hard, but enough to startle me. He strokes my clit and I moan, my eyes rolling back, my chest working.

He leaves a trail of rough kisses along my jaw, making his way to my neck, fingering me all the while. I'm a mess of stimulated nerve endings, crying out and trembling, chills of arousal hitting me on and off. I can't even think, I can only want. Need. Feel.

"Carter," I cry. I don't even know why; I don't know what I want to ask for.

"Feel good, princess?"

With my eyes closed, I nod my head. "Yeah."

"You want more?"

If I had the ability to think, I might consider what 'more' might entail and give him a resounding no, but I can't think, I can only feel, and what I feel is a building tension inside my body, a need I can't describe. It's like he's using his finger to drive me crazy and I'll explode without some outlet. Instead of saying no, I nod.

Carter chuckles, kissing me softly, like he finds me adorable. "You really haven't let anyone touch you before, have you? You've just been waiting for me to find you."

I spread my legs wider, moving against his hand. "Carter, please…"

"Please what, princess? Tell me what you want."

I shake my head, already flushed with all he's doing to my body, so at least I can't blush *more*.

"You want me to make you come?" he asks.

Licking my lips, I nod my head. My heart falters as I do, but I'm so close, I can feel it sneaking up on me. I need him to take me the rest of the way. I need it. "Please," I whisper.

"Mm, anything for you, princess," he hums against my lips, before claiming them again. His tongue sweeps into my mouth as his finger moves fast against my clit and I feel myself starting to come apart. In the same way he dismantled my shirt by drawing out the laces, he plays with me, teasing that sensitive place inside me like he knows just how to set me free.

And then he does. I cry out, helpless to keep the sounds in as pleasure so intense that I want to weep bursts open inside me. I moan and cry out against his mouth, the sharp pleasure taking its time moving through me. Oh, God, it feels incredible.

It finally stops, the sharpness ebbing, and I fall into a cocoon of blissful satisfaction. I need to be close to him. Gratitude consumes me, my body overriding my brain, wanting to thank him for that wonderful feeling he just gave me.

Carter must sense it—or I guess maybe he's just experienced this before, but I haven't. Either way, he rolls on his side and I immediately snuggle as close to him as I can get, wrapping my arm around his torso and nuzzling into his chest. At least for this moment, I am content as a kitten. I don't care what he is, I don't care about all he's made me feel—my body is in control, and it only cares about the most recent thing he made me feel, and that was intense, mind-melting pleasure.

Carter's arms settle around me and he keeps me close. I feel him kiss the top of my head, so I tip my head up, smiling at him softly, and give him a gentle kiss on the lips.

There are no words spoken between us, but after a moment, Carter reaches for one of my hands and guides it to the hardness between his legs. I got my release, but he's still turned on. Still consumed with gratitude and affection, I don't move my hand away. I rub him through the stiff fabric of his jeans, then I unbutton and unzip his pants so I can push my hand down inside.

I watch Carter close his eyes, see the pleasure on his face as I stroke him. His grip on me tightens as I work his dick. I can tell by the sounds he's making, by the way he fists his hand in my hair, what I'm doing is making him feel as good as he made me.

Then he says, "Zoey, I need your mouth."

I slide down the bed, tugging his jeans down. His cock springs free and I take it in my hand, pumping and stroking. Then I pull my hair over my shoulder and bend to take it into my mouth. He groans as soon as my mouth slides over half his length. I don't take him deep this time, but I don't need to. My hand has done most of the work, he just needed a place to come. With a couple more minutes of pumping and sucking, he grabs a fistful of my hair, groans, and empties himself in my mouth.

When he's done, he uses the fistful of hair in his hand to drag me back up next to him. I'm still pretty relaxed, so I let him drag me around like a ragdoll. I curl right up with him again, feeling strangely safe and secure when he wraps his arms around my waist and holds me, like he wants me as close as he can get me. I rest my face against his chest, still covered with his T-shirt.

It's probably indicative of our relationship that after what we just did, I'm stripped almost completely bare, while Carter is still almost fully dressed, only naked enough for me to service him.

I can't care about that right now. Closing my eyes, I let myself relax in his embrace and refuse to let my brain turn back on.

I DIDN'T MEAN to fall asleep, but I must have.

When my eyes drift open, I'm alone on the bed. My skirt and shirt are laid out down by my legs, so I sit up, slightly disoriented, and reach for them. I look around, not seeing Carter, and my stomach sinks. Did he leave me here? He was done with me, so he skipped out?

Probably. It would be stupid to expect anything less.

While I felt great in my brainless, post-orgasm moments, now reality comes back with a vengeance. I am a fucking moron if I thought I'd wake up and he would still be here, spooning me. Hell, while I'm expecting ridiculous things, I should just dream up a declaration of love and repentance, maybe a promise that we'll go to colleges close to each other, since we are clearly going to get married and have babies all because he fingered me and I sucked his dick to avoid rape for the second time.

"Get it together, Zoey," I mutter to myself, shaking my head and trying to orient myself to being awake. I'm still tired and I want to go back to bed. I will, but first I need to put my clothes on, go retrieve Grace, and take her home.

All the fun has died. My Carter high is wearing off and I am crashing, hard. Shit. That should not have happened. Well, there's little point beating myself up over it, I guess. What's done is done. Maybe now that Carter sort of got in my pants, he'll lose interest in this chase. Maybe now he'll leave me alone and I can get back to my life.

I'm able to look on the bright side, but as I'm walking down the stairs, I'm hit by a swell of dread. I keep my head down, hoping I can find Grace and slip out unnoticed.

Unfortunately, it becomes apparent that in order to get to the kitchen where I see her sitting on a stool next to Jake, I have to cross the living room full of teenagers. I don't know how long I was upstairs asleep, but if Carter came down without me, they probably have ideas—

Before I can even complete the thought, Shayne smirks at me and starts golf-clapping. I swallow down a lump of embarrassment, but I can't keep my eyes from darting around the room to see who else might have noticed, who else might be judging me.

Everybody. That seems to be the answer. Cartwright is smirking, red Solo cup in hand. Erika has her arms crossed. She's not clapping, she goes the more direct route and says, "Whore."

My stomach sinks and I head for the kitchen, trying to escape the lewd comments and additional mocking. Trying not to look for Carter. If I see him smirking and enjoying this, I won't even be able to hold on to a shred of a silver lining. This will be all regret and nothing nice, and I don't want to deal with that right now.

As if summoned by my thoughts, Carter steps into view. I didn't see him because he was in the kitchen with Grace and Jake, not in the living room with everyone else. He frowns, glancing around at his friends clapping, making comments, and generally being assholes, then he sees me and understands why.

"All right, that's enough of that," he tells them.

"Hey, we shouldn't be surprised," Cartwright says, smirking and lifting his chin in Carter's direction. "We all know Zoey the ho gets around."

"Nope," Carter replies, shaking his head. "We're done calling her that. Knock it off."

"Aww," Erika sneers, somewhat playfully—but passive aggressively playful. "Look at Carter, protecting his flavor of the week. How gallant."

This is more humiliating than I was prepared for. Just coming downstairs after falling asleep makes it so obvious I must have done *something* with him.

"She must have sucked that dick good, huh?" Shayne says, grinning.

My wide eyes snap to Carter's accusingly. "You *told* them?"

Grimacing faintly, Carter says, "Nope. You just did."

I can't even look at Grace. I cover my face with my hands while laughter and taunts fill the room at my back. "Nice one," they tell him.

"Way to slut it up in *my* bedroom," Erika chimes in, reviving the golf clap.

"You know what, Erika," Carter says, casually. "You've sucked my dick, too, so if you're handing out accolades, make sure to give yourself a pat on the back." His gaze shifts and he lifts an eyebrow. "Brianna, you wanna talk shit?"

Brianna immediately chirps, "Nope."

"Well, I ain't ever sucked your dick," Clemons states. "I'll talk all the shit I want."

"Yeah?" Carter asks. "The way you played tonight, you must be sucking *someone's* dick to stay on the team, you slow-ass motherfucker."

Cartwright barks with laughter. "Oh shit, that's cold, man."

Carter wraps an arm around me, pulling me close for a hug and looking down at me. "You okay?"

I can't entirely contain my surprise. Blinking a couple of times, I nod uncertainly.

Then, right here in front of everyone, he bends his head and kisses me. It's no long, lingering kiss like the ones he gave me in the bedroom, but when he pulls back, settles his arm around my shoulders, and looks back at his friends, no one says another unkind word. No more snide comments, no more teasing. They all fall silent, then slowly return to their own conversations.

It feels like I have heartburn, though. I can't believe everyone in this house now knows I did something so intimate with Carter. They don't just speculate or assume, they *know*. I'm afraid to look at Grace. This is exactly what I tried to warn her about—these parties are not for us. These *guys* are not for us. In under two weeks, I went from "I've never even French kissed" to Carter Mahoney's personal sex toy. Twice now, I've had to bargain with him for basic human decency. Now he's kissing me in public, and I'm not sure that's a good thing. I'm not his now. I don't belong to him just because I turned a potentially traumatic experience into something I could live with.

God, I need to get out of here. I need to leave this demented place and never come back.

Finally forcing my gaze to Grace, I ask, "Are you okay?"

She doesn't look as horrified as I expected her to look. The alcohol is probably helping all this insanity go down a little more easily. Dutifully picking up two empty water bottles, she tells me, "I am well hydrated."

Jake still gets a passive aggressive jab in, though. "Apparently Zoey is, too."

I glare at him, then look at Grace. "We need to go."

She nods, head down so she doesn't have to meet my gaze. "Yeah, we should. My mom's gonna kill me."

Carter follows me to the door, grabs me around the waist, and kisses me one more time. I don't know what to do or say, so I just offer a little smile, then haul ass out the door with Grace.

CHAPTER 15

"BREAKFAST IS READY!"

I squint at the bright light coming in through Grace's bedroom window. After I brought her home, I sent my mom a text to let her know I would be staying the night at Grace's. I managed to get her in the house without her parents (who were already in bed, not realizing she had left the house so late) finding out she was drunk, so I didn't want to leave her alone, just in case her body had a belated reaction to the alcohol or all the sugary punch.

I look over at her now. She's still sleeping, so I shake her awake. Even though I know she's okay, I still feel relieved when her eyes open and she frowns up at me. "Leave me alone."

I figure the alcohol probably has her feeling crappy, so I don't take offense. "Time to get up, party girl."

She groans. "Don't ever say party again."

Since I have no idea how much she had to drink, I ask, "Are you hung over?"

"No, I'm just livin' in the literal Hell of last night's memories." Opening her eyes and turning her gaze back to me, she says, "I am *so* sorry you had to come to that party because of me. I feel like I led you right into temptation, and you tried so hard to warn me."

It's not good for Grace to be stressed out, so I shake my head. "Everything is fine."

"You tried to tell me Carter was scheming to get you there, and then you ended up doing… things with him."

I don't even want her *thinking* about what Carter and I did. "It's over. It's done. It doesn't matter now. Don't worry about it, Grace. Honest. I mean, never do it again, but what's done is done."

"Are you and Carter, like… *together* now?"

"No." I push back the blankets, sitting on the edge of the bed and grabbing my phone off the end table. My battery is at 13% and I have to work in two hours. Fantastic.

"Did you really… do what you said last night?"

"I really don't want to talk about it, Grace," I tell her, clearing the notifications on my phone and opening the text my mom sent a half hour ago.

"Did you have sex with him?"

My shoulders tense, and I quickly text my mom back as I tell Grace, "No. I did not have sex with him."

"You fell asleep upstairs," she says in a leading way, like why would I fall asleep if I only went down on him? Valid question, I suppose.

Instead of answering her, I tell her, "Your mom said breakfast is ready, so we should probably go eat."

Before I make it to the door, she blurts, "I kissed Jake Parsons."

My eyes widen and I pivot to look at her. "You did what?"

Grace is grimacing, and now she hides her face in her hands. "I wasn't in my right mind. It was when you were upstairs with Carter, I just… I don't know what happened. He was getting me water and asking if I felt okay, and he has such pretty eyes…"

Still gaping, I say, "Pretty eyes?"

"I know, I know," she says, hiding her face again. "I'm a harlot. I'm so sorry, Zoey. After the crap he pulled with you, that dumb nickname and everything… I am the worst friend in the world."

I go back to the bed, taking a seat on the edge again. "When you say *kissed*…?"

She looks up with dread. "Like, really kissed. We made out. Body to body contact, tangled limbs, the whole nine yards."

"Oh, my God, Grace."

"I know! I'm sorry. It was so stupid."

I cradle my head in my hands, the various dangers of last night becoming harder and harder to ignore. We may have both emerged a little more tarnished than when we entered, but it could have been so much worse.

I didn't tell Grace that Jake cornered me in that classroom. She doesn't know how I got on Carter's radar, and I don't know how I can tell her now. After she heard last night that I did those things with him, after she saw him kiss me and shield me from the taunts of his friends. I don't know how to explain any of that. I don't know how to explain Carter. Whatever it is I've been doing with him, though, at least I've known what he's capable of. Grace doesn't have all the information about Jake.

Maybe I can implicate him without implicating Carter. I don't *want* to, but if Grace is attracted to him, she deserves to know the truth.

God, this is going to be so awkward.

"Look, Grace… I really didn't want to tell you this, but Jake didn't leave it at groping me the time you know about. After his football coach suspended him to punish him for his behavior, Jake got it in his mind that he needed to punish me back. He wanted to intimidate me into saying I lied so he'd be able to play, and… he and a couple of other guys from the team chased me into a classroom, cornered me, and—I won't go into details or anything, but it wasn't good. Jake isn't a good guy, Grace. He's not a safe guy."

Grace's brown eyes are wide with horror. "Oh, my gosh, Zoey. Did they… hurt you? I mean, did they…?"

I shake my head, looking down. "They stopped before it got that far, but just barely."

She covers her mouth, tears springing to her eyes. "I'm so sorry, Zoey. I didn't know. I would have never…. Are you okay?"

"It's fine. I'm fine. It's over. I don't want to think about it. The only reason I'm telling you is because, if you like Jake…"

Grace shakes her head, sniffling. "No, I don't. I don't. It was just a stupid, drunken thing. Alcohol really is evil, isn't it? Oh, my gosh, I just don't even know what to say, Zoey."

"You don't have to say anything. Honestly, I don't want you to get upset over it. I truly am fine. Thinkin' about it makes me feel icky, so I would feel better if we didn't. Let's move on. I just needed to tell you so you knew what Jake was capable of."

"Who were the other guys?"

That gives me pause. Maybe too obvious a pause, because there's no way I wouldn't know them all by name. Cartwright is an ass, but I'm not going to lie and say he did something he didn't.

"Shayne Sutton," I offer. "He was mostly just guarding the door. It doesn't even matter, the point was just—I wanted to warn you."

Her gaze drops to the comforter, then she swallows and meets my gaze again. "Was it Carter?"

Ignoring her question, I stand. "Let's go have breakfast."

Instead of letting it go, she presses. "Were you really sleeping last night, or were you... something else? Did he hurt you?"

"Grace, I'm fine," I say, a little more shortly than I intend. Attempting to smooth it over, I add in a more solicitous tone, "Now, let's go have breakfast or I need to go home. I work soon, and my phone is almost dead."

I'M in the middle of updating the "new release" display when my phone vibrates. I finish arranging the shelf, steal a glance at my manager to see if he's paying attention, then check my phone.

It's a direct message from Carter. It reads, "Seems like I should have your phone number, doesn't it?"

I type back, "I'm surprised you don't already, actually. You don't have devious alternate means of getting it? I'm disappointed."

"You always have to make me work extra hard for you, don't you, princess?"

I smile faintly. "It'll be good for you for to work for something in your life, QB."

"Hey, I earned that position," he tells me.

"Uh-huh. Didn't your parents buy the whole team new jerseys?"

"My mom thought the old ones were ugly. That had nothing to do with me making the team."

"Mm-hmm," I send back.

"If you'd ever bring your ass to one of my games, you'd see my skills."

"You invited me to ONE game," I point out. "It's a little premature to be throwing around 'ever' like this is a habit of mine."

"Last night I made a 31-yard touchdown pass to win the game. My parents didn't pay for that, now, did they?" he asks.

"Congratulations on throwing a ball kinda far."

"It's not my best pass," he assures me.

"I could not care less."

A few seconds later, he sends back, "Brutal. What do I have to do impress you, Ellis?"

"Get my phone number," I tease.

"Fine. I will. And when I text you, I'll tell you when I'm picking you up."

"Excuse me?" I send back, cocking an eyebrow at the screen.

"It's Saturday. I don't have practice. I thought we could catch an early showing of that movie."

"I can't, I'm at work until four," I reply without thought.

"Can't call off?"

I laugh a little, shaking my head at how out of touch he is. "No, I can't call off. I'm already here. That's not how jobs work."

"That's shitty. I can't go tonight. My parents are gonna be in Dallas, so I have to watch Chloe."

"The jokes would probably go over her head," I joke.

"Maybe slightly inappropriate."

Even though I didn't agree to go out with him, have not thought any more about this at all, and might not even *want* to go out with him, since he can't go anyway, I decide to keep the joke going. "Unless you wanted to go see the new Disney movie instead. I bet she'd like that one."

He sends back, "Are you serious?"

I grimace, not sure how he means that. The lack of tone leaves me thinking that joke didn't land as I reread it. If he really thinks I'm offering to go see a Disney movie with him and his kid sister, I would feel like sort of an asshole saying no. I don't hate being around him, I just can't trust him not to maul me. With Chloe there, that wouldn't be an issue. Besides, I have a little brother; it's not like I'm a stranger to Disney movies.

I don't know if his "are you serious?" was one of disbelief or actual interest. I decide to err on the side of actual interest, since at least if I'm wrong, I will look like the idiot and not him. I can handle it.

"Sure, why not? I think I might actually prefer to have a tiny buffer there. She's a sassy taskmaster; she'll keep you in line if you try to get all crazy."

"Until I bribe her with ice cream," he replies. "Then you're on your own."

"I'm glad to see her sense of girl power can only be bought out by frozen dairy."

"Everyone has their price," he states.

I crack a smile, glancing up as movement catches my eye and someone approaches the cash register. "All right, I have to get back to work. If you can manage to get my phone number, then I will talk to you later."

"You really want to hang out with a little hellion all night?" he asks, to be sure.

"Chloe will be there, too," I tease.

"Ha ha," he sends back, dryly.

"You walked right into it," I point out.

"I'll show you a hellion."

"You already have," I remind him, before slipping the phone in my pocket, pasting on a smile, and going to ring out the waiting customer.

CHAPTER 16

IT TAKES Carter just under an hour to get my phone number. He texts me a link to a trailer for the Disney movie we are apparently taking Chloe to with the message, "You asked for this."

"It looks heartwarming and adorable," I reply.

"This is definitely the first date you expected, right?" he answers.

"Actually, I never agreed to go out with you in the first place," I remind him.

"Details, details," he replies.

I clock out promptly at four and head home, figuring even if I'm not calling it a date, I should probably change out of my work T-shirt before I meet him and Chloe at the movie theater.

Before I even get out of my shirt, Carter texts me that there's been a change in plans, Chloe is hungry and she insists she needs to eat before the movie. He tells me to meet him at Chick-fil-A down the road from the theater.

"Not there," I text back.

"Why not?"

People from my church work there, and I don't really want to run into them while I'm out with Carter Mahoney. That's probably the wrong thing to say, so instead, I try a redirect. "How about wings again? Or Sonic?"

"Chloe thinks she's royalty, she can't be bothered to eat in a car. She requires sit-down dining and chicken nuggets. If you want to fight with a five-year-old about waffle fries, you be my guest. I've already traveled that road. It's a losing battle."

I crack a smile. "How about drive-thru Chick-fil-A and we take it to the park? I've never known a child to get mad about going to the park, no matter how prissy."

"Why don't you want to go inside Chick-fil-A? Do you know someone who works there or something? You like a boy, Ellis? It's okay, you can tell me."

Yeah, right. I can only imagine the torment he would inflict on a guy I admitted to liking who isn't him.

"Don't worry," I assure him. "Apparently I only go out with guys I DON'T like."

"Oh good, well then I'm all set," he replies.

I toss the phone down on my bed and turn to the closet, looking for a shirt he won't try to open while we're sitting in a theater with a small child. To stay on the safe side, I select a cran-berry ¾ sleeve ribbed sweater. The material is thin, but with the sleeves, it's more fitting for cooler weather. Today is a hot day, but it shows no cleavage and shouldn't tempt him. I can't believe I have to pick outfits based on what *won't* tempt my date. This is terrible. Good lord.

Shoving away that swell of common sense, I tug the top on and pick up my phone to see what Carter's last text says. "Your reluctance to go there has made me also want Chick-fil-A. You wanna meet there, or should I pick you up?"

"As always, I am bowled over by your concern for what I want," I reply.

"You're welcome," he replies.

I roll my eyes. "I'll meet you there."

———

CARTER'S MUSTANG is parked right up front. I park and approach it. Since it's hot outside, they have the windows rolled up and the air still on, so I make my presence known by knocking on the window.

Carter kills the engine and lets Chloe out. She slides down

off the leather seat, appraises me, then says, "You're the bookstore lady."

"That's me," I say with a nod. "Is it all right if I tag along to the movie theater with you today?"

"Sure," she says magnanimously, before taking her brother's hand and stopping at the edge of the sidewalk. I don't stop walking until I realize she isn't following, so she chastises me. "Gotta look both ways before you cross the street."

"That's right. Thank you for reminding me about that," I tell her.

Now that she's sure no cars are coming, she crosses. I walk ahead and open the door for her, all but forgetting the reason I hadn't wanted to come here in the first place.

Then I see my youth pastor's younger brother behind the counter and my hopes of not being seen are completely dashed.

"Hey, Zoey," he says brightly, flashing me a smile. "Lovely to see you, as always." His gaze drifts past me to Carter and his smile droops.

Steeling myself, I approach the counter and study the menu much harder than I need to. "Hi, Luke."

"I see you brought a friend," Luke remarks.

Because he's an asshole, Carter strides up to the counter and offers his hand. "Carter Mahoney."

"Yes, I know who you are," Luke says, his tone a touch reserved as he reluctantly shakes Carter's hand. His gaze drifts back to me and he makes a painful effort to inject something more like enthusiasm into his tone. "I didn't realize you were friends with the star quarterback."

Instead of making my life easier, Carter lets go of his sister's hand and drapes his arm around my waist, tugging me close. Like he did that first night he showed up at my house and blindsided me with soup and manipulation, he asks, "What looks good, babe?"

Luke's smile tightens, but he looks down at his cash register to keep from openly judging me, I think.

Great. Fantastic. I slide an unamused look at Carter, but he flashes me his bullshit golden boy smile.

Chloe decides she has been ignored for long enough, and she

puts her small hands on the edge of the counter and peers over at Luke. "We're going to the movies."

With his free hand, Carter ruffles her hair. "That's right. First, why don't you tell the nice cashier what you want to eat?"

Luke briefly meets Carter's gaze, letting him know he's aware of the subtle put-down, then he goes about taking our order. It's just as bad as I worried it would be, maybe worse. Somehow I did not expect Carter to call me *babe*. I knew just my association with someone in Carter's crowd—let alone Carter himself—wouldn't shine my halo any, but he may as well have stamped me with his seal to let Luke know we're together—even though we're not. I wanted to object, but that would have been even weirder. Better to ignore it and get to a booth as quickly as possible.

At least once we're seated and waiting for our food, I can glare at Carter in peace.

"What?" he asks, with a ridiculous attempt at innocence.

"That is my pastor's brother," I inform him.

"And?"

"And he goes to our school, so he knows who you are."

Carter cocks an eyebrow. "And?"

I shrug. "No big deal, I guess I'm just going to Hell now."

Carter smirks. "Because you've been seen in public with me? That seems a little dramatic."

"My pastor will hear all about it and stop praying for me. Decide I'm a lost cause."

"If your pastor knows enough about my life to know I'm bad news, I think he's got much bigger problems than the fate of your eternal soul. This town loves me. I can do no wrong around here."

"You do lots of wrong," I mutter. "What about that art teacher that had to move because of you? Grace told me, so he probably knows about that."

Carter waves off my concerns. "Who cares? I don't care what anyone thinks about me going out with you, do I? So why should you care?"

"Because, as you said, you can do no wrong in this town. I am in the opposite situation. My family and I are about one complaint away from being run out of town with pitchforks after the whole Jake debacle."

"I'm hungry," Chloe states, leaning forward on the table.

"Your food will be out in just a minute," he tells her.

"I want my milkshake," she says, looking up at him.

"You'll get it when it's ready. Be patient."

"I hate being patient," she tells him, resting her chin on her arms and sulking.

"Yeah, so do I," he says, winking at me.

I shake my head. "Terrible."

Poor Luke has to bring our food to the table when it's done. At least Carter is sitting on the opposite side of the booth with Chloe and not over here with me, I guess. Still, I can't shake the feeling that Luke doesn't approve of the company I'm keeping, and knowing all I know, I can't really fault him for it.

ONCE THE STRESS of being seen with Carter by my pastor's brother passes, the rest of the night is actually really nice. We take Chloe to the movie theater, get ice cream, then go back to their house and play Mario Kart with her until she passes out on the couch.

Carter takes Chloe upstairs and puts her in bed, so I make sure when he comes back down, I have my purse handy, my shoes on, and I'm standing, my body language clearly informing him that it's time for me to leave. Ordinarily, I wouldn't come back to his house at all, but I figured with Chloe in the room, I would be safe.

Now Chloe is asleep upstairs and we're in the house alone, so I am no longer protected by anything. Add to that the fact that he specifically said if he wanted to fuck me, he would take me to his house, and I'm feeling pretty antsy about getting out of here.

As he walks back into the great room, Carter eyes up my defensive position and faintly smirks. "Where do you think you're rushing off to, princess?"

I keep both hands fastened around the handles of my purse and take a step back. "I need to get home. I have some studying to do before bed, and I already texted my mom and told her I'd be on my way, so… she'll be waitin' for me."

"Nah," he says, moving directly into my space. "Not yet. We've been babysitting all night. Now we can spend some one-on-one time together."

"Yeah, well, I only really agreed to come out today because the little girl would be there, so…" I trail off as his hand closes around my wrist and he tugs me back toward the couch.

"Come on," he says.

My stomach drops as he pulls me forward. I put some effort into pulling back, but it's a measly resistance. Meeting his gaze, I say, "Come on, Carter. Let me go home."

"I'm not gonna hurt you," he tells me.

I swallow, watching him warily.

"I'm not," he insists, dragging me toward the couch. "I want to kiss you, that's all. Kissing didn't bother you last night, did it?"

Last night isn't something I even want to think about, but I'm more focused on *this* night. "You promise?"

His lips curve up and he pushes me down on the couch. "You believe my promises, princess?"

The breath rushes out of me as I ease back on the couch, watching him like a suicidal gazelle might watch the hungry lion as he approaches. "I don't have much of a choice, do I?" I ask, as he neatly moves my legs so I'm horizontal on the couch, then comes down on top of me. Once more, he pins me down, imprisoning my wrists against the soft couch cushion.

"Of course you have a choice," he says, bending his head to kiss my neck. "I can make you do a lot of things, but I can't *make* you trust me. That, you have to *give* me."

Does he want that? My trust? If so, boy, has he set some goals for himself. "Do you think it's easy to trust you when you're so willing to pounce on me?" I ask him.

"Didn't say it was easy," he remarks, nipping at the sensitive skin of my neck, sending a jolt straight through my body. "A challenge isn't enough to stop the magnificent Zoey Ellis though, is it?"

I crack a smile, even though I know he must be picking on me. "Magnificent, huh? I thought I was an ice princess."

"Sometimes," he acknowledges, his lips moving to my earlobe. Pleasurable shivers dance across the back of my neck and down my spine as he nips that, too. "But sometimes you're warm." He kisses my neck. "Sometimes you're sweet." Another kiss, trailing closer to my face. "Sometimes you're a real pain in the ass."

"How romantic," I say dryly, meeting his gaze as he pulls back to look at me.

His lips tug up in a faint smile. "You're a lot of different things, just like me."

That's true. We certainly aren't the same, he and I, but given we've experienced things with one another we haven't experienced with anyone else, we probably do have insight into layers that our friends and families haven't even peeked at.

That's interesting to think about. Intimacy seemed a little intimidating, but looking at it this way, as another way to bond with someone... well, maybe a little less so.

"Tell me something," I begin, holding his gaze. "What is it you want from me? You can be honest," I add, quickly. "I'd much prefer your honesty, even if it's... something unusual."

Smirking faintly at how carefully I worded that, he says, "I don't know if I want anything all that *unusual*. I want you. Simple, right?"

Instead of giving me time to answer, he restrains me a little more and bends his head, kissing his way up and down my neck again. Even held down and a little afraid, that feels good, so I close my eyes and soak it up.

My chest seems to tighten as I struggle to draw in enough air. It's not so much the physical weight of Carter crushing me that's the problem, it's the knowledge of how helpless I really am beneath him. He can make all the promises in the world, but he could decide not to honor them and make good on his initial threat right here, right now. I was even safer at the party than I am now. Right now, there is literally no one around to hear me scream.

That rational fear pierces the pleasurable sensation of his mouth traveling up and down my neck. I gasp like I'm coming up for air, and try to yank my wrists free.

I hear and dislike the trace of panic in my own voice as I tell him, "Carter, stop. I need to go. I need to go home."

Running his lips along my jaw, he murmurs, "What's the magic word?"

"Please," I add, pulling at my wrists, but he won't release me.

He smiles, then kisses me briefly on the lips. "No. But I appreciate you asking so nicely."

"Tell me somethin' else," I say, grasping for some kind of control over at least some part of this situation.

"What do you wanna know?" he asks.

"Did last night mean anything to you? I mean, you want to do it again, right?"

"I do," he verifies with a single nod, watching me to see where I'm going with this.

"So, I think you're right. I need to be able to trust you. That's the only way we'll ever get to a place where... where maybe I could see that happening again. I did some research—obviously informal research, and I don't have the proper educational background to wrap my head all the way around this. Or even all the information about you. I'm winging it, but I'm trying to figure out how to handle you. I'm trying, but I don't have all the information."

His voice lightens with amusement. "How to *handle* me?"

"You're not like other guys," I state, meeting his gaze. "Surely you realize that."

His amusement dissipates, and he watches me curiously. "And you're not like other girls," he states.

Lifting my eyebrows and looking pointedly at my arms pinned against his couch, I say, "That's a given, or we wouldn't be here right now."

"True. You'd probably be buried in a shallow grave somewhere."

The amusement in his voice is so wrong. I shake my head. "No. It's not funny to joke about murdering women. Can we not? I can't be completely sure you're joking, and I'd like to tackle one monstrous thing at a time."

"All right." He bends to kiss one of the wrists he has pinned down. Not just once, he lavishes the sensitive skin of my wrist with his mouth's attention. I struggle to stay focused, surprised at how good it feels. How sensual it is to have his lips running so tenderly over the area he's been restraining.

Focusing is harder when he does that, but I try anyway. This feels important, and I hate to hope I'm actually connecting with him, but I might as well try.

"I think the first thing I need to know is, what part of this appeals to you?"

He stops kissing my wrist and looks at me skeptically. "Which part of sex appeals to me?"

"No. Um…" I don't know exactly how to refer to it, so I tilt my head toward the wrist he still has restrained. "The force. I mean, do you really want to hurt me? Is it a power thing? A control thing? What makes it feel good to you?"

"Does it matter?"

Evasion, already. "Carter, I'm tryin' to understand you," I state, mild frustration entering my tone. "Even after everything, I am *trying*. If you want me to trust you, give me a reason to."

"I don't have to, though, do I?" he asks, letting his hand slide down between my legs. I'm wearing jeans today, so when he cups me this time, it's through two layers of fabric. "If I want to, I can take this right now."

Ignoring the sinking in my stomach, I hold his gaze. "You could. But it would only happen once. I would never let you get me alone again. Is that what you want? Is this a conquest thing? You said once you could fuck me and get me out of your system. Is that all this is to you? Some kind of drive to take my virginity, then you'll be done with me?"

Shaking his head noncommittally, he says, "Not really. Like I said, I like you."

"You like me, but you want to hurt me?" I question.

"It's not about hurting you."

Progress! "Hurting me doesn't… do anything for you?"

Frowning faintly, he shakes his head. "No, pain doesn't do much for me. It's the struggle, I guess. I do like overpowering you. Mentally, physically—I just like taking you on. I don't know why, exactly; I guess I've never felt so well-matched. Hell, I like doing it even when I know I'm not going to fuck you, just to see the fear in your eyes. That's fucked up, isn't it?"

While a brutal confession, it also strikes me as vulnerable, and I want to reinforce his honesty, so I tug free the wrist he kissed and touch his face tenderly. Holding his gaze, I shake my head. "Not necessarily. What do you see when you look at me? Do you think I'm weaker than you, someone easy to pick on? Or do you see me as strong?"

"Strong," he says, without hesitation. "One of the strongest people I've ever met, in ways I didn't even know people could be."

"And you like having me at your mercy," I say, to verify. "Maybe you like the power it gives *you*, overpowering someone you think is so strong?"

He nods, watching my face. His dark eyes are slightly hooded, either with lust or skepticism, I'm not sure.

"Does it turn you on to think of me helpless?" I ask.

"For me," he specifies. "Not helpless in general, only for me."

I nod my head, swallowing. "Does it lessen your arousal to think of me enjoying it?"

"No. I want you to enjoy it. I like the cute little helpless sounds you make when you come."

Flushing, I drop my gaze to his chest and try to focus on my train of thought without the distraction of bashfulness. "Does it lessen your arousal to picture me crying? Begging you to stop? Meaning it?"

He hesitates for a second, deliberating over whether or not he wants to be honest, but then says, "No."

I let out a breath, but try to keep hold of my objectivity.

So, he can take or leave my pleasure, but he prefers it. All right. My stomach sinks from the weight of all my nerves as I try to find the courage for this next part. "Okay, so, what if you could go through all the motions, but it was just playing? Have you ever…" I clear my throat, trying again. "You've obviously had some sexual experiences, so have you ever explored these desires with any of them?"

Carter shakes his head, still watching me. "I told you, you were the first."

"Okay, so, something I came across——" God, this is awkward. Might as well just spit it out. "Different people obviously like different things. Sexuality is a spectrum, and sexual interests vary and evolve, and… just because you may be into something that not everyone considers normal, it doesn't mean it has to be criminal. You would just have to have a certain kind of partner. You can engage in safer play that would indulge the same…" I have no idea how to say what I'm trying to say. My head is a jumbled mess, I don't know if he's even receptive to it, and I just feel so awkward.

He isn't ridiculing me when he speaks, though, and he uses my actual name, which does encourage me. "Just spit it out, Zoey."

"I just wonder what might happen if you had someone who understood your desires, someone who *consented* to playing with you the way you like. If you like taking someone's power, maybe you could try it with someone who would happily *surrender* her power to you."

I glance up at his face to make sure he's still with me, and when he appears to be, I continue.

"But the thing is, in any kind of situation where power is given over to you like that, it requires a lot of trust. More than average relationships require. It would have to be with someone open-minded, but most importantly, you would have to invest in them. You would have to really care, because it might not always go so well, and if you push too far and actually hurt your plaything, then you need to take care of them after. You can't just disregard their needs or their limits; you'd have to make it right. I think your needs can be met if you look to satisfy them in the right place, but in the wrong place… you're going to become someone's nightmare. There is a line between abuse and rough play, but you have predatory tendencies, Carter. I can say with reasonable certainty, if you don't legitimately care about your partner, that line will disappear."

His dark eyes light up with interest. "Plaything?"

I was testing his response, and I'm not shocked to find he likes that phrase. I swallow. "I imagine your ideal partner would have to find some pleasure in being your plaything."

Cocking his head, he asks, "Are you volunteering?"

I shake my head quickly to disabuse him of that notion. "No. We're just talking, that's all. I'm tryin' to get a read on what you're interested in, what your specific needs are to see if maybe…"

"Have I said yes to anything that's a deal-breaker for you yet?"

The faint trace of hope evident in his asking that strikes a sympathetic chord and gives me pause. "I don't think so, but I haven't even experienced normal sex yet, so I can't be sure. The fact that I'm here right now after everything you've done to me makes me think I might be able to handle it. It doesn't start with sex, though." I lift my eyebrows, eyeing him sternly. "It starts with building trust and a relationship. Like any relationship. I know you don't have many of those, but *normally* before having sex, people connect with one another as human beings, build up their emotional attachment, and sex happens afterward."

His nose wrinkles up with exaggerated disinterest. "That's not really my style."

"Well, it is mine," I inform him. "Trust is central to any solid relationship, but especially one like this. If I'm going to trust someone with unfettered access to my body, I have to be able to trust them with everything else first. Let's get to know each other more and see if it's something we're even interested in pursuing."

"But knowing what you know already, you might be?" he asks.

I don't know if my acceptance matters, but these flecks of vulnerability make me think it does, so I nod my head. "Maybe."

Nodding his head, he says, "Interesting," as if he's conducting his own study. "I guess I can be patient."

"How magnanimous of you," I offer, lightly.

He smiles down at me. "Isn't it?"

CHAPTER 17

MOST WEEKS, I don't dread going to church. It's not really *my* thing, but Grace is in her element there, and the church we go to is a good one. They do lots of community outreach and offer plenty of volunteer opportunities. All that stuff fills Grace's cup, and when you love someone, sometimes you do things for them, to make them happy, to fill them up. It's not like I dislike it, and I wouldn't be doing anything better with my time, anyway.

This week is different, though. This week Grace is dodging my gaze, and when I daydream while the pastor talks, my mind drifts to last night. To Carter Mahoney's couch, pinned beneath his strong body, his mouth claiming mine, his hand pushed down inside my jeans. After all my coaching to get him out of a dysfunctional place, he persuaded me that just because we weren't ready for sex yet didn't mean we couldn't fool around. He told me he wanted to make me come again, told me he owed me one since the first time I got him off, he hadn't returned the favor.

So as my pastor talks about sin and temptation, memories flash through my mind of moaning Carter's name, my eyes closed, my body writhing while his fingers sent me somewhere magical.

Sitting in a church pew with those memories running through my head, I'm flushed and uncomfortable. I smooth a wrinkle out of my skirt, trying to expel those thoughts at least until I leave this building.

When the service is over, I pull out my phone to check it. There's a message from Carter, asking what I'm up to this afternoon.

"Stuck at church," I tell him. "We have a youth group meeting today, we have a new project and we're trying to organize it quickly so we can get funds together."

"For what?"

"This lady and her baby are staying with the pastor and his wife because there was a fire at their place. It destroyed all their stuff and they have nowhere to live, so we're going to raise some funds to help her get back on her feet."

"Aren't you an angel," he replies.

I can practically hear the sarcasm, even in text. "Not in the least," I reply. "You don't have to be an angel to help people."

"When is it over? How about we meet for lunch and you can tell me all about it."

I'm so used to telling him no, I have my thumbs poised over the keypad, prepared to make an excuse before I realize I don't have one, and I don't need to make one up. If I'm going to give the guy a chance, lunch is a good starting place.

"All right," I text back instead.

"Zoey."

The voice in front of me pulls me out of my text conversation. I flush, seeing the friendly, smiling face of the youth pastor, James. I slip my phone back into my purse and flash him a smile. "Good morning, pastor."

Glancing down the hall, he says, "I saw Grace headed off to youth group without you today."

"Did she?" I must have missed her exit while I was texting. "Well, you know Grace, always eager and willing to see how she can help."

Nodding his head, he says, "She's a good one, that Grace."

"She sure is," I agree.

"How are you doing, Zoey?" he asks, a slight emphasis in his question.

"I'm good," I tell him.

"Are you?"

I look down at the ground, clutching the handle of my purse a little more tightly in my hands. Dammit, Luke. This has to be because Luke saw me yesterday.

"I don't want you to think we were gossiping about you, because I assure you that was not the intent at all, but Luke confided in me that you've been having some trouble at school with some of the kids. Calling you names and—"

I cut him off, nodding my head. "Yeah, for a while, but I don't think that'll be happening anymore."

Instead of looking in any way reassured, he looks even more concerned. "Because you've made new friends?"

Knowing he already has the answer, I respond with stony silence. I know exactly what this is, and I really don't want to hear it. I may not be able to argue convincingly that Carter *isn't* bad news, but it's no one else's decision to make. It's mine. I'm the one who will bear the consequences if I'm wrong to give him a chance, so I don't need to be told what to do, or who to spend my time with. I'm perfectly capable of deciding that on my own, and anyone who doesn't like it can mind their own business.

Instead of saying anything I expect, Pastor James nods firmly and says, "Well, I trust your judgment."

I blink in surprise. "You do?"

He smiles again. "Of course I do. You're a bright young woman, Zoey. You have a good head on your shoulders. You have a respect for people I find quite admirable. I only hope you'll insist on that same respect being shown back to you, because you deserve no less. You're at an age of exploration, of self-discovery and expansion, so it's natural to try new things and meet new people. I also want to remind you that my door is always open if you ever want to talk about anything—whether you need guidance or just to bounce your own ideas off some-one. Sometimes we hear our own thoughts better if they're said out loud. Even if you just need a friend other than Grace to talk to. My door is open, always."

"I appreciate that," I tell him, and I mean it. I don't know why I expected Pastor James to get all stodgy and judgmental. He's not like that; it's one of the things I like about him.

"Well, we should probably get to youth group before they start without us," he says lightly.

I can't help smiling. "Better be careful, Grace might take your job."

***

MY MEETING RUNS MUCH LONGER than I anticipated. I wasn't able to text Carter and let him know. I tried twice, but as soon as I got my phone out, someone would start talking to me. My mom already left after the service when I told her I was going to lunch with Carter afterward, but Carter isn't at the church to pick me up since I never texted him to tell him when to be here.

Pastor James came outside with Grace talking his ear off about the fundraiser we're organizing for next weekend. We have a youth group meeting on Wednesday, but Grace insisted since we have to have all this done by weekend, we should have a couple of team leaders who would help out more, and then she volunteered me to help her.

So, my week is looking a lot busier now.

"We could go with you to buy supplies," Grace volunteers, as Pastor James walks us toward her car. "We'll need a bunch of stuff, so more hands are always helpful, and since you have that big SUV, me and Zoey could easily fit with all the cookout supplies."

Faint amusement in his tone, James assures her, "I think we've got the shopping under control, but thank you, Grace. We'll touch base again on Wednesday and see what everybody has donation-wise."

"I work tomorrow," I volunteer. "So I can ask about the gift card from my work."

"I'll make sure I hit up every other place on our list tomorrow," Grace assures him. "I'll have answers from everyone by Tuesday."

"Great, then we'll talk about it Wednesday," he says.

Grace shrugs. "I'm just saying, I could come Tuesday if we wanted to get a head start on things."

"Wednesday will suffice," he assures her.

While he fends off Grace's enthusiasm a little more, Carter finally texts me back. He's still interested in going to lunch, so he asks which church I go to and tells me he'll swing by and pick me up.

By the time I'm done on my phone, Grace is calling out, "Text me later," and ducking into the driver's side seat of her car.

I wave as she drives off, then turn to Pastor James when he remarks, "She is aggressively excited about this idea."

Nodding my head, I reply without thought, "She went to a party over the weekend; I think she feels guilty about it. Grace is always a lot, but even I started to get annoyed by her enthusiasm today."

James glances over at me. "A party, huh? Did you go, too?"

"I didn't want to go, but when she went without me, I had to go pick her up."

"You're a good friend," he tells me. Casually shoving his hands into his suit pockets, he asks, "Did you stay a while?"

I don't want to talk to him about the party, and I don't want to tell him anything about Grace that she wouldn't share herself, so I clam up again.

Apparently sensing that, James goes on like he's not waiting for my response. "I remember my first high school party—not the kind like we have in youth group, obviously," he adds, a bit knowingly. "There was a girl from church that I liked. She wasn't in my crowd of friends, wasn't involved in the church beyond Sunday service, but she was pretty, and she had the nicest smile. Made me happy just looking at her, you know?"

I crack a smile and nod my head.

"But she had this awful boyfriend. Football player, on the wrestling team—his whole family was. Three brothers, every last one of them Longhorns. I don't know if you knew him because he's a year ahead of you, but his younger brother was a halfback, just graduated last year, went off to Penn State. Duncan Bradwell?"

"Oh, yeah, I remember that name."

He nods. "Yeah, well, his older brother was in my class, and all the girls loved him. I'm sure you know how that goes."

Carter immediately flashes to mind and I nod my head. "Yeah, I know how that goes."

"He was a real jerk, though," he says, glancing down and shaking his head. "A real rage-monster. He got mad over everything. Something didn't go his way, he couldn't handle it. Bad attitude, but Mandi must've seen something in him. So, anyway, when I got invited to this party, I thought maybe it'd be a chance to talk to her, or maybe I would see Duncan in a different light when I saw him on his downtime, and I'd be able to understand what she saw in him and make my peace with it. Maybe kill that ill-fated crush, or if it was my path to be with her, then maybe start a friendship. I was open to either outcome. I wanted to follow the path I was meant for, not force my own will."

I nod my understanding.

"It was a rough night. Everyone was drinking alcohol and makin' questionable decisions. Duncan and Mandi got in a fight and he stormed off, yelling about what a bitch she was being—pardon my language. Mandi was in tears, telling her friend she was only trying to make him happy and she didn't know what she'd done wrong."

I grimace. "That doesn't sound like much fun at all."

He smiles, shaking his head. "It wasn't. I, uh… I'll admit I wasn't completely sober myself at that point, and when I saw Mandi crying and her friend assuring her that Duncan would calm down and come back, I had just enough liquid courage in my veins that I wanted to go tell her not to wait for that guy, that I thought he was a real jerk and she deserved someone who would never treat her the way he did."

That sounds like James. It's not like high school was that long ago for him, so I guess I shouldn't be surprised he's mostly the same person. "Did you tell her that?"

He nods his head. "I did. I marched right over there, took her off to the side away from her friend, and told her how great I thought she was, how mad it made me to see someone treating her that way and making her cry. She accepted my comfort, hugged me, I thought I was walkin' on sunshine." His voice levels out with a slightly self-deprecating edge. "Then Duncan came back, and all the sense I thought I'd talked into her leaked right out, and she went running right back to him."

"That stinks," I murmur sympathetically.

He shrugs. "You can't save everybody," he tells me. "Mandi had her own path to follow, and she learned her lesson the hard way. He kept treating her badly because she allowed him to, then he cheated on her with one of her friends and broke her heart."

"That's terrible."

He nods his agreement. "Some people aren't good-hearted, Zoey. We might want them to be, we might offer our hand and try to pull them up, but you know what? It's much easier for them to pull us down. Mandi thought she could change Duncan, but all she got for her effort was broken. Following Duncan led her onto a different path than the one she started out on. Even after they broke up, she was stuck on that sinful path. She never made it back. When her first crisis occurred and she realized Duncan had led her somewhere bad, she could have made a change and turned back around. She could have come back to church, picked up the pieces after that painful mistake, and made better choices going forward, but she didn't. Now she's 23 with 2 kids by 2 different men, not married to either of 'em. Her life isn't what she wants it to be, but she allows it to stay that way. That's the thing that determines your path. It's not mistakes you might make, it's not detours off the straight and narrow. It's knowing when to say enough is enough, when to stop taking that crap, and when to turn back toward the light and away from whatever tempts you to stray from it."

As if on cue, Carter's Mustang pulls into the mostly empty church parking lot. Since James and I are the only ones still standing out here, he drives right up and stops in front of us. Carter's dark gaze rakes over James appraisingly, then slides over to me.

"Hop in, babe."

Heat creeps up my neck and stains my cheeks. He had to call me babe, didn't he? Why does he live to torment me? I shoot him a look of warning, then look back over at Pastor James. "I'll see you Wednesday."

"Yes, I'll see you then," he replies, his voice faintly resigned.

I open the passenger door and slide in. I no more than get it shut and I feel Carter's hand move to the nape of my neck. He grabs me and pulls me in for an aggressive kiss, just in case the "babe" didn't get his point across.

When he finishes kissing me and nips my bottom lip, I want to sink into the seat and disappear. Carter looks out my window, shooting my pastor a little smile. I can't even look at Pastor James, still standing there, but thankfully Carter doesn't feel like lingering either. He puts the car back in drive and peels out of the church parking lot like a raging asshole.

Great. That's just wonderful.

"Was that necessary?" I ask him.

"I think it was," he remarks. Barely missing a beat, he continues, "Who was that guy? Why are you seeing him Wednesday?"

"Oh, the guy you just mauled me in front of? That's my youth pastor," I state, glaring at him. "I'll see him Wednesday at youth group, and now he's going to have a mental image of you kissing my face off and then driving away like a Neanderthal, so thanks very much for that."

"Neanderthals didn't drive; get your facts straight. And that guy did not look old enough to be a pastor."

"He's 23."

"Like I said," Carter replies.

"If you were tryin' to make my life less pleasant, congratulations, you've done that. The cashier you 'babed' me in front of yesterday? His younger brother. Now their whole family is going to be prayin' for my soul."

Carter grins, like this brings him pleasure instead of embarrassment. "Happy to help, princess."

"Terrible," I inform him, shaking my head in disapproval. "I think Pastor James has some kind of savior boner for fallen women, so now he's probably gonna be all over my ass at youth group for the next couple of weeks. I can usually keep to myself and just help out the minimum amount." Sighing dramatically, I let my head fall back against the seat. "Men are the worst. I hate all of you."

"That guy seemed like the worst," Carter says with a nod.

"You shouldn't hang out with him. His boring might rub off on you."

"I will hang out with whomever I want to hang out with, thank you very much," I inform him.

He shrugs. "We'll see. I don't like the way he looked at you."

"That's absurd."

"I know what I saw," Carter replies.

"James is a pastor. A *married* pastor. You can relax, he doesn't want to pin me to his couch and have his way with me. He wants to save me from bad influences who *might* want to do those sorts of things."

"Either way, he doesn't sound like someone who should be watching your ass when you get into my car. And that look on his face when I kissed you? It wasn't judgment, it was envy."

"Stop," I say, covering my ears. "Stop trying to pervert everything in my life. I need some things to stay pure, dammit."

"People aren't pure, princess," he tells me, shaking his head as he hits his turn signal. "When are you ever gonna accept that?"

CHAPTER 18

CARTER PICKS at the basket of fries between us on the table, listening as I explain about the themed baskets we're going to make and auction off at the church cook-out next weekend. It's all part of the fundraiser—we'll make the food and the baskets, people will buy the food and raffle tickets for the baskets, and all the money raised will go to help the woman and her baby get the bare necessities and a new place to live.

Carter leans back in his chair, shaking his head. "Look at you, shining up that halo. You must be fixing to blind somebody with it."

I flash him a smile, stealing a fry. "No, but I might be tryin' to keep up with all the tarnish you're inflicting on it."

"I've tarnished your halo?" he asks with ludicrous innocence. "That doesn't sound like me at all."

"I was sittin' in church today thinking about what you did to me on your couch last night. These are not distractions I've ever had before."

"Eh, part of growing up," he says dismissively. "You and your little group of Bible-thumpers are just a little behind in the process, that's all."

"We aren't Bible-thumpers," I mutter.

"Grace would thump me with a Bible in a heartbeat."

"Someone should thump you with something," I shoot back.

Carter smiles another one of those smiles that starts slow and spreads, drawing me right into his mischief.

"Can I ask you something?" I inquire.

He grabs another fry. "Shoot."

"It's personal," I warn him. "I was just wondering… how many girls have you been with?"

"How many have I actually had sex with? Or that *plus* girls who have blown me, but I haven't fucked them?" My eyes are wide, so he doesn't wait for my response. "You know what, let's just go with the first number."

"So, I won't be part of this count," I state.

"Correct." He pauses in thought, running through a mental list and ticking off fingers on his hands. I watch all 10 get used up quickly, then he starts over. Oh, shit.

I grab my Diet Coke and take a sip, eyeing his fingers.

"Nineteen," he finally says.

"Nineteen," I repeat, a bit dumbly.

"Wait." He runs back through the count again, then he shakes his head and grabs another salty fry. "Twenty. I forgot Melissa. That was a one-nighter. Still counts."

"Wow. That's… more than one for every year you've been alive."

Shrugging, he says, "It's spread out over six years. It's not that many. Could have been a lot more, but football keeps me busy."

"Your first time was 13?"

He nods. "Two that year. When I was 14, I dated a 16-year-old. Then 15 was the year I got a little more active, 16 was pretty active. Last year was the highest. Not the best year to date Erika; I fucked around on her a lot."

I grimace. "Wonderful. I love hearing that."

"Hey, I assumed you wanted the truth."

Nodding reluctantly, I assure him, "I did. I do. I'm just not terribly excited about the prospect of dating a serial cheater."

"I am not a serial cheater. She was a pain in the ass. I tried to break up with her a bunch of times and she wouldn't let go. Desperate times call for desperate measures. I wasn't going to be forced into a relationship, so I did whatever the hell I wanted, and if she wanted to keep being crazy, then she would have to deal with it. Otherwise, she could accept that I didn't want to be with her and I could do my own thing."

"Like the teacher," I offer.

"Yeah, that one really pissed her off. Anyway, as long as I'm being honest with you, you don't have to worry. Honest men don't cheat."

"Who cheats?" I ask, curious to get his viewpoint.

"Well, men who don't want to be in the relationship, obviously. Bad communicators, or men too timid to tell a woman what they really want—clearly not something I struggle with. There are exceptions to every rule, but generally men who cheat are the cowards, the weaklings, the needy assholes. No one worth missing once they're gone."

His brutal dismissal of unfaithful men brings a relieved smile to my face. "Oh, good. I assume you don't consider yourself any of those things?"

"Nah," he says, shaking his head. "I want to manhandle you, not cheat on you."

I think I can handle the former far better than the latter. I'd dump him on the spot for the latter, but since he's already expressed his stance, I see no reason to add that.

"Have you ever slept with your rally girl?" I ask him.

"Yes."

I tense a little, but I nod, trying to stay grounded. "But you won't now?"

"Of course not. That'd be a lousy way to earn your trust, wouldn't it?"

He's saying all the right things, and it makes me want to kiss him. I will refrain since we're in public, but I do currently want to. This is a nice change from him saying all the *wrong* things, and me trying to deflect his missiles of impropriety like an indestructible human wall.

That thought triggers a rogue strain of doubt. My mind digs through the Carter files and reminds me that I know he has been manipulative before, that I watched him play Jake like a fiddle, saying exactly the right things to turn the tides in the direction he wanted. Jake walked into that classroom wanting me to recant my story, got me desperate enough to give in and give him *exactly* what he wanted, and Carter convinced him not to take it by playing to his weaknesses.

Keeping my eyes on the French fry I'm breaking apart, I ask Carter, "What do you think my weaknesses are?"

"What?"

I glance up at him, but he looks genuinely confused by my question. "My weaknesses. When you look at me, when you appraise me the way I've seen you do other people, you sum me up and slide my traits and tendencies into boxes. We all do it, it's how we process people. In your opinion, what are my weaknesses?"

This question makes him uncomfortable. I see it in the way he shifts his position and breaks my gaze. Uncomfortable because he wants to get into my pants and figures offending me isn't the best way to get there, or uncomfortable because he's using my weaknesses to his advantage, and doesn't want to tip his hand?

If it's the latter, he'll lie. Try to misdirect my attention to some weakness he doesn't find useful, maybe something that isn't even a weakness at all.

"I don't think you're weak. I told you, I think you're strong as hell."

"I know. I believe you. But every person, no matter how strong, has weaknesses. That's part of being human. People are imperfect. What do you think mine are?"

"You don't like football."

I slant him a mildly unamused look. "I'm serious."

"You steal all the flat wings and leave me with the drumsticks," he states.

"That's what you get for making me share. Come on, something real."

He ignores me, as is his way. "Why are they called drumsticks, anyway? Drumsticks are long and skinny, they don't look a thing like chicken legs."

"I will Google it later," I state, cocking an eyebrow. "Come on, Mahoney, answer my question. I promise not to feel attacked. I'm the one who initiated this conversation; I'm *inviting you* to answer my question. I won't hold it against you. I just want to see myself through your eyes."

"Fine." He sits back in his seat, crossing his arms and meeting my gaze across the table. "I'm not complaining, I actually really like this about you, but I'll label it a weakness because it makes you easy to take advantage of. You try too hard to see the good in people, which is weird as hell, because one of the things I like *most* about you is that you don't seem to give a single fuck what anyone thinks of you. I've seen people bullied with far less venom than you have been fold under the scrutiny, but you sail through the halls like a queen, like we're all beneath you, and our opinions legitimately don't matter. People call you stuck-up, but you're not stuck up. You're too nice to be stuck up. I don't know what you are. Well-insulated, maybe? Secure as hell in who you are? It's awesome, but if you're so isolated, so apart from the rest of us, why do you care so much about other people? Why aren't you selfish? You should be selfish."

"My flaw is that I'm not selfish enough?" I ask, skeptically.

"You'd be a hell of a lot safer from people who seek to hurt you if you were more selfish. You make yourself vulnerable. It's not like you're oblivious to the danger around you. You *know* you're doing it, but you're willing to; you'll take that risk for someone else's sake, to try to help them, even if they've never helped you."

"Bravery," I deadpan. "Bravery and unselfishness are my worst qualities? This isn't a job interview. Don't bullshit me, Carter."

"I'm not bullshitting you," he tells me. "I like your flaws, so maybe I'm putting a nicer spin on them. Someone who didn't like you would probably call them something different. They'd say stuck up instead of secure, they'd call your bravery stupidity because they don't have your guts. They'd put you down because they don't like you, or they don't like those things about you, but I do. They're beneficial to me, because they're the only reason you even talk to me, but… if pressed, that's why I'd call them weaknesses."

He regards me across the table to see how I'm taking this. When he sees I'm not offended, he goes on.

"Technically speaking, I'm someone you shouldn't have let into your world. After our first interaction, you should've locked yourself away from me and barred all the doors, but instead you let me in to see what I'd do. You knew the danger I presented, but... I don't know. You're like the vet brave enough to tend to wounded animals even though they might bite you, because you know they've been hurt, and you know no one else will help them if you don't. Those qualities are like chinks in your armor, but you know they're there, and you don't care to fix them. You're willing to take a little damage to reach out to someone else." He shrugs. "I don't know, I like that about you, but you asked, so there it is."

I like his comparison. I picture myself with a medical bag, coming across Carter Mahoney with an injured limb in the woods. "I can handle a few nips. I've got thick skin."

"Exactly," he says, smiling at me. It's a real smile, not his golden boy bullshit smile, not his mischievous smirk. "It takes some serious balls to be that brave. Either you've never been hurt before, or you've got balls of steel; either way, I've never met anyone like you."

"Of course I've been hurt before," I offer, a tad dismissively. "You know that, you're one of the people who hurt me. I just don't let bad things that happen have enough power over me to keep me down. It's not my natural inclination, it wasn't always easy; I just learned at an early age I needed to fight my own human instincts on some things or I'd be an unhappy person. I chose not to be unhappy. I fought my natural instincts, I fought teachings that had been instilled in me from birth, and I won. I guess maybe that's why you perceive me as being so strong. I *am* strong; I can even conquer myself, if I set my mind to it."

"That's why you're not afraid of me?"

I shrug. "Sometimes I *am* afraid of you," I offer, since we're being honest. "I don't know exactly what you're capable of, what your limits are, if you even have any. You're definitely a gamble. But as long as you don't actually, physically kill me, I'll survive you. I'll survive everybody. I don't give outsiders enough access to my inner world to destroy me. They could torch everything they're able to reach, and I'd still have a lot left. I have an abundance of mental strength, gained the same way all strength is acquired—by working out the muscle. Physically, you can overpower me, but not mentally. I'll always rise, from everything. I'm unconquerable."

Shaking his head with a fond smile on his face, Carter reaches forward for a fry. "If I didn't like you so much, I'd take that as a challenge."

Reaching for another fry, I flash him an answering smile. "Then let's hope you keep liking me."

"Let's."

CHAPTER 19

IN FRONT OF ME, Carter holds up a bag of Twizzlers and a bag of Jolly Ranchers.

"Which one?" he asks.

"Trick question? We should obviously get both."

Tossing both bags of candy into the blue shopping basket on his arm, he nods. "Respectable choice. I would've picked Jolly Ranchers."

"I think it would be mean to make the Twizzlers homeless," I offer.

He smiles down at me, wraps an arm around me, and leans in for a kiss.

A heavy sigh of irritation interrupts us as Erika Martin drops a box of 100-calorie snacks into the shopping basket. "Must be nice not to think about keeping your figure," she comments. "We'll have to meet up when we're like 30, see if that sweet tooth catches up to you."

I sigh, wrapping an arm around Carter's waist. Erika narrows her eyes at me like I did it on purpose, but I don't really care. She's been such a bitch all night long, confirming my suspicions that hanging out with Carter and his friends was *not* a good idea.

He insisted, though. Made a good point that if we're going to date, I'm going to have to be around his friends sometimes. Tonight, Cartwright invited a few people over to have a bonfire in his backyard, then watch a movie afterward. That sounded more accessible than one of their parties or a football game, so I decided this was the time to give in.

Even the least terrible thing I can do with these people is unpleasant. Carter and I have such vastly different taste in friends.

"Got the marshmallows," Brianna announces merrily, dropping them into Carter's basket. "Oh, my God, I cannot wait for these s'mores." Flashing me a smile, she asks, "Do you like s'mores, Zoey?"

"I do, but I don't like my marshmallow burned," I tell her. "I like it just warmed up, maybe a little bit brown."

Brianna seems pretty okay. I was prepared for her to be standoffish like Erika since Carter called her out as someone he has also been intimate with, but theirs must have been a more casual arrangement—or she just didn't care when it ended— because she has made several pleasant attempts to talk to me since Carter picked me up, and no one else has.

"So particular about what you put in your mouth," Erika remarks.

"Can it, Erika," Carter says.

Raising innocent eyes, she shoots him a wounded look. "What? We were talking about s'mores."

"Keep being bitchy, you can haul your ass home," he tells her.

Cartwright has no warmth for me either, but you wouldn't know it now as he joins Carter's team, dropping a pack of Hershey bars in the basket and mocking her. "What's wrong, Erika? Is it that time of the month? Maybe we should open up these candy bars right here. When we get to the register, we can just tell 'em it was a lady emergency."

Erika rolls her eyes at him. "Ugh, spare me, Sparky. Do you fetch Carter his house slippers and the Sunday paper, too?"

"Pretty sure you're the one who used to be his bitch, not me," Cartwright offers back.

"Can we *not* start this again?" Brianna pleads. "Can you both just take a chill pill? Honestly."

"Let's see what Jake thinks—oh wait, he wasn't invited," Erika says, feigning surprise. "Bunch of fucking traitors."

"Keep it up," Carter tells her, his tone light enough, but carrying enough legitimate warning that she finally shuts her mouth and walks ahead of us.

Leaning in closer so I can address him without Erika overhearing, I say, "So, hangin' out with your ex is super fun. We should do this more."

Carter smirks. "See why I fucked the art teacher?"

"I might've fucked the art teacher too, if it was the only way to get away from her," I admit.

"Oof, would watch," he murmurs.

I grin, my cheeks flushing, and bump him in the side. "Behave yourself, Mr. Mahoney."

"Never," he murmurs back.

"Do we need anything else?" Erika calls back to us, halting at the end of the aisle, unsure which direction to turn.

"Yes," Brianna volunteers. "Nail polish."

"Nail polish?" Carter questions, looking over at her. "I said I'd buy you snacks, not make-up."

Brianna rolls her eyes. "It's not for me, it's for Zoey." She nods at my fingernails, bare of shiny, pigmented coating. "We need to get her a bottle of Longhorn blue. Duh. She's gotta show her support for the team somehow, doesn't she?"

"Good call," Carter tells her, nodding. Glancing back at Erika, he says, "To the nail polish, wherever that is."

Erika sighs as loudly as she can at him, but turns and leads us to the cosmetics, anyway.

I did not sign up for supporting the team in any way, shape, or form, but I suppose since Carter is the quarterback, brushing some blue polish on my nails won't kill me. As Brianna squats down and compares shades of blues to find the right one, she asks me, "You're comin' to the game tomorrow night, right?"

It's a home game, so it would be an easy one to go to. The problem is, I really don't want to. Not only because I can't think of anything more boring than watching a football game, but because showing up at the sporting event that got me terrorized in the first place seems like a terrible idea.

"Of course she's coming to the game," Carter answers for me, his arm around me tightening ever so slightly.

Erika disappears for a couple minutes while Brianna outfits me with Longhorn-appropriate cosmetics, but I don't think much of it. I know Erika doesn't like me being here. I don't entirely blame her; I wouldn't like hanging out with my ex and the girl he's dating now either, but then, I wouldn't date someone in my friend group for that very reason. If I did and it bothered me, I would stop hanging out with him. I didn't even know Carter when he dated her, so it's not like I was one of the girls he cheated with. If she wants to be nasty to someone, she should be nasty to him. He's the one bringing a new girl around with no consideration for her feelings. He's the only one of us who might owe her something—I sure don't.

When Erika comes sauntering back over to us, it's with a sly smile on her face, the kind that belies a trick up her sleeve. She stops in front of us, her audience, and dangles a blue thong from her index finger.

"Something else for Zoey's new Longhorn kit," Erika offers, smirking at Carter. "Remember last time we bought these for her? I bet she never got to wear that pair."

The sight of the panties didn't register, but her words do. I look at them again and realize they're the same panties that someone dropped off on my doorstep with the "slut" message stapled to them.

So, those were from Carter.

It's not like it's news that he was in on my weeks of torment, but having it thrown in my face like this sours my mood. I ease my arm from around him and step away, moving forward to look at some eyeshadows as a cover. I don't look back at Carter over my shoulder, but I do catch a glimpse of him in one of the cosmetic mirrors. His features are hard as he looks at Erika, his eyes cold.

Erika tries to brush it off, muttering about how none of us can take a joke, but no one is amused.

Awkwardness falls over the evening. Cartwright has no idea which side he's supposed to be on anymore, so he gets out his phone and plays on it to keep from having to commit. Brianna stays near me and looks at the makeup, but she offers me an apologetic grimace. I'm not mad at her. Brianna seems mellow; I'm sure she just went along with whatever her friends did and didn't want to raise a fuss.

I hate the idea of Erika and Carter plotting against me together, though. I'm not jealous of Erika, not at all, but I am aware they were together before. I'm even more aware that she doesn't like me, and I just hate having that mental image in my head. Were the panties her idea, and Carter just bought them? Did Erika write "slut" in her girly handwriting? Did Carter laugh at the idea of my embarrassment as they drove away?

They're all dicks. I want to go home.

Without asking, I know Carter won't let me. I know I could probably force the issue, but it wouldn't be pleasant, and it probably wouldn't be worth the fight. Maybe I can text my mom on the sly and ask her to send me an emergency message of some kind to bail me out.

No, what am I saying? She knows I'm with Carter tonight; she won't help.

Maybe Grace.

If both of those options fail, I can text Pastor James. Hell, if I really need to, I can ask him to come pick me up from Carter's house. Carter holds a lot of influence in this town, but so does the church. How likely is it Carter will blatantly stop my pastor from giving me a safe ride home?

We all wander quietly to the register, then back out to Carter's car. It's not actually his car tonight, he drove a red Escalade from his dad's dealership since his Mustang isn't exactly roomy enough for five people. Erika refuses to budge. Her attitude is the loudest thing in the car as Carter drives us away from the store. The only other sound we hear is the rustling of bags when Cartwright proves too hungry to wait for snacks, but other than that, dead silence.

I'm debating telling Carter I'd like for him to take me home when he turns onto Erika's road. I sit up a little straighter, a little more alert, and sure enough, he coasts to a stop in front of Erika's house.

After a moment of stunned silence, she demands, "Are you serious?"

"Do I bluff?" Carter asks simply.

Erika laugh-scoffs, looking to her friends for support, clearly expecting them to tell Carter he's being a little harsh, and he shouldn't kick her out of the group hang. That does not happen, though. Cartwright's eyeballs are glued to his cell phone screen, and he pretends he doesn't notice what's happening. Brianna picks at invisible lint on her jeans.

"Wow, that's real nice," Erika mutters, before finally shoving the back door open and climbing out.

"Learn to play nice, or lose your invitation permanently," Carter tells her.

"Fuck you," she flings back at him. "Next time your prude girlfriend leaves you hard-up after some heavy petting, you better call Brianna to get you off, not me. Asshole," she mutters, before slamming the door and storming up to her front door.

My stomach sinks and my heart kicks into overdrive. What the hell does that mean? Has Carter been with Erika since we got together? I guess we're only *sort of* together, we haven't said anything official, but…

It takes a few seconds before I work up the nerve to look over at Carter in the driver's seat. He's massaging the bridge of his nose, his eyes closed.

I turn my gaze back to the road and tell myself not to read too much into it, but I feel my investment in Carter Mahoney dropping like a rock. After all the shit he fed me about how men like him only cheat when they're not afraid to lose the woman, what other conclusion can I possibly draw if he's sleeping with his ex behind my back? He certainly hasn't mentioned that to me, and she implied he turned to her after I left him unsatisfied. There has only been one time he got me off and I didn't return the favor, and at that point in our journey toward a relationship, official or not, I would have expected him not to sleep with anyone else.

Not unless I'm just a conquest, anyway.

"I'd like to go home, too," I finally tell him, breaking the silence.

"No," Carter says immediately, dropping his hand and looking over at me.

"I wasn't asking for permission," I inform him. "I'm sorry if that was unclear."

"Zoey, this is exactly what she wanted. Come on, you know that."

Not a denial.

Since I know his track record of respecting my wishes, I don't waste this opportunity to get away. There are better witnesses present this time, so he can't force his will on me.

I push open the passenger door and climb out. I'm not that far from home, I can just walk.

"Jesus Christ," he mutters, throwing his door open and coming out after me. "I did not sleep with her, Zoey."

"You're a minute too late in sayin' that, Carter."

"I assumed you were smart enough to see through her bullshit," he states, coming around the car and grabbing my arm to stop me.

"Don't do that," I say, shaking my head. "Don't act like the only reason to believe what she said is stupidity. What she said was damn specific. That *she* got you off when *I* didn't after some heavy petting. That's an awfully accurate description of the part of our date that I was there for. That's a hell of a guess, Carter."

"Zoey, stop," he says, putting more muscle into his hold.

I jerk to a stop, so I glare at him over my shoulder. "Let me go, or I'll scream."

"Go ahead," he challenges. "Scream your head off. As soon as the first person out of their house sees it's *you* screaming, they'll go back inside and shut their blinds."

That is so accurate and so infuriating that I want to slap him. "Go to Hell, Carter."

While his comeback was clearly meant to hit below the belt, he must not want to fight with me. Instead of lobbing more meanness, he pulls me close and turns me around to face him. "I did not sleep with Erika."

"She didn't say you slept with her," I state. "She said she got you off."

"She did not get me off," he assures me, meeting my gaze. "I told you, I'm trying to build your trust, not break it down. You know me. I may be unscrupulous when I'm going after something I want, but I'm not a fucking moron. Why would I squander your trust for a blow job from an ex I don't care about? What kind of sense would that make, Zoey?"

"Just because it's stupid doesn't mean you didn't do it," I fire back. "Don't try to use logic to bail yourself out."

Carter blinks at me. "I... do not know how to respond to that. What else am I supposed to use?"

"Don't bullshit me," I tell him, shoving him in the chest. He doesn't budge. "If you did anything with her, tell me that right now. Not later after you've thought it over, weighed the pros and cons. Now. We weren't technically official, so I guess... this is a gray area, but it isn't gray if you lie to me. I will never trust you if I find out you're lyin' about this. I won't date you either. You can terrorize me all you want, I'll shut you down so fast, my relationship with Jake will look warm and fuzzy."

Instead of being offended that I'm reaming him, Carter smiles and grabs my shoulders, yanking me into his chest. "Come here, you."

"Tell me the truth," I say, refusing to hug him back.

"I *am* telling you the truth," he insists calmly. He keeps one hand secured around me to keep me from escaping his hold and runs the other one up and down my back in a reassuringly tender gesture. "Nothing happened between me and Erika," he continues. "It's a coincidence that part of the scenario she tossed out actually happened. You know me. If I had wanted to get off, I would've made you do it, not called in a sub."

I would've made you do it shouldn't reassure me, but it's so damn true, it's kind of hard to refute. "You promise?" I mutter.

Carter tips my chin up so I have to look into his hypnotically beautiful face. A little piece of me gives under the power of it, but my stubborn brain points out that he knows the effect he has on girls, that he's probably spent years perfecting the look he's giving me right now. That enticing glimmer of fond affection dancing in his dark eyes has probably been launched at dozens of girls before me, and each of them probably felt this same tug on all their heartstrings, urging their hearts to leap into his waiting hands.

Only Carter isn't some handsome prince with gentle, loving hands made of flesh and bone. He's a predator with talons designed to keep his prey from escaping his powerful grip. How many of those girls who fell into his trap made it out with their hearts intact? Do I really expect I'll be the first?

His faintly amused words from that very night flit across my mind: *"You believe my promises, princess?"*

In the present, he caresses my face tenderly, all the affection of a guy who is legitimately invested glimmering in his endless brown eyes. "I promise."

CHAPTER 20

ORANGE FLAMES jump in front of me, the only light in the isolated clearing. We had to trek through woods for so long that I had the passing thought I might be heading to my own murder scene, but then we came upon this clearing, and the guys commenced putting their Boy Scout skills to good use. There's forest all around us, but not close enough to the fire to pose a danger.

The fire roars taller as Cartwright throws more shit on it. Heat blasts my face, like the singeing heat from an open portal to Hell.

The real portal to Hell is behind me, though. Carter's strong arms wrapped snugly around my body, me sitting between his legs like I belong here.

He and Brianna are bullshitting. I'm quiet. I'm drunk. That was stupid. I know that was stupid, and I know my chances of escaping with my virginity intact dropped drastically with alcohol consumption, because on a clear stroke of genius, I at some point decided it would be an okay idea to start dating the guy privately voted most likely to date rape. Fabulous. I make fabulous choices.

I giggle into my red Solo cup. My friend Solo doesn't judge me. She understands. Carter has dark eyes and a damaged soul. I probably won't be the last smart girl to go dumb for him, especially since he's getting blow jobs from exes already and we're barely dating.

I lift my cup and give it a stern look. "Whoa, Solo, way to take it to a depressing place. Let's take it down a notch."

Carter leans forward, murmuring in my ear, "Did you just talk to your cup?"

"No?"

Chuckling, he pulls me back against his chest. "You're drunk."

"I would never," I offer with mock outrage.

I should be at home. Or with Grace, assembling baskets for the raffle this weekend. Or doing literally anything other than sitting here with Carter Mahoney in front of a roaring bonfire, consuming alcohol with his jock friends.

I didn't like the taste of beer, but Carter poured something from a flask into my cup, and it tastes delicious. I thought maybe it was roofie soup and I shouldn't drink it, but then I remembered Carter has no use for roofie soup because he likes when I fight him.

Kinky bastard.

Why is his brain the way it is?

Why is my cup empty?

I scowl at Solo for letting me down and lean back against Carter's hard chest. "I'm out."

"You want more?" he asks.

"Might as well."

Unexpectedly, Brianna interrupts before he can pour more of whatever he keeps in that flask into my cup. "Why don't you drink some water? Carter's flask is deceptive; sometimes you consume a lot more than you realize."

"Of course she's also had her lips around your flask," I mutter. A little louder, I say, "No offense, Brianna. I like you. You're cool."

She cracks a smile and pushes up out of her canvas chair. Approaching me, she offers me her hand. "Come on. I have to pee, why don't you come back to the house with me and we'll get you some water while we're there?"

"I will take Zoey back to the house when she's ready," Carter states.

"I know," she says easily. "I'm not tryin' to steal her from you. I'll bring her back, I promise."

I get the feeling she's trying to save me, and since that means she knows there's something to save me *from*, I pull myself through the slog of drunkenness and stumble to my feet. "I'm gonna go with her. I'll be back."

Carter's gaze drops to my hand now in Brianna's and he cocks an eyebrow at her. "No funny business. That's mine."

I snort-laugh, assuming he's joking. Brianna is a girl, and a girl he has had sexual intimacies with. Real funny, Carter.

"I'll try to behave myself," Brianna tells him with a wink, tugging on my hand. "Come on, sweetie."

It takes forever to get back to the house. When we do, Brianna starts taking care of me like I'm someone who needs taking care of. She gets me some water and opens the fridge to find me a snack. She settles on some strawberries and a hastily made peanut butter sandwich.

"I'm not hungry," I tell her.

"You need the bread to soak up the alcohol. Are you planning to stay the night, or are you going home?"

"I dunno," I murmur, grabbing a strawberry and sinking my teeth into it. "Oh, God, so good," I murmur, taking another bite. Maybe I *am* hungry. "That's not how the bread thing works, though," I add. "If you eat before you go drinking it takes longer to get drunk than you would on an empty stomach, but that's because the food and alcohol are both competing to be processed, and also the..." I trail off, completely losing my train of thought. "What was I saying?"

Brianna giggles, patting me on the arm as she walks past. "Eat your food, sweetie. I'm gonna go pee."

While she uses the bathroom, I stand at the counter and devour the food she gave me. I didn't think I was hungry, but every bite is more magical than the next. I'm just about finished when the sliding door in the kitchen opens and Carter steps inside.

His predatory gaze lands on me immediately. He walks over and stops behind me, securing his arms around my waist and hugging me from behind. "How are you feeling?"

"Super drunk," I announce. "Brianna made me a sandwich."

"How wifely of her," he remarks.

"She's tryin' to sober me up."

"Yes, she is," he agrees.

"Why do you have an accent?"

Carter pauses. "Excuse me?"

"You live here, but you definitely sound like a Yankee."

Catching up to my drunk girl stream of thought, he answers, "Ah. I *am* a Yankee, I suppose. I live here now, but I'm not *from* Texas originally. This is the state my father does the most business in besides New York, where we lived before, so it made sense to move here when we relocated."

"When did you relocate?" I ask him.

"When I was 13. My mom needed a change in scenery." He misses a beat, then adds, "Dad had an affair."

"Oh. But you look down on men who have affairs," I remind him.

"Sure do," he agrees. "Never said I liked my father."

Sighing, I settle my hands on his arms around my waist and lean back into him. "I really want to like you."

Nuzzling his face into my neck, he murmurs, "You should. I recommend it."

"I really don't want you making me feel stupid and letting other girls blow you."

"I didn't. I swear." He presses his lips against the sensitive skin of my neck, sending shivers of pleasure down my spine. "The only lips I want around my dick are yours."

Desire pours through me, my normal inhibitions melted away by the alcohol he's supplied me with all night long. I turn in his arms so I can wind mine around his neck, leaning up on my tiptoes and kissing him. He presses a hand against the small of my back, pulling my body closer to his. His mouth easily overpowers mine, turning my tender kiss into something more ravenous. Lust squeezes my insides and a faint moan escapes me when Carter's hand brushes my ass.

Growling low in his throat, Carter breaks the kiss and pulls back, leaning his forehead against mine and closing his eyes. I sigh happily and lean in to kiss him again, not sober enough to notice he's trying to slow down, and I'm haplessly inviting him to speed back up. His lips are just so kissable.

"All right, come on," Carter says, grabbing my hand and pulling me across the kitchen.

"Where are we going?" I ask, following after him.

He opens a door off the kitchen and flips a switch. Then he starts down the stairs. "Hold on to my hand so you don't fall."

I *am* holding onto his hand. I roll my eyes but don't comment, following him down the stairs and into the basement. We take a right as soon as we get down there. The basement is finished and seems to serve as a second family room. Facing a big screen television, there's a gray, custom sectional that probably seats a dozen people.

The sight of the television reminds me that we were supposed to be watching a movie. That was the whole reason I agreed to come over, the reason we bought movie snacks.

"We forgot the Twizzlers and Jolly Ranchers upstairs," I tell him.

"We're not going to need them," he assures me.

"Are we going to watch a movie now?"

Carter shakes his head, leading me around the sectional, over to the farthest side. He tugs me close, gives me a kiss, then pushes me back onto the soft surface. I giggle to myself when I land on my back with a thud, then open my eyes when I feel Carter climbing on top of me.

Still feeling languid and operating without running actions through the proper channels of my mind, I smile up at him. "Hi."

His lips curve up in faint amusement as he looks down at me. "Hi."

His fingers find the button of my jeans, and a second later, they loosen around my hips as he unzips them.

"Wait, aren't we going to kiss some more?" I ask him.

"Would you like to kiss some more?"

I nod my head. "Yes, please."

Carter smirks, coming down on top of me, moving his arms on either side of my head so I'm completely boxed inside a Carter prison. "Well, since you said please."

"You like when I say please," I murmur. His lips touch mine and I close my eyes, looping my arms around his neck. It's so much easier to kiss him when we're lying down and I can reach him.

"I do," he murmurs, breaking away from my lips to kiss his way across my jawline before coming back to my lips. He kisses me hard, then nips my bottom lip. I gasp at the bite of pain, but he makes it all better, leaving tender kisses afterward.

His body suddenly tenses mid-kiss, and I don't immediately understand why. Once he stops kissing me, my senses stop working, but they turn back on when I hear the sound of Brianna's voice.

"Not a good time, Brianna," Carter tells her.

Ignoring him, she drops onto the opposite side of the sectional with some candy and a remote control. "Weren't we supposed to watch a movie?"

"Where is Cartwright?" I ask, realizing I haven't seen him lately. "Did we leave him in the woods?"

"He had to put out the fire," Carter mutters, easing back on my hips and looking down at me.

"For sure," Brianna volunteers, flashing us both an innocent smile. "Gotta put out those dangerous fires."

Carter shakes his head at her, climbing off me. "Fucking cockblock."

"You'll thank me tomorrow when she's sober," she advises him.

"Don't count on it," he replies, sinking into the corner of the couch behind me. Once he's situated, he drags me between his legs like we were by the fire, only this time, I can feel how hard he is. That reminds me that my pants are unzipped, so I zip them back up and pop the button back through the hole before leaning back against his warm body.

"What movie should we watch?" Brianna asks, scrolling through a collection of available movies on the screen.

My eyes feel so heavy all of a sudden. I can't even be bothered to look at the screen to see which movies we have to choose from. Leaning my head back against Carter, I tell myself I'll just rest my eyes for a few seconds, then I'll be able to pay attention to the movie.

CHAPTER 21

I WAKE to the sounds of soft moans and wet, sloppy impact. I'm disoriented for a moment, and I don't understand what I'm hearing. A masculine grunt joins the mix and she moans again, more sharply this time.

My eyes pop open and I turn my face in the direction of the noises. The basement is dark now, the TV and all the lights off. On the sectional opposite me, Brianna is naked and riding someone. I jerk upright, half-prepared to see Carter beneath her, but when I jerk, one of Carter's arms falls from around my body.

Another groan and a few murmured, filthy words.

Cartwright. I sink back down in relief, but confusion follows right on its tail. Why is Brianna riding Cartwright? I didn't think they were dating.

Now that it hits me the sounds are absolutely the sounds of them having sex, my whole body heats with embarrassment. Carter stirs behind me, and I tip my head back to look up at him. He's still in the corner seat of the couch with me between his legs, so we must have fallen asleep while the movie was on.

"Mm, that's right, just like that. Fuck, Bri," Cartwright says as she slams down onto him again.

I should not be awake listening to this. I feel like a voyeur, but I don't know what to do. Would it be rude to interrupt so I can slip away and give them privacy? What is the proper etiquette for something like this?

Carter moves some more, and a moment later I feel him stretch, so I look up at him. He glances at Brianna and Cartwright, but seems much less surprised, and not at all embarrassed.

"Movie must not have been very good," he murmurs to me.

I have *no idea* what to say right now. I'm still playing with the idea that if I don't speak, we can all pretend I haven't witnessed this.

Carter is not awkward or confused. Leaning forward, he tells me, "Come on," then climbs off the couch.

Brianna and Cartwright do not stop now that they realize we're awake, like I expected. They keep at it like nothing changed.

"You two have fun," Carter tells them, taking my hand and leading me around the sectional. "We're going to bed."

"Wait, what time is it?" I ask, realizing it must be pretty late. I need to text my mom. I told her we were watching a movie, not that I was staying the night.

I pat my pockets with my free hand, but find no phone. Did I have my phone in my pocket, or in my purse? Where is my purse? My head throbs and I wish I had my bottle of water, but I left it upstairs.

Carter doesn't lead me back upstairs, he takes me to the opposite end of the basement where there is a room with a door. He opens the door but doesn't bother flipping on that light.

"Spare bedroom," he explains. "Comes in handy when we drink too much to drive home."

"I didn't tell my mom I would be spending the night. I need to call her, or at least send her a text so she knows I'm okay."

Carter closes the door, and everything turns pitch black. Out in the larger part of the basement, there is at least a sliver of light from the windows, but this room *has* no windows. With the door closed, I can't see anything.

My heart hammers in my chest at the sudden loss of a sense, and my hand shoots out in the dark, feeling for a surface to orient myself.

"Carter," I say uncertainly.

He finds my hand in the dark and tugs me forward. While my tone is infused with an edge of fear, Carter's is smooth like honey. "Right here."

"Can we turn on the light?"

He ignores my request, pulling me closer, then puts his hands on my shoulders to stop me. His hands slide to the hem of my shirt and he tugs it up over my head. I swallow, doing my best to ignore a flashback of Jake doing the same thing in the empty classroom that day. He unzips my pants and drags my jeans down next. When I go to step out of a leg hole, I lose my balance. He catches me to keep me from falling in the wrong direction, but then pushes me back onto the bed.

Apprehension tickles at me. "Carter, wait. I don't want—I'm not ready—"

"Relax," he tells me smoothly, pushing me closer to the center of the bed. I hear the zipper of his dark wash jeans, the rustle of fabric as he takes his clothes off, too.

Shit.

The bed dips as Carter climbs on. His dick brushes my leg, so I know he's naked, but I'm still wearing a bra and panties. I don't like not being able to see anything.

"Carter, I don't want to lose my virginity like this," I tell him, panic starting to make its way up my throat.

"I won't take your virginity yet," he assures me, catching my hand and pressing his lips against it. "Relax. We're just going to have a little fun."

I do relax a little, but I don't know what he means by *yet*. "You mean, tonight? I don't want to lose my virginity *tonight*," I specify.

"All right."

"You won't—you won't take it?" I ask, needing verification.

"Not tonight," he tells me.

Relief settles over me and I can breathe a little easier. Now that he's reassured me he won't take more than I'm willing to allow, the tenseness leaves my body. Carter feels around to find the outline of me in the dark, then he slides down, hooks his fingers inside my panties, and drags them down.

I'm not surprised when he presses the palm of his hand against the inside of my leg and follows the path up to the juncture between my thighs. I expect that. What I *don't* expect is for him to then plant himself between my legs, hook one arm around my thigh, spread the other one wider, and lean in until I can feel his breath on my pussy.

I jump, startled. Before I can muster an objection, he spreads me open and pushes his tongue inside me, lighting my nerve endings up as effectively as a finger plugged into a socket. I gasp, clutching fistfuls of bed sheet, and throw my head back into the cool pillow beneath my head.

"Oh, Carter," I say, breathless.

His tongue is as aggressive inside my pussy as it is inside my mouth. I've never felt anything like this—not when I've touched myself, not even when he touched me. I can't keep still, twisting and writhing away from his tongue. It's a counterintuitive thing to do because I love what he's doing to me with it, but my body is too lit up to be sensible.

Carter's grip on me tightens and he yanks me a little closer. "Stay put," he orders.

Instead of obeying, I tell him, "No."

He lifts his head and cocks an eyebrow. "No?"

"That's right, no," I say, infusing just enough playfulness into my tone to invite him to play along. "I'm not here to be your *plaything*, Carter. Get off me."

Catching on, he moves up my body, grabs my wrists, and pins them to the bed, hard. His voice is low and infused with more danger than I expect when he says, "Don't tell me no, princess."

My heart races, even though I invited this. I'm not scared, not really, but my body's signals are all knotted up, excitement firing from the wrong cylinders. Wetness gathers between my legs, and not just from him teasing me with his tongue.

Since I don't say anything back, he hovers close and asks, "Now, are you going to stop fighting me and be a good girl?"

"Make me," I shoot back.

I'm improvising as I go, walking a tightrope, hoping there's a safety net beneath me. There's nothing tentative in Carter, though. He's like a bull I just waved a red flag in front of. My hands are suddenly free, but before I can decide what I should do with them, Carter grabs me and flips me over onto my stomach.

My heart somersaults as his body comes down on top of mine, then he murmurs low in my ear, like a secret can be kept even though we're the only ones in the room, "Fight me."

My stomach plummets with the danger and excitement of it. I do, though. I try to push off the bed, to shoulder him off me. I don't know how hard to fight because I don't actually want to hurt him, but that's probably an absurd worry. Carter can handle me at full force like it's nothing, so I can probably fight as hard as I want.

My skin heats with the surge of energy rushing through my veins and I try harder to shove him off. "Get off me or I'll scream," I threaten.

"Try it, princess. I'll fill that pretty little throat so full of my cock, you'll scarcely be able to breathe."

That threat pierces the playfulness for me, because I remember when he actually did that to me, and it wasn't fun, it was terrifying. It occurs to me that before deciding on a whim to cannonball into this sort of game, I should have told him what I don't like, or established some sort of signal that I'm serious so I can stop him if I need to.

Before I decide whether or not to break the game and try now, Carter grabs me and throws me down on the bed so hard, my teeth rattle. Shit, that's a little rough. It's too dark for me to realize what's happening until it's too late. Until Carter's thighs are on either side of my head and his cock is in my face.

"Carter, no—"

His hand covers my mouth. "Open this mouth again, and it's gonna be to take my cock."

As soon as he removes his hand, I say, "No, Carter, I'm—"

He grasps his cock and guides it into my mouth. I try to object, but he expects me to, so he ignores it.

"Suck," he tells me.

I remember that disobeying that order is how shit got so out of hand before, so I wrap my tongue around his dick and suck. As long as I do, maybe he won't shove so deep that I can't breathe.

"Touch yourself while you get me off," he demands.

There's an answering throb between my legs, but I don't reach my hand down between them. Maybe he'll assume I'm obeying and I won't actually have to do it. I can't finger myself in front of him. That's too… I don't know, but I just can't.

A minute passes and I think he's too wrapped up in his own pleasure to worry about mine. Now that I'm not panicked he's going to choke me, I actually like this position. I like him on top of me like this, taking my mouth. I like the power he has over me, and knowing he won't go further than I want him to.

I like sucking him, too. I like the low sounds of pleasure from his throat, his dark head tipped back as he thrusts his hips against my face. Unthinkingly, I reach up and grab his ass to cradle him closer, giving me just a little more control as I work his dick with my mouth.

But I shouldn't have both hands free, because I should be using one to touch myself, like he told me. His cock is still in my mouth, but he reaches back and grabs both of my wrists with his hands, verifying my disobedience.

"Huh," he says.

Seeking to distract him, I inch him a little deeper and swallow around his cock. He hisses, grabbing a fistful of my hair and thrusting harder into my throat, but I don't object. It doesn't make me feel like I'm dying this time. Even though there's discomfort when he does it, I feel another throb of arousal at his dominance. In fact, I want him to thrust into my throat like that again.

He does, several times. He keeps hold of my hair and fucks my face, hard. I struggle to take it, but there's something different about this time. I know when he pushed this hard before, he hit my limits. He's pushing the same distance now, but my limits… they've moved. Inched back to accommodate him, to allow me to enjoy rather than fear him.

It feels like a breakthrough, but maybe it's something simpler.

Maybe it's corruption.

When he had me on my knees in that classroom making me suck him, I was so much more innocent than I am now. Maybe he hasn't completely busted through the physical barrier of my innocence yet, but like my limits, he's inching his way there.

Carter pulls out of my mouth, and I lie there, breathing heavily, trying to adjust to sucking in breath without the huge obstruction of his cock in my airway. He didn't come, so I don't know why he's stopping.

He doesn't immediately move off me; he stays right where he was and strokes his cock, watching me. "You like that, Ellis? You like being treated like my little whore?"

Ellis? No, no, I don't want to go back to Ellis. Call me princess. That's what you call me when you're doing degrading things; Ellis is what you call me when you keep me at a distance.

I don't deserve distance for the nasty shit I'm letting him do to me right now.

Impulsively reaching up and dragging my nails down his back, I tell him, "I'm not your little whore. I'm your princess."

He sighs with pleasure as my nails scrape his flesh. "Fuck, Zoey."

That's better. "Let me suck you again," I request, lifting my head to kiss his thigh, since that's what I can reach. "Take my throat. Make me yours."

He pushes his fingers through my hair, letting go of his cock and leaning down to kiss me. It's a tender kiss—passionate, but not rough and hard. Possessive. When he breaks the kiss, he murmurs against me, "You *are* mine."

CHAPTER 22

I EXPECT him to let me finish sucking him off now, but he repositions himself between my legs instead. He's up on his knees, too close to go down on me again. I sigh when his blunt fingers spread me, anticipating his finger inside me next.

Instead, I'm invaded by something larger. My heart stalls at the realization that has to be the head of his cock. *Inside me.*

"Carter, you promised," I say quickly.

"I'm not going to fuck you," he assures me just as quickly, to calm me down. "I want to, I *really* want to, but if you don't want me to, I won't."

I swallow, wanting to believe him, but... he's inside me, and he shouldn't be. "What are you doing?"

Rather than answer me right away with words, he rubs the tip of his cock against my clit. The friction makes me jump like his tongue did. "I don't suggest you fight me while I do this, princess," he tells me, his tone even as he slides his cock lower, slipping just the head of his cock inside me. "You struggle and I might go deeper than I intend to."

I swallow, deliberately still, while my heart hammers in my chest. It's the strangest sensation as he pulls out and rocks into me again. I know I shouldn't, but my body tries to draw him deeper inside. I don't know how much I can move without him slipping—and it's not lost on me that he could just pretend to slip. Once he's inside me, it's not like I'm going to make him stop. It's not like I'm sure he would, even if I told him to.

He pulls out and my cheeks burn at the wet sound of it. "You probably shouldn't be doing that without a condom on," I tell him.

"I'm clean, and you're a virgin," he replies, rubbing his cock up and down my entrance. Then, with dark amusement, he adds, "At least for a few more minutes."

"Not funny," I reprimand, wishing I could see better.

"Feels good, doesn't it?" he asks.

It *does* feel good. I like the feel of his smooth head rubbing against me, but I could live without the stress of wondering if he's going to take more than I said he could.

"Would you hate me if I fucked you right now?" he asks.

I sigh, half-expecting the pain of full penetration to follow this exploration of his boundaries. "No, I wouldn't hate you. But I don't want you to. Not yet. Not like this. Not in Cartwright's basement."

"Do you know how hard it is to hold back, Zoey?" he asks, slowly sliding out and back into me. "You're so fucking wet. I know you want it."

I don't offer confirmation or denial. He took control as soon as he pushed the tip of his cock inside me, and I let him keep it when I told him I wouldn't hate him if he didn't respect my wishes.

I should probably care more than I do, but at this point, telling him no is more a test than anything. If I could handle what he did to me in that classroom, I can handle sex. I just don't want to be one of his many casual hook-ups. I don't want to be some girl he goes through and gets bored with. If that's all I am, then no, I don't want to give him my virginity; I'm just aware he might take it whether I want him to or not, so if he does, I need to be prepared.

"I'm not even officially your girlfriend," I tell him. "I think it's premature to give you my virginity when we're not even technically together. When just earlier tonight another girl——"

"Don't." His tone is laced with enough warning that I stop. "I told you, that didn't happen."

"I know. I'm just saying. I know you're used to moving faster than me, I understand that. But if I'm not moving at the pace you need, I need to know you're going to bring that to me, not take the decision out of my hands and delegate it to someone else. If I'm not even your girlfriend, I guess you don't owe me anything, but—"

"Do you *want* to be my girlfriend?" he asks, butting himself against my clit.

I gasp as he rubs me, closing my eyes. "Once I have the title, how long do I have to come to terms with losing my virginity? I feel like the clock starts ticking faster if we're official."

"You're going to like sex, Zoey. I don't know why you're so afraid of it."

"I'm not afraid of sex. I'm afraid of being used and discarded," I blurt. "You said you wanted my virginity, and now you're takin' the fastest path you can to get to it. What else am I supposed to think?"

"That I want to fuck you for the first time, because then I will get to keep fucking you, and it won't be such a fucking event?" he suggests. Shaking his head in vague aggravation, he says, "Fuck this."

My heart kicks up and I half-expect him to pull out of my body and leave me here alone on the bed, but instead he drives his hips forward. I cry out at the unexpected pain as he tears into me, my upper body arching off the bed.

Carter comes down to meet me, bracing a hand behind my back and pulling me against his chest to comfort me. He's not moving inside me, trying to give my body a chance to adjust to his brutal invasion, but it still hurts.

"You said you wouldn't."

"I know," he murmurs, caressing my hair and kissing the side of my face. "I'm sorry. But you're not going to start trusting me until after I've fucked you. You think everything I do is suspect because I only want your virginity. I do want it, but it's getting in the way."

I swallow, lean my forehead against his shoulder, and mutter, "Not anymore."

"No," he agrees, petting me again. "Not anymore."

He holds me for a couple minutes while I wrestle with the pain accompanying the loss of my innocence, then he lays me back down on the bed. I feel more vulnerable now in every way, emotionally and physically. He starts to move inside me, but it's such a tight fit that it stings when he pulls back and pushes inside me again.

I don't know how to feel, but he doesn't give me long to debate. He takes my hands and moves them, pinning them beside me on the bed, but he links our fingers together, too. He puts more weight into holding me down, but it doesn't feel mean with our fingers intertwined. His hips move slowly at first as I get accustomed to the way my body stretches to accommodate him. I've never felt so full in my life.

"Does it still hurt?" he asks.

I swallow and shake my head. "Not really."

"I need to move faster. Tell me if it starts hurting, okay?"

I nod my head and go to reach for him, but he still has my arms pinned to the bed, and he doesn't let go when I try to pull them free. I don't try hard, figuring we've already come this far, I might as well let him do this his way.

It turns out, his way isn't terrible. I love the feeling of his weight on top of me, his masculine scent, the sounds of his plea- sure as he pumps into me. Being held down doesn't bother me now that there's nothing left to lose. He still kisses me—hard, fierce kisses that punctuate his thrusts. I still get the impression he's holding back, not pounding into me as hard as he wants to, but as the friction of him rubbing against my walls starts to build up inside *me*, I need more.

"Harder," I tell him, somewhat breathlessly.

He misses a thrust, looking down at me with surprise. "Yeah?"

"Can I—?" I nod at my wrists.

He releases them and I immediately wind them around his neck, pulling him down for a kiss, then repositioning my hands on his muscular shoulders so I have something to hold on to. He pulls his hips back and drives himself inside me full force. My whole body moves up the bed, then he does it again and again and again. That delicious friction starts building again and I welcome it with open arms. It's a life raft thrown at me when I was drowning in an ocean of uncertainty. Everything feels scarier now, like he unlocked new levels when he thrust through the barrier I asked him to leave intact, but with higher risks come a chance at higher rewards.

I can't think about all that right now. I can't think about anything but the way it feels like my insides are being stretched tighter and tighter, preparing to snap. The way I ache, yet still crave every impact when he slams inside me. In that way, sex with Carter is exactly like him.

The tension radiates through my core and before long I'm panting and gasping, my fingers digging into his skin unintentionally this time. Carter's thumb brushes over my nipple and that extra jolt of unexpected pleasure sweeps over me, triggering the tension between my legs. I cry out as a deafening wave crashes through me, sending white-hot ripples of pleasure through my whole body. It's like an explosion went off and I was standing too close; for a few seconds, I can't hear, can't think, can't function beyond receiving pleasure.

When I can finally feel my skin again, I feel the bite of Carter's fingers digging into my hips, his warm breath in my neck as he groans my name. He's still inside me, as deep as he can get, his body tense. I blink a few times to orient myself, then take stock. Carter relaxes against me, settling his face in the crook of my neck while he recovers.

I'm feeling tender, so I wrap my arms around him and hold him close. My body feels hot everywhere except between my legs, where it feels… wet.

He didn't use a condom, and he didn't pull out. I didn't want him to pull out, but I shouldn't have let him come inside me, either.

I almost laugh at my own thoughts. *Let him.* I barely *let him* have sex with me in the first place.

Carter pulls back, and I realize the short laugh must have escaped me. "What's funny?" he asks.

"Nothing. I'm kind of surprised you didn't have a condom on you, though. You have been planning to fuck me since that day in the classroom; I expected you'd have one handy at all times."

"There's a condom in my wallet," he says, before resting his head against my shoulder again.

"What?" I blink. "Then why didn't we *use* it?"

He shifts his weight and carefully pulls his dick out of me. "I wanted to come inside you," he states, like that's a valid reason.

"Well, I'm not on the pill," I inform him.

"Well, you should probably get on it then, huh?" he returns, reaching over and snaking an arm under me so he can gather me against his chest.

"Future birth control doesn't do any good tonight," I mutter at him.

"It'll be all right," he says, with unreasonable confidence.

I shake my head at him, but snuggle into the crook of his arm anyway. "You're not actually invincible, you know? The world won't *always* bend to your will."

He doesn't bother to argue with me. I hope it's because in every other sexual scenario he has been safe, and this was a fluke. I'm going to be really pissed off if he only *assumed* he was clean, and he actually gives me Chlamydia.

I'll be doubly pissed if he gives me a baby. He'll never hear the end of it.

I know that's a paranoid thought to have when we've only had unprotected sex one time, but he's so quiet, my mind has nowhere else to wander. It takes the direst road, leading me down the path of teenage pregnancy. Would I still be able to go to college? Probably, but only part-time; it would take twice as long to graduate, and I would feel like such a failure.

And Carter—would it even impact his life? What are his post-high school plans? He told me football wasn't his end game, that it was just a stop along the way, but what *are* his future plans? Why didn't I make him tell me that before I slept with him?

Well, because I had no intention of sleeping with him, but tonight got away from me. Wow, what a cluster-fuck of bad decision-making.

Swallowing, I tip my head back to look up at him. "Do you have any idea where you'll be going to school next year? I mean, where do you want to go?"

"It's not officially official yet because of the rules and regulations, but I've already made a commitment. There are schools with better teams that want me, but I'm not going to college to play football, I'm going for the degree. I lucked out that their quarterback is a senior this year, so they needed someone to fill the spot, and I'm the best they can get. Didn't actually plan to play college ball, to be honest, certainly don't need the scholarship, but Hell, it's a guaranteed in at the school I wanted to go to anyway, so why not?"

I nod. "Which school is that?"

"Columbia."

My stomach sinks. "Columbia. Like, Columbia University. In New York."

"That's the one," he verifies.

A lead balloon seems to rest in my gut. I manage a faint nod, but icy regret starts to spread through my veins like it's being pumped in through an IV. He's not staying here. Of course he's not staying here. Why would he? If I had a scholarship to go to an Ivy League school in New York, nothing could keep me in Texas.

I just gave my virginity to someone I have absolutely no future with. That isn't what I wanted. I'm not Grace, I won't be devastated if the man I gave myself to the first time isn't the man I'll marry and spend the rest of my life with, but I wanted more than this. I wanted to be positive I wasn't a conquest, I wanted it to be with someone I trusted, a relationship I would always remember fondly, even after it ended.

I wanted to be in love.

With the icy fingers of regret already prodding me, I can't bear to remain snuggled up against him like we're lovers. I guess we are now in the technical sense, but it was too soon. I knew it was too soon, and he didn't want to hear it. He decided for us that my virginity was in the way, and then he removed it.

I don't know what happens now.

I pull back the corner of the made up bed so I can crawl under the sheets once I'm out of his embrace. It occurs to me that I am still wearing my bra. He never got around to taking it off.

It's quiet for a long time. I don't like the need that swells up inside me, that hopes he'll ask if I'm okay, or if it was okay that he did that, or even just simply decide to be pushy in the way that will reassure me—by reaching over and grabbing me, by pulling me close and snuggling me despite my concerns. Maybe that would melt some of them away.

He doesn't, though. He lets me have my space, and every inch between us feels like a cold slab of concrete. After a few minutes, he climbs off the bed and walks naked toward the door. When it opens, the low light from the basement creeps in and I pull the sheets up to my neck like a vampire, hiding from the light. Wordlessly, Carter leaves the room. I have no idea where he's going, for what, or if he'll be back.

He does come back though, after just a couple of minutes. He shuts the door behind him so it's pitch black in here again. I hear the crinkling of flimsy plastic and him gulping down some water.

"Can I have a sip of that?" I ask him.

"Of course," he replies, reaching over and handing me the bottle.

I take a few good gulps, remembering how parched I felt when we entered this bedroom, prior to all that physical exertion. I hand the bottle back to Carter when I'm done and he caps it, putting it down on what must be an end table. Then he pulls back the sheets on his side of the bed and climbs underneath with me.

I expect him to keep to his side, but he scoots over and drags me close to him. "Don't tell me you hate cuddling; I won't believe you."

I crack a smile. "I didn't say I hate cuddling."

"You certainly rolled away fast enough," he remarks. Then, as if we entered into a binding contract, he reminds me, "You said you wouldn't hate me."

"I don't hate you." Then I can't help reminding him, "*You* said you wouldn't do it."

"I know. Circumstances changed. I really didn't intend to. Not tonight, anyway."

I offer a faint nod and rest my head against his bicep. There's little point raising a fuss now, when it's already done. I'm tired, emotionally and physically. I have no idea what tomorrow has in store for me. I know I don't trust Carter enough for this to have happened, but it did, and now I'll just have to deal with it.

I don't like the doubts that hide at the back of my mind, though. The doubts that paint an ugly picture of the bully who bought those panties and left the "slut" message on my doorstep. It's not unfathomable to consider that this could have all been some sick game, that he has been lying, and that he pushed so hard tonight because he could feel his act starting to come apart. If it was all a game, it didn't even take him long to win.

In the darkness, I feel him look over at me. "Who do you think you would have been if you'd never met me?"

It's a loaded question with implications I can't ignore. He knows he has changed me in the short time we've known each other, and he's not just asking who I think I would have been, but if I would have *preferred* it that way. If I miss the more sheltered version of myself that existed before he tangled his twisted desires all around my sense of normalcy, before he dirtied me up and perverted me with his damage and his darkness.

I trail my fingers over the ridges of muscles along his naked torso, offering the only response that feels like the truth. "It doesn't matter anymore."

CHAPTER 23

WHEN I WAKE UP AGAIN, the room is still dark. I climb out of bed as gently as I can so as not to wake Carter, then walk around to his side of the bed and retrieve my clothes from off the floor.

When I slipped out last night to go to the bathroom, I didn't bother getting fully dressed, I just slipped on Carter's T-shirt on the off chance someone saw me. No one did, and I climbed back into bed in only my bra and panties.

Dressed in my wrinkled clothes from yesterday, I slip out of the bedroom and head for the bathroom. When I get to the top of the basement stairs, I come across a man in the kitchen. He's older, looks enough like Cartwright that I assume it's his dad. He pauses in pouring his coffee to glance at me, but it must not be too rare an occasion to have random girls in his house, because he doesn't look in the least bit stunned.

"Good morning," he offers amiably.

"Good morning," I murmur, tucking a chunk of hair behind my ear and looking down a tad awkwardly.

Indicating the coffee pot, he says, "I made coffee, if you want some."

"I'm okay, thank you." I pause, then glance toward the bathroom. "I'm just gonna…" I point in that direction.

"Oh, sure, don't mind me," he says, going back to fixing his coffee.

What an odd thing to be so comfortable with strangers in your house.

Even though it's hopeless, I do my best in the bathroom to make myself look presentable. My long blonde hair is a tangled mess, so I finger comb it, but it doesn't look much better than when I began. There's a tube of toothpaste on the edge of the sink. Since I don't have a toothbrush but I also don't want to greet Carter with morning breath, I squeeze some out onto my fingertip and rub it around my teeth and tongue. I run some water into a plastic-coated paper cup to rinse, then hold my hand up to my mouth, trying to test my own breath. Not as thorough a job as I would like, but depending on what time it is, hopefully I'll have time to shower and brush my teeth the right way before school.

That reminds me that I have no idea what time it is and school could start anytime, so I hustle back to the kitchen to look for my purse. I find it, but after rummaging through it, my phone is nowhere to be found.

The clock on the stove says I have a little over an hour before I need to be on my way to school, so I slide my purse strap onto my shoulder and head back to the basement.

I must have woken Carter on my way up, because when I come back down, he's dressed and sitting on the sectional with Brianna and Cartwright. This morning they look nothing like a couple again, just two friends, if that.

Carter looks up at me when I come into view. His dark hair is mussed and he looks a little sleepy. Tenderness rushes over me before I can remember my hesitance to entirely accept what happened as real. I guess I'll find out today. Until then, what's the harm in hoping it is?

Even if it is real, it's incredibly temporary. We have a few months together, then he'll go off to New York, and I'll struggle to pay tuition, even though it's 10% the cost of his—which he will undoubtedly never have to pay for, anyway.

Gonna try really hard not to be jealous about that, but probably going to be unsuccessful in that endeavor.

As I come closer, Carter stands up. "I should probably get you home so you can get dressed," he tells me.

"Probably," I agree. Since it wasn't in my purse, I ask, "Have you by chance seen my phone?"

Carter reaches into his own pocket and walks over to hand it to me.

I cock a questioning eyebrow.

Shrugging his shoulders, he says, "You left it out on the counter last night. I grabbed it before we came down."

"Funny, I could swear I had it in my purse," I tell him.

"And I could swear you were white girl wasted, so you probably shouldn't trust your own account of events."

I shake my head at him. "You didn't seem to think I was too white girl wasted for rational thought last night, as I recall."

Carter loops an arm around my waist and pulls me in, gazing down at me rather fondly, given the topic of discussion. "You know who I am, princess. You knew what you signed up for."

I can't exactly argue that in this case, so I don't try to. I glance past him at his friends and offer loudly enough for everyone to hear, "I'm ready when you guys are."

We all head upstairs. Carter bullshits with Cartwright's dad for a few minutes and listens to his advice about tonight's game with a polite nod. Cartwright is less polite since it's his own father, rolling his eyes and telling him they know how to play the damn game.

Brianna nods at me and places a guiding hand on my back, so I follow her to the refrigerator where she opens it and grabs a bottle of water.

"You okay?" she asks quietly.

I nod my head, my gaze darting to hers. "Yeah. Why wouldn't I be?"

"You just seemed really drunk last night. I tried to keep you away from Carter, but obviously it didn't hold."

Cracking a smile, I tell her, "I appreciate the attempt."

She grabs my hand and inspects my bare nails. "We never did paint your nails. I'll do it in the car on the way back to your house if you trust me to paint you in a moving vehicle while slightly hungover."

"I do like to live dangerously," I tell her.

Carter and Cartwright come walking over, their male gazes

on our touching hands. "You two over here gettin' friendly? Shit, invite us to watch next time."

Brianna rolls her eyes. "In your dreams."

"In many of my dreams," Cartwright agrees. "You're mud-wrestlin' in bikinis, too. Damndest thing."

"Ugh," Brianna mutters, uncapping her water and taking a sip. Regarding Carter, she says, "I need a shower. Can you drop me off first?"

Carter nods. "I was planning to, anyway."

Cartwright and Brianna don't kiss or even hug goodbye. I try to reconcile that with the knowledge that they had sex last night, but there are no social cues indicating it happened. I wonder if that's what it was like between her and Carter—just some extremely casual thing? It didn't seem to bother Carter at all that someone he had been intimate with was being intimate with someone else.

My head hurts too much to ponder Carter's sex life at the present moment. I slide into the backseat with Brianna so she can paint my nails on the way to her house, but when we drop her off, I climb back up front with Carter.

Silence falls and I can't tell who's initiating it. I stop myself a few times from stealing glances over at him in the driver's seat, but ultimately give in to the temptation. He still looks tired, his hand on top of the wheel. He's wearing his letter jacket. It's not cold out, but it is still that grayish hue of morning, before the sun fully lights up the sky.

Carter feels me looking at him and his dark eyes snap to mine.

Finally, he asks, "How do you feel this morning?"

"Tired," I tell him.

He nods his agreement. "I'll stop and grab us a couple of coffees on the way to your house."

That's probably a bad idea. If anyone sees us there this early in what are clearly yesterday's clothes, they'll know we spent the night together. Then if by chance Carter fucks me over today, people will run their mouths even faster about what a ho I am.

Oh well. I'm probably going to need to some coffee if I want to make it through this morning without falling asleep at my desk.

Carter and I stop at Grace's favorite coffee shop. He buys me an iced coffee, himself a black coffee, and we both get muffins—chocolate chip for me, banana nut for him. Not that we actually have the time, but Carter leads us over to a table so we can eat here before he takes me home.

I check my phone real quick. Apparently noticing, he asks, "Your mom?"

I glance up at him and shake my head. "No, I was just checking the time. I'm going to have to take the quickest shower of all time."

Instead of asking if I'd even wanted to sit for breakfast, he smirks. "That's all right, I kinda like knowing I'll still be on you when I see you later today."

I widen my eyes at him. "That's... I don't know how to respond to that."

Breaking off a piece of his muffin, he asks, "You're coming to the game tonight, right?"

I still have no desire to go to a football game, but I guess if I'm going to be his girlfriend, I should do the supportive thing and show up. At least, I think I'm his girlfriend. We definitely discussed it prior to his decision to remove the obstacle of my virginity, and I think that's where we landed.

My fears got the best of me while I slept, though. In my dreams, I was standing at my locker getting out my books for class, and Carter came up behind me. He held up a bouquet of Longhorn blue flowers and said, "For my beautiful girlfriend." Flushing with pleasure, I naturally assumed he meant me, but when I went to take them, Erika appeared out of nowhere and grabbed them away, saying, "You wish, freak." Then they both laughed at me. His arm slid around her waist, she leaned into him and smelled her flowers. With a sinking stomach, I realized it had all been an incredibly cruel joke, that they *were* just playing me, and there was no limit to the levels of their corruption.

"Where'd you go?"

My gaze jerks back to Carter. "Hm?"

He's watching me get lost in the memory of that awful dream, so I shake it off and take a drink of my coffee.

Since I can't tell him what I *was* thinking about, I ask, "Are Brianna and Cartwright a thing?"

Carter shakes his head, taking a sip of his coffee. "Not really. Only when they're bored or lonely. Sometimes when they're both single, they hook up."

"Was that how it was when you guys…?"

"More or less." He smiles faintly. "We're not as sexually reserved as you are."

"Yes, I noticed," I agree.

"Does that bother you?" he asks.

"No. It's just not what I'm used to, that's all."

MY MOM SHOULD PROBABLY BE mad when I return home. I had a half dozen texts from her when I got my phone back, wanting to know if I was okay, so by the time I show up at the front door, she already knows I'm alive.

She isn't mad, though. She knows I spent the night with Carter since he's the one who dropped me off, and she's still hung up on the idea of him being our redemption. I don't tell her anything. There's no time, even if I wanted to. Coffee with Carter has me running seriously late, and I barely have time to shower and get dressed before I'm on my way out the door again.

My mind is foggy all morning. Carter doesn't show up with flowers or Erika at my locker; in fact, I don't see him at all until history class.

I'm still pretty fogged when Mr. Hassenfeld approaches with his stack of graded papers, slides mine across the surface of my desk, and says, "Stay for a minute when class lets out."

My heart slides into my stomach. I'm confused, but I nod, anyway. As soon as he walks past, I peel back the sheet to see my grade.

C-

Tightness in my chest makes it harder to breathe. I've never seen a C grade on one of my own papers before, let alone with a *minus* attached. I don't even know how to process it.

The fog clears, but alarm sets in. I tell myself it's just one test, just one grade, that my overall grade in this class is strong enough to survive a single C, but my face is hot with adrenaline and embarrassment.

Sitting through the rest of class is like sitting on a bed of nails and trying not to move. I struggle from one moment to the next, one second paying extra attention to the teacher, the next searching my textbook for the right answer to a question I missed. The problem is, I can't even remember reading this chapter. I know I did, but I also know when, and I couldn't concentrate.

When class finally ends, everyone files toward the door except me. I approach Mr. Hassenfeld's desk. Carter frowns at me questioningly as he passes by, but I ignore him.

This is really his fault.

The teacher waits until the last student has cleared out, then he leans back in his chair, crosses his arms, and nods at the sheet of paper clutched tightly in my fist. "What happened, Zoey?"

I shake my head, feeling my face heat up again. "This was a fluke," I assure him. "I was havin' some personal problems. I couldn't get my head straight. I *did* study for this test. I know you can't tell, but I did. The problem is, my memory... it just wouldn't work. I couldn't concentrate, I couldn't retain anything. I was..."

"Distracted," he offers, kindly, but knowingly.

Distraction is the closest approximation of an explanation I can offer, so I nod my head. My throat is clogged with all the reasons I can't give, but none of them matter now.

"Look, Zoey, I know you're a bright girl with a good head on your shoulders, but I've seen a lot of bright girls make massive mistakes around this point in their lives, and I really hope you won't be one of them. I know things haven't been easy for you lately, that other kids don't like that Jake got suspended from the team because you spoke up for yourself. But this is only high school. There's a whole world out there after this, and you are going to accomplish great things. It won't even matter to you how a bunch of jocks acted your senior year of high school. Jake Parsons is gonna be doin' oil changes down at the Lube Stop and you'll be settin' the world on fire. Don't lose sight of your goals, Zoey. Don't let them distract you and drag you off the right path."

I swallow, unable to formulate a response. I never really thought Mr. Hassenfeld noticed me, so I'm surprised to hear such a passionate plea for my future from him.

Without waiting for me to respond, he leans forward and opens a manila folder on his desk. "Take this. It's extra credit. I'm not going to keep giving you chances if you choose to screw up your future," he warns me. "But everyone messes up once in a while, and I know you were out sick for a couple of days right before, so I want to help you get back some credit you lost on the test."

Taking the paper with a sigh of relief, I tell him, "It won't happen again. Thank you so much."

Mr. Hassenfeld spends another minute going over the assignment with me, then I'm finally free to go to lunch. I feel terrible as I leave the classroom, like Hester Prynne walking through town with a scarlet letter on her chest. There's no one even around to witness my shame, but I see it, and that's what matters. It burns inside me, picking out the worst of Mr. Hassenfeld's insights. All the mistakes I'm making. Potentially screwing up my future over stupid shit in high school. Getting a single C on a single test might not be the end of the world, but it's far from the only bad decision I've made lately. Last night I got drunk at a near-stranger's house with Carter Mahoney. That very same troublemaker took my virginity and didn't even bother to wear a condom.

I don't care what my classmates think about me, but thinking of the disappointment on Mr. Hassenfeld's face if I showed up to class pregnant makes me feel wretched.

Such a shame. She had such a bright future ahead of her.

I pull my phone out of my pocket with unsteady hands. I need to make an appointment to get birth control. I need to never sleep with Carter again. I need to—

"Zoey."

Carter.

I look up and see him walking in this direction from the cafeteria.

Frowning with mild concern, he asks, "What was that all about?"

"Oh, nothin' major. Mr. Hassenfeld just wanted to remind me not to be a dumbass and ruin my own life."

Carter cocks an eyebrow, clearly not sure if I'm serious. "Did he offer specific instructions on how to avoid that dour fate?"

I hold up the crinkled paper so he can see the test, a lump in my throat. "It's the test we took right after…" I shake my head, swallowing the words down. "I couldn't concentrate. I thought I did okay, but I bombed it."

"It's just a C," Carter offers, his gaze drifting from the test back to my face. "I mean, it's not great, but it's not the end of the world, either. He pulled you aside for *that?*"

"This is my first C. *Ever.* In the entire history of my education, I have never…"

His dark eyes widen. "Seriously? Not once?"

"You didn't use a condom," I toss out a little wildly. "You can't have sex with me if you're not gonna use a condom. It doesn't matter to you, you won't be stuck with the consequences, but I will. You'll ruin my life and then go off to Columbia and never think of me again; you'll graduate and get a wife, have a family who will never know about me, and I'll be stuck here all by myself, working two jobs and too exhausted to study for my community college courses with my stingy little Carter clone undoubtedly demanding all my time and attention."

"Whoa," Carter says, glancing around the halls, then settling an arm around my shoulders and hauling me toward the doors out of the school. "I was going to say you should sit with us today, but after that speech, I think you need to get some air. These are isolated incidents, Zoey. One shitty grade, one fuck without a condom. I'm not going to ruin your life. You're overreacting a little, don't you think?"

"Has telling someone 'you're overreacting' ever *stopped* someone from overreacting?" I ask him. "In my experience, it only makes it worse."

Nodding casually as he pushes open the door and ushers me through it, he says, "You're right, this is a perfectly adequate response to one mediocre grade. I don't know what I was thinking before."

"It's not just the grade," I tell him, as we stop on the cement pad in front of the school. "You and I are completely different people. You have all these privileges, so maybe it doesn't seem like such a big deal to you, but there's no one there to catch me if I fall. There's no cushion; I'll just hit the ground. I don't have the luxury of fucking up, because it could cost me the only chance I have to get out of here. I have a 4.5 GPA, Carter. Do you think it's because I derive pleasure from studyin' my ass off? It's not. It's because scholarships are the only chance I have of getting the hell out of this godforsaken town. I don't have a golden ticket to one of the best schools in the country, I don't have rich parents to pay for it even if I did—the world is not my fuckin' oyster. I cannot afford to blow everything I've worked so hard for over a guy."

Given the blistering unkindness of my rant and Carter's penchant for turning defensive when he feels attacked, I do not expect this to end well. In fact, I expect him to break up with me, making this less-than-12-hour-long relationship possibly the shortest in the history of relationships. I dread that I gave away my virginity to something so disposable, but that's nothing compared to what I'll feel a year from now if I give up even more for him.

It's time to cut my losses, not sink more energy into this just because I've already invested more than I intended.

Calmly, he asks, "Are you done?"

A bit deflated, I nod and look at the ground. "Yeah. I'm done."

"Okay." Carter misses a beat, then says, "Why don't we go get some lunch?"

I look back up at him blankly. "Lunch?"

"You're hangry. You need food. Come on," he says, nodding toward his car, then taking off in that direction, confident I'll follow.

My feet remain planted to the cement pad. "I'm not gonna ditch classes."

"I'll have you back when lunch is over," he calls back.

Since he hasn't missed a step, I take off a little faster to catch up to him. He opens his passenger door, gestures for me to get in, then walks around to the driver's side.

CHAPTER 24

I DUNK a fry in cheese sauce, then drag it through a pool of ketchup, creating a cheesy ketchup marriage in my French fry boat.

"I used to be a perfectionist," I announce, figuring I should probably explain my outburst.

"Well, thank God you overcame that," Carter shoots back wryly.

"I didn't mean to yell at you," I add. "Although it is largely your fault I failed that test."

He nods. "It is. I'm sorry."

"No condom was also your fault. Even if I'd asked you to stop, I'm sure you wouldn't have."

Not bothering to confirm or deny, Carter grabs a fry and dips it into my cheesy ketchup. "I'll buy you the morning-after pill, if you're that worried about it."

Sitting back in my seat, I demand, "Why are you so calm?"

Carter regards me warily, pausing with his drink halfway to his lips. "Do you not want me to be calm?"

"The natural reaction to me yellin' at you about possible pregnancy and blamin' you for potentially ruining my life does not seem like placidity—especially mere hours into a brand-new relationship. You should be runnin' for the hills right now."

Shrugging, Carter takes a sip of his drink, then says, "Getting yelled at sometimes is part of the girlfriend package. I knew what I was signing up for. To be honest, I've given you more reasons than most *to* yell at me, so it was probably past due." He puts his drink cup down and glances up at me. "You're scared. I'm not gonna get mad at you for getting scared."

"I am not scared," I shoot back, on instinct. Missing a beat, I ask for clarification, "What do you mean, I'm scared?"

"You freaked out about the test, but that's not what you started yelling at me about. That was just the thing that decimated your composure. You've told me everything that scares you about me in tiny increments. I think I might finally have the whole picture." He grabs a fry and points it at me. "Curiously, the event responsible for you bombing that test isn't even on the list anymore. If it is, it's the last item, and only added on because you're already mad at me and looking for reasons. That's odd, but cool. Works out well for me. I can snip the wires of all the things that *do* have you freaked out, but if I had to cut that one, you'd be just like any other girl. You're not, so you're worth more to me, and you should relax. I'm in no hurry to get rid of you. I'm not interested in anyone else, and I am not going to ruin your life. Change it a little, maybe, but not ruin."

"That's easy for you to say now," I mutter. "You think you're invincible. I've had visions of onesies dancing through my mind all day. I can't handle the stress of risky sex. We can't do that again. I'll go on the pill or the shot or something, but it takes a good month to kick in, so for the foreseeable future, if we're going to have sex, you need to wrap it up."

"I don't think I'm invincible," he disagrees. "It just doesn't scare me as much as it does you. We don't see it the same way. You view an accidental pregnancy as something that would automatically ruin your life. I don't. While I'm certainly not trying to get you pregnant, if it happened, I wouldn't fling myself off a bridge over it."

"No, you'd fling *me* off the bridge," I mutter at him.

Carter smirks. "I wouldn't fling you off a bridge, either. I'm an asshole in a lot of ways, but not when it comes to kids. I like kids. If I knocked you up, I'd take responsibility. I wouldn't run off and leave you here slaving away and taking care of my

'Carter clone' all by yourself. And you're too smart to go to community college, anyway," he adds dismissively.

"Just for the first two years," I defend. "To save money. I'd only be takin' general education classes anyway, then for my last two years, I'll transfer somewhere else."

Carter's eyebrows rise. "Wait, that's your actual plan? Not just your teen mom horror scenario, but what you *actually* plan to do?"

"Unless I can get a full scholarship elsewhere, yeah. I mean, I'm still hoping for that, but I'm trying to stay realistic to avoid being crushed if it doesn't happen. I can't afford tuition at out-of-state schools without financial aid. There's a school in PA where students in the top 10 percent of their classes get free rides. Out of all the schools I've looked at, that one seems like the best fit for me, so I'm hoping I can go there. The campus is beautiful, too. You should see pictures of it in fall, with all the trees." I sigh. "I want to go to school up north so badly."

"Fall's my favorite, too," he agrees. "You ever experienced a northern fall?"

I shake my head. "I've always lived here. Never even visited. For my 18th birthday present, my mom wanted to surprise me with a weekend in New York, but she couldn't come up with enough money to pull it off."

"That sucks. A weekend in New York isn't long for a first visit, but better than nothing. Where were you planning to stay?"

"I don't know," I offer, eyeing the basket, debating whether or not I want to keep eating. "We never got that far. Somewhere in Manhattan, I imagine."

"When the season's over, I'm going for a visit. You should come with me."

I'm glad I'm not eating or drinking anything when he says that, because I might actually choke. "Come with you? In a few months? To New York?"

Nodding like it's no big deal to make plans for us a few months out, he says, "Yeah, why not? I'll be going anyway, and it'll be more fun with company. I can show you around that corner of the city, show you around campus. I've gone for school visits already, but this time I've gotta go check out the apartment and sign some papers."

"What apartment? Columbia is setting you up with your own apartment?"

"No, not Columbia. My parents. It's my graduation present."

Blinking, I reiterate flatly, "Your graduation present is an apartment in New York?"

As if that's a normal gift, he casually reaches for a French fry. "My dad got a pretty good deal on it. Ugly divorce. NYC real estate is always a good investment," he explains when I continue to stare. "It's a 10-minute walk from the school, and since I'm going to be there for many years, it makes more sense to buy than to rent, anyway. We aren't renters."

Still struggling to wrap my head around the ability to buy your son a New York City apartment, I offer, "I guess four years of rent in New York would be pretty pricey. Does that mean you won't come home for summers?"

"Not just four years. After I graduate, I plan to go on to Columbia Law. I'm sure I'll come home for visits, but not the whole summer. I'll have a life there, not here. New York is home; Texas is just a pit stop."

Every part of what he just said is fodder for some *intense* dissection, but I am stuck on the absolute hilarity of the first part. "Did you just say, Columbia Law?"

His brown eyes sparkle with a hint of shared amusement. "I did."

"You're going to law school," I repeat, dumbstruck. "*You* are going to *law school?*"

Flashing me a grin, he says, "That's right. I'm going to be a trial lawyer. Not what you expected?"

I throw my head back and laugh. It's probably an inappropriate response for a *lot* of reasons, but I can't help myself. When I catch my breath, I bring my gaze back to him. Seeing he's not offended by my laughter, I ask, "Are you at least going to be gettin' the bad guys off, or are you the one puttin' them away? I have to know how deep your hypocrisy runs."

"Does it really count as hypocrisy if I'm well-aware of it?" he shoots back. "Most hypocrites are in denial, fumbling around with bullshit justifications and empty reasons why they're special and breaking the rules doesn't make them a bad person. People who do bad things but need to *believe* they're still good—that's a hypocrite. That's not me. I don't lie to myself like that. I don't have to justify my actions in order to sleep at night. I don't blame anyone else for the way I behave, or pretend I'm being fair when I'm not. I know I'm fucked up, I just don't care."

Sighing, I tell him, "You're shameless. I think that's one of the reasons I like you, though."

"Probably. One of the many," he half-jokes.

"Oh, so many," I mockingly agree. "It's impossible to keep track of all the reasons. I should really keep a spreadsheet for all of them. Update it every time I think of one."

Smirking, he grabs the last fry and drags it through my cheesy ketchup concoction as he stands up. "You're such a nerd."

"Better than being a sociopath," I tell him, watching as he gathers up all our garbage and takes it over to toss in the trash. I grab my drink and follow him, taking a few quick gulps so I can finish it before we leave.

Carter glances back at me over his shoulder. "I told you before, I'm not a sociopath."

"You're something abnormal," I tell him.

"I protect my inner world from people, that's all," he offers. "Give them something easier to swallow, since that's what they need. Keeps everybody happy."

I shake my head as he opens the door for me. "You can't make everybody happy. That's impossible. If you try to, eventually you'll snap."

"Well, I did nearly rape a girl in an empty classroom. Does that count?"

My heart free falls and my jaw drops. I look at him with wide eyes, but he merely shrugs and heads for his car like referring to what he did to me is no big deal. Trailing along behind him, I say, "Wow, I don't even know what to say to that."

Because he's absolutely depraved, he follows up that reminder of our first encounter by stopping in front of my car door, locking an arm around my waist to draw me against him, and giving me a lingering kiss.

Because my depravity apparently matches his on some level, I wrap my arms around his neck and kiss him back, allowing myself an intoxicating hit of his affection. His free hand moves to cradle my face and he deepens the kiss. His tongue tangles with mine and sends an answering jolt of electricity through my veins. Thoughts of last night suddenly spring to mind, memories of his hands on my body, the tightness of arousal in my core, that incredible fullness when he pushed himself inside me.

That tightness is back, twisting and tugging. Carter's arm around my waist loosens and his hand drops lower so he can grab my ass while he kisses me. I gasp against his mouth, closing my eyes and dropping down from my tiptoes to break the kiss before we get too carried away.

Breathing a little unevenly, I tell him, "We need to get back to school."

Instead of agreeing, he caresses my face and gives me another briefer kiss. "Or I could fuck you in the backseat now, and *then* we could go back to school," he suggests.

Smiling faintly, I shake my head and step out of his embrace. "There's no time. Mr. Fitz is waiting."

"Mr. Fitz likes me," Carter insists, but he lets me move away. "I can just tell him I need your assistance for something football-related. I bet he'd let you skip the whole period."

"Don't even try it, Mahoney. You're bad enough for me without tanking my grades. If you ruin my GPA, I'll follow you to Columbia just to cock block you. I'll follow you everywhere you go and tell all your potential wives that you have a small penis."

"That's not true," he points out.

"But they'll never know that because my methods will be so effective, they will stay far, far away from it. I'll bring a Tootsie Roll for visual aid. I will become the bane of your existence, and then I'll be like, 'Well, you should've let me maintain my GPA and then I'd be at college in PA right now, but nooooo.'"

Carter smirks, catching me around the waist again and pressing me up against his car. "One small flaw in your plan, princess."

I let him smash me against the warm metal at my back.

Holding his gaze as he leans in until our chests are touching, I ask, "Oh yeah? What's that?"

"If no one else is paying my dick any attention, I'll make you pick up the slack."

It shouldn't send a thrill through me when he tells me he'd 'make me,' because he's him, and I know he actually would. He seems to have twisted something in my brain though, because instead of wanting to push him away for saying something so perverse, I want to hook my leg around his hip and draw him closer. I want to spread my thighs and feel his heat between them. I want to play with him, egg him on, tell him to go on and do it, then.

But I can't, because I really do need to get to class.

"Maybe that was my diabolical plan all along," I tease, lightly.

"Maybe it was." Carter smiles, dragging the back of his hand along the curve of my jaw. "Well played, Ellis. I hope you read the fine print, though. Now you've locked yourself inside a cage with the beast."

"That's okay," I joke, just before his lips brush mine. "I've got thick skin, and I'm beginning to like when you nibble on me."

CHAPTER 25

THE MIDDLE-AGED MAN beside me hasn't washed his Longhorns jersey since the season started. He's afraid if he does, it will interrupt the team's winning streak. I would have been able to guess his jersey was unwashed from the faint musk wafting in my direction every time he stands and calls out encouragement to the guys on the field anyway, but I know it for a fact because in the slower moments, he strikes up conversation with me since we're both here alone.

Given all Grace knows about Carter, I didn't feel right asking her to come to the game with me tonight. Grace knows I have absolutely no interest in football, and that after everything went down with Jake, I would never attend a game. Yet, here I sit in the bleachers, my nails painted blue, and wearing a Longhorns tank top on top of it all. I certainly didn't own one, but Carter brought me one after school, telling me I needed some team gear.

I don't care about football. I still hate all of this. But I want to be supportive, so here I sit.

The team must have scored or something, because the man beside me jumps up and hollers at the top of his lungs. I wince, covering my ears to protect them from the roar of the crowd. I look out at the field, then the score board, trying to figure out what happened. There's still time on the clock, so the game must not be over. I think the score changed, but I wasn't really paying attention to what it was before.

I really need to do some research and figure out at the very least how the game is divided up, and how scoring works. I think football is four quarters, but to be honest, I'm not entirely sure.

Pushing up off the metal bench, I ease my way out of the row and down the concrete steps. I need a break from the football aspect of this game, so I'll go to the concession stand and get something to drink. Carter says we're all going for food afterward, so I won't get myself a snack, but I'm so bored, I'm tempted to get food just because eating would give me something to do.

Technically, I brought a book in my purse and I was hoping I could sneak a few chapters between plays. The stands are too noisy though, and every time I look at my purse and think about getting it out, I figure *that* will inevitably be the moment Carter looks up at me. Then he'll think I spent the whole game reading and not even paying attention to his whole golden arm thing.

Not that I really understand what he's doing when he throws. I don't know a good pass from a shitty one. The only barometer I have is the noise level. When the crowd goes nuts, I figure something good happened. When they're quiet, I guess not.

There are two people in line when I get to the concession stand, so I pull out my phone to text Grace while I wait. I was supposed to head over to the church early tomorrow morning and put the finishing touches on the baskets, but Grace decided to go tonight and get a head start. While I wait to hear how it's going, I move forward in line.

"Well, I'll be damned."

My shoulders drop with disappointment, and I turn to face Jake Parsons. I assumed he would be on the bench, not in the crowd, so crossing paths with him hadn't even crossed my mind.

He's smiling at me, his amused gaze raking over my Longhorn gear. "Did Hell have to freeze over to get you here, or is Carter really that good and he's already made his way between your legs?"

My face flames at the truth in that comment, but I narrow my eyes at him, anyway. "Nice to see you, too, Jake."

He steps into line behind me, even though he's already holding a Longhorn water bottle. Judging from the smell of his breath when he gets close to me, it's not water he poured into it. "Oh, it's always nice to see you, Zo."

I fight the instinct to take a step back, but he's too close. Jake is taller than me—not as tall as Carter, but still taller than me—and like Carter, when he wants to make himself look more intimidating, he uses every inch of his height.

"Don't be a jerk," I tell him, my tone low. I really don't want trouble with him, but I'm not unarmed anymore. I have more than my own voice to protect me—I have Carter, and I'm not afraid to wield him.

Jake's arm comes to settle around my shoulders, and I stiffen. "Am I bein' a jerk?"

"Get your arm off my shoulder."

"Is that sexual harassment now, too?"

"You know what, Jake?" I snap back. "Touching a girl who doesn't want you to touch her *anywhere* is pathetic, no matter what you want to call it. It's pitiful."

His blue eyes harden, turning from oceans as warm as summertime to little chips of ice. "Only when it's me, though, right? I seem to remember Carter touching you an awful lot when you didn't want him to, and you're datin' him now. All comes down to what you can get out of it, I guess."

"Tell yourself what you need to, Jake," I tell him, shrugging his arm off. "Carter also happens to be a hell of a lot more interesting than you, but yeah, obviously, that couldn't have anything to do with me liking him."

"Interesting, my ass. It's his money or his dick that has you singin' a different tune, and I hate to think you'd sell out for the latter," Jake tells me, smirking a little, eyeing up my tank top and shaking his head.

"I'm bein' supportive. That's what you do when you're with someone who's into shit you don't care about."

"You don't have to defend yourself, darlin'. I get it. You're certainly not the first girl to chase after him, I just thought you were smart enough not to. Guess I was wrong."

I open my mouth to point out I am not chasing Carter, that

he is the one who pursued me, but I stop because it doesn't matter. My words will fall on deaf ears. Jake has already made up his mind and sold himself on a narrative he needs to believe. The truth isn't just irrelevant, it's something he is actively disinterested in.

That his position is rooted in the idea that he and Carter are equally entitled to me and *my* desires are beside the point is a whole heap of sexist bullshit, but there's no point trying to engage him in conversation about it.

Unlike Carter, Jake is close-minded and set on viewing himself as a good guy, regardless of his actions. As crazy as it seems, given his behavior and tendencies, Carter can be reasoned with. Without the emergence of a genuine desire to grow and evolve as a human being, Jake is a lost cause.

Telling Jake he's not currently smart enough to interest me despite his boorish behavior—while true—wouldn't help, so instead of responding, I turn my back to him and wait for the person at the counter to finish up.

"If you have fucked him, he'll get bored with you now. Cast you aside like any other slut he goes through," Jake continues, ignoring the cue that I no longer want to talk to him. "That's what he does. You were nothin' more than a novelty, some little virgin he wanted to nail. If you gave it up, you don't have anything left to hold his interest."

"Actually, I think I have a lot to offer regardless of my virginity, but my sex life is none of your business, so…"

"That's your problem," he states, moving to stand beside me. "You're so damn full of yourself."

"Thinking I have more to offer a guy than orgasms isn't being full of myself, it's having a healthier sense of self-worth than a snug napkin ring." Meeting his gaze, I tell him, "Maybe if you *had* looked at me as something more than a pair of boobs and a vagina, *you* would have been the one to catch my interest. You didn't. I'm not interested. I can't be any clearer. Move along."

Laughing despite himself, he says, "A snug napkin ring?"

Looking up at him through my eyelashes, I ask, "Oh, are not all dicks that thick? Sorry, I've only seen Carter's."

Now he loses his smile.

The alcohol compels him to act on his wounded ego rather than common sense, and he grabs me around the waist, yanking me against his side. "That so? Well, come with me and I'll be happy to introduce you to another one."

My heart tumbles out of its cavity, but I don't betray my nervousness. "Let go of me. I'm not some defenseless girl alone in a classroom tonight, Jake. If you don't get your hands off me this time, I won't tell Coach, I'll tell Carter. Remember when he threatened me? He doesn't want to fuck you, so I bet his threats for you would be even less pleasant."

"You think you got him wrapped around your little finger that tight, huh?"

"Why don't you try me and find out," I challenge.

Jake shakes his head, his hooded gaze dropping to my lips. I don't like the interest I see there as he murmurs, "So fuckin' mouthy."

Ahead of us, a woman calls out, "Next!"

I break eye contact with Jake and look ahead at the woman standing behind the concession counter. Jake doesn't move to release me, but the woman caught his attention too, so I use the distraction to shove his arm away and step forward.

I order myself a drink and keep my gaze trained straight ahead, hoping if I stop feeding Jake attention, he'll go away. I'm not sure whether or not he'll still be standing there when I turn around, but I really don't feel like dealing with him anymore tonight.

Thankfully, when I turn around to head back to my seat, he's gone.

CHAPTER 26

THE LONGHORNS USHER in a crushing defeat: 42-14, and the crowd goes wild.

Kasey Jones from the school paper is standing on the sidelines looking through shots from the game when I make my way up there. I'm not exactly sure about the proper etiquette of post-game madness. The cheerleaders are team-adjacent, so they probably head inside with the guys, but I don't know what a non-cheerleader girlfriend is supposed to do while she waits for her quarterback boyfriend.

So, I linger with Kasey and wait for Carter to spot me and hopefully fill me in on what I'm supposed to do next.

"Oh, that's a good one," she murmurs.

Without thought, I lean over to sneak a peek. It's a shot of Carter mid-throw, and yeah, it's a damn good one. I'm not even into athletes, really, but the way his muscular body looks in that uniform, his arm poised to throw the ball… damn.

Noticing my unsubtle spying, she turns the preview screen so I can see it better. "Not to pat myself on the back, but look at this shit."

Cracking a smile, I tell her, "No, you're right. You deserve a back-pat; that is some fine picture-taking, right there."

Shaking her head as she turns the screen back and scrolls through, she says, "That is one damn fine specimen."

"He's pretty nice to look at," I agree. "Not bad to talk to either, but if all else fails, at least he has his looks to fall back on."

"And like a bazillion dollars. I think he's gonna be okay."

I nod my head, glancing her over. She doesn't exactly look like his type, but then I've only seen two of his past lovers. "Are you friends?"

Snort-laughing, she says, "With Carter? God no, he doesn't know I exist." She misses a beat, then says, "What about you? How do you have the balls to show up at a football game? I mean, damn, kudos on your enormous lady balls, but how?"

I sort of thought I was flying under the radar tonight, so I'm surprised and a little unsure how to proceed. There's no hostility in her tone, though, so I open my mouth to answer.

Before I have a chance, Carter comes running over, a shit-eating grin on his face. He's sweaty and happy, and he doesn't hesitate to grab me around the waist and pull me right up against him in all his gear.

"You see that?" he asks. "I told you I made better passes. A 71-yard touchdown pass to win the game? Not too shabby, right?"

His enthusiasm is catching and I can't help grinning up at him. "You might as well be speaking in Latin, but I'm glad you won."

Carter shakes his head, dark eyes sparkling with amusement. He leans down to give me a kiss, then says, "I need to teach you about football."

"My education on that particular subject *is* clearly lacking," I admit.

His hand comes up to tenderly caress my face, and he kisses me again. "I've gotta head back to the locker room, but we'll be out as soon as we can. Is it cool with you if Erika tags along tonight? I'll tell her no if you don't want her to."

Ugh, Erika. I'll feel mean saying she can't come though, so I offer back, "It's up to you."

"That's a no," he interprets, nodding. "All right, no problem." He kisses me again, then releases me before I can respond and jogs back out on the field where his teammates are still celebrating.

I look over to where the cheerleaders are gathered and see Erika eyeing me up. Resisting the urge to glare back, I turn my attention back to Kasey, realizing Carter *did* just act like he couldn't even see her. I don't know why I'm surprised. Carter is well known, but not too long ago, I was one of those dust specks he couldn't even see.

Kasey is staring at me. "How did *that* happen?"

"Long story."

Her eyebrows rise, then fall, then she shakes her head. "Well, be careful. Erika has been known to play dirty. Last year she slashed some girl's tires for daring show up to a game and steal Carter's attention, and I did an expose on the actual effects of sugar in a gas tank after she caramelized the art teacher's pistons like she was making a nice car part crème brulèe. Of course, I had to pretend I didn't know it was her or risk inciting her wrath myself, but she treats bitchiness like a competition, and she aims to win it."

"Yeah, I've noticed," I murmur. "I'm not afraid of Erika."

"You probably should be. She's fucking crazy."

Cocking my head to the side, I ask, "Why don't I know you?"

Blushing and cracking a wry smile, she says, "We clearly don't run in the same circles. I've been photographing these games for two years, and if pressed, I doubt anyone on the team could come up with my name."

Unfortunately, that sounds about right. Rolling my eyes, I tell her, "They can be really oblivious, can't they?"

She nods, but her gaze isn't trained on me, it's focused behind me with a hint of concern glistening in her eyes. I turn my head to see where she's looking, and see something out of a nightmare —Jake and Erika approaching, side by side.

"Ugh, really?" I mutter.

Erika looks smug. That can't be good. She smirks at me as she comes to a stop. "Hey, buddy."

"What's up, pal?" I offer back.

"Just thought I'd come over and say hi. How was the party after I left?"

"Somehow, we still managed to have fun," I tell her.

"Oh, I bet you did. Judgin' by your presence at the game

tonight, I guess you fucked Carter, huh? You must feel pretty proud of yourself."

Frowning, I say, "That seems like an odd feeling to accompany intimacy with my boyfriend."

"Boyfriend?" Her eyes widen and she stares at me, but maintains her superior sense of amusement. "Oh, honey. He's gonna chew you up and spit you out."

"Well, if he does, I'm sure you'll enjoy the show," I offer. I barely miss a beat, not wanting to give her a chance to further engage me. "Anyway, good cheering. I've got plans, so I have to—"

Interrupting before I can leave, she says, "You know what Jake and I were just discussin'?"

Sighing, I spin back around and offer back a tight smile. "How neither of you are invited to the group-hang tonight, so maybe you should both stop acting like assholes before you lose all your friends?"

Erika's gaze dims, then sharpens. "No, whore. We were talkin' about how surprisingly kinky you must be, how much you like a little… struggle."

Her word choice alone wouldn't be enough to set me on edge, but the way her eyes dance with delight in the shit she thinks she's about to stir up… Jake couldn't have actually *told her*, right? They all behaved like randy assholes. That's not a story you share with anyone, not even Erika.

She goes on, "And Jake here had a thought. We all know Carter has double standards; he's allowed to fuck around, no problem, but his girl? Oh, no. She has to be the pinnacle of morality, a real one-man woman."

"I don't think Carter's that hung up on *morality*, but if there's a point anywhere in the near vicinity…"

"I just think if Carter knew you were still flirtin' with Jake, he might get… angry. Brianna said he got you drunk last night, so I don't know what he's done to you already, but you know what? I bet it gets worse with jealousy and anger."

My jaw hangs open as I stare in absolute shock at the awful human being before me. "Wow, Erika. Really?"

She shrugs. "Lorraine saw you and Jake touchin' and lockin'

eyes at the concession stand. Said you were givin' him fuck-me eyes. Now, I would say that Carter would never believe you could be romantically interested in someone who supposedly sexually harassed you." She pauses, propping a hand on her hip and tapping her chin in mock thought. "But, you know what, maybe he *would* believe that."

My chest starts to tighten as it hits me that Erika really does know what Carter did to me that day in that classroom. Something about keeping that experience locked away inside me—a secret kept between me and those three assholes—made it easier to deal with, but now it's not just out there, it's in *Erika's* hands.

Erika's opinion doesn't mean anything to me, but her having that knowledge makes me sick. It's not safe anymore. It's not like she'll keep her mouth shut. I want to punch Jake in the face for exploiting my bad experience this way, but that would require breathing, and I'm struggling with that right now.

A flash goes off and Erika jumps, her gaze darting to Kasey like she, too, hadn't even noticed her there. "What the hell? Did you just take my picture?"

Kasey nods, looking down at her display screen. "Yep. I'm a photographer for the school yearbook, and I thought you just looked so pretty. My bad, I actually had the video function on before, so... whoops. Anyway, after I accidentally recorded you threatening Carter's girlfriend, I got a really great shot of you. Your jawline looks killer. Wanna see?"

Glaring, Erika says, "Delete that right now."

"Um, no," she says, shaking her head with something like regret. "This girl's been dragged through the mud enough by you guys. Carter really seems to like her, so I hate to think what he'd do if I showed it to him. He'd probably knock you so far down the social ladder, you'd actually have to learn my name."

"Oh, I'll learn your name, all right." Erika glares and huffs like a beautiful raging bull. "You're gonna live to regret this. Mark my words."

Her targeting my new friend shakes my voice loose. "I wouldn't, if I were you. I *am* going to tell Carter about this, and he won't believe I was flirting with Jake, but even without video evidence, he *will* believe you threatened me, especially after that lie you told last night when he pissed you off."

"Wasn't a lie," she states. "You know it wasn't a lie. You just have blinders on right now. You're gonna feel dumb as hell when they fall off, and you're the one watchin' from a distance while he kisses *me* like *you* don't exist."

"Why would you want him back? I'm not even tryin' to be mean, but he told me how awful he was to you. He knows you'll put up with it, so it wouldn't change. Carter only plays within boundaries if he has to, and you've already shown him you don't have any. If he cheats on you with some girl, you'll be vicious to her and try to hold on to him. That's crazy. Alienating the symptom won't eliminate the disease."

My words only serve to further infuriate her. "You think you're so much different? I literally *told you* he fucked around with me when you left him high and dry, and you *still* fucked him last night. You may have some genius GPA, but don't fool yourself, Zoey; you're no smarter than I am when it comes to Carter."

Shaking my head, at a loss for how to grasp this situation, I say, "This is a bizarre conversation. You're calling both of us stupid. You're not just insulting me, you're including yourself."

"I'm not stupid, I'm realistic," she states, lifting her chin with an infusion of stubbornness. "That's why I'm the one who will end up keeping Carter. You have unrealistic expectations about him, and he'll never live up to them. As soon as he disappoints you, as soon as you stop believin' his bullshit and withdraw, he'll drop your ass and come runnin' back to me. I've seen this dog and pony show before, Zoey. You're not the first. You won't be the last. But *I* will be."

I shake my head, unwilling to stand here and listen to her a moment longer. I can't leave Kasey here now either, so I glance at her. "Are you done taking pictures? I've gotta meet Carter, so we should probably go."

She stares blankly for a moment, then nods. "Yeah. I'm done."

I nod and turn, walking away. "Come on, then."

She jogs a few steps to catch up, then falls into step beside me. Her cheeks are rosy and she sighs, telling me, "I shouldn't have done that. Standing up to Erika. She's going to shiv me in the kidney."

Cracking a smile, I tell her, "Don't worry, I'll tell Carter everything she said. I'll tell him you stuck up for me. I'm sure he'll tell her to leave you alone, too. You may have noticed, but Carter carries a lot of weight around here, especially with that psycho."

"Well, yeah, since apparently she aspires to be his constantly cheated-on Stepford wife," Kasey volunteers.

"Right? Strange goals. I hate when she says shit like that though. She gets in my head," I admit, since she was there, too. Maybe I'm too biased to see the truth clearly, but this girl has no investment in the situation, so perhaps she sees something I don't.

"I get that, but honestly, I think she's gaslighting you," she tells me. "Being a jealous girlfriend herself, she knows exactly how to access that part of your brain. She knows which seeds of doubt to plant, she knows how to fertilize them for optimal damage... I mean, I don't know, Carter could be cheating on you, but I wouldn't take her word for it. She would absolutely lie about that. Hell, she'd run you off the road and into a ditch. The cheerleader is crazy."

CHAPTER 27

CARTER DROVE his Mustang to school today, so I ride with him and everyone else meets us at the nearby café where they gather after Friday night games. When we get there, the place is packed. The café stays open late on game nights because so many locals come here—partially to eat, even though they could have eaten similar food at the concession stand, and partially to see the players, exchange smiles with the guys responsible for putting them in such a good mood, and extend the high of the big win they usually ushered in.

Accordingly, I almost never come here. Grace and I prefer the coffee shop, far away from the jocks and their fans—even before they all hated me, but now, definitely.

Only when I walk through the doors tonight, it's with Carter's arm draped around my shoulder like a mantle of protection, and his friends crowded around me like my own personal entourage.

When we come into view, a few people call out comments like, "Hell of a game, son," and "that's some arm you've got there!" No one notices me, so my anxiety about a lukewarm reception melts. They all have Carter vision, and he's playing his role well. I have my Carter, and they have theirs, and tonight, he has to convey his golden jock façade, not the more truthful face of my boyfriend/tormentor.

I feel a strange closeness to him, though, knowing I see a side of him other people don't have access to. I hate all of this—even his arm around me while all these people gush at him makes me feel like I'm on display, even though they're paying me no attention whatsoever. I'm the girl on his arm, and I'm so not that girl.

But he's not really that guy, either. I tell myself that as we finally make our way to the table. Carter had to stop and bullshit with people at three different tables before we made it to ours.

When we finally slide into our seats—the same side of the booth, with Cartwright and Brianna across from us—I lean into Carter and murmur, "Do you think you'll miss this?"

His gaze meets mine. "Miss what?"

I blink, figuring it's clear, but I guess this is his normal. Gesturing around, I say, "The fanfare. The small-town celebrity status. You're a big fish here. When you go off to college, you'll be in a significantly bigger pond."

Stretching his arm around me and leaning back in the booth, he says, "Bigger pond just offers more room to grow."

He's so confident, so unshakably sure of his future. I'm confident in myself, but I wonder what it's like to be like him, to literally have no doubts because you know there's a safety net if you ever fall.

On one hand, I tell myself it's better I'll have to work for everything I get, that I'll appreciate it more, but on the other hand, it really would be nice if things could just be easy for once. Nothing is ever easy for me, and everything is always easy for him.

We are such different people.

Our minds are in very different places, too, because Carter smirks and leans in to kiss the side of my face, murmuring, "You're not already worried about me going off to school, are you?"

"What? No, of course not."

"Kinda sounds like you want me to stay in the small pond."

I shake my head, glancing down at the table. "Of course not. Columbia is an amazing opportunity; I know you'd never even think of passing it up. I don't blame you. I wouldn't either, if I were in your place."

"Do you resent not having my opportunities?" he asks casually.

"Of course not." Since he appears unconvinced, I add, "Remember, I'm going to stow away and come to New York so I can chase off all your potential wives anyway, so I'm sure I'll see you around."

I pluck a menu off the table and nonchalantly beginning to peruse it.

Chuckling warmly, Carter tugs me closer against his side, but doesn't offer further comment.

THE REST of the group-hang is uneventful. Carter gets more attention here and there, and Cartwright and Brianna behave as if I have always been part of their crew. It becomes pretty clear to me that Carter is shifting his favor to these two now *because* of their easy acceptance of me, their willingness to turn on a dime and welcome me into the fold after happily hating me before. Partially to reward behavior he likes, and therefore encourage more of it, but also to show the friends of his he's currently leaving out how they need to behave if they want back on the inside.

It's appealing, his ability to subtly shift the world and take *what* he wants from *whomever* he wants.

I know I'm one of those things he subtly shifts from time to time, and I know it would be extremely unpleasant to fall from Carter's good graces and suddenly be on the outside looking in, but that's just who Carter is. High risk, high reward. I can't pick and choose the pieces and parts of him I like and leave the rest. He is who he is.

It makes him scary, though. Carter isn't going to be an easy man to trust, and he isn't going to be an easy man to control. On one hand, I tell myself I should be glad I'm only dealing with the high school version of him, because all grown up, he will be a force of nature for whoever has the bad luck of falling in love with him. But on the other hand… well, I'm not one to shy away from a challenge.

It's pointless to think about, though. When he brought up him going away to school at dinner, of course I shot it down and acted as if it had barely crossed my mind. We've been dating for like three minutes; it's entirely too early to worry about our future.

He complicated things, though, by deciding to take my virginity so quickly. I figured once I agreed to date him, I would have time to come around to it, time to figure out if there was even a remote possibility of a future—and if not, if I would be okay with that. As is his way, Carter yanked the reins out of my hands. We weren't ready to move this far, this fast, but now we have, and the natural progression of our relationship is a bit topsy-turvy.

Carter brings me back to my car at the stadium and it's just the two of us, standing here under the lights. As always, he invades my personal space, following me to my car and backing me up against it. I can tell by the way he lingers he doesn't want me to go, but it's late and I have to go to church tomorrow. Not quite as early as I would have prior to Grace's overachieving tonight, but still.

Carter grasps me by the shoulder and runs his hands down my arms, his gaze perusing my body before returning to my face.

"I like you in Longhorn gear."

"Yeah?" I murmur, resisting the urge to touch him, because then it'll take me even longer to get out of here.

He nods. "I know you didn't want to come, but I'm glad you did."

"It's not that I didn't want to come," I offer, making an attempt at sounding convincing, but failing horribly.

Smiling faintly, Carter shakes his head. "Don't lie to me. It's all right. I know you're not into all this. Still, it's nice you came."

I glance down at the pavement beneath our feet, scuffing the toe of my shoes on the asphalt. Erika's words from the other night flourish, making me wonder if sending him home after kissing him by my car counts as "leaving him high and dry."

Carter's thoughts aren't entirely in line with mine, but as if he can pick up on the fact that I want to kiss him, he catches the back of my neck and pulls me close, bending his head to kiss me just like he did at lunch today.

My heart gallops in my chest, half from the sensation of Carter's lips on mine, half from the fear of getting him excited. I try to shake it off, tell myself I won't be blackmailed by my own imagination into... into what? I don't even know. Getting in the back seat with him? I don't want to do that, but Carter has maybe three fucks to give about what I want, and whether or not I want to have sex at any given time is not on the distribution list.

When he pulls back, he stays close. There's genuine tenderness on his face that makes me feel mean for having those thoughts, but I'm stuck inside my own head and I can't get out.

"Why don't you come back to my house?" Carter suggests.

There it is. The invitation. The trap. I feel nervous, and it bugs the shit out of me. Before I can stop myself, I bring up what I've meant to bring up, but couldn't in front of Carter's friends.

"Erika came over to me after the game tonight."

I watch his face for some sign of guilt like he's a normal guy, like that feeling might register, but naturally, it doesn't. His expression doesn't change at all. "And?"

I swallow and glance down, then meet his gaze again, desperate for the truth, and knowing only he has it. A truth I'll believe, anyway. "And she insists she wasn't lying last night."

"Of course she does," he says, sounding unsurprised. "Erika doesn't confess and repent when she's caught in a lie, Zoey, she doubles down."

"Well, it makes me uncomfortable," I tell him.

"What would you like me to do about it?" he asks, wrapping his arms around my waist and tugging me against him.

"She thinks I'm a passing fad, that you were into my virginity more than me, and that now I'll lose your interest and you'll go back to her."

"No, she's worried you're *not* a passing fad, and that's why she's putting work into scaring you off. Come on, you can deduce that without my help, can't you?"

"She's tapping into my existing concerns and exacerbating them," I state.

"Only if you let her," he says simply. "I realize I'm not the easiest guy in the world to trust, but you really wanna trust her more?" he adds, cocking his head skeptically. "She thinks I'm her ticket out of here, Zoey. She wants to use me as a stepping stone so she's not stuck here, knocked up two years from now, waiting tables six days a week and going home to some washed up former Longhorn who's probably fucking around on her anyway —but with him, there are a lot fewer perks for dealing with it. Erika doesn't like me, she likes what I can do for her. You think she doesn't know where I'm headed? She wants to hitch her star to my wagon. That's all it is. I promise. I already told you nothing happened, and I can tell you ten more times, but why are we still wasting our time talking about this?"

I sigh, training my eyes on his abdomen instead of his face. "I think Jake told her. About that day in the classroom. About what you did to me."

Silence.

My gaze darts to his, hoping for some reaction, but his face is carefully blank, the thoughts behind his dark eyes as transparent as brick walls. "She said some stuff, made it sound like she was gonna try to convince you Jake and I had some kind of… I don't know. Then she said how ordinarily no one would believe I'd be romantically interested in someone who sexually harassed me, but hey, maybe you would believe that. It was clear she was talkin' about you and what happened. Jake was with her, so I think he—"

"All right. I'll handle it," he says, cutting me off. The back of his hand moves along my jawline. I sigh, enjoying the faint tickle, the rush of tenderness. "Let's not think about either of them anymore tonight."

"There's one more thing. There was a girl, the football photographer from the school paper."

"She overheard as well?"

"Well, yeah, but she didn't know what they were talkin' about. That's not the problem. We were talking when Erika came up and she seemed nice. Actually, she was standing right there when you kissed me, but you didn't seem to notice her. Anyway, she stood up for me, but Erika got really pissy about it and told her she'd regret it. So, if you're going to talk to Erika about takin' her psycho bitchiness down a few levels, tell her to leave Kasey alone, too."

"Done," he agrees, gazing down at me. Hardly a moment passes, then he says, "Come home with me."

"It's late," I tell him.

"You can spend the night. It's the weekend, so you don't have to go to school tomorrow. I don't have practice. We could hang out, maybe head into the city. I have to be back in the evening to watch Chloe, but we could spend the better part of the day together."

"You seem to watch your sister a lot," I remark.

"Yeah. We don't do babysitters, so if my parents go out, it's up to me or my older sister. It's easier for me, since I live there."

"Well, I would like to go out with you tomorrow, but I can't. I have the cook-out and basket fundraiser at the church, remember?"

"Ah, yes. With the pastor who wants to bone you."

I roll my eyes. "With my married pastor who definitely does not want to bone me."

Nodding and completely ignoring my objection, he asks, "When does Pastor Boner want you there?"

"Pastor *James* and his lovely *wife* asked us to come around ten so we can help set up. Grace went tonight, so I don't know how much there will be left to do, but I'm gonna go then anyway, just to be safe."

"That's plenty of time. It's settled. You're coming to my house."

I shake my head. "I'm not, though."

He ignores me. "You're going to climb your pretty little ass in my bed so I can fuck you, then we can fall asleep together like last night, but in a much more comfortable bed. I really like this plan."

"This is not the plan at all. The plan is for me to go to my house alone, curl up in bed wearin' flannel pajamas, and sleep all by myself."

Glancing beyond me, Carter gazes absently into my car. "Now, do I trust you to drive yourself to my house, or do I drag you to my car and bring you back for yours tomorrow?"

I lift my eyebrows. "I am for sure not leaving my car here. I'll probably come back to the windows busted out and the inside strewn with cheap blue panties."

Nodding slowly and talking to himself, as if I'm not even contributing to this conversation, he says, "Then again, if you go to your house, I can always just follow you. Your mom loves me, so I'll just tell her we came to ask permission for you to spend the night. Bet she'd love that, huh?"

I cock my head. "Do you actually want me to respond, or are you just gonna keep pretendin' I'm not here?"

"I think I can keep it can going by myself, but thanks for the offer," he returns lightly.

"I can't spend the night," I state.

"Why not?"

"Because I'm not allowed to have sleepovers with boys."

"Was your mom mad about last night?" he asks.

"Well, no…"

Latching onto it, he says, "See, she doesn't care. If you think she'll care, call her now and ask. I'll take the phone. Promise to be on my best behavior."

I know he's right, so I do not pull out my phone. "Lies. *Your* best behavior is way below the acceptable threshold, anyway."

Releasing me, Carter takes a step back. "Meet me at my house. If you don't follow me, I'll show up at yours—you know I will."

"Pushy," I tell him, running a hand down his chest.

Catching my hand, he replies, "You like it."

"I don't *hate* it. Jury's still out on whether or not I *like* it," I tease.

"Well, meet me at my house and we can work on figuring it out."

CHAPTER 28

CARTER'S HOUSE is enormous in broad daylight, but somehow at night, it looks even more intimidating. I think it's because of the glow. In daylight, it's like any other big house, but at night, Carter's home *glows.* Illuminated by strategically placed lighting, Carter's house sets itself apart from other homes with their paltry porch lights.

I got stuck by a couple of red lights, so Carter made it here first. He's standing outside his car, his face lit by the glow of the cell phone in his hands. His fingers are moving like he's typing something. A message? A text? Who is he texting this late at night?

God, what an annoying immediate thought to have.

I turn off my car with a sigh and grab my purse from the passenger seat. I wanted to buy a pack of condoms before I found myself alone with Carter again, just in case, but I don't want to buy them in town. I'd rather buy them one day when I go to work, so I can stop at Wal-Mart and be an anonymous condom-buyer, as opposed to the local drugstore where it would be further advertised that I'm sleeping with Carter Mahoney.

I'm sleeping with Carter Mahoney. Wow, that's a weird thing to wrap my head around.

Carter slips his phone into his pocket as I approach and flashes me a smile. Wordlessly, we make our way up the stairs to his front door. He catches my hand in his once he gets the door unlocked and then we make our way inside.

While he's locking up and setting the security alarm, I ask, "Were your parents at the game tonight?"

"Yeah, they come to most of the games. If my dad's out of town on business, he might miss one, but then my big sister usually comes to keep Mom company."

"Are you close to your mom?" I ask, since he hasn't told me much about her.

"We have a touchy relationship. We're family, but we're polar opposite people with polar opposite views of the world. I love her because she's my mother, but I don't always like her, if that makes sense."

"That does make sense," I murmur, following him up the stairs. "I always felt like my mom had more potential, but she was limited by her own upbringing, and she never pushed past that to grow into her own. I wondered what she might have been like if she had taken a different path, made different choices. It's the same with anyone, though, you know? Our paths curve, and who we become isn't always who we thought we would be."

Glancing back at me as he leads me up the stairs, he asks, "Who do you want to be?"

Good question. "Still trying to figure it out, I guess. I have a few different destinations in mind, but I'm trying to be realistic. I know my ultimate destination depends on a lot of different things, so I'm making a few different plans that I could be happy with."

His tone amused, he remarks, "You're always prepared, aren't you, Ellis?"

"No one can be prepared for every eventuality, but I do my best."

"Throw out the conditions. If you could be anything, if the world would just open up and let you have anything—what do you want?"

I ponder that as I follow him to his room, trying on different lives, sifting through all the daydreams I've had about my future to see where they lead. "Well, I want to live somewhere with a cool, colorful fall, as we discussed before. Snow at Christmas. The whole nine yards."

Nodding briefly, he says, "That's a given."

"I'll probably want to get married and have a child or two. To play in the fall leaf piles," I add.

"A solid reason for procreation, if I ever heard one."

I crack a smile as he turns on the light in his bedroom, then I go over and climb onto his bed. "I want a job in a field I'm interested in, something I can continue to study so I'll never get bored, but I also want to make a positive difference in other people's lives. Ideally, I would like to be a professor or maybe a psychologist. Then I could study what interests me, and also apply what I learn to help others, either by teaching them or actively counseling them. The mind is a complex beast, and I'm fascinated by it."

"Never would have guessed," he remarks, smirking faintly. "Am I your first experiment, future Dr. Ellis?"

I crack a smile. "Maybe someday I'll write a paper about you. We'll have a dinner party to celebrate its publication, and my like-minded colleagues will be intrigued rather than scandalized."

Pushing me back on the bed and climbing on top of me, he says, "Might want to change my name to protect my identity. Otherwise, it will be pretty awkward when I'm sitting at the dinner table next to you."

My heart kicks up as he prowls over me, but not in the bad way. "Why are you sitting next to me in this scenario? Are you stalking me? Do we have a bad break-up and you just can't let go? I cheat on you with Erika, don't I?"

Cocking his head, he says, "I'd watch that."

I roll my eyes and shove him in the shoulder. "Ew."

"Anyway, no, I'm not stalking you. We're married."

Laughter bubbles up and I can't quite keep it in. "We are?"

Offering a confident nod only *he* could pull off when saying something so crazy, one single day into our relationship, he says, "Yep. You're the one who stalked me, remember? Followed me to Columbia so you could chase off all my potential wives."

"Ah, right. How could I forget? And that led to marriage?

Clingy exes 'round the world are going to be really excited to hear this works."

"It worked for you," he verifies. "I didn't want to leave you behind, anyway, so I was happy to see you peeking around pillars on campus. In fact, I flirted with a couple of girls just to get a rise out of you. Once you scared them off with your Tootsie Roll, I hauled your ass back to my apartment and made you mine. Eventually we got married, something about you wanting babies to play in leaf piles. They're asleep upstairs while my accomplished wife celebrates her big brain with her snobby friends. I don't like many of them, myself, but I have plenty of snobby friends you don't like, too."

"Oh, well, that seems fair, then."

He nods. "It works out. Then, at the end of the day, we can both take off our public faces, shake off our snobby colleagues, and reconnect with what's real. Every night, I curl up with a woman who knows me and likes me anyway, and every night, you get to curl up beside a man who finds you as endlessly fascinating as you find your work."

Even though I know he's just playing with me, his words wrap around me like vines. They shake me like nothing he's ever said before, tempt me like no words ever have.

I want that.

I know logically it's much too soon to know whether or not I could ever have that with him, but that it's *his* scenario... maybe.

"You find me endlessly fascinating?" I ask.

Bending his head to kiss my neck, he murmurs near my ear, "I've never met anyone I could talk to the way I can with you. You know exactly who you are and what you stand for, but you have an openness I've never encountered before. You're not stubborn like most people; it's not your way or the highway. You're curious and flexible, you'll try out new ways of approaching things rather than accepting the beaten path as the only way. I love the breadth of your mind. I love just hanging out and talking with you, and..." He unbuttons my jeans. "I'm a pretty big fan of everything else we do, too."

This time, I don't even stall. He unbuttons and unzips my pants, sliding his hand down inside. Lust twists low in my belly and I let my eyes drift closed as his hand cups me, his fingers sliding under the fabric of my panties so he can touch me.

Pushing a finger inside me, he leans close and catches my gasp in his mouth. "I love the way you feel," he mumbles against my lips. "The way you taste. I love your little cries when I make you come."

With his words warming me up so effectively, my response to his touch is immediate and electrifying. His finger rubs against my clit and my whole body jerks, lightning rods of pleasure coursing straight through me. I grab onto his shoulders and pull him closer, feeling the pronounced rise and fall of my chest as I breathe harder.

"I spend every day of my life with people who like the look of a mask I wear, Zoey. You're the only person who likes what's underneath better."

"Carter," I murmur, needing to kiss him, to express affection. I bend to reach him, brushing my lips against his. His words massage my mind and my heart, his fingers work my body, and in no time at all, I cry out against his mouth as I come apart.

My body is boneless in the aftermath, and my eyes drift closed. I'm tired, satisfied, and Carter's bed is so comfortable. He moves down the bed and pulls off my jeans. My panties come off next, then he starts tugging my new Longhorns tank top up my midriff.

"You don't want to leave my Longhorns shirt on and pretend I'm an eager-to-please Carter Mahoney fan?" I tease.

"And miss the chance to watch your tits bounce while I fuck you? I don't think so."

I sit up enough for him to drag the tank top off over my head, then start to recline against the mattress again. Before I can, Carter gets his hand around my back and unsnaps my bra, then he drags that off, too.

Once more, I'm stripped bare, and Carter is still fully dressed. He comes down on top of me, the smooth fabric of his T-shirt soft against my skin. The sensation of the fabric dragging across my nipples causes them to harden. On instinct, I arch my breasts closer to him, craving his touch.

His hand slides down my side and he anchors it on my hip,

pulling me as he rolls onto his back so that I end up on top of him.

"Are you sore from last night?" he asks.

"Yeah, but it's okay," I assure him.

Carter smirks. "I wasn't offering to stop."

I roll my eyes at him. "Of course you weren't."

"Take out your ponytail. I like your hair down."

As I reach back to pull the elastic band out and free my hair from the heavy pony tail, I murmur sarcastically, "Yes, master."

Naturally, Carter is not offended by my playful rebuff—he relishes it. "Damn right."

"I've never met anyone who could say things that make me want to smack them, but also kiss them. You're the first."

"That's because when I say it, you know we're on the same side."

"*Are* we on the same side?" I ask lightly, sliding down so that I'm lying on top of him, my hair down around my shoulders now.

"Of course we are," he murmurs, bringing a hand up to caress the ball of my shoulder, then playing with a lock of my hair. "Believe me, Zoey, it's easy to tell when you're on my bad side. You haven't been since the first time I actually saw you, volleying back and forth with me in the middle of your greatest humiliation. You know when to fight and when to stand down. You're perfect for me."

"Do you want me to fight tonight?" I inquire.

Carter shakes his head. "Nah. I want to make love to you tonight."

His words make my tummy bottom out. He's saying all the nice things tonight, and I like it. Suspicion whispers at the back of my mind though, trying to convince me he's saying nice words because he knows he needs to, just to melt away my reasonable doubts.

I don't want to let suspicion ruin this, but I don't want to turn a blind eye, either. Looking at his chest instead of his face, playing with the fabric of his T-shirt, I ask, "How do I know you're not playing me like you play everyone else?"

"You don't," he says, simply.

I meet his gaze. "That's scary, you know."

"Anything that isn't safe can be scary," he states. "I'll never be the safe bet, Zoey."

"I know," I murmur. "I just…" I try to think of how to explain the simplest thing in the world, that like all people entering into a new relationship, I don't want to get hurt. I don't want him to smash my heart into pieces so small, it will never be the same, and land a massive blow to my pride on top of it, because the red flags were out in the open, blowing in the breeze, and I ignored all of them to try to connect with him.

"You just need to start trusting me," he finishes for me.

"Trust the scary, unpredictable sociopath?" I ask lightly, leaning down to kiss him to take any potential sting out of my words.

Carter reaches up and grabs a fistful of my hair, dragging me off him and rolling me onto my back. "Not a sociopath."

"Right," I murmur. "You're just manipulative, fine with exploiting and violating the rights of others, callously disregarding—"

Rather than allow me to continue my diagnosis, Carter kisses me. Then he finally undresses, flinging his clothes onto the floor with mine and coming back down on top of me, this time, naked.

"I know we joke about this from time to time, but I need you to know it's a *joke*. If you think I'm pathological, you're never going to trust me."

"Girlfriend Zoey agrees that what you said makes sense. Watchdog Zoey says of course it's true—you need me to trust you so you can keep manipulating me and getting your way while doin' whatever the hell you want."

"I wasn't born this way," he assures me. "I used to be more normal, then I realized the world sucks, everyone in it sucks, and I needed to toughen up and look out for myself, because no one else is gonna look out for me. Can't be a sociopath, because they're born, not made. My brain wasn't wired this way."

That's the most revealing thing he has ever said to me. "You rewired it. That's a lot of work. Why?"

"Doesn't matter. The point is, I protect myself and my own interests. You're one of my interests. You're safe. I *want* you; I'm not going to hurt you. If I just wanted some dopey doormat I could cheat on, I could find one, easily. That's not what I want, and I'd never try to turn you into one. I only cut down people I don't like or don't give a shit about. You don't fall into either category."

Cracking a smile as I look up at him, I tease, "You saying you care about me, Mahoney?"

Picking up the teasing gauntlet while imprisoning me with his body, he says, "Maybe a little bit."

He's still a little scary despite his reassuring words, because he's right—he'll never be the safe bet, and maybe that means I'll always be aware of his capacity for damage. Maybe he's feeding me lies, and they taste better than the truth, so I want to swallow them, even though it will undoubtedly mean trouble later.

But maybe he's telling the truth, and Erika is just doing what some girls do when they still want a guy who doesn't want them anymore—scaring off the competition, like my not-at-all-serious joke about stalking Carter at Columbia. I, personally, would never do something like that because it's desperate, and any man who made me feel desperate to keep him when he's desperate to get away would be a man better cut loose, anyway.

That's a personal choice though, and one I would abide no matter how painful for the sake of my own self-respect. My ability to feel good about myself is crucial to my own identity, and I know the parameters. I know what I expect from myself, where the line is drawn and what I can't bend to tolerate. A cheating boyfriend tops the "hell no" list.

Just because I feel that way about it doesn't mean Erika does, though. Like Carter pointed out, putting up with his shit comes with perks. I haven't taken as much advantage of them yet—I'm not even sure I want to—but Erika was with him for a while, so surely she knows all the ins and outs of being Carter's girlfriend.

Me, I'm still in the 101 class, and some days I don't even feel qualified for that one. I need Remedial Mahoney 099 or something. Maybe grab up an elective—Carter's Backstory 089.

Carter leans in and kisses his way up my neck, lighting up my nerve endings and drawing a shudder of pleasure out of me. He follows up the assault to my senses by pulling back and looking down at me with unrestrained tenderness. When he looks at me like that, all I want to do is kiss him.

"I must care about you a little bit, too," I offer back.

Carter smiles. "Just a little bit, huh?"

I hold up my thumb and forefinger to show a miniscule distance between them.

"Let's see what I can do to change that," he murmurs, before resuming his trail of kisses—but this time, down my abdomen, across my pelvic bone, and finally, between my thighs.

CHAPTER 29

CARTER'S BODY SHIFTS, the bicep that serves as my pillow moving and displacing my head. It wasn't easy finding a comfortable way to lay on him to begin with, so I grumble and curl into him even harder.

"Stop squirming," I mutter.

Chuckling, he leans in and kisses my forehead. "It's time to get up, sleeping beauty."

"Never."

"Not a morning person?"

"Mornings are the devil's work. Your bed is so comfortable. Your bedding is so soft. I don't understand why you ever leave your bed."

"It's much more tempting to stay in it when you're here with me," he offers. "Wanna blow off your church thing and stay here all day?"

Aw, man. I was nestled up in a comfy sleep fog and I totally forgot I volunteered to help out at the church this morning. Instead of getting up, I keep my eyes closed. "I should tell Grace I'll be late. She probably already did everything last night, anyway. Grace enjoys mornings—you know, like a psycho."

I nearly jump out of my skin as Carter's bedroom door flies open. I grab the blanket on top of us and yank it against my breasts, my heart stalling as I look up into the face of a middle-aged woman with copper-colored hair and a tired smile.

"Good morning, dear." She glances at me and nods. "Carter's friend."

I blink, confounded by her calmness at finding a girl naked in her son's bed. Surely this is Carter's mom. She doesn't resemble him much at all, but she called him dear.

Before another word can be said, a much smaller female hauls an armful of stuffed animals into the bedroom. Carter's little sister is wearing a crown, a princess dress over her clothing, and blue sparkly eye shadow that has been smeared clear up to her tiny, dark eyebrows.

"Don't I look pretty?" she demands.

Dutifully, Carter looks her over. "Looking sharp, kiddo. What are you all dressed up for?"

"Breakfast. My princess in the book Mama read me last night dresses up before she goes down to breakfast, so I did, too. Come on, it's time to eat. Hi, bookstore lady," she adds, an apparent afterthought.

Swallowing down my awkwardness, I offer a much more sheepish, "Hi, Chloe."

Turning on her plastic sparkle heels, she announces, "I'm taking my animals down to breakfast, but we'll save you guys a seat."

"How considerate," Carter says, dryly. "We'll be down in a minute."

We?

Carter's mom flashes me a bland smile and pulls his door closed once Chloe vacates the room.

Wide-eyed, I prop myself up on an elbow and stare at Carter. "That was so weird."

"What?"

My eyes widen even more. "That! Is your mom used to finding random girls in your bed?"

"She's not *used to it*, but it's not like she thinks I'm a virgin. House guests don't bother her." Drawing the blanket off his abdomen, he sits on the edge of the bed and stretches. "We should go downstairs. Chloe will come back up to get us if we take too long. She's an assertive little shit."

I sit up, pulling the bed sheets around me rather than dropping them. "I wasn't planning to stay for breakfast. I don't think you were planning that either, were you? I mean, your parents were *at* the game last night and I didn't meet them. Awkward morning after breakfast sounds much less ideal."

"It won't be awkward," he says dismissively, standing with his back to me so that I get distracted admiring his ass and forget about the horrible prospect of sitting there with his parents. They would both know their son banged me last night. How could it not be awkward?

Following his lead despite my hesitance, I climb off the bed. I'd really prefer a shower before we go downstairs. Carter came inside me again last night, despite my asking him to pull out. He reasoned that pulling out was kind of pointless, and ignored me when I asked him to do it, anyway. Consequently, my thighs still feel a little sticky, and I can't imagine sitting there with his parents and little sister, still feeling Carter between my legs.

"I have to shower. I can be fast, but considering you're bound and determined to make your mother a grandma, I'd like to make a better first impression than this."

Carter chokes on laughter, but since he told me Chloe would come get us if we dawdled, I don't wait to hear his response.

AFTER THE WORLD'S quickest shower, I put on last night's clothes and head downstairs with Carter. One more reason I shouldn't be going to this breakfast is that I can't go to church in what I'm wearing, so I'll have to stop home first.

I text Grace to let her know I might be a little late as Carter leads me toward the dining room. I haven't been in this room yet, but his house is pretty big, so there are quite a few rooms I haven't seen.

The dining room is gray and white with a chandelier hanging over the table, dark hardwood flooring, and a wall of windows, letting in a stream of light from the big backyard. I see patio furniture out there, but my gaze snaps right back to the table. There's a dark-haired man with his back to us. He has Carter's broad shoulders, a matured version of his physique, and he's wearing a pristine navy-blue suit. There's a newspaper open in his hands and the table is quiet. Carter's mom is just sitting down, so she glances up at us with another weak smile as she takes her seat. Chloe is seated and poking her eggs with a fork, but there's a scowl on her cute little face, telegraphing her displeasure.

"Good morning," Carter offers to the room as he leads me straight past the table and into the next room. It's the kitchen—a big kitchen. I wish I had this kitchen.

At the center of the cooking area is an island with a wooden surface, polished and gleaming. There are chairs all around that, and I would really rather eat there, but that would probably be rude.

There's a fancy coffee machine on the counter beyond the island, and a line of breakfast dishes. Carter opens a cupboard and grabs two plates, then passes one to me.

"Wow, does your mom make breakfast like this every morning?" I ask him.

"Most mornings."

"My mom buys Pop-Tarts," I offer, smiling wryly as I eye up the steaming dishes.

Carter is spoiled and does not adequately appreciate this breakfast feast. I do, and my mouth waters as I scoop a bit of everything up and put it on my plate. I didn't even know how hungry I was, but man, it all looks and smells so good.

Carter glances at my plate and smirks. "Hungry?"

"I need the extra nourishment," I inform him, lifting my eyebrows. "I'm probably eatin' for two."

"Jesus Christ," he says, rolling his eyes.

"If I keep talkin' about it, maybe it will finally sink in that you need to wear a damn condom. I know you get a kick out of ignorin' me when I tell you not to do something sexual, but refusing to wear a condom shouldn't be included in your deviance."

"I like being inside you without a condom."

"You're gonna like it a whole lot less when you're explainin' to your Columbia wife five years from now why you're paying child support to some girl you used to know in Texas."

"I'm getting married in five years? To someone else? Why are you still in Texas? I feel like you left a lot out of the missing years, here. Anyway, you could just get an abortion and go on about your life," he points out.

"I'm spendin' both of my weekend days at *church*, Carter. You really think I'm gonna get an abortion because you can't be bothered to wrap it up? Nope. I would have the baby and curse you forever."

"You wanted one or two to play in the leaf piles, anyway. Jeeze, does nothing make you happy? It *is* like we're married."

"Next time you fuck me without a condom, I'm buyin' myself a 'baby on board' maternity shirt, and it's all I'm ever going to wear around you."

"You are a real pain in my ass, you know that?" he asks, opening a drawer and grabbing some silverware.

I grab some while he has it open. "Wait until my pregnancy hormones kick in."

"For fuck's sake, you are not pregnant."

"No thanks to you," I mutter.

Carter shakes his head, puts his plate down, and moves close. I move my plate aside just in time for him to close in. His chest brushes mine and he grabs the back of my neck, pulling me in for a kiss. "No discussing our impending family at the breakfast table," he tells me when he pulls back. "I'm sure you can guess, but my parents would be decidedly less amused."

"You know when you're going to be decidedly less amused? When I'm sendin' you to the store at 3am because I'm craving a certain brand of pickles."

Carter takes a step back, rolls his eyes at me again, and grabs his plate. "Come on, wifey."

"And my back is already aching from carrying around your spawn. I hope you're plannin' to give me a back rub later."

"Are your feet swelling up, too? Maybe I should just buy you a whole spa day."

"I mean, it's the least you could do for the mother of your child."

Carter walks ahead of me, shaking his head, but I let the joke die since we're walking back into the dining room. I *should* tell on him to his parents; maybe they could convince him that safe sex is the only sex we should be having, because I don't seem to be getting through.

Obviously, I'm not going to do that, though.

Carter's father glances up from his paper to look me over, and I immediately see where both kids got all their looks from. Carter and Chloe both favor their father and got little to no physical characteristics from their mom.

"Mom, Dad, this is Zoey," Carter offers as he drops into his seat next to Chloe.

I flash his mom a smile, then his father. "Zoey Ellis. It's nice to meet you both."

"I'm Angela," his mother tells me. "This is Carter's father, Kevin."

Carter's father doesn't greet me, but when I look at him, his gaze is either resting on my breasts, or my Longhorns tank. I hope it's the latter, and breathe a sigh of relief that it is when a moment later he says, "Zoey Ellis, huh? Bet Jake's not happy about that."

I take a seat, looking awkwardly to Carter.

Carter shrugs. "Didn't ask him. Don't care."

"You should care," his father states. "Jake's suspension could've thrown off your whole season."

"Could've—if the team depended on *his* talent. Since it relies on mine, we're just fine," Carter replies.

His gaze slides past Carter and comes back to me. "Well, in any case, it's good you got that whole misunderstanding cleared up."

My fingers tighten around the fork like it's the blade of a knife that I'm about to plant in Carter's father's jugular. "There was no misunderstanding. Jake behaved in a less than gentlemanly manner, and I didn't appreciate it. Anyway, I'm also glad it's behind us."

"Maybe an overreaction to ruin the boy's last season of foot-ball," Kevin tells me.

"I don't think it was," I offer back, with a painfully polite smile. "Personally, I think his behavior warranted a time-out. Since that's the only punishment that seemed to affect him, I'm glad Coach took it seriously and took away something Jake enjoyed."

"Did he get grounded?" Chloe asks.

I nod my head. "He sure did."

"I bet he didn't like that. I wouldn't like to be grounded," she informs me.

"No, I wouldn't either," I agree, turning my attention to her, since her company is far more pleasant. Carter's dad already has my cheeks flushing with defensive annoyance, and that is not the foot I intended to start out on. Carter could have given me a heads up his dad was on the anti-Zoey, pitchfork-wielding side. Not only would I not have come to this breakfast, I would have avoided meeting his parents at all, at least until the season ended.

I am starting to understand now why he didn't introduce them to me at the game last night, though. His father condescending to me at the table in private is one thing, but in front of everyone at the stadium? That would have been doubly embarrassing.

"Zoey's a good girl," Carter tells Chloe, or his dad, I'm not sure. He's talking to Chloe, but it sounds more like it's aimed at his dad. "I'm sure she's never done anything to get herself grounded."

"She can't be that good, if she's having sleepovers with you," his dad murmurs, lifting his coffee to his lips and turning his attention back to his paper.

"Oh, Kevin," his mom finally fusses, shaking her head. Offering me an apologetic smile, she says, "Don't mind him, dear. He's a grump before he's finished his morning coffee. He doesn't mean any of that."

"Mm-hmm," his dad mutters. "We'll see what you say when it's our son she's trying to drag through the mud."

"Would you stop it?" Carter snaps. "Jesus Christ, I'm intro-ducing you to my girlfriend and you have to act like an ass."

His father's eyebrows rise, but with something closer to amusement than I would expect upon getting a lecture from his own son. "Girlfriend? Christ, what's this girl doing to you boys to make you behave like fucking idiots?"

"Kevin," his mother chides.

"She accuses his friend, and he says 'hey, I think I'll make her my girlfriend.'" Kevin shakes his head. "Boy has no sense of loyalty."

Carter's fork drops to the plate with a clatter, and he leans back in his chair. "Oh, that is rich coming from you."

"Carter, please," his mother says, trying to take his reins, since his father's are clearly beyond her reach.

I get the impression that Carter's are, too, but he must not want to bring up something he knows will pain *her* at the breakfast table. Shaking his head, he grabs his fork and starts eating a little faster.

"I wanna go to Disney World," Chloe announces. "Alicia said her parents took her there, and she got to eat breakfast at the *castle* with *princesses*. Can you imagine if we lived in a castle?"

"You basically do," I tell her, offering a little smile. "Your house is a lot bigger than mine, that's for sure."

"I bet it is," Carter's dad murmurs.

Carter's jaw locks and he glares.

His mom fidgets with her napkin.

Yep, totally not awkward at all, Carter. Good call on making me come to family breakfast.

Carter's mom clutches onto an invisible tangent. "Speaking of, Carter, can you take Chloe to ballet today? You'll have to clean all that makeup off her first, she can't go like that. I intended to take her, but I'm just too tired."

"You're always tired," his dad mutters. "Never do anything, but tired all the damn time."

With every syllable that leaves his lips, I dislike Carter's father a little more.

"Mama does stuff," Chloe defends. "She's great."

Offering a smile that doesn't reach her eyes, Angela says, "Thank you, Chloe."

The rest of breakfast passes awkwardly, but at least it doesn't get worse. When I've consumed my food as quickly as possible without appearing to be training for my career as a competitive eater, Carter walks me out to my car.

Once we're a safe distance from the house, he shoves his hands into the pockets of his jeans and tells me, "I owe you an apology. I did not think that would go the way it did."

I shrug, feeling relieved to be out of the house, but bad for Carter, Chloe, and Carter's mom, because they're all stuck here. "It's fine. Your dad is awful, though. Like, truly awful. Was not prepared for that."

Carter shakes his head, glancing back at the house. "I told you, I don't know why she won't leave the bastard."

"Well… I thought you were exaggerating, but no. I don't know why either. I would leave him, then I'd come back just so I could leave him again. Every morning, come over just to leave. Maybe after a month or so it would feel like I had left him a sufficient number of times, but… I'm not sure."

Carter cracks a smile, then leans in and kisses me. "Well, I'm glad we got that over with, at least."

"I have officially met the parents. I hope you don't think we're bringin' the baby back here for holidays though, because… no."

"Chloe's gonna have a bedroom at my place in New York. We'll invite my mom to stay on an air mattress in her room. My father can spend the holidays alone like the miserable bastard he is."

"We'll send him a card to thank him for the apartment, just to be polite. But bar him from ever visiting, on account of his personality."

Now Carter's smile widens, and he leans in and kisses me. "Have fun getting ready for church with Pastor Boner."

"You're goin' to Hell for callin' him that," I inform him.

"I'm going to Hell for a lot of things," he assures me.

CHAPTER 30

ON MY WAY back to the table with a fresh dish of sliced tomatoes, I spot the last thing I ever expected to see—Carter Mahoney at church.

Well, okay, he's outside of church, technically. The cookout is outside, and there aren't many people here, but I certainly didn't expect him to be one of them. My steps slow, my forehead creasing with a frown as I take in the sight of Carter talking to Pastor James, then I remember last time Carter encountered him and I pick up the pace.

"Hey, what are you doin' here?" I call out as I approach.

Carter turns to watch me approach. "Came to see your basket."

Now I notice James is also holding a basket I haven't seen before—which shouldn't be possible, since I'm one of the volunteers who put the baskets together. This one is wrapped in cellophane and tied with Longhorn blue ribbon. Inside, with a Longhorns shirt nestled around it, I see a football with marks all over it. Signatures?

An autographed football.

I put it together at the same time James offers a mild smile and says, "Carter here brought another basket for the auction."

"Sure did," Carter says, sounding pretty satisfied with himself.

I don't even know what to say. I did tell him all about the baskets and what each basket would contain, so I guess he had the information, but he certainly didn't say he would contribute anything. "That was generous of you, Carter. Thank you," I tell him.

"It's well put together, too," James offers, nodding as he looks over the contents of the basket. "Seems you have a knack for arts and crafts, Carter."

Carter chuckles to himself and shakes his head. "I can't take credit for the assembly. I bought the stuff, my rally girl put it together. *She* has a knack for arts and crafts."

"Oh, okay," James returns, nodding. "Well, that's real nice of your girlfriend to help you out."

Okay, that's enough of that. Nodding my head toward the tables before Carter can rise to the bait and kiss my face off right here in front of the assembled members of my congregation, I say, "I've gotta walk these tomatoes over here. You wanna follow me?"

Carter allows me to rein him in, thankfully, and he follows me over to the folding table set up with all the fixings. "Are more people supposed to show up?"

I sigh, looking around the empty church lawn. We've all done our parts to spread the word about the cookout and basket auction, but so far, the turnout hasn't been great. As sad as it is, at this point, we would have been better off just giving the woman we're raising funds for the money we spent doing all this.

"Hopefully more people will show up in the afternoon."

"How long is this thing going?" he asks.

"We close everything up at four."

Carter nods, pulling out his phone and checking the display. "Still got some time, then. I've gotta run over and pick up Chloe from ballet in a few minutes, but I'll bring her over and buy her a burger after."

I flash him a grateful smile. "Thanks. Every little bit helps. It was nice of you to do the basket, too. You didn't even tell me you were doin' that."

"It's nothing," he says dismissively. "How does this basket auction thing work?"

"You buy tickets, fill them out with your name and phone number, and then put as many as you want into the canister by each basket you'd like to win. If you win and you're not here for the drawing, we call you and you can come pick up your prize."

"Great." He flashes me a smile. "I wanna buy like $20 worth of tickets for the Longhorn basket."

"For... the basket you donated yourself?"

"Yep."

"Why?"

"Because the ball is signed by all of this year's Longhorns. I wanna buy the tickets for Jake, not myself."

"Why do you want to buy tickets for Jake?" I ask, not following.

"Because he's the only one who didn't get to sign the ball; being excluded will piss him off."

Amusement bubbles up inside me, but I tamp it down and try to bite back a smile. "That's mean," I inform him.

"I'm still gonna do it," he states. "Where do I buy tickets?"

I shake my head, indicating the other end of the table where the pastor's wife is seated. "Right over there. Don't tell her about your extremely unchristian ulterior motives."

"I'll pretend to be a good person," he promises.

AFTER CARTER LEAVES to pick up Chloe, business picks up a bit. Her ballet school must not be far, because he comes back pretty fast. Chloe comes bounding up to my table, full of energy despite the dance class she just finished. As if she's not cute enough, today her dark hair is pulled back in a ponytail and she's wearing a pink leotard with a sheer skirt that bounces and sways with every step she takes. She's clutching Carter's hand as she walks this way, and it sends my thoughts to the unprotected sex I've had twice with her brother.

Obviously, I hope I'm not pregnant, but I'm aware of the risk. I don't really want to have kids for probably ten more years, but I don't know what to do about Carter's unwillingness to be reasonable. If he were a normal guy, I would refuse to have sex with him until a month has passed and I can get some birth control in my system, or he decides to put a condom on his dick before we have sex. Given he's Carter, that won't work. I don't want to break up with him. I like dating him so far, but I don't like all the shots he's taking at my womb.

Frankly, it doesn't make sense. It doesn't seem like he thinks he's invincible, yet he doesn't seem worried about it happening, either. Not in the oblivious way of teenage guys who think they can have unprotected sex with impunity, but trying to sober him up by mentioning the real possibility of him making me a mother —and himself a father—before either of us have a diploma doesn't freak him out, either. Wouldn't thinking about the *result* of unprotected sex freak out most teenage guys? I realize Carter isn't ordinary, but why doesn't *this* scare him?

Why does it feel like he regards a potential accidental teen pregnancy like no big deal... almost in the way someone regards something terrifying that they've survived before, so it no longer has the power it had over you the first time?

I cock my head, watching Chloe grin up at Carter and reach her free hand across to show him something that sparkles in the sun. Probably a sticker. He regards her with warmth, like always. Then he points in my direction and Chloe looks ahead, then waves at me with her sticker hand.

"Hi, bookstore lady!"

Hi, Carter clone.

Sudden horror grips me, and I look from her to him again.

Thirteen. He was thirteen the first time he had sex. Chloe is five.

Erika flashes to mind, since she always hangs out in the dark pockets of my brain, waiting to torment me and fill me full of doubts. They weren't a thing back then though, right? He couldn't have possibly gotten Erika pregnant when they were little more than kids... but if he did, it would explain some things. It would explain why she's so attached to him, why she thinks he belongs to her. Maybe she went along with everything he wanted her to do, everything his family told her to do, and she thinks it's her due to end up with him.

It would also explain why she's the only girl he's ever given girlfriend status, even though it doesn't seem like he wanted a girlfriend. Maybe it was part of her perks package. Maybe he was being nice because… well, knocking up a 13-year-old is a shitty thing to do, even if you are also only 13. This just isn't a thing that should happen.

Carter doesn't seem like someone who would insist a meaningless fling he knocked up keep a pregnancy though, and if Erika didn't want it… why is Chloe here?

Now I look at the little girl, and if I look hard enough, I can see some Erika. Erika has blue eyes and brown hair, but Carter's genes clearly run strong, given how much he looks like his father. Erika is pretty, and Chloe is adorable. While their shades are different, they both have pin-straight hair and cute little button noses.

Carter cocks an eyebrow. "Earth to Zoey."

I shake myself out of my rush of paranoid thoughts and try to remember what was just said. "Uh, sorry. What?"

"I said hi, and you didn't say hi back," Chloe announces.

"I'm so sorry about that. I was daydreaming. Hi, Chloe."

My mind is still in overdrive though, kicking up new thoughts. When Carter walked me to my car, he said Chloe will have a bedroom at his apartment. I assumed he meant it as part of our joking scenario, similar to our kids sleeping upstairs at my dinner scenario last night, but the apartment is actually happening. Does she really have a bedroom at his apartment in New York? That doesn't seem normal. How many older brothers have actual bedrooms set up for their five-year-old sisters? In case of what? A visit? How often would she be visiting to warrant her own bedroom?

Is this too crazy to ask him? This is definitely too crazy to ask him. If I'm right, I don't even know what I would do with that, and if I'm wrong, he would think I'm a paranoid, overthinking psycho. I've already theorized he cheated and he's only been my boyfriend for a day and a half. For our two-day anniversary, I can't ask, "Also, did you by chance impregnate Erika in middle school and Chloe is actually your daughter? Asking for a friend."

"You wanna see my dance moves?" Chloe asks.

"Sure, I'd love to see your moves."

She takes a step back away from the table, then does a series of attempts at ballet moves. I'm not sure she actually nails any of them, but she's five; who cares?

Upon finishing, she plants a hand on her hip and does an end pose.

Clapping my hands, I say, "Encore!"

"I don't know that word," she tells me, coming up to the table and looking at the food. Her nose instantly wrinkles up. "I don't want any of this, either."

"How about a cheeseburger?" Carter suggests.

"No," she says.

"Hot dog?"

"Nuh uh."

"Chips. You love chips."

Chloe shakes her head and looks up at him. "I want to go to a restaurant. I want chicken tenders or spaghetti."

"We can go to a restaurant for dinner," he tells her. "It's not dinnertime yet."

"I'll wait," she tells him. "How 'bout some dessert first? I want a cookie."

Carter shakes his head. "This is a cookout, not a bake sale."

"Well, I want a cookie," Chloe announces, like this should be sufficient reason for cookies to appear.

I'm not sure I should offer cookies to the five-year-old who hasn't even eaten yet, but I give her brother metaphorical cookies before dinner all the time, so what the hell? "We do have cookies," I tell Carter. "Chocolate chip. Two for a dollar."

"Two cookies! I want two cookies," she tells him.

Carter pulls out his wallet, fishes out a dollar, and hands it to her. "Here you go. See that girl with brown hair?" he asks, pointing. "That's Grace. Give her the dollar and tell her you want to buy two cookies."

Chloe snatches the money and runs over to Grace's side of the table.

Shaking his head, Carter stays right where he is. "Picky little shit."

I grin. "Hey, I don't blame her. Pasta is delicious. I would probably choose that over a boring burger, too."

"You don't work tonight, do you?"

I shake my head. "I work tomorrow, but I'm off today."

"Perfect. When you're done doing all this, I'll take you both out for dinner."

"Are your parents still going out?" I ask, mildly surprised. After seeing them at breakfast, I assumed they weren't getting along today and might cancel whatever they had planned that meant Carter had to babysit.

"Yeah, they're still going. Mom's having an episode, though, so she and my dad will end up fighting before he eventually drags her out of the house. Just better for Chloe not to be there for all that."

"How is that all going to work when you go off to school? It seems like you're a crucial cog in Chloe's life."

He glances over at her, paying for her cookies in her cute little ballet outfit. "Yeah, I'm not sure yet. Caroline says she'll help out, but she and her husband are planning to start their own family soon and she doesn't have enough time as it is." He shakes his head. "I don't know."

"Are you really going to have a spare bedroom at your apartment for her?"

Carter brings his gaze back to me. "Yeah. It's a three bedroom, so there's enough space to set one aside for her. I figure bedroom, office, Chloe's room. Unless I knock you up, of course. Then we'll probably need a nursery."

I widen my eyes and look around to make sure no one overheard, then glare at him. "Really? At a church function?"

Carter smirks. "Hey, you were doing it in my kitchen with my parents in the next room."

"I was trying to scare you straight; you're just bein' a troublemaker."

"No, I'm being a problem-solver," he offers back, lightly. "If I knock you up, we already have to accommodate one kid. We could probably just have Chloe move to New York with us, wouldn't be much added trouble."

"I'm growing increasingly worried that you're startin' to view knockin' me up as a way to lock down a dedicated nanny."

"And lover," he adds. "I'm seeing a lot of perks."

"You are an insane person," I tell him. "I want to go to college, not be trapped at home with Carter clones, watching you become successful. Especially because come your mid-life crisis, you would undoubtedly leave me for a co-ed after I gave you my best years and gave up my own goals to accommodate you and raise your babies. Sorry, it's a hard no. I'll be focusin' on my own goals, thank you very much."

"Pessimist," he accuses. "I already told you I wouldn't ruin your life. It's like you don't believe me or something."

"Go figure," I toss back.

Chloe comes running back over with a cookie in each hand. "Look what I got!"

Carter's attention is still on me, though. He's studying me again, a look on his face like the one that was probably on mine while I was theorizing about his relation to Chloe. "Where's your father?"

"What?"

"Your dad. You live with your mom and a stepdad, right? You've never mentioned your father. What happened to him?"

I don't like that question. It's unreasonable to be annoyed by such a common inquiry, but I know what he's doing. He's trying to pin my fears about him on an absent, disappointing father—and I *have* an absent, disappointing father, so if I tell him that, he'll be able to.

"I don't have daddy issues," I say instead.

"Then tell me what happened to him," he counters.

"I don't want to."

Carter smirks. "Because then I'll be able to logically argue against your fears. Right. Why would you want that?"

"My fears have nothin' to do with my father, Dr. Mahoney," I say, dryly. "My fears have everything to do with what I know about you as a person, your life goals, and men just like you. Selfish people can't be relied on, and a relationship is not a life plan. It's important to do your own thing, that way you never come to a point where you've built your whole life around someone else and then they decide to leave and your whole world crumbles. A romantic relationship can be the icing on the life-cake, not the flour in the batter."

"So, he left you and your mom for some other woman," Carter surmises. "Do you ever see him?"

"I have no desire to," I mutter, annoyed at him now for digging. "He broke my mom's heart and abandoned all of his responsibilities. He's dead to me."

"I would never do that," Carter states. He seems sincere enough, but of course he does. No one would admit they would ever do that to begin with, but most people probably also don't think they *would* until they've slid so far down a moral hill, all of a sudden it's acceptable. "Say what you will about me, Zoey, but I don't abandon my responsibilities. Never have, never will."

As if to illustrate his point, Chloe goes, "Mm, this cookie is delicious."

Baby sister, secret daughter—whatever she is to him, he does help take care of her. It doesn't seem like anyone forces him to. Even today, he has her out of the house because he knows things will be tense there and that wouldn't be good for her to be around. That is absolutely responsible behavior, and it sounds like his motivation to do it comes from within, not his mother or anyone else pressuring him to do it.

Instead of saying any of that, I pointedly start rearranging condiments, hoping he'll see I'm busy and go away for the time being. "I don't have daddy issues," I tell him again. "And you don't have any responsibilities attached to me. Behave yourself and we can keep it that way."

CHAPTER 31

WHAT BEGAN AS AN EASY—IF boring—day volunteering at
the church quickly turned into a crush of people. Carter bought
a cheeseburger he only took one bite of before tossing in the
trash, but he utilized that one bite like a marketing pro—to take
a posed picture of him and Chloe, then post it online with a call
to all his followers to come on out to the church and support a
good cause… plus, get to hang out with him, and score a chance
at an autographed ball signed by the football team.

Boy, did they show up. We sold out of burgers and had only
four hot dogs left by the time the last person had ordered and we
could finally clean up. Carter also directed people to the baskets,
so we ended up selling a *lot* more tickets than we expected to.

I'm hot, sticky, and exhausted by the time I'm done working.
I tell Carter I have to swing by my house and take a shower first,
and he takes Chloe home to change out of her ballet clothes
before we go out to dinner.

Carter picks me up. I'm too tired and worn out from the heat
of the sun beating down on me while I worked all day to even
ask where we're going, but before long, the Dallas skyline comes
into view.

"We're goin' into the city for dinner?" I ask, finally sitting up
and taking notice.

"Yep." He misses a beat, then he says, "We're going to Porter's."

Remembering he said his sister *owns* Porter's, dread snakes through me. "Haven't I met enough of your family members for one day? Give a girl a break, would ya?"

The corners of Carter's mouth tilt up. "This is a make-up meeting. Since the one earlier went so poorly, I wanted to bring you to meet my sister. She's cool, you'll like her."

"I wish you'd've told me that," I tell him, glancing down at my outfit. I'm wearing jeans with a snag in the knee and a worn T-shirt. "I'm not exactly dressed to impress."

"I'm taking care of it," he assures me.

"What does that mean?"

He doesn't answer. I'm growing accustomed to him outright ignoring me when he doesn't want to answer, so I turn my attention out the window and watch as we drive into the city. A short time later, we arrive at a shopping mall and Carter parks the car. I've never been to Porter's, but I know it's not located inside a shopping mall, so I know we aren't here to eat.

"Are we going shopping?" Chloe asks cheerfully, clearly delighted at the prospect.

"We're just making a quick stop," he tells her, taking her hand as he leads her around the car. "We're going to buy Zoey a dress to wear to dinner. You want to help her pick it out?"

"Yeah," Chloe says, nodding. "And I want a new dress, too."

"We're here for Zoey today," he informs her.

"But *please*," she drawls passionately.

After a brief shopping excursion, we head to the register with a pretty—though a touch sexier than I would have selected for myself—little black dress for me, and a new dress with Minnie Mouse on it for Chloe.

"This dress is so pretty," Chloe announces, holding it up in the air so the red tulle doesn't drag on the ground. "I'm gonna wear it all the time."

Still feeling self-conscious about letting Carter buy me an outfit, I tell him, "I think I should pay for this myself."

Carter slows down, falling into step beside me and letting Chloe take the lead. "No," he says, simply.

"You can't veto me," I tell him. "You're not my boss, Carter Mahoney."

"You don't have the money. I do," he says, simply. "Besides, I'm not even using my own money. I'm charging all this to my credit card. The bill goes to my father. Technically, my dad is buying you a new dress, and don't you think that's the least he could do after being so rude to you at breakfast?"

I *do* dislike his dad.

"I mean, all that shit he said about your *misunderstanding* with Jake?" Carter continues, shaking his head. "Guy's a dick. Let him pay for it."

Even though he's right, I recognize his techniques as the same ones he used on Jake when Carter was trying to persuade him to do his bidding, even in spite of Jake's best interest. Shaking my head at his second nature manipulation, I envision Carter's future. Without any training, he's already a shark. What kind of man will he be after an Ivy League law school teaches him new tips and tricks?

"What?" he asks since I'm shaking my head at him.

"I just can't decide if I should be envious of or feel bad for your future wife."

Smiling, Carter drapes an arm around my shoulder. "I'm gonna marry you, remember? You don't strike me as the type to spend a lot of time feeling sorry for yourself."

"I won't. Not even after our divorce when you're shacking up with a 20-year-old yoga instructor," I tell him, exaggerated pride dripping from my tone. "I'll just take half of your shit in the divorce—the good half. I think we should buy a vacation home somewhere with a beach, that way I can lounge by the ocean with a hot young thing of my own. Even up the score, you know."

"Of course. That seems fair."

"Even though it'll be *your* mid-life crisis that causes it, *I'll* win the divorce," I inform him.

"I don't doubt it. Give it a month, I'll be so annoyed at how well you're doing without me—not to mention I'll miss you so much—I'll come crawling right back."

Grinning over at him, I ask, "Do you crawl?"

"Well, no," he admits. "But I'll stride in, throw you over my shoulder caveman style, haul you to the bedroom, and reclaim you as my wife. That's about as close to crawling as I can get."

"Will you at least slouch?"

"Probably not. Gotta show your dumb fucking boyfriend what an imposing man I am. After I reclaim you in the bedroom, I'm gonna drown him in the ocean for daring to touch you," he adds casually.

"That seems reasonable. Do I get to kill the yoga instructor for touching you?"

"I already did. Thought I might have to, in order to atone for being such a massive douchebag." Leaning close, he murmurs in my ear, "Turns out, the make-up sex was sufficient. Oh well."

He's crazy, but that he even manages to charm me in this jaded, imaginary scenario where I should hate him is as exasperating as it is endearing. I wrap my arm around his waist so I can lean in closer. "That's why you're my favorite sociopath," I inform him.

His arm tightens around me and he jokes, "I better be. I'm not afraid to take out the competition."

WHEN WE GET to Porter's, I'm really glad Carter made me get the dress. I tug at the hem absently as I walk beside him and Chloe into the lavish dining area. A neatly coiffed hostess in a black dress walks ahead of us, clutching menus to her chest. I steal glimpses here and there as we walk past tables and booths full of patrons, most of them in attire ranging from business-casual to cocktail. Even the few open tables in the room are set with bone-white plates, folded cloth napkins, and spotless clear goblets, maybe for water or wine.

There's a silver-haired man in a tuxedo playing the piano along the back wall. Behind him, an entire floor-to-ceiling wall of wine bottles, like the inside of a well-stocked wine cellar, but on steroids.

"This place is beautiful," I tell Carter.

Carter stops where the hostess halted and lets Chloe climb

into the booth first. Glancing around with the casualness of someone already accustomed to the setting and unable to see its charm, he nods his head. "Yeah, it's a nice place."

"I want banana pudding," Chloe informs us, her little brown eyes lit up with anticipation.

"For dessert," Carter says. "As long as you finish your dinner."

"But the pudding is the best! We should have dessert first, just in case we run out of room," she informs him.

He shakes his head at her, but doesn't bother arguing. Instead, he looks back at me and catches me checking him out.

Carter is still wearing jeans, but before he came to pick me up, he changed into a black button-down shirt, since he had the advantage of knowing where we were going. The sleeves are rolled up to his elbows since it's hot outside, and the pronounced veins in his strong, lean arms... well, they do things to me.

My cheeks warm up since I'm caught, but I don't back down when he smirks at me. Instead, I shrug. "What? You're gorgeous. This isn't news."

He smiles and leans back a step, wrapping his arm around me and drawing me against him so he can give me a kiss.

"Well, well, well, look what the cat dragged in."

I break away and turn, startled, at the sound of a woman's voice. A stunning woman with dark hair and classic red lips stands there smiling as she looks from Carter to Chloe. Chloe climbs back down and runs the short distance to throw her arms around the woman.

"Hi, Caroline," Chloe greets, squeezing her.

"Hey, baby," the woman offers back, reaching a hand down and rubbing Chloe's back.

"Carter said I can have pudding," Chloe informs her.

"For dessert," Carter reminds her.

"And he said we could have dessert first," Chloe adds optimistically.

"That's not true," Carter states.

Caroline grins. "She gets that from you, you know. You can't even be mad about it."

Given my earlier line of thoughts, I want to jump on that and pry, but before I can, Carter intervenes, telling Chloe to sit back down. Then he rests his hand on my hip and tells his sister, "Caroline, this is my lovely girlfriend, Zoey."

"Girlfriend?" she asks with interest, looking me over before extending her hand. "Well, how about that? It's nice to meet you, Zoey. You must have jumped through some high hoops to lock my little brother down. He's a handful, this one," she adds as she drops my hand, in case I didn't already know.

"Oh, I know he is," I assure her. "Don't worry, I can handle him."

"Most of Carter's lady friends don't get introductions, so I believe you. You two go to school together?"

I nod my head. "We're in the same history class."

"Are you a cheerleader?"

"God, no." The words tumble right out before I can think better of them. I don't know Carter's sister, but since Carter is on the team, maybe she was a cheerleader in high school. Attempting to backtrack so as not to offend her, I add, "Not that there's anything wrong with cheerleading. I'm just not a big fan of having more eyes on me than necessary. I'm not really the cheering on the sidelines type, I'm more the... stay home and read type."

Caroline's eyebrows rise like that's the last thing she expected to hear. "Really? Not a social butterfly, huh? How did you and my brother meet again?" she half-jokes.

"It was an accident of fate," I assure her. "I'm not his type."

"You are now," Carter assures me, putting slight pressure on my back to urge me toward the booth. "Anyway, I introduced her to Mom and Dad this morning, and it did not go well. I thought I'd show her we're not all assholes."

Chloe shakes her head and passes him a pack of crayons wrapped in plastic wrap to open. "You owe me a dollar, Carter."

Taking the pack and ripping it open, he tells her, "You already spent your dollar on cookies, rugrat."

"You used a adult word," she tells him, eyebrows rising. "You owe me *another* dollar."

"You should really just give her a twenty and tell her it's a down payment," Caroline offers. "That's what Chris does when we watch her. He knows he's going to fail to clean up that dirty mouth, so he just forks down his penance and gets it out of the way."

Chloe looks at me. "I make a lot of money off the boys."

I bite back a grin as I slide into the booth across from her. "I bet you do."

"I'm saving it up. I'm gonna buy a pony named Lucy and put a unicorn horn on her," Chloe tells me.

"That's not going to happen," Carter informs her, sliding into the booth beside her.

"Yeah, it is. I'm gonna have a pet unicorn. I just have to save up a lot of dollars."

"That wouldn't be a unicorn, it would be a pony with a weird hat," Carter tells her. "Why don't you aim a little lower? Start with a pet fish."

"I would name it Sharky," she announces. Then she nods, already sold on the idea. "Okay, I want a pet fish. Can we go get one today?"

"You've gotta save up your money first," he tells her, passing me a menu. "You'll have to buy it a bowl and fish food."

"Can it go places with us? We should get it a cage, like a dog. But that water will stay in, so we can bring Sharky."

Sighing, Carter murmurs, "I'm already regretting this suggestion." Glancing her way, he says, "How about instead of buying a fish today, we all watch *The Little Mermaid* when we get home?"

"Yeah, yeah, yeah," she says, bouncing in her seat as she colors on her place setting.

Now that we're all seated, Caroline says, "I'll grab you guys a waitress. You're actually in Marla's section, but I'll get you a different one."

"Yes, please do," Carter says.

As soon as Caroline walks away, I ask, "Who is Marla?"

"Number 19," he offers back.

Oh. "Did you date, or…?"

"Or," he answers, shooting me a little smirk and winking at me.

Shameless. Carter Mahoney is shameless.

CHAPTER 32

HAVING WATCHED *The Little Mermaid* many times as a child, I watch the beginning until Chloe is engrossed and no longer paying me any attention, then I get on my phone and review some of my notes to prepare for class on Monday. Carter has cut way into my studying time and I have to work tomorrow. In preparation, I took pictures of all my notes and put them in a folder in my phone, that way if I got some free time by the register, I could study.

It turned out to be a great plan. By the time Ariel is getting married and living happily ever after, I feel a little less stressed about spending almost my whole entire weekend with Carter.

I am a little surprised I'm not sick of him yet, though. As much as I like Carter and find him interesting, spending this much time with someone without interruption is a lot. Most anyone would be getting on my nerves by now, but I'm still thoroughly enjoying Carter's company.

"Can you hand me the remote?"

I'm sitting on the floor in front of the couch Carter is lying on. I only intend to glimpse at him before leaning forward to grab the remote control for him, but what I see makes my heart stop, drop, and roll right out of my body.

Chloe got sleepy while the movie was on, so she decided to lie down on Carter and use him as a makeshift bed. Currently, she is fast asleep like a little angel, with one small arm curled around his neck. Her other hand is wrapped around his side so that she's basically hugging him while she sleeps.

I can't handle it. Instead of moving toward the end table where Carter put the remote before lying down with Chloe, I just sit here, half-turned, and stare.

"This is so adorable, I can't stand it," I inform him.

Carter rolls his eyes. "Yeah, I'm losing feeling in my throwing arm—real adorable."

Since he's immobile with Chloe sleeping on him and he can't stop me, I scoot back, turn around, and slide my phone to camera mode. I tap the screen to focus and take a picture of them.

"Are you gonna help me, or ogle me some more?" Carter asks when I'm done.

"I'm still deciding," I admit. "Since you've probably impregnated me, my heart is seizing up at the image of you being so paternal with her."

"I guess you won't make me wear a condom tonight, huh?" he murmurs.

"No, I'm still gonna make you wear a condom," I say, since I can't be sure he's joking. "This will surely get less endearing after I've lived as your unpaid nanny for a while, and you've snuffed out all my aspirations and replaced them with baby diapers."

"You're cynical as hell about any chance of a future with me, aren't you?"

"I'm not bein' cynical, just realistic. Why doesn't the prospect of teenage pregnancy scare you?" I ask, since he gave me a solid opening.

"Babies aren't scary."

"I know, they're adorable, but they're also an enormous responsibility, not to mention a lifelong commitment. You and I wouldn't just be stuck tryin' to live our lives around a newborn's schedule, we would be stuck with *each other* forever. I'm not saying we couldn't make it work, but it would be far from ideal, and I don't understand why it doesn't terrify you. It terrifies *me*."

"Because you have it in your head it would ruin your life," he says, simply.

"Why don't you?" This is the part I don't understand.

"Because I know it *doesn't.*"

"*How* do you know that? Have you knocked a girl up before?"

His dark eyes shutter with something like annoyance. Instead of answering me, he braces a hand on Chloe's back and sits up. Her little head lolls, but he stands and readjusts her weight. She stirs just enough to wrap her arms around his neck, but her eyes drift closed immediately, and she rests her head on his shoulder.

"I'm taking her up to bed," he tells me.

My hammering heart sinks down into my gut. It took so much courage to push that question out, and he's ignoring it. It's also a completely crazy question. Even if the answer turns out to be yes, it's still a crazy thing to have to ask my 18-year-old boyfriend of roughly 3 minutes.

I know I can't ask it again, either. I don't like that he won't just give me satisfactory answers to certain questions so I can put them to bed. I don't like that he keeps me uncertain and makes me feel crazy. Pre-Carter, I didn't have fits of insecurity thinking my boyfriend might already be unfaithful. I didn't worry that I would get pregnant, or that my grades would drop and tank my future, or about almost any of the things I worry about now.

I let Carter off the hook a lot, but he has to know that some-times he has to cut the evasive bullshit and actually *answer* me. The only way he'll learn is if I show him, so not for the first time, while he carries Chloe up to bed, I grab my purse, slip my shoes on, and get ready to leave.

When Carter comes back, he slows down as he takes in the fact that I'm ready to go. "Where do you think you're going?" he asks casually as he approaches.

"Home," I tell him, sliding my purse onto my shoulder. "I have a long day of work and studying ahead of me tomorrow, so I need to get some sleep."

Wrapping his arms around my waist and tugging me close, he asks, "And you don't think I'll let you get any sleep if you stay here?"

Cracking a smile despite myself, I tell him, "I cannot stay here *again*."

"Why not?"

"Because I don't live here. I told my mom I was helpin' you babysit your little sister and then I'd be home. Babysitting is finished. Time for me to go."

"You can't just ask a guy if he's ever knocked someone up and then bail," Carter states.

"Why not? Didn't seem like you planned to answer me, anyway. If the answer was no, it would have been pretty simple to just say that. If the answer is yes…" I trail off, shaking my head, because I don't even know how to keep going.

It's one of those thoughts I don't expect I'll have to finish, because despite the insanity of this even being a question, the answer *has* to be no. I have no frame of reference for where to even go after this if it isn't.

Instead of immediately setting my mind at ease, Carter asks, "If the answer is yes…?"

My stomach knots up and lightens all at once, like I just jumped off a ledge and now I'm anticipating the *splat* of my body hitting pavement. "I don't…" I shake my head, searching for words. "I don't know. Then I have about a million more questions."

"What's at the top of the list?"

I try to pull back, but he doesn't let me go. "Is the answer yes, then? Who? When? Did she keep it? Was it Erika? Is that why you literally make her crazy? Is Chloe really your little sister? My God. You're *eighteen*."

"Breathe," he says mildly, watching my face.

I'm too busy freaking out to breathe. He needs to start answering some of my questions, but at the same time, I'm afraid of my own reaction if he does.

As much as I've been able to swallow, there's something about this I can't get down. I'll feel bad pushing him away for telling me the truth, but some truths are just too hard to swallow.

It's not even Chloe. If she is his, it's wild that he could possibly be my age and have a five-year-old, but it's more the idea that he has already experienced that milestone with someone else that bothers me—especially if it was Erika. I *need* to know if it was Erika. She'll never leave me alone, not in a million years, if it was her.

Much more calmly, Carter tells me, "It's too soon to have this conversation. I know that's a shitty answer and I'm sorry for it, but it's too soon."

"I mean, this is the conversation, Carter. You can't just leave me hanging from the edge of a cliff like that. Whether you want to give me details or not, you basically answered the question. It's yes."

"It's not as simple as that," he states, running his hands down my arms in a stabilizing rhythm.

"Was it Erika?"

"No, it wasn't Erika. She has nothing to do with this," he answers. "I didn't get anyone—" He stops, shaking his head and looking away from me. "I just need you to trust me on this, all right? It's not what you're imagining. I'll explain it to you some-day, but you know all you need to know right now."

"Did you love her? The girl you…?"

"No."

"Do you still… I mean, is she around? Do you see her?"

"No. I promise you, you have nothing to worry about. There's nothing about this that will ever affect you. There are no hidden strings waiting to trip you. There's no baby mama drama, nothing like that. I have no ties to her. She's gone, and she's not coming back."

"Is it Chloe? Is she actually your…?" I can't quite get the word 'daughter' out of my mouth. It's too bizarre.

He hesitates briefly, then nods once.

I pieced that together myself, and I still feel I was just hit with a bagful of bricks.

"She doesn't know," he adds, like that might help. "She thinks I'm her brother. She's little, so she doesn't question it."

I need to sit down. Backing out of his embrace, I walk over to the couch and take a seat, holding onto the edge and remem-bering just a few minutes ago, when he was lying there on the couch with her.

Carter follows me over to the couch, but he doesn't sit beside me. He crosses his arms and stands there regarding me like a flight risk.

I *am* a flight risk. This verification of what felt like a far-fetched suspicion is opening up wormholes I don't want to fall through. I have to, though. I'm not going to be that girl. I'm not going to stick my head in the sand so I don't have to make the hard decisions.

I try to filter through all the things Carter has ever said that could pertain to this situation, but believing any of those things is predicated on accepting that he was being truthful when he told me he hadn't lied to me. When had he said it? I'm trying to remember which of his claims came before, and which ones came after. Even if he hadn't lied to me at the time he said that, it doesn't mean he didn't afterward.

"Why isn't she around anymore? The girl you got pregnant. That's an ominous statement coming from anyone, but coming from you…" I look up at him, dread weighing me down. "What does that mean?"

His jaw locks, and that doesn't fill me with optimism. "I've answered as many questions about this as I want to," he tells me.

"I have done a *lot* of things I haven't wanted to do for you," I point out. "I think, in fairness, you should have a single conversation you don't want to have for me."

"This doesn't have anything to do with you," he informs me, apparently immovable. "I don't want to fight with you. I'm not trying to close you out or hurt your feelings, but I don't want to talk about this, and I need you to respect that."

Launching up off the couch, wide-eyed, I tell him, "And I didn't want to blow you in front of your douchebag teammates or give you my virginity in Cartwright's basement. Sometimes you don't get what you want, and all you can do is fucking deal with it."

That should be the truth, that should be the winning hand. As much as I've overlooked for him, I really feel like he *owes me* a few minutes of discomfort. Telling me about some hook-up he impregnated is not even close to the level of what I've had to process and put away. I don't have a problem making risky emotional investments in him, but if he can't occasionally repay the favor... well, fuck that. That's not a relationship, it's emotional charity, and I'm not here for that.

I'm just about to say that, too. I swear to God, I am, but before I can, Carter grabs me by the throat. Not hard, not to hurt me, just enough to startle me. Then he takes advantage of my shock to guide me until my back is pressed against a wall. The alarm coursing through me steals my words for a moment. I'm just about to open my mouth and tell him to get his hands off me when his hand falls away from my throat.

I swallow and take in his expression, his energy, to gauge potential danger now that he's not a moment away from choking me.

"Maybe I was unclear," he says evenly, his fingertips skating down my left arm. I pull it away from him and his dark eyes snap to my face. "This isn't a debate. The topic is closed."

Glaring at him and moving my arm away from his touch, I tell him, "Well, so are my legs."

A slow, dark smile spreads across his sensual lips. "Until I pry them open, sure."

"Don't you dare. I'm not playing with you right now, Carter. This isn't a game. This is not a relationship if you get the upper hand all the damn time and I get whatever scraps you want to throw me. I didn't sign up for that. I'm not interested in that. If you want me to trust you, you have to be willing to open up *some* corner of yourself to me. I can't be the only one bending in every single scenario. This can't be all work for me, and all fun for you. I can't trust that."

"You don't trust me, anyway," he states. "Even when I do things right, it doesn't matter."

"That's not true," I say, my stomach sinking at his words.

"Yes, it is. If you want to hold a grudge, Zoey, at least be honest about it. I'm not blaming you. It's normal. I thought you were giving me a chance, but hey, maybe I was wrong. Maybe you were just holding onto ammunition so you could use it against me when the right opportunity presented itself. Maybe you're just like everyone else."

Ouch. "Don't say that. You don't believe that."

"Maybe I do. Everyone wants something, Zoey," he says,

trailing the back of his hand along my jaw line. "What do you want from me?"

I hate that I feel my insides collapsing under the chill of his response, but there's danger in what he's saying. Not real, physical danger, but his words highlight the risk of extinguishing his main interest in me—and extinguishing it wrongly, because I *am* what he thinks I am. It's not self-interest that compels me to try to reach him or to put up with his shit, but he's already pretty convinced most people are users. Once he puts me in that category, I have a feeling there's no getting back out of it.

"You want to be the special one?" he asks, his gaze raking over me before returning back to my face. "I've given you that, haven't I? You wanted people to leave you alone about Jake, so I stopped it. I helped you with your stupid church fundraiser. I introduced you to my family so you'd know I was serious. I think it's unfair to say I never give, Zoey. I think I do, just in a different way than you do."

I want to mutter that the fundraiser wasn't stupid, but that's not the right thing to be defensive about right now. "I wasn't implying you never do anything nice for me," I tell him. "But you pick and choose. You give when it doesn't cost you anything. I give when the cost is high. This is the first thing that's ever seemed like it cost you anything, and you don't want to talk to me about it."

He doesn't bother to disagree. "That's right, I don't. I respect your boundaries when you tell me I have to, so respect mine."

"When, Carter? When have you *really* respected my boundaries because I said no? Certainly not in the classroom."

"That doesn't count. It was before."

"Fine. Not when I told you I didn't want to go to a party at your ex's house and you vaguely threatened to rape my best friend if I didn't show up to take her place. Not when I said 'I don't want to lose my virginity tonight' and you said 'fuck this' and took it anyway. Definitely not when I asked you not to come inside me and you did, twice. I can come up with more examples if you need me to."

Instead of looking remotely ashamed, Carter says, "I never threatened to rape Grace."

"Yes, you did. After that, and what you did to me, and what you said you *wanted* to do to me, how am I supposed to just... not worry about this skeleton in your closet? What did you do to that girl? What happened to her? Why is she not around anymore? Why do you have Chloe and no concerns that her mom might resurface? Is she not *able* to resurface? We make jokes about where your moral line is, but to be honest, I have no idea. I don't know if you have one. You're a slippery slope, and I do look for the best in you, but I'm not going to close my eyes to reality in order to lie to myself."

His voice drops, a hint of menace creeping in as he snaps, "Don't pussyfoot around the question, Ellis. If you're trying to ask me something, go ahead and fucking ask."

Every cell in my body shrieks at me to drop it and extract myself from this situation as peacefully as I'm able, but the part of my brain that has become familiar with Carter is less afraid, despite his tone. "Did you hurt her?" I ask, my voice wobbling. I don't know if I *want* the answer, but I need it. "You told me you had never done anything like that to someone before, but you also told me Chloe was your sister, so... it's not true that you've never lied to me, and if this is one of the things you've lied about, maybe that was, too."

Now I've pissed him off. I can see it in the tenseness of his muscles, in the clenched jaw and flaring of his nostrils as he breathes. Judging by appearances, not throttling me is taking intense physical restraint on his part, and while I find it a little worrying, apparently not enough, because instead of running, I remain plastered against the wall and wait for him to answer my question.

"Did I hurt her?" he repeats calmly, slowly, like he's savoring the anger that question stokes inside. He moves closer and plants his arms on the wall on either of me to frame me in. I stiffen, knowing he's trying to intimidate me. To punish me for asking such an ugly question.

He closes the distance, leaning in and bending his head like he's going to kiss me. Instead, he buries his face in the curve of my neck. I shiver at the sensation of his warm breath against the sensitive skin. My nerve endings come alive when he presses his lips there, but I push him away. He's evading the question, and that's terrifying.

"I need you to answer this one, Carter. I need the truth."

Grabbing my wrists, he roughly pins them to the wall over my head. "Did I *rape* her?" he asks, cocking an eyebrow.

I refuse to flinch. "Did you?"

Disdain drips from his tone as he answers, "No."

I want to feel relieved. Maybe I *should* feel relieved, but it's hard to manufacture the sensation of relief when confronted with an angry Carter Mahoney. "Okay. I just had to ask. You know how scary it is to trust you, Carter. We're still technically gettin' to know each other, so… I mean, I had to ask."

"Do you believe me?"

His tone is even, but it sets off alarm bells, anyway. "Yes. Should I?"

He shrugs. "I'm telling the truth. Doesn't necessarily mean you have to believe it."

"Is she… alive?"

His lips curve up faintly. There's a look in his eyes that makes me want to take the question back, but he doesn't answer me. Not with words, anyway. He shrugs his shoulders slowly, a hard expression on his handsome face. His response could mean it's none of my business and he's not going to tell me, or it could indicate he doesn't know if she's alive and doesn't care.

This is torture. Piecing out the truth like this, offering what's affordable and withholding the rest. I want the whole truth, not just fragments of it. I want him to go all in on me, not stick with the safer bets. I want to know all of him, every dark corner; I don't want to be relegated to the surface layer like everybody else.

Maybe he's right, maybe I do want to be the special one, but only because that's the only way I can really *know* him. You wouldn't think it seeing him surrounded by friends in the halls at school, but Carter Mahoney is a fortress, and he keeps everyone locked out.

I want in.

I realize I've been escalating his resistance by battling him for the truth. I will never win openly fighting him like this. He won't suddenly back down because I bitched about it enough—that's not Carter. He doesn't operate that way. Fighting him will only lessen my chances of getting what I want, and never getting the truth raises the chances I'm going to lose my damn mind trying to keep up with this asshole.

His hands are still on me. That's important. As annoyed as he is with me, as agitated as I'm making him, he still wants to touch me.

I tug my wrists free of his hold and lean toward him, arching away from the wall just enough to reach the zipper on the back of my dress. Carter's eyes narrow with suspicion as I drag it down and the fabric around me loosens. Without a word, I push the top of the dress down my arms, then pull on the fabric until it falls to the floor.

Carter's gaze turns hot as he looks over my offering, at first lingering on my breasts, then drifting down my abdomen, finally settling between my thighs before returning to my face. There's a glint of distrust in his dark eyes, but he doesn't say anything.

Wordlessly, I step forward, bringing my body against his. His heat sears me and my blood warms as I hold his gaze, refusing to waver. I loop one arm around his neck and rest the other over his strong shoulder, then I bend my head and kiss my way along his strong jaw. I kiss his neck the way he tried to kiss mine just a moment ago, but his body is rigid and unresponsive. That just makes me try harder. My arm over his shoulder drifts down to his waist and I pull him against me, subtly rubbing my breasts against his hard chest, then kissing my way along his jaw again.

In a violent burst, he grabs a fistful of my hair and yanks my head back. My heart pounds as he backs me up the few remaining inches toward the wall, then pushes my shoulder until I drop to my knees. It's scary knowing he *could* hurt me if he wanted to, but not knowing if he will. I'm all twisted up, because it's not fear I feel the strongest. Lust stirs inside me as I look up at him, a need, newly awakened, pulsating in my core.

Carter holds my gaze as he unbuttons and unzips his pants, daring me to look away. Daring me to run. I don't know if I should. I don't know if he wants me to. Does he want to chase me? Does he want to punish me, to take out his aggressions? My breath quickens at the thought, so rather than wait for him to shove his cock in my face, I break his gaze and try to crawl away.

He's on me in an instant, his sharp reflexes and physical strength making it so easy to trap me. I'm caught beneath his body, tummy down, as he forces his hand between my legs and slides it inside my panties. I try to crawl away again, but he keeps me right where he wants me. My stomach twists up with desire, and I groan as he pushes a finger inside me. I struggle by instinct, even though I'll die of disappointment if he takes that pressure off my clit.

"You like that?" he asks roughly, still holding me down. "I sure do."

I'm breathing too heavily to respond, but I don't know what he'd want me to say, anyway. I don't care. All I care about is the pleasurable sensations coursing through my body as he touches me.

I never know what to expect when Carter opens his mouth, but right now as he fingers me, he yanks on my hair again and leans close to my ear, telling me in a low, gravelly murmur. "I think about that day in the classroom all the time, you know?"

My heart rate jumps, but I don't move. I don't speak. I just wait to see where he's going with this. A strangely timed apology, or a barbed taunt, intended to further punish me for pushing him tonight?

"You looked so fucking pretty, all outraged and helpless. You know what I never understood, though? You could've stopped it. All you had to do was lie to Jake, pretend you liked him for five minutes. He would've called me off and protected you, but you stood by your fucking principles and told the poor bastard the truth."

I don't know if he actually expects me to answer him while he's doing this, but I swallow and offer one up, anyway. "It would've only been a temporary fix. If I pretended to like him when I didn't, then I would've had to deal with it later."

"Maybe. Or maybe you wanted to play with me," he offers.

Even though I do *currently* want to play with him, I damn sure didn't then, so I shake my head. "That wasn't it. You've obviously grown on me, but you're an acquired taste."

"You like me now though, don't you, princess?" His finger circles my clit and I throw my head back against his shoulder, a faint noise of pleasure escaping my throat. "You like when I hold you down and play with you, when I treat you like my little whore. You're good at that role, aren't you?"

His words combined with his fingers toying with me send a naughty spike of pleasure soaring through me, but I remain on edge. I don't know where he's going with this. I don't know if he's in the mood to be nice or mean, but my money is on mean.

His touch is rougher than I want it to be, but I don't complain. I'm pretty sure he doesn't care in this moment, even if he will later. My body is still responsive; spikes of pleasure still hit me as he toys with me. Then the pleasure ratchets up and I lean back against him, feeling my body building toward orgasm.

Carter bites my neck, keeping the pressure on my clit. I gasp at the unexpected sting of pain, but I'm entirely focused on the pleasure I know is coming my way.

"You like that?" he demands.

"Yes." My response is rushed, my breathing heavy.

The stimulation intensifies, my breaths come in short bursts. Then, just as I'm about to fall over the edge into an abyss of pleasure, Carter withdraws his finger from between my thighs.

"No," I groan, hugging the hardwood floor.

Behind me, Carter pulls down my panties and smacks my ass. "Up."

"You're mean," I inform him, wanting to glare at him, but too disappointed to move.

"I'm gonna get meaner if you don't fucking listen," he tells me, smacking my ass hard enough that I jump. Since my skin is stinging and another slap might follow further disobedience, I push myself up on my forearms and thrust my ass in the air.

"Better, master?" I ask dryly.

His voice is warm and rich, and his satisfaction washes over me like liquefied pleasure as he runs his hand over the stinging skin of my ass, appeased. "It sure is. Beautiful."

A warm flush crawls up my chest and neck, no doubt coloring my cheeks. "Thank you," I murmur, a bit uncertainly.

There's a rustling of stiff fabric as he shoves down his jeans and then I feel him move closer. He rubs the head of his cock against my entrance, then pushes it inside me. I can tell by the way it feels, the stretch of my skin, he's going in bare again. I sigh, but don't bother bitching about it. He's going to do it either way, so what's the point?

"Will you hate me if I get you pregnant?" he asks.

He's not deep, just pushing the smooth tip inside me and pulling out. Just playing with me. Carter's exploration of my boundaries is hard, because he forces me to be brutally honest— not just with him, but myself. He won't let me have a comfort zone. I know he'll interpret me telling him I won't hate him as permission, but I also know if I start telling him too many things will make me hate him, the threat will lose all meaning and become ineffective. I can only tell him I'll hate him for doing something if I really will. I can only say no if he's really *at* my limit. With Carter, you can only tap out if you literally can't take anymore. Anything before a hard limit is fair game.

"I won't right now," I tell him, carefully. "I probably will someday."

He rubs his hand over my ass again. "Good answer."

I roll my eyes, even though he can't see me. Leave it to Carter to test me when he's about to have sex with me.

He pushes himself deeper and I have to flatten one hand against the floor to brace myself. This position on the floor is hard on my knees. I wish he would've moved us to the couch first. Wish he would've put a condom on, too. I have to figure out how to get things I want out of Carter. Arguing doesn't work. Asking certainly hasn't worked. I guess submission doesn't entirely work either, because I more or less submitted, and he is thrusting deep with no protection. I don't know what else to try.

Carter grabs hold of my hair and pushes me down until my cheek is pressed against the floor. My stomach pitches as he holds me down even more roughly and thrusts his cock inside me. This is rougher, dirtier, even less comfortable, but a shudder of pleasure moves right through me as he pumps inside me, as he fills me up. He's holding me down and using me. Punishing me. I should hate this. Why don't I hate this?

"This pussy belongs to me, doesn't it, princess?" Carter asks.

I swallow, trying to hold on to the floor to stay in one place as he fucks me.

His fist tightens in my hair, and he thrusts so brutally a little yelp slips out of me. "Answer me."

"Yes," I offer promptly.

"I can do whatever I want to it, can't I?"

I try to get a better hold on the floor. This time I know he wants a response, and I know which one, too. "Anything you want."

The challenge melts out of his voice and it's warm again, so it washes over me like the reward it is when he says, "Mm, good girl."

He's trying to train me. That's funny, since I'm trying to train him, too. Oh well. I guess it works out if we train each other. I certainly can't claim his training isn't working, because it is. But so is mine. Kinda. I may not be getting my way all the time, but I'm pretty sure I'm making more progress with him than anyone else ever has.

My belief is strengthened when, after I've taken a few more brutal pumps without complaint, Carter lets go of my hair and pulls out of my body. I wait, breathing heavily, to see what comes next. I stay in position because he hasn't told me to move. Then I hear something that sounds suspiciously like a foil packet being torn open and my heart leaps. Is he…?

Carter's hands settle on my hips, and he nudges me. "On your back."

I roll over onto my back so I'm looking up at him. My stomach rocks with a strange mix of feelings when I see the condom wrapper discarded on the ground beside us. I want to kiss him, so I do. I arch up, grab his face, and kiss him, the flavor of gratitude on my lips as they soften under his.

Beneath the gratitude, I feel victorious. Submission *did* work, he just had to prove his point first, show me he'd take what he wanted and see how I responded. Naturally, I responded the right way, so now he'll respect my wishes.

Warmth spreads through me. I love his twisted ways. Carter may be difficult to maneuver sometimes, but he fascinates me.

Carter breaks the kiss and slides his hands down the outside of my thighs. Then he lifts my legs and moves until he's hovering over me with my bent legs resting on his shoulders. He leans down and brushes his lips across mine, then braces his weight on one arm while he reaches down with the other and guides his cock between my legs.

His condom-covered cock.

I can't help smiling. I can't help kissing him again. Then as I'm kissing him, he shoves inside me and steals my breath. Steals my *soul*.

"Oh, Carter," I murmur, struggling to adjust as he fills me in a way he never has before. "Oh, God."

Pressing his forehead to mine in a show of tenderness, he moves inside me. As the breadth of his cock steadily rubs my walls, intense pleasure courses through my body. Again and again and again. I can't stop moaning as he moves in and out of me, as the pleasure builds and builds.

It's not just the pleasure that feels so incredible, but the intimacy between us. Having him so close fills me with affection while he uses his body to fill me with pleasure. Between all that, the submission of my position juxtaposed with the dominance of his, and the faint background feeling of finally getting my hands on a hard-won reward, my heart opens up like a flower, unafraid of exposing its delicacy to damage from such a potentially dangerous visitor.

When my body can't take anymore, it vaults over the precipice, free-falling into pleasure. I cry out and Carter kisses me, catching the sounds of my pleasure against his lips. The pleasure goes on as he rubs my sensitive walls, extending the pleasure.

"Fuck, Zoey," he murmurs, closing his eyes.

All the strength rushes out of my body. I slide a bit on the floor as Carter continues to pump into me, but I don't have the energy to try to hold myself in place. Turns out I don't have to; a moment later he groans, his muscles go taut, and he thrusts deep. I don't feel him come this time because he's wearing the condom, but once he's spent, he collapses on top of me like before.

Thoroughly satisfied and still bursting with affection, I wrap my arms around Carter and hold him close. I love the feeling of his warm, muscular back beneath my fingers. When I get the energy back, I want him to roll over so I can kiss him everywhere, trail my lips over the ridges of his washboard abs, kiss my way down the V framing his pelvic area. Hell, I'll take him in my mouth again and really show my gratitude for all that pleasure.

I sigh blissfully, caught up in a sexy thought bubble of all the things I want to do to his body, then he lifts his head up just enough to kiss me.

My brain sees where I'm going and makes a valiant effort to stop my mouth from moving, but it gets ignored. When my determined mouth opens, I let crazy, reckless words tumble right out.

"I think I love you."

My stomach bottoms out even though my tone was light and dreamy, far from a heavy declaration. He'll still probably take it a weird way. My brain immediately starts generating justifications and excuses. This explosion of hormones and affection has left me vulnerable; the hit of oxytocin makes me feel fonder of him, the flood of dopamine to my brain has clearly impaired my ability to reason. I might as well be on drugs! He can't hold me responsible for things I say during sex, just like I don't hold him accountable for things he says during sex—the only difference is that he says mean stuff and I say nice stuff. Besides, I'm a Christian; I love everybody! It doesn't have to *mean* anything dramatic…

Instead of getting freaked out, though, Carter grins. "Oh yeah? Damn, I must have fucked you good."

I smile back with faint relief and nod my head. "So good."

After a lingering kiss, he tells me, "Spend the night and I'll do it again."

Mm, that's tempting. "I'll ask my mom," I tell him. "In any case, could we move this production off the floor? It's not the most comfortable place in the world. Usually when I'm lyin' on the floor, I at least have a nice, cushiony yoga mat beneath me."

"Yeah," he murmurs, climbing off me. "I've gotta go get rid of this stupid fucking condom, anyway."

I offer him another glowing smile. "Thank you."

Since he gets up first, I allow myself a moment to admire his well-sculpted ass as he walks away. He's so sexy. I want to say all the nice things to him right now.

I wish I could bottle up these lovey post-orgasm feelings so I can take hits later, when he's testing my patience.

Oh well, might as well enjoy the dopamine rush while it lasts.

CHAPTER 33

AFTER A BRIEF TEXT exchange with my mom grants me permission to stay the night, Carter does, in fact, sex me into a stupor again.

This time, we're in his bed, and he doesn't bother with a condom, but at least I won one round. I already have an appointment Monday after school to get on birth control, so I'll ask the doctor for whatever starts working immediately.

Once he's finished putting me in a blissful pleasure coma, Carter curls his arms around me and pulls my back snugly against his chest, keeping me close.

"Tell me something I don't know about you," I request.

"Something you don't know? Hm. I like rough sex."

I chuckle, lightly smacking the hand he has settled on my hip. "Very funny."

"I like blondes," he offers, playing with a flaxen lock of my hair.

"Carter Mahoney. Something real."

"I don't know what you want me to tell you," he says, being difficult, just because he's him.

"I'd like to know everything, so feel free to start anywhere—except 'my favorite color is blue,' because that doesn't really tell me anything."

"Tells you what color lingerie you should invest in," he offers.

Cocking an eyebrow, I look over my shoulder at him and say sweetly, "Oh, but you've already bought me Longhorn blue panties. Remember, baby?"

Sliding me an unamused look, he says, "I've never had a pet. How's that?"

I'll take that, I suppose. "Really? Why not? Allergies? Just didn't want one?"

"Until I was 13, we lived in Manhattan. It's harder to have a dog in the city and my dad doesn't like cats. Mom said I could get a fish, but that's a pretty lame pet, don't you think?"

"I had a fish, actually. A goldfish named Juniper. Unfortunately, it didn't live for much longer than a year. I wouldn't mind having fish again as an adult, if I had an actual aquarium with a filtration system and all that. Colorful gravel in the bottom, some of those cute coral things for them to play hide and seek in when I'm trying to find them in the tank."

Curling his hand around my hip, he says, "See, you even make fish sound like fun. I always imagined it floating in the tank all bug-eyed and getting bored with it in ten minutes."

I crack a smile. "You probably would. My fish would be my reading buddy. I'd set up a comfy chair in the corner by its aquarium and read it some of my favorite passages. When I'm so tired of studying for classes that I wanna die, I would turn to my fish for moral support. My fish would feel very important, and it would like me a lot more than yours would like you."

"Without a doubt. You'd probably chop up fucking broccoli to feed it snacks. I *might* remember to put some fish flakes in its bowl."

I shake my head. "You're never allowed to have fish unless we live together or you have hired help, tasked with caring for the fish. Promise me."

"Aw, come on. Chloe would probably like a fish if it had all that colorful shit in the tank. She'd name it something stupid like Princess Penelope. It'd be great."

"Chloe would probably take better care of it than you, and she's five." Since we're back on the subject of Chloe, though, I take advantage and guide us back to more important things. "Speaking of Chloe…"

"There it is," he murmurs, knowing what's coming.

"What's the plan?" I ask him. "You're actually going to set up a bedroom for her at your place." I pause, rolling onto my back so I can look at him less awkwardly. "So, are you planning for her to move in with you at some point? Is this custody situation with your parents temporary, or permanent? Are they just caring for her while you're in school, or…?"

Carter sighs heavily, like this weighs on his mind, too. I imagine him losing sleep thinking about it nights when I'm not here. "I don't know. It's kind of a mess. The original plan was for them to take her on permanently, full-time. I didn't want any part of it. But then she was born, y'know? She was a cute little shit, right out of the gate. My mom, she's the one who insisted on raising her, but she goes through these bouts of depression. When they hit her, sometimes she can't even get out of bed, and one hit her when Chloe was six weeks old. My sister tried to come over and help as much as she could, but she had her own stuff going on, so I ended up spending a lot of time with Chloe without meaning to. I'd just prop her up on her pillow on my bed while I did homework. She'd chew on her fist and watch me like a cute little creep."

I grin at the mental image of a baby keeping an eye on Carter.

"Anyway, she grew on me before long. I didn't worry much about her living situation until moving back to New York for college became a reality. Now it's something I've gotta think about, but it's not exactly simple. If I move away, she'll get used to never seeing me. Then my parents will be her only caregivers, and I'll pretty much… I can never tell her the truth if we do that. She'll feel like I abandoned her—especially since my parents aren't exactly the best, temperament-wise. My mom means well, but she's all fucked up. My dad's mean. Chloe's a tough cookie, I know she'd be all right if I left her here, but… I don't know."

"You don't want to leave her here," I say simply. If his clear affection for her didn't give me a strong enough vibe, his lowkey attempts to impregnate me and lock down a nanny—I'm certain now that's his end game, whether he realizes it or not—certainly do.

"I don't know if it'd be fair to take her though, either. I mean, *should* I really tell her the truth? I'm her brother, as far as she knows. She wouldn't have a mother if she went with me. I'd have to make something up to explain why hers isn't around."

"The mother, I take it she's from New York. Does she still live there?"

Smiling faintly, he shakes his head. "Nice try. I told you I didn't want to talk about that."

"But then I let you have rapey sex with me. If that doesn't buy me information, what am I doin' it for?"

Biting back an even bigger smile, he leans over and gives me a kiss. "My affection."

"Mm, so high maintenance," I murmur against his lips.

Tugging my bottom lip into his mouth, he sucks on it for a few seconds, then releases it. Still hovering over me, he tells me, "I didn't hear you complaining."

"No complaints here," I agree. "It could be you've broken my brain, but no complaints, all the same." He burrows into my neck next. I'm already naked from the last round, so when he pushes his hand under the thin cover of his crisp sheets, his palm comes directly into contact with my breast. He cups it, massaging it as he kisses my neck. My eyes drift closed as a shudder of pleasure moves through me.

As tempted as I am to let him pull me under, I resist. Puzzling out Carter's motivations is a game I feel like I'll be playing for as long as I keep him around, but right now, I'm fairly certain I need to block my womb.

Pulling back so he knows I want to talk more, I tell him, "Obviously, you're not going to try to ruin my life so you have a babysitter though, because that would be a really shitty thing to do."

"Obviously," he offers, lightly, playfully. "I would never do anything shitty."

"Of course not. You're an angel."

"Shiniest halo on the block," he agrees.

"But just in case you *were* thinking about doing that, don't. If you and I are still together when you go off to college, we'll figure something out. I looked it up, and it's about a 7 hour drive from—*hopefully*—my college to yours, so I don't think frequent visits would be a realistic possibility. But if you're staying in the city once the semester is over, maybe I could come stay with you during breaks from school." Not wanting him to think I'm banking on us lasting forever, I add, "And that's obviously a very big if, but I'm just saying. If we still want to be together, we'll figure out a way. No one has to do anything drastic."

Dragging the tip of his finger over my curve of my shoulder, he watches my face and asks, "How would you feel about the Chloe situation?"

"I would feel better if you told me everything about it."

He rolls his eyes. "I know that. I meant, how would you feel about her potentially living with me? That's a lot to ask of you. I've had years to get used to all this, but you haven't. Probably didn't think when you started dating me, *this* would be something you'd have to deal with."

"No, of all the things I knew I would have to deal with, this certainly wasn't one," I admit. "But that's entirely up to you, don't factor me into that decision. Do whatever you think is best for you and Chloe. I'm flexible. I can adjust."

"It's not a deal-breaker, though?" he asks, for verification.

"No, of course not. Chloe's adorable and I like kids. It wasn't my plan, certainly, but it's definitely not a deal-breaker, either. Still no deal-breakers as far as I can see."

"Huh," he murmurs, bending his head so he can brush his lips against mine. "Good."

Looping my arm around his neck, I tug him even closer. "Very good."

CHAPTER 34

I CAN'T SHAKE the vague sense of dread brought on by the dwindling of my remaining weekend hours. It has been so nice spending my time with Carter and not having to deal with reality. Monday will bring with it the stress of homework, the inevitability of Erika glaring at me in the halls, Jake lurking in the shadows like an irritant that won't stop, and Grace not knowing what to think or how to respond to my being with Carter. Then after all that, I have to endure the awkwardness of going to get birth control and trying to explain to my doctor that I need the fast-acting stuff because I have an uncontrollable boyfriend… but without setting off any alarm bells that will have her handing me domestic abuse pamphlets I don't need.

Sunday I have to work, but the bookstore is empty. By the time I've finished sorting fiction for clearance and reorganizing the books around the register, I'm bored out of my mind. I already studied my notes on my phone at Carter's last night, but with nothing else to do, I pull them out and start reading through them again.

"What's a guy gotta do to get a little service around here?"

I smile at the sound of Carter's voice and look up, clearing my phone screen and sliding it into the pocket of my jeans as I step toward the counter. "What are you doin' here, troublemaker?"

"Checking out this hot cashier who works here," he says, letting his gaze travel over my body. "Don't tell my girlfriend."

I play along, asking, "Is she a real ball-buster?"

"She'd kick my ass."

Bracing my palms on the countertop, I lean in and give him a kiss. "All right, I'll keep your secret. But only if you don't tell my boyfriend. He's fucking crazy."

Carter chuckles against my lips before murmuring, "Damn right he is."

Since I shouldn't really be kissing him at work, I pull back. There's really no one around to see, anyway. Even the manager went in the back to do paperwork, since no one is coming in to sell any books.

Not seeing Chloe anywhere, I ask, "No cute little sidekick today, huh?"

He shakes his head. "Didn't think I'd need one this time." Glancing around the empty aisles of books, he asks, "Has it been this dead all day?"

"Yep. I've done every bit of side work that belongs to me, *and* some that belongs to other people. I'm just watchin' the minutes tick by at this point."

"Why don't you recommend me some books," he suggests. "Surely a nerd like you has wet dreams about bookstore dates. Let's squeeze one in since no one's here."

Rolling my eyes as I walk around to the outside of the counter, I tell him, "Whatever, you like my nerdy ass."

Coming up behind me, he grabs my butt. "I sure do. And what was that thing you said to me last night?" he muses.

"I don't know what you're talking about. I didn't say anything last night. Zero words were spoken by me."

Playing along, he says, "No, there was something. Something about how you felt about me. An l-word?"

"Get your hands off my butt before you get me fired," I say, pushing his hand away.

"You're the only one in the store."

"The manager is in the back, and we do have cameras."

Carter glances up at the ceiling, checking to see where the

cameras are pointed. "And he'll fire *you* because a customer groped you?"

"Probably. This world is a fucked-up place," I tell him, shaking my head. Glancing back at him over my shoulder as I lead him toward the small Beats section where many of the books that make me think of him reside, I inquire, "Have you ever read Bukowski?"

"Nope. Should I have?"

"I have a feeling you might like him," I tell him, leading him down to the end of the aisle, then squatting down to peruse the limited selection. "*Tales of Ordinary Madness* makes me think of you," I add, pulling our single copy from the shelf. It's a weathered copy with aged pages, but that's okay. Handing it to Carter, I explain, "His writing style isn't for everyone, but if you can get into it, my hunch is you might enjoy his stuff. I'm gonna be really basic here for a minute, but I also think you'd like *Catcher in the Rye* if you haven't read it already."

"If it hasn't been assigned in class, I haven't read it."

"That has been assigned."

"If it has been assigned in class, I also might not have read it," he amends.

I shake my head disapprovingly. "You can't rally girl your way through law school, you know? Someday you might actually have to do your own work."

"Nah, doing all the work is for plebs. I'm a delegator," he tells me, only half-joking.

"What's your plan when you leave high school? Bang all your professors?"

"Only the lady professors."

I wrinkle my nose up and turn to smack him in the abdomen. He smiles like a rogue, not even grunting from the impact. "This is why we're getting divorced."

"Because I'm charming?" he asks, innocently.

"Because you're a rule-flouting whore," I inform him. Turning on my heel, I lead him back through fiction toward Salinger. "*Franny and Zooey* is good, too. So is *Nine Stories*, actually. I bet you'd like Salinger."

"Man, you jump tracks like a ninja."

"My brain is sharp from all those years of doing my own work," I tell him sweetly over my shoulder.

"Work smarter, not harder," he offers back.

I shake my head, stopping and running my fingers down spines until I find what I'm looking for. "I have a hunch the real world is going to be quite an adjustment for you."

He turns to watch me peruse the shelves, shoving his hands into his pockets. "And *I* have a feeling you're the one who will be disillusioned, not me. You and I don't have the same 'real world,' princess. Haven't you figured that out by now?"

I drop my hand, momentarily abandoning my search. "That's only because we're in high school and you get to be Mr. Popularity. After high school is over—"

"After high school is over, I'll be Mr. Whatever I Have to be Next," he interrupts, looking almost sympathetic. "The world's not gonna change, Zo. What, you think we'll swap positions of power? After graduation, you'll be on top just because you work harder? Because you deserve it more? Because you're a better person? It doesn't mean anything, babe. I mean, it does to you, it's who you are, but that's not the world. I'll be on top long after high school has ended. Not because I'll deserve it any more then than I do now, but because I'll bring the right toolbox. That's it. It's that simple."

Given I *like* Carter, my stomach shouldn't feel so unsettled, but I hate the possibility that he's right. My mind and heart both reject his version of reality, stubbornly insisting it means something to be a good person. Someday, somehow... it will matter that I do the right thing and he does the wrong thing.

I don't like making us competitors right now because I know he would win every time, but surely *someday* I would be the victor. He's right—I work harder. I do the right thing. I *deserve it* more than he does.

He must be able to see he has poked a small hole in my dreams, because he reaches out to grab me and tugs me into his chest. "I'm sorry, I'm just being cynical," he says, although I know he doesn't mean it. Settling his arm around my shoulder to keep me close, he nods at the bookshelf. "Come on, pick out some books. Educate me."

"Why?" I mutter, glancing up at him. "So you can have your rally girl read them to you while you're practicing?"

"I'll read them all by myself, I promise," he says lightly, a small smile on his perfect lips. It's a smile he intends to be reassuring, but knowing he's only trying to placate me makes the gesture feel hollow.

Displeasure is leaking out of me now, and I can't put a stopper in it. Frowning up at him, I tell him, "It's not stupid to try. It's not stupid to be nice to people and do the right thing instead of the wrong thing. The world would be a lousy place if nobody cared. You obviously don't, but someone has to."

"I was just messing with you, Zoey," he assures me.

"But it was the truth," I state, staring at him. "You weren't messing with me, you told the truth and when I didn't like it, you tried to backpedal like you always do, because it wasn't worth it to you to stand your ground on this one. You're not invested in whether I agree or disagree because it doesn't affect you."

"Yes, Zoey, I'm a selfish monster. I think only of myself, always. None of your opinions or worldviews matter to me. You're just a trophy I can fuck."

My stomach drops at the possibility of truth in those words, and I take a step back.

Raking a hand through his hair, Carter says, "Jesus Christ. It was a joke, Zoey."

"That's a weird joke," I tell him. "Trophy? That's not a term I would've associated with myself. I'm not exactly a catch in this town. What makes me a trophy?"

This time, he knows better than to answer, but the gleam in his eye fuels my own suspicions and all of a sudden I know. It still doesn't make sense, but I know the answer.

"Jake," I say, softly. "He made me a trophy."

"I was joking," he says again, slowly. "I don't view you as a trophy. I don't even fucking value trophies—do you know how many of them I have?"

"Yeah, but you didn't have a Zoey," I say, shaking my head. "Not me. Not the stuck-up, church-going bookworm who didn't give a damn about how impressive you are. Despite all your accomplishments and easy-pickings, I wasn't on the menu for you, was I?"

Carter's jaw locks. I see the tick, so I shouldn't be surprised when he gets a little mean. "I don't know, Zoey, if memory serves, I put you on the menu. I've had *several* servings at this point," he reminds me.

That pisses me off. Plucking a book off the shelf, I shove a small paperback against his chest. "There's your book. Buy it or don't. I need to get back to the register."

"Why are you doing this?" he demands, following me. "Why are you picking a fight with me over nothing?"

"I'm not picking a fight with you, I'm doing my job."

He grabs my arm, pulling me backward and into the cooking section. "Stop."

I turn and glare up at him. "Don't tell me what to do."

Carter rolls his eyes, tugging me into the corner, then switching our positions. Now he's on the dominant side and I'm cornered between him and an intersection of books. Rather than argue with me, he grabs a fistful of my hair, yanks my head to the side, and kisses me. My heart hammers in my chest and I push against him, trying to shove him away. Carter drops his paperbacks and grabs my wrist, twisting it behind me and pinning me against the hard shelf of books.

It shouldn't turn me on, but being manhandled by him turns my blood hot. It should be anger, but it's something else. Interest stirs in my loins as he dominates my mouth, still firmly holding onto my hair. It only intensifies when he uses my hair to yank my head back and break the kiss, then pushes me down until I'm on my knees.

Then I hear him unzipping his jeans and my stomach bottoms out. My eyes widen as I look up at him. "Carter, what are you doing?"

"What does it look like I'm doing?" he asks evenly. Like the shameless bastard he is, he takes his cock out. "Open up, princess."

"Carter, I'm at *work*. I can't—"

"Next time you wanna be a pain in my ass, do it somewhere more convenient then," he says, unapologetically. His dark gaze lingers on my swollen lips, then darts back to my eyes. "Now, open that pretty mouth or I'll do it for you."

Despite the steel in his tone, I do open my mouth—to tell him no way, he's crazy, he's going to get me fired. I have a litany of incredibly valid reasons on the tip of my tongue. Before I can share a single one, Carter pushes the smooth tip of his cock between my lips.

"Watch your teeth," he warns, in case I've forgotten since last time.

I look up at him, adrenaline surging through my veins. We're in such a calm, ordinary space, a place I spend several boring hours every week, and Carter is defiling it just like he defiles everything else. Given he pushed me into the corner, we *are* in one of the blind spots of the security cameras, but anyone could walk in. The manager could come out of the back and walk right past. Carter could get me fired, and there's nothing I could say to defend myself in this scenario.

I should bite him. Not hard, not to hurt him, just to scare him, the fucking jerk. Making me give him a blow job while I'm on the clock. He's got some damn nerve.

I like his nerve, though. I don't know why, but his raging asshole side does things to me. The roughness of his hand fisted in my hair, the way he holds onto my head and uses my mouth for his own pleasure. Even if I tried to stop him right now, I doubt he would, and that should make me want to bite his dick right off, but instead it melts something in my brain. Instead, I find myself thinking, what the hell? If I'm risking getting fired, I might as well make it good.

Cornered in the cooking section, Carter fucks my face. There's no other way to put it. Calling this a blow job would be irrationally generous. He punishes my mouth for all the annoying things that come out of it, then pushes deep into my throat and makes me choke down his cum. It's filthy, harsh, and somehow hot. Tears leak out of the corners of my eyes from the brutality of it as I pull back and look up at him, swallowing down the last salty remnants of his pleasure.

Carter caresses my face affectionately, looking down at me. "Good girl."

His voice is warm and approving. I'm tempted to melt into his touch, but now that he's done, I'm more concerned about not getting caught. I bend to retrieve the paperbacks he dropped. He takes them, and I push up off the ground, swiping at the moisture under my eyes with the backs of my fingers.

"You okay?" he asks, somewhat reluctantly.

I nod my head, wiping my damp hands on the sides of my T-shirt. "Yeah. If I get fired, I'm going to murder you."

Offering a smile as he zips back up, he says, "If you get fired, I'll just give you the, what, 60 bucks a week you probably make here? I'm not too worried about it."

"You should be." I nod toward the ceiling, but don't point, lest I draw attention. "There are security cameras. If they caught what you just did, that's gotta count as indecent exposure, at the very least. That's not gonna look very good, Mr. Future Lawyer."

Carter shrugs and drapes an arm across my shoulder, tugging me into his side and kissing the crown of my head. "If the cameras caught it and anyone actually watches the tapes, my dad will just buy them. Your manager gets a nice, big bonus, the tape accidentally gets lost. Whoops."

"You have an answer for everything, don't you?" I ask, leaning into his side and wrapping my arm around him, nonetheless.

"Sure do. You like that about me."

He's right, I do. Still, I say, "Not when the things you say piss me off."

"It's bound to happen sometimes," he replies, unconcerned. "At least until you accept that you don't have to oppose me. You can be my partner. All my perks are your perks. It's not me vs. you, Zoey. We aren't opponents. When I win, you win."

"Until we *are* opponents. Then what?"

"I crush my opponents," he informs me casually, meeting my gaze. "Don't be one of them and you have nothing to worry about."

CHAPTER 35

AFTER SLEEPING in my own bed again, Monday morning I grab myself a cup of cold milk and a pack of Pop-Tarts for breakfast. It's quite a change from the feast-like breakfasts at Carter's house. I find myself thinking about the future, the one Carter likes to talk about like we really have one. Will Carter expect his live-in girlfriend to feed him like a king, too? I bet he will. He probably thinks that's normal. Meanwhile, I think cold Pop-Tarts for breakfast are normal. Chloe is used to the big breakfast spread, too. If she did move in with Carter and I stayed with them for any length of time, I would probably have to step up my breakfast game.

I almost hate thinking about it—not because I have a grudge against breakfast, but because I feel crazy to even consider it a possibility. It's tempting, not only because I like Carter, but because I like the life I could see us having together. I really do enjoy him as a person. He's spoiled, devious, and the mirror opposite of me in many ways, but we connect on a lot of levels, too. I would have never envisioned myself feeling genuine friendship with Carter Mahoney, but I genuinely like him, even when I think he's a pain in the ass. I don't want to get carried away daydreaming about a future that will never exist, though. A future he's not at all serious about, despite the things he says that lead me to believe maybe he is.

I don't know why it feels like things have to move so fast with Carter. Maybe it's because he *is* a lot to handle, he is a big gamble, and *he* moves fast. He blows past normal relationship checkpoints like they're made for other people, not for him. It's so easy to get swept up in his lightning speed, to fly as high as he does while he shares his powers, but I'm all too aware of how hard I'll fall if he suddenly lets go and I go plummeting back to earth.

"Hey, stranger," my mom says, smiling as she comes into the kitchen.

My cheeks flush faintly at the reminder of my sleepovers. "Good morning."

Crossing to the counter, not looking back at me, she says, "So, Dr. Lucker's office left an appointment reminder for you today. Something I should know about?"

She turns around to gauge my reaction. I'm frozen in awkwardness, horrified at the idea of the conversation that would undoubtedly follow the truth. I guess I should just tell her, though. She already knows I have spent the night at Carter's house, and Carter isn't a girl. She probably knows that wasn't innocent.

"I made an appointment to get on birth control," I tell her, looking at my Pop-Tart as I break it in half.

"I see," she returns evenly. "I guess this means your overnights with Carter...?"

"Yeah," I offer, but nothing else.

Mom nods again. "Do we need to talk about it?"

"Nope. I've got it under control," I assure her quickly, grabbing my glass of milk and taking a sip.

Rather than accepting it and letting it go that easily, she asks, "Is this—I mean, have you already... taken that step?" she asks, haltingly. "Or are you just getting ready in case it comes up?"

I would rather crawl right out of my skin than have this conversation with my mom. "I'm doing everything I can to be responsible," I tell her.

"How long have you two been dating?" she asks me. "You never tell me about anything. I have to hear about my own daughter's love life through gossip. How is it other people know more about you than I know myself?"

Rolling my eyes as I take a sip, I point out, "People generally don't *know*, they just talk and talk and talk. Carter and I are dating, and he is more accustomed to… a faster type of girl. It's hard to slow down when you're with him, and I would rather be safe than pregnant. That's a pretty detailed summary of my situation right now."

Her gaze shifts away awkwardly, but then she moves closer to the table to tell me, "Well, you know, sometimes it works better to make him chase you a little bit. You don't have to speed up to meet his pace. Make him slow down to meet yours. Show him you're a girl worth waiting for."

I don't bother telling her that ship has already sailed, or that Carter doesn't really switch speeds to accommodate other people. I'm not worried about making her dislike him—given who he is, I know it would take a lot—but it would be pointless. At best, it would make her stop asking questions and awkwardly leave the room. At worst, it would make her worry that I'm not in a safe relationship.

Actually, maybe the "at worst" is that she would tell me to suck it up because I've landed a whale, and then I would be annoyed at her for giving me even more bad advice than she already has.

No good can come of it, that's the point.

"I've got it under control," I say instead, flashing her a brief smile before turning my attention back to my breakfast.

ALTHOUGH THERE WAS nothing *normal* about my weekend, it finally feels like things are getting back to normal at school. There is no "Zoey the ho" greeting waiting for me today as I head for the school's entrance doors. A couple of jocks are lingering around the stone wall where Carter sometimes holds court, but he's not there to command them. Even so, when they notice me, rather than taunts, I get a nod of acknowledgement and a friendly, rhetorical "what's up?"

My, how the tides have changed. I walk through the halls without being obviously stared at, glared at, or talked about. When I open my locker, there is no vandalism. It's starting to feel just a little too good.

Then I hear, "Hey, whore."

My shoulders sag with displeasure at the ruination of this perfect arrival. I finish stuffing the books I don't need yet into my locker, then I close the metal door and meet the blue-eyed gaze of Erika Martin.

"Hey, friend," I offer back.

Erika smiles, her eyes twinkling. Why is she so happy? "Did you kick a puppy this morning?" I inquire. "You seem awfully cheerful."

"A whole litter. Ugly little things."

I crack a smile. "Not quite Dalmatian coat material, huh? Too bad."

"No new coat for me. There's a killer shoe sale going on this week, though. That's pretty good consolation."

"It is. We should go. I could use a new pair of shoes."

Erika blinks and looks over at me. "Are you joking? I can't always tell with you. You have a weird sense of humor."

Hanging out with Erika is the last thing I would *ever* choose to do, but I shrug noncommittally. "Hey, if you'd rather be friends than enemies, shoe shopping could be a good first step. We could get iced coffee, maybe grab lunch. There's really no reason for us to hate each other."

"Except the fact that we're fucking the same guy," she offers.

Sighing with disappointment, I shake my head. "You're still on that? Seriously? It didn't work, Erika. Move on."

"See, that's the thing. I know a lot of girls would just put up with Carter's bullshit because he's Carter. He won't stop *doing* it, so you just have to deal if you wanna be with him. But I think you *actually* believe him. You really believe he changed for you or some shit, and that's just sad."

"I don't care what you think of me, Erika." Pointing to a random spot across the hall, away from me, I add, "Just judge me from way over there. Honestly, your opinion of me is not my business and I couldn't be less interested."

"I'm really not trying to be mean," she states.

"Just naturally bitchy, huh?" I murmur. I can't imagine why Carter didn't want to be with her. She's such a delight!

"I've been there before," she tells me. "I wasn't always like this. Carter made me... he changed me, because of the way he acts. I had to compromise a lot to be with him, and it never ends. He just takes and takes and takes. Just when you've finally adjusted and you think you'll break if you bend another inch, he demands it. He's... He drives me fucking crazy."

That I can understand. Nodding and glancing over at her, I assure her, "I don't doubt that at all. That just means he's not right for you, though. I think Carter isn't right for the majority of women. He's a difficult guy. If that isn't something you enjoy, you should really let him go. Wouldn't you be happier? Why keep fighting to hang onto someone who *literally* drives you crazy? You couldn't have had any peace with him. Were you always worried about other girls?"

"Constantly. If they so much as looked at him, I wanted to claw out their eyeballs. I lived in a constant state of terror that some bitch would steal him away from me."

I'm surprised by the honesty of her answer, by her ability to *admit* that, but it triggers a strain of real sympathy for her. I completely get Carter making someone lose their damn mind. "You couldn't trust him. It wasn't your fault, Erika. He's a hard person to trust. *Not* trusting him is probably the smart thing to do."

Her eyes widen like she didn't expect me to agree with her. "So, if you know that, then what are you doing with him?"

Sighing to myself, I sift through a few possible responses, but she won't like any of them. *He's different with me* would sound moronic. It's an oversimplification for the better explanation, *I fit him better than you do.* She would hate that, though. It would make her feel like I'm putting the weight of their relationship's failure on *her* shoulders, saying she was somehow inadequate. It's not inadequacy, they just weren't compatible. Carter is a handful, and the average woman is not equipped to deal with him. I don't think Carter could make an average woman happy; luckily for him, I'm just a weirdo.

"I'm of the belief that *why* someone does something is super important. If you want to understand who someone really is, you don't just need to know what they've done, you need to know *why* they've done it. I don't know why Carter has done every bad thing he has done, but I *do* know why he cheated on you. Without being mean or hurting your feelings, I'll just say the same circumstances do not apply to our relationship. You and I are very different people, and I think that's why Carter behaves differently with each of us. It's not that I'm better or worse than you, we are just different, and I am more what Carter needs."

I tried really hard not to offend her, but that last line slipped out, and now her eyes gleam with an embarrassed kind of anger that lets me know she feels attacked. "You think you're so much better than me, Zoey, but you fall for the same shit. You think he always *openly* cheated on me? No. That was at the end, when everything had gone to hell and he didn't care anymore. When it first started, when he still wanted to keep me, he lied about it. He tried to cover his ass, just like he's doing with you. Carter is incapable of fidelity. He's too damn selfish."

That does not logically fit with what I already know about Carter's opinions on cheating. Lying and trying to scare me off *does* fit with what I know about Erika though, so it's easy enough to dodge this particular dollop of bullshit.

"I've gotta get to class, Erika," I tell her. "I don't believe you more than I believe him, I'm sorry. I think your motivation to lie to me about this is much stronger than his, so please, stop wasting your time with this. It's gettin' old."

When I start to speed up so I can walk away from her, she stops and calls out, "I have proof."

My steps slow. *Proof?* That's a pretty bold claim to make baselessly.

Pivoting on my heel, I cock my head to the side and ask, "What kind of proof?"

CHAPTER 36

I DON'T KNOW what to expect when Erika pulls out her cell phone, but the smug look on her face tells me she has something up her sleeve. Something she thinks will work.

On one hand, I don't believe her words, but on the other hand, I'm not about to stick my head in the sand just to protect my idea of Carter, either. Even though class is starting any minute and I need to hustle if I don't want to be late, I fall back and stop beside Erika, glancing curiously at her phone for this supposed evidence.

She opens up her photos and leans closer so I can see. "Now, I figured you wouldn't want to believe me, so I was pretty thorough." First, she pulls up a photo of her and Carter to show me. They are on her bed, Carter is wearing a white T-shirt, his arm stretched around her. Erika is wearing a thin sleep top and no bra. Her head is tilted in toward his, a little smile on her face. Carter is asleep, and she's snuggling with him, but this picture could have been taken literally anytime. It could have been taken when they were together.

Raising my gaze back to hers and cocking an eyebrow, I ask, "This is your proof?"

Pointing a well-manicured fingertip at various spots she wants me to pay attention to, she says, "Take it all in. This is a current picture. See what we're wearing? I'm just giving you all the groundwork you need. This is Carter at my house that night." Now she drags the picture up to show the data. A little square of the picture on a map to show where it was taken, the day, and the time.

My brow furrows because that *is* the day of our date, and the time is about an hour and a half after I left Carter's. That could be a coincidence, though. I'm not sure how the metadata of a photo works, but Erika probably could have taken a screenshot of an older photo on her cell phone that evening to get a recent time stamp. It could just be convenient timing—that seems more likely to me than the alternative.

"Nice try," I tell her, shaking my head.

"I'm not done," she assures me, not sounding worried about my current dismissal of her *evidence*. "Now, this is the evidence. This is the video. I just wanted to show you that pic first." Meeting my gaze and flashing me a smile, she says, "It's cute, right?"

I give her a dead look.

"Okay," she says, tapping her screen. "So, this is the same night, a couple minutes later," she says, dragging the video up to show me the metadata on that, too. Same night, a couple minutes later. "Now, obviously, I had to be sly taking this. Carter's not dumb enough to have let me do it. Anyway, once things get going, we bumped the headboard and the phone fell down so you can't *see* what's happening anymore, but trust me, you'll be able to tell by listening."

Suddenly overcome with wariness, I take a step back and shake my head. Common sense tells me I *should* watch that video and see what's on it, but between her absolute confidence and how eager she is for me to watch this video… this doesn't feel like a trick. That means whatever is on this video is going to be really bad. A screen shot might have explained the photo having the right time stamp, but a video?

Taking a step toward me, Erika tilts the screen and presses play. Despite my misgivings, I can't help looking at the screen.

"Hi, Zoey," Erika whispers to the camera. She is nestled in the crook of Carter's arm and he is lying propped against her pillow, like he was in the picture. The camera is pointed at both of them for a moment, then Erika

*flashes her audience a little smile and the footage gets shaky for a moment.
Her gaze keeps drifting to Carter like she's checking to make sure he isn't
awake as she crawls on her knees carefully, turning around and positioning
the camera on the shelf on her headboard. There is some noise as she settles it
as quietly as possible.*

*The position isn't perfect, but since she had to hide the phone, that's not
surprising. I can still see the back of Carter's head and over his shoulder. So
the view is perfectly clear when Erika climbs back to her previous position and
slides an arm affectionately around his waist.*

I swallow, discomfort enveloping me. I can feel myself
growing tense while my mind screams that he's asleep. Even
though I want to slap her for even touching him so affectionately,
he isn't doing anything wrong. He's asleep, and she's caressing
him like a lover—if this is her proof, it's only proof that she's a
creep.

On the video, Carter stirs, making a faint noise.

*"Shh, baby," she murmurs, shifting her body so that she's half on top of
him. Erika cradles the back of his neck tenderly and leans in, kissing her way
along his neck.*

Rage surges through my body, leaving a trail of blistering
heat in its wake. I can feel the warmth of anger traveling up my
neck and suffusing my face.

"Right now, I'm leaning more toward punching you in the
face than dumping Carter, if I'm being honest," I tell her.

Smiling faintly, eyes on the screen, she says, "Keep
watching."

My stomach twists in protest, telling me whatever I do, I
should *not* continue watching this. I won't be able to unsee it, and
I am starting to worry that what Erika views as proof of Carter's
infidelity is going to feel a lot more like sexual assault to me.

"Is he asleep the whole time?" I ask, looking away from the
video to her. "If so, I'm afraid to tell you, male rape is not my
kink."

Fury leaps in her gaze. "Rape? Are you fucking delusional?"

"If you had sex with him while he was literally unconscious,
that's not cheating. It's a felony, and you should be locked up
for it."

She gapes at me for the longest moment, but finally pulls

herself out of it and shakes her head. "I didn't rape anybody, psycho. I think you have *your* sex life with Carter and *mine* severely mixed up if that's the first place your mind goes, you little freak. Keep watching. He wakes up."

Taking a step away from her, I shake my head. "I don't want to watch this. This is making me uncomfortable, and not in the way you intended. I'm going to tell Carter about this tape. You can show it to him, and he can decide what to do with you."

"You're being ridiculous," she states, following after me. "I've made a lot of leaps in my time tryin' to defend his ass, but this? You're insane. There's something wrong with you."

"I'm not the one who forced herself on an unconscious ex because he doesn't want me when he's awake," I tell her.

"You fucking idiot." She grabs my arm, yanking me back. "Watch the video. That is not what this is."

I don't want to look at the phone. There's no possible positive outcome. Either she shows me something horrible that verifies she violated my boyfriend, or she shows me something horrible that shows this turning into something else. Something Carter vehemently denied happening.

The agony of wondering which it is might be worse, though, so I force my gaze back to the screen. She unpauses it and I try to keep control of the anger pulsating through me.

"Mm, I'm gonna take good care of you, baby," Erika murmurs in the *video. I missed the transition, but she's on top of Carter now, straddling him. She sits back, grabs the hem of her shirt, and pulls it off over her head. After tossing it back on the floor, she leans down to kiss him again.*

His hands move, coming to rest on her sides. Now he is clearly awake, because he's… kissing her back. It goes on for what feels like an endless measure of time, then Erika grinds her hips and Carter groans.

I'm going to be sick. My heart can't beat properly and my stomach is so twisted up, I want to vomit.

Finally, they break the kiss and I wait, my aching heart hoping for some-thing from Carter that will make this sting less. He'll tell her to get off him, to stop, that he was still half-asleep and didn't realize…

Instead, he grabs her around the waist with one arm, braces his weight on the bed with the other, and flips her on her back so he can be on top. He climbs between her legs and leans down, so close he smashes her bare breasts against his chest. Erika giggles and locks a leg around his hips. She tilts her head and I see him bending to kiss her neck the way she did a moment ago.

Because of Carter's movement, the phone slips and falls flat. Now all I can see is the wood of the top shelf. She's right, though, I can still hear it. I can still hear Erika moaning as my boyfriend kisses her neck.

The bell rings, alerting me that I'm late to class. I pull myself out of the video, but I can't shake the weight of sadness. The icky sensation of complete and utter disappointment.

My limbs feel shaky and not up to the job of walking to class. I still feel like I'm going to vomit. I really should race to a restroom, but Erika could follow me in there. The last thing I'm going to give her is the satisfaction of standing outside the stalls listening to me throw up my guts.

Swallowing down the anger, hurt, and bile rising inside me, I walk away from Erika without a word. Well, I intend to walk away without a word, but I'm feeling too exposed right now to hold my temper.

"Don't you wanna watch the rest?" she calls out innocently.

"Fuck off, Erika."

I'm so angry that I can *hear* it. The blood surging through my veins, the discomfort oozing as my head feels close to combusting. I replay Carter's bullshit words in my mind, his insistence that nothing happened between him and Erika, that she was making it all up, saying things she knew would make me doubt him.

I believed him. I struggled with it, but ultimately, I chose to give him the benefit of the doubt. I chose to trust him instead of her.

And he fucking lied to me.

Once I've turned the corner so Erika can't see me anymore, I pull out my cell phone. My hands tremble and my fingers shake, making it difficult to navigate where I want to go. Frustration surges at the delay, at the difficulty to click a damn button because I'm so upset, but I finally get my message chain with Carter open.

"Where are you?" I type without thought.

I stare at the screen as I approach my class. I don't know how I'll focus on schoolwork when I'm this upset. I don't know how talking to Carter will make it any better, but all these feelings are trapped inside me and I feel like I'm going to explode if I don't find some outlet for them.

Finally, three little gray bubbles move across the screen and Carter types back, "What? I'm in class. Where are you?"

Now that I have him, I don't know what to say. I guess we can't have this conversation via text, and we don't have a free period until lunch.

How am I supposed to sit in class with him today?

How am I supposed to look at him ever again and not want to scream at him for being such a miserable liar?

I don't know. I can't think straight. Rather than send back a thoughtless, hasty response, I slide my cell phone into the pocket of my jeans and head into class. I've let him fuck up enough of my life. I have to try to clear my head so I can concentrate.

I'll deal with Carter later.

CHAPTER 37

THE MORNING PASSES in a foggy blur. Random memory assaults hit me at odd times—Carter and me tangled in the dark, his skin against mine the night he took my virginity. Sleeping over at his house this weekend, the way I woke up next to his warm body. The way he held me down in his living room and fucked me brutally, without mercy.

The faint stirring of lust should feel better than the sadness that has been following me around, but instead, it intensifies my loss. No more of that. No more of him.

I have to be done now. I know Carter needs firm boundaries, and if I say I'm not like Erika but I do exactly what she did, he'll only keep hurting me. Carter is a predator, and that's what predators do. I'm not even sure he can help it, not anymore.

There was no reason for him to do what he did. No reason that I can see, anyway. None but the obvious one.

I don't really matter to him. He's not afraid to lose me. I *am* just another girl to him, but it's the kind of thing you only realize in hindsight, not when you're swept up in his lies. Carter only tells the truth when he's tired of you and wants you to go away, just like he did with Erika. I don't think he *wants* to get rid of me yet, so he'll probably lie more, and I need to be braced for that. I know how convincing he can be. I have vivid recall of the night

Erika first told me about this, the way Carter looked when he promised me nothing happened between them.

I knew Carter was a gamble, so I shouldn't be so surprised I lost.

By the time I get to history class, I'm drained. It has been a long, sad, angering day, and I just want to go home and curl up in bed. Sleep off the disappointment. Sleep off Carter's spell so I can get back to living my ordinary, Carter-less life.

I've spent so much of my day with this new reality already that I'm taken off guard when Carter stops by my desk, a smile on his face, a twinkle in his eyes like everything is normal.

Then I realize it is for him. I've had to live with this new reality, but he doesn't even know anything has changed. I didn't text him back once I got to class late, and I didn't text him after that because I didn't want to.

"Hey, you," Carter says, bending down to kiss me.

I should pull away or turn my head, but since I know it's the last kiss I'll get from him, I go ahead and take it. Closing my eyes for the briefest of moments, I kiss him back.

Unexpectedly, the brush of his lips causes tears to sting behind my eyes. A fist of sadness seems to have punched me in the stomach. I pull back and look down at my desk, trying to get my bearings.

I shouldn't have done that. I should have let whichever kiss we shared before I knew be the last one. It doesn't matter that I can't remember it. God willing, someday I won't remember *him*.

I know that won't happen, though. I'll never forget Carter Mahoney. He may not reside inside me as a *good* memory, but he'll certainly be there.

Carter touches my arm to get my attention. His dark brows are furrowed in confusion, and he frowns. "Hey, you okay?"

His presence right now is unbearable. I'm suddenly overwhelmed by the idea of having this conversation face-to-face. Maybe I *should* just text it to him. Maybe there's no bravery in facing him, only more hurt. Only more chances for him to fill my head with bullshit. The smartest thing to do is probably to cut him off, to never listen to another word he says. Never speak another word to him.

"You should probably get to your seat," I murmur, flipping open my notebook to a clean page. I grab my pen and write the date in the top right corner, doing my best to ignore Carter.

Rather than going to his seat, he squats down by my desk and frowns at me more intensely. "Zoey, what's wrong? Did something happen?"

"Carter, please," I say, finally meeting his gaze. "Just…"

"Just what?" he asks, completely lost.

His confusion makes me ache with sympathy, and that's infuriating. He doesn't deserve my sympathy. He deserves a slap in the face, but I can see in his eyes that he's genuinely confused. He wants to know what's wrong, and he doesn't understand why I'm not telling him.

"Just leave me alone," I say, shaking my head. My heart drops saying that, so I look at my empty sheet of notebook paper instead of his face. I don't need any additional torture material; my heart is already being a real jerk to me.

Carter rises slowly, even more confused now. I don't look up, but I can feel him wanting to stay. Wanting to haul me out of this seat, drag me out into the hall, and demand to know what's wrong.

The teacher is standing right up front, though. In general, Carter has a lot of leeway, but this particular teacher doesn't give Carter as long a leash and has already advised me to be careful with my 'new friends.' I doubt Mr. Hassenfeld would *let* Carter drag me out into the hall when he's watching, especially if I gave any resistance. Carter must think the same thing, because after a moment's consideration, he finally turns and walks slowly to his desk a couple of rows over.

I look up and watch him walk away, but once he sits down, I don't look at him again for the rest of the period. On the off chance he's looking my way, I don't want to get caught.

This history class is at once the longest and shortest of my life. I try vehemently to concentrate, but I can't. I'm so frustrated by it, but my mind keeps wandering. On top of the massive distraction that is Carter Mahoney on a normal day, today I have images of him in bed with Erika flitting through my mind.

Maybe this *is* for the best. Carter has my head more messed up than Jake ever did. Even with virtually the whole school against me, I never let them get to me before. I never let them shake me.

Now, I am shaken.

Predictably, the moment class lets out, Carter is out of his seat and on his way to me. I gather all my things quickly and make a beeline for the door, but he's right on my heels.

"Zoey," he calls out, grabbing my arm and tugging me back to stop me running away. "What the hell is going on?"

Sucking in a fortifying breath, I turn on my heel and tug my arm free from his grasp. There are a million things I could say and I'm sure I'll have to explain beyond this, but I decide to open with the bold truth. "We're breaking up."

Carter rears back a bit, completely flabbergasted. "What? We are not."

"Yes, we are."

"No, we most assuredly are not," he says, more firmly.

"I know you went to Erika's that night," I state, impressed by how calm and even I'm able to keep my voice. "I know you've been lying to me. I know we agreed it might be a gray area because we weren't official yet, but I specifically told you that if you lied to me about it, then it was no longer a gray area for me." I shake my head, hugging my books tightly to my chest and looking down at the speckled linoleum floor. "I can't trust you, and I can't be with someone I can't trust."

"Zoey…" He trails off, for once, unsure what to say. Raking a hand through his dark locks, he tries to come up with something, but I really don't want to hear it. "Nothing happened—"

I interrupt. "No. Come on, Carter, don't make it worse. Don't pile on the lies. I saw evidence. She took a sneaky video and showed it to me this morning. I saw… much more than I wanted to see." The memory of Carter flipping Erika on her back hits me, and heat suffuses my face. "I'm just… I'm done. I have to be. I'm sorry," I offer, before turning on my heel.

Rather than let it go, Carter follows me. "What the fuck are you talking about, she took a sneaky video?"

"It was on her headboard," I state, flatly. "Now I know what Erika's bare breasts look like. Yay for me."

"Oh, fuck," he mutters.

A wave of cynicism hits me, but I manage a cool nod. "Yeah. Fuck, indeed. It's fine. It's over, it's done. Whatever. I really can't expend much more emotional energy on you, Carter. I'm done."

"Zoey, it is not what you think," he says. "I don't know what you saw on that video, but didn't you see me stop? I woke up to a half-naked girl I used to date kissing me. I was disoriented, and… Trust me, the minute I realized what I was doing, I stopped. It was a stupid fucking mistake. I'm not lying when I say nothing happened. Nothing did, so it wasn't worth admitting to you. It wasn't worth hurting your feelings over what amounts to sleep fog and nothing else."

I stop walking and turn back to look at him, my eyes flashing. "I gave you the benefit of the doubt, Carter. I initially thought she took advantage of you because you were asleep, but the problem with that is, you woke up. And when you woke up, you *kept going.* Not only did you kiss her back, let her grind against you without a shirt on and touch her, I watched you take charge. If you had enough of your bearings to take control, you had enough not to do it in the first place. But you expect me to believe you didn't know what was happening? Was the feel of her naked breasts not a big enough clue? Maybe I could have let you off the hook for just kissing her back when you woke up because I can believe that your head wasn't clear yet, I can believe you were disoriented for a minute. I *can't* believe that you didn't know what you were doing after that, though. That doesn't check out."

"Haven't you ever woken up exhausted and not thinking clearly?"

"Of course, but I didn't roll over and maul anyone by accident."

Grabbing my arm lightly, he pulls me closer to him, trying to suck me into his vortex. His voice calms, like he knows he needs to take control of the wheel before I navigate us into a brick wall. "Zoey, I'm sorry. I'm sorry for whatever you saw. Believe me, I will have words with her about this bullshit, but this is not worth breaking up over. I wasn't lying to you. I told you nothing happened, and from my perspective, nothing did. Not really. As soon as I realized what I was doing, I stopped."

"And as soon as I realized I can't trust you and this relationship will never *not* be hard and stressful, I stopped," I shoot back, firmly. Pulling away, I take a couple of steps back and shake my head. "There's nothing you can say to change my mind. I've thought about it all morning, and I honestly think this is for the best."

"You *can* trust me," he says, his eyes flashing with irritation. "I didn't *cheat*, I didn't even really lie."

Shaking my head, I ask the question that's really been on my mind all morning. "Why were you even at her house in the first place, Carter?"

That takes some of the wind out of his sails.

"It was after our date, exactly like she said. It was late. I don't understand why you were there, and honestly, I don't think you should have been."

It takes him a moment to answer that one. He looks away from me for a few seconds, then brings his gaze back. "You're right. I shouldn't have been there."

"But you were. Why?"

Sighing, he shakes his head and avoids my gaze. "It was before we slept together, Zoey. We weren't 100 percent certain yet. Erika was texting me, and... it was stupid, incredibly stupid, and I regretted it immediately. That's why I didn't want to say anything to you. I knew it was a mistake, I knew it could only possibly hurt your feelings, and I... I didn't want you to find out. I didn't plan on doing anything, but I did think about it."

That *sucks*. I should probably say something back, but anger and disappointment fuse together and begin to bubble under the surface of my skin. I really don't want to get emotional, especially in front of him. I think he'll take advantage of it the second I stop being logical and let him access my feelings. So, I won't. I seal myself behind a wall Carter can't penetrate and tell him evenly, "Well, I wish you all the best. Goodbye, Carter."

"I'm just being honest, Zoey," he states.

"Maybe, but it's too late." With that, I summon every ounce of grace I can scrape up and walk away.

CHAPTER 38

FLIPPING THROUGH THE DENTED, glossy pages of an old magazine, I do my best to focus on the reading material. The wait at the doctor's office is taking forever. I've already thumbed through the trashy celebrity gossip magazines and the single issue of *Time*, so that only left me with a fitness magazine from last year, or the current parenting magazine with an adorable baby on the cover offering me a big, gummy grin.

Currently, I am trying to focus on how to banish that stubborn tricep fat so I can rock a tank top like the hottest Hollywood starlets.

Glancing up from the magazine, I look at the reception desk again. The woman closed the frosted window after checking in the last patient, and now I can't keep my gaze from drifting over to them. A woman and her husband are seated on the other side. Her stomach is protruding, her hand absently rubbing the big bump.

I should have probably just gone to my general practitioner, but given Carter has had unprotected sex with me, I thought the gynecologist would be best. I should probably ask for a full panel of STD testing, regardless of Carter's claim that he's clean. Carter is a lying whore, so maybe he's crawling with infections and just doesn't know it.

Ugh.

Scowling, I flip past a few more pages before coming to the end of the magazine.

With a sigh, I put it back on the end table beside me and glance at the cute baby cover again. I refuse to touch it, as if distancing myself will somehow lessen the risk of unprotected sex. Now that I've broken up with Carter, I'm not even sure I need birth control, but it's better to be safe than sorry.

Not to mention, while I assume Carter will accept the break-up and move on, there's always the off chance he won't. Given our first interaction, if he decides to go back to bullying me now that I'm not sleeping with him, it's possible he'll take it to a new level. It's possible Carter could get angry at my rejection once he realizes I'm serious and I'm sticking to my guns. It's possible Carter could be inside me again before it's all over with, whether I want him to be or not.

Just to cover all my bases, I think getting on birth control is the right choice.

"Zoey Ellis."

I look up at the woman in scrubs holding a clipboard. She flashes me a quick, polite smile. I grab my purse and stand, then approach her with a quick, polite smile of my own. "Hello."

Holding the door open, she nods inside. "Follow me this way."

I follow her and go through the routine. Afterward she takes me to an exam room. Given what I've told her, she tells me I can undress because the doctor will probably want to give me a pelvic exam.

Once I'm changed into the thin paper gown and perched on the exam table, there's nothing to do but wait. Waiting leads to thinking, and waiting in a paper gown on a table at my OB-GYN's office leads my thoughts back to babies. I can't shake the dread of having to tell even a doctor I had unprotected sex several times like an idiot. Logically I know the doctor doesn't care and isn't going to judge me, but it's not something I would have done on my own, it's not something *I* approve of myself doing, so in my imagination the sensible doctor is similarly horrified.

When she actually comes in, it's with a polite, distracted smile, and a clipboard in hand. "Hi, how are you today?"

Stupid. "Good," I say, mirroring back her polite smile. I fold my hands together awkwardly in my lap. I have never actually been to the OB-GYN before. Usually, my general practitioner is sufficient.

"So, what brings you in today, Zoey?" she asks, glancing at the clipboard, then back at me. "I see you want to get on some birth control."

I nod my head, absently squeezing my knees together. "Yes, that's the main thing. I was also thinkin' if it's something you can do now, maybe I should get tested. I don't think I have anything," I offer quickly. "But just to be safe."

Dr. Lucker nods. "Have you had unprotected sex recently?"

Swallowing, I nod my head. "Yes. A couple of times. I know it was dumb," I assure her, lest she feel the need to tell me. "It was spontaneous. If you can do something spontaneous multiple times…"

Smiling kindly at my somewhat apologetic tone, she tells me, "Accidents happen. When was this?" she asks, uncapping her pen and taking notes on her clipboard.

"Over the weekend."

She nods. "And did you take anything afterward?"

"You mean like the morning-after pill? No."

"How long have you been sexually active?" she inquires.

"Since over the weekend," I offer dryly.

She nods and glances up from the clipboard to look at me. "How many partners?"

"Just the one."

Pressing the nub of her pen to paper, she jots a few more casual notes. She asks a few more common questions about when my last period was and how long I generally go between cycles. Then she declares—like an afterthought—that it's possible I was ovulating over the weekend, and if not, I will be soon.

With my heart in my throat, I ask her, "Can you—I mean, it hasn't been—Is there a blood test or something you could take to make sure I'm not?"

This time, she shakes her head. "It's too early. It's actually early enough that you don't have to worry about it. If the earliest you had unprotected sex was 3 days ago, I can write you a prescription for emergency birth control, if you'd like. As long as you take it up to five days after possible conception, and it's very effective."

I wish I hadn't let paranoia compel me to search online for information about how soon an embryo can actually implant. There were just enough delusionally excited expectant moms insisting they knew they were pregnant the day after conception for me to let my more logical side win this particular argument. "Wouldn't that be more of an early abortion pill than preventative birth control?"

Her gaze drifts to mine a little more warily. "It's emergency birth control."

"It's not 100% effective though, right? So, if I took it and I *was* pregnant, and I happened to be one of the people it wasn't effective for, would it harm the baby?" I shake my head, waving her off. "Never mind. It doesn't matter. I don't need that. I'm sure I'm not pregnant. I'd rather not have to make a decision about that unless I absolutely have to, so why don't we just wait and see. I don't need the emergency birth control, but I would like to get birth control that is effective as soon as possible. The guy and I already broke up, so I don't think I'll actually be having sex in the immediate future, but I wanna be prepared just in case. I don't want to go through worrying like this again."

The polite doctor nods her head. "All right."

I'M EXHAUSTED by the time I get home. Someone called off at work while I was at the doctor's appointment, so as soon as I left, I had to head straight to work and stay until close. Carter has been blowing up my phone since school. Telling me we need to talk, that he's sorry, that I didn't give him a chance to adequately explain.

I don't want to hear any of it and I'm too tired, so I do the smartest thing—delete the message so all of his texts are gone. I plug the charger into my dying phone and climb into bed, then I sigh and arrange all my books around me. Since I had to work unexpectedly, I have a crap ton of homework to catch up on. The good thing about that is it makes me feel like I'm on the right track—and gives me absolutely no time to think of Carter.

A couple minutes after midnight when I'm finished, I finally check my phone before I crawl into bed. I expect to see more messages from Carter, but there aren't any. I don't know whether to be relieved or disappointed, but foolishly, I feel more of the latter emotion than I want to. I can't help thinking how today might have gone if Erika hadn't accosted me with reality this morning. I would have come home from a long day of life, curled up in bed, and wasted a bunch of time talking to Carter. I would have told him about my doctor's appointment and insisted he probably already planted a little Carter clone inside me to try and make him sweat, but he wouldn't have because he's crazy.

I already miss him. That's annoying. It was so hurtful to see him with Erika. I was so angry when it became clear he lied to me, so disappointed that he even went over there at all, but my heart hasn't caught up to my new reality as completely as I thought it had. Now, in the quiet, in the complete aloneness, I recall the feeling of Carter's warm body snuggled up against mine. My memory brings to life the feel of his featherlight touch as he trailed a finger along the curve of my shoulder. The tickle along my nape when his lips brushed that sensitive spot.

In the absence of Carter's arms, temptation wraps itself around me. I lie awake telling myself to go to sleep, but my phone beckons me. I resist for a while, tossing and turning, but the lure of Carter keeps me awake.

Finally, I reach for the phone. My eyes are heavy, but my mind won't quiet down, so rather than try resisting temptation, I decide to check in on Carter. He'll never know I did it, so it doesn't matter. Rather than text him, I check out his social media. It's hardly a window to his soul most of the time, so I don't know what I expect to find.

I find nothing. It's unusual for Carter not to keep up appearances, but he hasn't updated any of his social media since I dumped him.

Sighing, I put my phone back on charge and snuggle up

under my blanket. I'm too warm with it on, but I crave the cocoon-like comfort.

My bedroom door eases open, but the light stays off. My mom must be checking in on me before she goes to bed. I didn't tell her I broke up with Carter, but I've been in a surly mood since I walked in the door tonight. I don't feel like talking about it though, least of all with her, so I don't roll over. I keep my back to the door and let her think I'm asleep already.

After a few seconds, she accepts that I'm asleep and doesn't want to disturb me. The door closes with a soft click, and I breathe a little sigh of relief.

At least, until my bed sags with the weight of someone climbing on it. My mom might open the door to check on me, but she wouldn't come in and sit down on my bed when she thinks I'm asleep. I turn to investigate, but I already have a wild suspicion who I'll find there.

Sure enough, when I roll over, I see the dark silhouette of Carter Mahoney climbing onto my bed.

CHAPTER 39

MY BEDROOM IS DARK, but the sliver of moonlight coming in through the window illuminates Carter's intense features. Faced with the reality of him in my room, my stomach bottoms out. With my heart in my throat, I open my mouth to… well, I'm not exactly sure, but before I can say anything, Carter does.

"Caught your mom before she went to bed. Told her we were fighting, and I really needed to talk to you. She let me come right up." Crawling forward, he adds, "Your mom kind of sucks."

"She doesn't suck," I defend, easing up on my elbows to move back away from him. "She's just…" I don't know how to finish that sentence, so I don't bother. "More importantly, what are you doing here?"

"You weren't answering my texts," he tells me, as if sneaking into my bedroom is a reasonable response. "I know you can't ignore me in person, so here I am."

He's so damn pushy. Shaking my head, I tell him, "You need to leave. I don't want to talk to you. That's what it means when you text someone and they don't text back. Hard to interpret, I realize."

"Definitely a mixed signal," he says lightly, playing along. "I figured you were just busy."

"You did not."

Carter smiles, grabbing my hips and dragging me to the middle of the bed.

My defenses go up. I know Carter isn't above using any means at his disposal, but if he thinks he can use his body to short circuit my brain, he has another thing coming. "Carter, you really need to leave. I'm not playin' around. We broke up. I'm not your plaything anymore. This is no longer appropriate by any stretch of the imagination."

"Now, that's where we disagree," he tells me, pulling me beneath him and straddling my hips. "*You* broke up. I didn't agree to it."

"You can't reject my break-up. When one person initiates a break-up, the other person has no choice but to accept it. Have you never been dumped before?"

"Of course I haven't," he answers. "I've only ever dated Erika, and, well, you know how that went down."

That's the wrong person to bring up right now. Glaring up at him, I say, "Yes, I do. And speaking of Erika, get the fuck off me before I grab my phone and call the police to report an intruder in my house."

Utterly unconcerned, Carter says, "Feel free to try, princess. If you think my reflexes are so shitty I won't be able to stop you, go ahead and reach for your phone. Let's find out if you're right."

Huffing at him, I glare harder. "Just tell me what you want to tell me so you can leave."

Cocking a dark eyebrow, he tells me, "Now, that's not very hospitable."

"You are not my guest. You're not welcome here. I don't *want* you here," I offer more firmly.

"Now you're just being mean," he tells me. "It doesn't suit you."

"I'm not bein' mean. I'm telling my erratic *ex* to get off me and get out of my bedroom. That's perfectly reasonable."

"Ouch. Ex? No, I don't like that."

"I'm not playin' around, Carter," I tell him seriously. "I know I've let you get away with some stuff in the past, but not this. Not her. You won't talk me out of this. You and I are over, done, finished. I don't trust you anymore. I'm sorry to tell you, no matter what you say or do, you're not getting your way this time."

I'm only wearing shorts and a thin, baby blue cami top to sleep in, no bra underneath. Because he's a dick, Carter covers my breasts with his big hands and squeezes. "No matter what I do, huh?" he asks, a note of challenge in his tone.

An answering pulse of arousal rears its ugly head at the feel of his hands on me, but I ignore it. There's little point in dancing around the obvious, so I meet his gaze and tell him evenly, "You and I both know you can take what you want physically, if you want to. That's not what I'm talking about. You may be able to force your way inside my body, Carter, but you can't force your way back into my heart."

Aware of the force field Carter usually erects when he needs to defend himself, I don't really expect much of a reaction to my words. I'm surprised when he looks down and I see something like disappointment in his eyes. "You got rid of me that fast, huh? Just the other night, you were saying you loved me."

There's enough hurt in his words that I drop some of my own defenses. Even if he is the one who put us in this situation, I feel bad for him. I don't *hate* Carter, I just can't be in a relationship with him if I know it will drive me crazy. Now that I know he went over to her house and I saw what happened, I could never trust Carter with Erika again, not even as friends. I know he was willing to cut her out of group hangs, but she's a cheerleader and he's on the football team. What about away games? I refuse to babysit him, and I don't want a version of Carter I would *have* to babysit. When I started falling for him, I fell for what he sold me—an imperfect person, absolutely, but one I would never have to worry about cheating.

I don't know what to say. I want to take the sting out of my words and make him feel better, but I don't want to give him false hope, either.

"I still care about you," I offer, carefully. "I just can't be with you. Whether you intended to or not, you damaged my ability to trust you. Knowing you're unscrupulous with other people is one thing, but you're right, in order for me to accept all your baggage, I needed to be the exception. I needed to be the one you treated like a teammate, like I was in on the joke you're playing on the world, not the one you're lying to and plotting against. That's a deal-breaker for me, Carter. I liked feeling that you respected me and had my back. I would've had yours, too. But I didn't sign up for this. I didn't sign up to be like every other inconsequential girl you didn't care about. And if that's all I am, that's fine. I can't dictate how you feel about me. I'm not sayin' I *am* special, but if I'm just like all the others, then I'm not interested. You can't make me interested again, because I never wanted that in the first place."

Carter's hot gaze burns into me. "You are *not* just another girl to me, Zoey. Can't you see that? In a world full of phony bullshit, you're the only thing that's real. I *do* respect you immensely. What happened with her was before we officially got together. I know that's a technicality, I know it still fucking sucks, and I'm sorry for that. But this is not something you and I break up over. I don't care about Erika. She's dead to me. I'll never be alone with her again, you have my word on that. I care about you, I care about us, I care about the future I can see us having, and I'm not about to let you chuck it all out the fucking window when we're just getting started. If you couldn't handle *me*, that would be one thing, but not over this. Not over her."

I know there's little point arguing with Carter. I've volleyed back and forth in a battle of wills with him before, but I'm tired, I'm sad, and I'm done. I don't want to play these games with him anymore. I don't want to defend my worldview and explore his. I just want him to leave and let me get back to my life.

Since I know he already expects that the only reason I'm doing this is because he hurt me with the Erika thing, I offer him the rest of the story. "You're too much of a distraction, Carter. I get so wrapped up in you and everything else gets moved to the back burner, and it never stops. It never slows down. It's not like it's just a bumpy road getting to the relationship and then things calm down. There's a dark secret lurking around every corner. There is *so much* I still don't know about you, and… after this Erika thing, I am just at capacity. I don't have enough interest left to keep going through things with you. I'm sorry if that sounds hard-hearted, but you know what? Less than a week ago, you put your whims ahead of me. I have to put my future ahead of you. I have to keep my grades up so I can graduate at the top of our class, get that scholarship, and get the hell out of this town. That's my only chance, and I really believe that if I stay with you, I'll blow it. I know you like the idea of a future with me, but we were together for like 5 minutes, Carter. It probably wouldn't end up workin' out between us, and then where does that leave me? Drowning in an ocean of regret because I allowed my high school boyfriend to distract me with his endless drama and my focus slipped. I can't have that. I won't."

"How many times do I have to tell you, I'm not going to ruin your life?" he asks.

"That's the problem, Carter. It doesn't matter how many times you say it, because I can't believe it. I think you're a lot of things, and I *have* enjoyed… whatever this has been between us. I don't know what that says about me, but I have. The problem is, you are a slippery slope, and I can see a future between us too, but I think mine looks a lot different than yours. At this point, I can't see a version of my life where you are not my downfall."

Shaking his head, visibly aggravated, Carter says, "You didn't feel this way before you saw that fucking video. You can act like you have all these solid reasons, Zoey, but you were ready to do this before Erika fucked it up. These excuses are bullshit. You can study and have a boyfriend. Literally everyone else manages."

"It doesn't matter if you believe me," I state, done with explaining myself. "It doesn't matter if you like my reasons. Our relationship is over and so is this conversation. Now, please leave. I have had the longest day ever. I'm tired, and I want to go to sleep."

"You don't have to do this, you know," he says, suddenly calm and meeting my gaze. "If you think your dignity demands this response, it doesn't. I will make it up to you. I can fix this. One mistake is not who I am, and it damn sure isn't the sum total of our fucking relationship. Throwing it all away… it's a waste."

I wish I could argue that, but I can't. No, I can't be positive I'm making the right decision, but I think the chances are good I would regret staying with Carter more than I'll ever regret leaving him. I'm not going to say that to him. I've said enough and I really don't feel like being mean.

Instead, I meet his gaze and offer simply, "I'm sorry."

Carter watches me for a moment, still straddling my hips. Finally, he shakes his head and climbs off me. "Fine."

My stomach rocks at his acquiescence, but I remind myself this is what I wanted. It's still jarring that he's not only doing what I asked him to do, but doing it so quickly. Now that he's off me, off my bed, he doesn't linger. He goes straight to the door and pulls it open, preparing to leave.

Out of place disappointment creeps up on me, but only fleetingly. I shove it down, pointing out to myself I should be glad Carter is respecting my wishes for once. And I am. I meant what I said, it's just… a little voice in the back of my mind whispers that for all he claims to see a future with me, he sure didn't fight very hard for me.

Oh well. I didn't *want* him to fight me, I wanted him to go away, and now he is. If there's still a small part of me that wants to call him back, that's just an impulse I'll have to ignore.

Carter doesn't say goodbye, and he doesn't look back. I'm so focused on holding onto my control, on guarding myself in case he pivots at the last second, it's not until he's so far gone he must be out the front door that I feel it for the first time.

This crazy ride I have been taking with him… it's finally over. Carter and I are *really* over, and God help me, I'm gonna miss him.

CHAPTER 40

TUESDAY PASSES IN A SLOG. My morning classes crawl by, then I have to see Carter again for the first time as an ex. He doesn't look at me once in history class, and he doesn't look sad either. He has bounced right back, his mask has slid right back into place, and he sits over there like he used to up until a few weeks ago, blissfully unaware of my existence.

Since he showed up in my bedroom last night, it crosses my mind a couple times that maybe he will hang back after class like he used to when he was pursuing me, drape an arm around my shoulder and lightly harass me before I make my way out to my car for lunch.

He doesn't. He walks right past me toward the cafeteria, and I go out to my car in peace. Too much peace. I miss his stupid harassment.

Slamming my car door shut once I'm inside, I lean my head forward and rest my forehead against the steering wheel, trying to get my bearings. I can't be the only one sad about the break-up I initiated. Carter wanted to stay together, I'm the one who said no. I can't be the one sitting in my car feeling rejected while he is laughing with his friends at lunch.

Shaking off the light grasp of misery, I tell myself I have two days. Two days to be sad and mourn the relationship that barely got to happen, then I'm done, and I move on with my life.

Work helps the evening hours pass, and Wednesday passes more quickly because of youth group in the evening. It's a light night and we end up playing games. I beat Luke's ass at air hockey twice, then we break for snacks.

"Wanna go a little easier on me next time? Man, you're an air hockey beast," he tells me, shaking his head as he takes a seat on the couch beside me.

I smile, looking down at my plate. Grace was on snack duty tonight, and Grace just can't help doing too much. Last time I was on snack duty, I brought chocolate chip cookies and a gallon of milk. Grace set up an apple dipper buffet. Every different kind of apple wedge, a trio of dips—peanut butter, caramel, and chocolate—and an assortment of toppings to sprinkle on top for the adventurous. I got adventurous. I have a peanut butter dipped McIntosh slice coated in graham cracker crumbs, a chocolate dipped slice coated in crushed up Oreos, and a caramel Granny Smith slice covered with salted peanuts. I also grabbed a spoonful of baby marshmallows, for good measure.

"I don't know, I think after all this sugar, I might be even more ruthless," I tell him.

Cracking a smile, he looks down at his own plate. He was less adventurous. Three identical wedges covered in caramel with no toppings. "That spread sure is something, isn't it?" he remarks.

"Grace always goes all out. She knows no other way, I swear."

"That's for sure," he agrees.

I feel a touch awkward eating with him watching me, but I want to try this Oreo-coated deliciousness, so I go ahead and take a bite anyway.

"You should bring Carter to youth group one of these weeks," Luke says, suddenly.

Just as my tastebuds are dancing with glee at the combination of flavors, he has to go and bring up Carter. "Oh, I don't think so," I offer, shaking my head faintly. "Youth group isn't really Carter's scene."

"Sure, maybe it isn't, but guys tend to do things they don't always want to do to please their girlfriends," he tells me, smiling faintly. "I'm sure we'd all like the chance to get to know him. There must be somethin' we're not seeing if you think he's—"

"We're not together anymore," I blurt, wanting out of this conversation promptly.

"Oh." Concern transforms his features. "I'm sorry to hear that. Are you okay?"

"Yep." I take another bite of my Oreo apple, then lean forward to grab my bottle of water so I can take a drink.

Seeing that I'm not in a sharing mood, he lets it go, simply telling me, "Well, if you ever need to talk about it…"

"I don't." I flash him a smile that I hope doesn't look as stiff as it feels. "Thanks."

THURSDAY MARKS my official End of Sadness deadline, so I start the day with gumption and sail through with intentional joyfulness. I make it to history, but my mood takes a hit when I see Carter turned around at his desk, offering a charming smile to some girl he is chatting up at the desk behind him. A leggy blonde in snug jeans smiles back, twirling a lock of her chin-length hair and mooning at him.

Two days. God, he doesn't take long to move onto the next, does he? He might be doing it just to spite me, but it's entirely possible he's not, too. The more he projects that he doesn't care, the more I can't help believing him.

Oh well. Doesn't matter. It's deadline day, and no matter how much flirting is probably going on over there, I will be happy, dammit!

That's the plan, but I underestimated Carter's evilness. Throughout the whole class—to the point of the teacher shooting him an evil eye that warns Carter Mahoney or not, he's about to say something—Carter and Blondie are shameless. She does stupid things to get his attention, and boy, does he give it to her. She pretends to accidentally kick the leg of his chair, so he shoots her a playfully devious look over his shoulder. She drops her pen on the floor in front of her desk, and he oh-so-gallantly bends to pick it up. Cutesy smiling bullshit, casual playfulness—I hate *everything*.

I can hardly sit still for the bell. When it finally rings, I already have my stuff hugged close to my chest. I'm up and out of my seat, pushing my way down the aisle with mumbled apologies, but I have to get out of this classroom. I can't *breathe*.

I practically run to the bathroom, locking myself inside a stall, dropping my books on the floor, and taking a few deep breaths. My tummy is twisted up in knots, my heart beats entirely too fast, and Carter Mahoney is an *asshole*.

I hate him. He is the absolute worst and I hate him. He knew I could see that shit. Even if he actually likes that girl, he didn't have to make a spectacle right in front of me when our break-up is still so fresh. He did that shit on purpose, and he is an asshole.

Once I'm calm enough to hold my shit together until I can get to my car—and enough time has passed that the bathroom has emptied of other girls—I collect my things and make my way out of the bathroom.

"Upset stomach?"

I nearly jump out of my skin at the sound of Carter's voice. When I look back over my shoulder, I see him leaning against the wall. He's wearing jeans and a white T-shirt today. His arms are crossed, his well-shaped biceps grabbing my attention. I might enjoy the sight of them a little more, if not for the new memory of Blondie *touching* that bicep when she leaned forward to get Carter's attention about 20 minutes ago.

It's not enough to ignore him—I want to ignore him so hard it hurts. I want him to feel a sudden Arctic chill from the blast of my coldness. I'm too riled to think straight though, so I settle for glaring at him wordlessly and turning to walk away.

Kicking off the wall, Carter follows after me. "Whoa, princess, what's that look for?"

"Do *not* call me that. My name is Zoey. Call me Zoey or Ellis, don't call me princess."

"Hm, irritable, too," he muses. "Maybe I *did* knock you up."

"Or maybe I had to pee and I just don't like you," I suggest. "Much simpler explanations."

"That can't be it. You liked me fine a couple of days ago. Oh, wait," he drawls, annoying the ever-loving fuck out of me. "You're not salty because of me and Jenna, are you?"

I want to tell him to go die, but that would only verify I am annoyed by his flirting. "Nope. Don't even know who Jenna is. New girlfriend already?"

"Nah, you know me. Not big on girlfriends. I prefer playthings."

Somehow, that hurts more than hearing he has a new girlfriend. My heart shrivels up until it's too small to fit inside its natural cavity, then it drops into my gut with a painful thud. I can't come up with anything quick and snappy to toss back. My mind assaults me with a vision of him and the blonde, her in his bed just like I was, her arms wound around his neck, his lips blazing a hot path along her bare skin.

Now I really *do* want to throw up. Maybe I'm just imagining it, but I can feel his satisfaction. Whether it's real or imagined, I want to demolish it. That's the only excuse I have for the lie that tumbles out of my mouth next.

"Good. I'm seein' someone else already, too. I'm glad we're both movin' on."

"Bullshit," he fires back.

I cock an eyebrow and look over at him. "Bullshit? You think you're the only guy in the world, Carter? Not hardly. Plenty of other fish in the sea. Fish that *won't* fuck around with their ex-girlfriends, crazily enough. I know, I was surprised, too. Turns out you just have to date the *good* guys if you don't want endless drama and heartache."

That dig seems to do more to legitimize my lie. He stares at me, openly confounded, then snaps, "Who?"

"None of your business," I tell him. "You have your new plaything, I have someone who meets my needs… we both win."

"Meets your *needs*?" he snaps, grabbing me by the arm and yanking me closer.

My gaze drops to his hand on my arm, then moves to his face. "Let me go."

Instead, he glances around the hall, locates the nearest empty classroom, and drags me into it.

CHAPTER 41

"CARTER," I object, trying to pull my arm out of his steel grip. Given what happened last time I was alone in a classroom with him, I'm not eager to see why he needs privacy today. "Get your hands off me."

"I'll put my hands wherever I damn well please," he tells me, shutting the door with a quiet click, then hauling me away from it so we aren't visible through the window.

"No," I say firmly, trying in vain to free my arm from his grasp. "We are not doing this again."

"Why not? Afraid your boring new boyfriend might get jealous?" he shoots back.

Narrowing my eyes, ridiculously protective of this made-up person, I admonish, "He is not *boring*. I didn't say boring."

"Sure you did," he disagrees. "You said he was a *good guy*," he says sarcastically, rolling his eyes. "I damn near fell asleep."

"Spend enough time with a depraved sociopath, you might be surprised how nice *good guys* start to sound," I shoot back.

"He's a palate cleanser, at best," Carter states, dismissive of my imaginary boyfriend. "You need someone who stimulates you, not someone who puts you to sleep. You might not want to admit it, but you *liked* all my fucking damage. You *craved* my depravity. You don't *want* a good guy, Zoey. You want me."

Since he was pretty damn mean to me in class, I feel like

giving him a little dose of his own medicine. "And yet when you asked me to stay with you, I told you no thanks." I cock my head, tapping my chin as if confused. "Funny, that doesn't *sound* like someone who wants you."

Easily deflecting my well-placed shot, Carter smiles at me. "I can do 'mean' a whole lot better than you, princess. I wouldn't go there, if I were you."

"You think so?" I ask, lifting an eyebrow. "You make me feel pretty mean sometimes. For instance, right now. I'd like to scratch your face off."

"How 'bout you drag those nails down my back instead?" he suggests.

"How 'bout I drag them down someone *else's* back?" I return bitingly. "You're not the only one with urges, you know. You're not the only one who can *play*."

"Let me make something crystal clear, Zoey," he says, shifting his hold on me. He releases my arm and takes my books, setting them on a nearby desk. Then he drags me fully against him, locks his arms around me, and gazes down at me patiently, like a teacher with an unruly pupil. "If you fuck someone else just to spite me, you will regret it. Not as much as he will though," he adds, silkily. "I might not have the heart to destroy you, but I damn sure won't feel so merciful toward him. Any asshole who is seen alone with you from now on will wind up between *my* crosshairs. Understand?"

Rage bubbles up inside me, heating my skin. "How dare you. You're allowed to do whatever you want with any damn girl you want, and I'm, what, supposed to stay home and *knit*?"

"No, you're supposed to stay home and study. That's why you dumped me, right? Can't have a boyfriend and do well in school? Well, I'd say that applies to other guys, too. I'm just looking out for your best interests."

Glaring up at him, I tell him, "No, you're being a jealous asshole, and over a girl who isn't even yours. How would your new *toy* feel about that?"

I'm caught off guard when his arms drop from around me and he grabs a fistful of my hair. I gasp as he uses it to pull my neck back. Leaning forward, he doesn't stop until his head is bent, his lips hovering mere inches from mine. My heart thuds in my chest and I try to pull away, but that only causes his grip on my hair to tighten.

"Not mine?" he asks lowly, dangerously. "Oh, you're still mine, Zoey. You'll always be mine. You made the mistake of letting me be the first. No matter what happens, no matter the circumstances, you never forget your first. They always own a little piece of you, whether you want them to or not." With his free hand, he grabs me between the legs. I gasp, surprised, but my body is so accustomed to his roughness already, it responds with interest. Arousal swirls inside me and my eyelids grow heavy. They want to drift closed, to give him free rein, since he'll take it even if I don't. My body doesn't care about the stupid words he's saying, it cares about the warmth of his hand against my pussy, the closeness of his lips and the lovely things he can do with them.

Shit, I need to get out of this classroom.

"I think 'letting you' might be a slight overstatement," I tell him, my chest starting to work too hard. Hopefully, if he notices, he attributes it to anger and not the stirring of arousal. "Now, get your hands off of me."

"Who is the guy?" he asks again.

"There is no guy," I state evenly. It's the truth, but the funny thing is, now he doesn't believe me. Now he thinks I'm just protecting someone else because he threatened to target them for daring traipse on his territory.

"All right, I'll guess. Can't be the pastor; he's married and you're too Christian to do something like that without immense shame. No shame, so… Not Jake, you don't like him. I guess you could go out with him out of spite, but I don't think you'd do that. Too principled to use someone so blatantly." When I show no signs of guilt, I guess, he nods. I see him going through the mental inventory, then his gaze sharpens and his eyes lock on mine. "The cashier. The pastor's brother. The one you didn't want to see us together."

"No," I say quickly. *Too* quickly. Carter's eyes light up with momentary victory, then dull a little, then shift to amusement. "Really? That fucking guy? He's gotta be a virgin."

I'm tempted to say *"He was,"* just to piss him off, but I don't want to put a target on Luke's back, so I hold my tongue.

"I'm telling the truth, Carter, there's no guy. I made it up. I was… mad. It doesn't matter," I say, trying to shake my head, but pulling my own hair in the process. "There's no guy. Don't start watching me, trying to figure it out. There's nothing to figure out."

Instead of accepting the truth, Carter gets angry enough that his jaw locks. "Do not try to protect some other guy from me, Zoey."

"I'm not tryin' to protect anyone," I insist.

"I'm gonna have a talk with Luke."

My eyes widen with panic at the mental image of him accosting poor Luke in the hall. He wouldn't even know what was happening. "Don't you dare!"

"When did he even have time to move on you? You had youth group on Wednesday, didn't you?" he muses. "Did he hit on you at youth group? That's fucking lame."

"Why aren't you listening to me?" I demand. "It isn't Luke. I'm not with Luke. I'm not with anybody. I lied before, but I'm tellin' the truth now."

Carter is having another one of his conversations with himself, though, ignoring my contribution at this point. "Doesn't matter. I'll handle it. I'm gonna scare the choir boy off, and if you try to date anyone else, I'll scare him off, too. And the next one. And the next one. And the next," he finishes, dipping closer.

Before I can pull away, he kisses me. I jerk away and his hand between my legs moves to cradle my neck, to give him better control. He walks me backward as his lips claim mine, soft and sensual, but possessive and demanding at the same time. My heart races, but I don't know which instinct is more pressing. I can't see where I'm going and I'm not sure I trust him to navigate. I gasp into his mouth when the backs of my legs hit a desk.

I'm wearing a cream-colored top and a caramel brown skirt, just like the first day he had me in this room. Memories of that encounter flash to mind, so when he finally breaks the kiss, my gaze is a little more guarded as it rises to meet his.

I'm so conflicted on so many fronts. I can't get my head and my heart on the same page when he's around. Right now, looking up into his handsome face, all I want to do is thread my fingers through his dark hair and pull him close. I want his strong arm to lock around my waist, his other hand to cradle my face. I want things I can't want anymore, and it's incredibly frustrating.

Carter's brown eyes move down my body, surveying the property he claims belongs to him. If we were still together, I might find that sexy, but I'm trying so hard to dump him, and he's not making it easy.

"This is the same skirt I peeled off you before," he realizes.

"Which time?" I ask dryly, since I have two similar looking skirts, and the jerk has peeled both of them off me against my will.

His lips tug up like he finds that amusing. "We need to get you some new clothes."

"Clothes cost money," I mutter. "I don't need new clothes, anyway. I have perfectly good clothes already. If you don't like my skirt, don't look at it."

"You're being pretty mouthy for someone so completely at my mercy," he observes.

"I'd say do your worst, but you already have."

"Nah, I haven't done my worst," he says dismissively. "Not to you. Don't intend to. I like you too much."

If he hasn't done his worst to me, I'm not sure I even *want* to know what his worst entails. I am curious, though. On his damage scale, where do I fall? I have to score pretty high. He already told me he never did to anyone else what he did to me, and while I'm not *sure* where his limits are, I *hope* they stop somewhere before murder. He never did give me the details about Chloe's mother, but for all that I quasi-joke about him being a sociopath, I can't imagine he has ever *actually* killed someone. He probably wouldn't dirty his own hands even if he did have a problem he needed to get rid of. There's an aura of darkness around his past, but it's a locked door and he wouldn't give me the key even when we were together, so there's no chance he'll give it to me now.

While I'm thinking about the darkness in his past, the darkness in his present emerges. I don't immediately notice, too distracted by my own thoughts, but then I feel his fingers slipping the buttons through the holes of my skirt. My skirt loosens and before I can reach to grab it, it falls down my hips.

"Don't," I object, grabbing at the material.

"Let it go," Carter commands, grabbing my hip and turning me around.

"What are you doing?" I ask, catching my palms on the desk when Carter pushes me down.

Before he even has time to answer, I realize he is bending me over the desk. I have enough time to piece it together, but not enough time to move out of the way. The sound of his zipper is so loud in this empty room—nearly as loud as the blood surging through my veins like a tidal wave.

"Carter—"

"No," he interrupts, pressing on my back until I'm flat against the surface. Kicking my legs apart, he moves up behind me. He's still holding me down against the desk, and it reminds me of the night he held me down on his living room floor. Lust grabs hold of me, but I try to fight it off, to remain focused on getting away. "You're a good girl, aren't you, Zoey?" he asks, almost soothingly as he works my panties down with one hand. "So why don't you act like one. Close that pretty little mouth, spread your legs, and take your punishment."

Struggling to push against his hand, I bark, "You don't get to punish me. I didn't do anything wrong, and you're not my—"

Smack. Before I can finish that sentence, his hand comes down hard across my bottom. I yelp at the bite of pain and grab onto the edge of the desk.

"Try again," he tells me, rubbing his hand over the smarting skin to soothe it.

Fuck. I miss this bullshit, and I didn't even have time to get used to it in the first place. Fury snakes through me again, but this time not at what he's doing. This time, the live wire of anger is what he cheated us both out of with his assholery.

"Fuck you," I fling back.

His hand comes down across my ass again, then again, and again. By the third time, I'm squirming, trying in earnest to get away. The strikes are hard, clearly some anger on his end, too.

Another smack lands and it feels like my skin is on fire. "Carter, stop," I beg, pushing against the hand on my back. He presses even harder, then spanks me again. I'm starting to notice the harder I squirm, the harder he smacks.

Another smack makes me yelp, but instead of fighting, I stop. I hold on to the desk, but I stop pushing against his hand, trying to move from the position he put me in. I'm breathing heavily, so I take a couple of calming breaths. Carter's hand moves across my burning ass again. "Had enough yet?"

Swallowing down my feelings of rebellion, I nod my head. "Yes, please."

"Mm, good girl," he says, rubbing my back with the hand that was holding me down only a moment ago. "You're fucking perfect, you know that?"

He asks the question casually, but it still makes my achy heart drop. If I'm so perfect, why did he jeopardize what he was building with me over something he didn't give a damn about?

I can't ask, so I ignore his comment like he ignores me when I say things he doesn't like. I don't know exactly what to do. On one hand, I don't want to let him fuck me when we're no longer together and I don't know where he's been since. On the other hand, I probably don't have a say in the matter.

My heart thunders in my chest as Carter slowly slides a finger inside me. "Carter," I say on a gasp.

"Yes, princess?" His tone is patient while he caresses me.

Trying to get my bearings, I keep my tone soft despite my words. "I'm not your plaything anymore. You can't do this. You lost the right."

"And yet, here I am," he tells me.

"You have to stop before this goes any further. This isn't right."

"If you want to stop me, you're going to have to scream," he advises. "Maybe you'll luck out and a teacher will be walking by on their way to the lounge."

"I—I don't want to get you in trouble, I just want you to stop."

"Are you experiencing déjà vu?" he asks lightly. "I am."

He withdraws his finger from between my legs, but before I

can have more than a passing thought that maybe he'll honor my wishes, he guides his cock between my legs in its place. He shoves inside me, filling me up in one brutal plunge. The friction sends shivers of pleasure dancing down my spine, weakens the muscles in my legs. Thank God this desk is beneath me, supporting my weight.

A moan slips out of me as he pulls back, then I cry out when he thrusts forward and drives himself inside me again.

"Fuck, I missed your pussy." Bracing one hand on my hip and grabbing a fistful of my hair with the other, he holds onto me more firmly as he thrusts into me. "Haven't even been away long, and still missed it. That's mildly alarming, isn't it?"

I don't bother answering him. I don't know what to do. I really don't want to get him in trouble. My body is flying with the exhilaration of having him inside me again, but my mind balks at the mental image of him with Jenna, then the slightly older one of him with Erika. Not to mention, he isn't wearing a condom again. I'm protected by birth control now, but the idea of him inside me after being with someone else makes my skin crawl.

"Get off me," I tell him. "This is your last warning, Carter."

He sounds amused. "My last warning?" he asks, pulling back then shoving forward so hard, the desk skids across the floor. "And you'll do what, exactly, if I don't listen?"

I can only shake my head at his stubborn arrogance. He's already told me he won't go all out on me, that he doesn't want to turn the full brunt of his wickedness on me, that he doesn't have the heart to destroy me because he likes me too much.

Carter doesn't have the terrifying element of surprise in his hands this time, like he had the first time he locked me inside a classroom with him. Then, I was legitimately afraid he might be a monster, and I didn't want him chasing me.

Now I *know* he's a monster, but I'm not afraid of the chase.

I scream. At the top of my lungs, I scream for help.

Carter pulls right out of me, grabbing me off the desk and yanking me back against his chest. "What the *fuck* are you doing?" he demands.

Turning my head just enough to look back at him, I say calmly, "Stopping you."

Fire leaps in his eyes, and the sight of his anger unleashes warring feelings inside me. On one hand, it's terrifying. I don't like to see Carter angry, even if I don't believe he would actually hurt me anymore.

It also warms my blood, the silent promise of his violence. His lip curls up in a sneer and my heart leaps in response. He grabs the front of my shirt, balling it in his hand, and shoves me back against the wall.

"You think that was fucking cute?" he demands.

"Nope," I answer, holding his gaze. "I think I don't want you inside me when you've been God knows where since last time we were together. I just got a full panel of STD tests done; I'd prefer not to have to go back so soon."

He cocks an eyebrow in surprise, but he's too annoyed to ask me about it. "I haven't been with anyone else yet," he tells me.

Yet. That word does more to bottom out my stomach than him bending me over the desk and making me take his cock. I hate that specific part of his statement, but I love the rest. Warmth washes over me at the knowledge that he hasn't had sex with anyone else since me. I know it hasn't been long, but in Carter time, it has been a while.

"But you said you had a new plaything," I point out.

"I didn't say I've already tested out the equipment," he states, glancing at the door. Enough seconds have passed that there must not have been anyone in the immediate vicinity, but someone down the hall could still be walking this way to investigate the noise.

I shouldn't give him the satisfaction, wouldn't if I could control myself, but my shoulders sag with relief, my head drops back against the wall, and my eyes drift closed with a sort of nonverbal "Oh, thank God."

I don't want to get back together, but I don't want him to sleep with that stupid girl in class, either. I don't know what to do with that, but I don't have time to figure it out and there are more pressing matters to attend to.

I'm about to pull away, walk back to the desk, and reposition myself the way he had me. I don't think it's a *good* idea to have sex with him, but he has already been inside me. I don't think I'll be in much hotter water just for letting him finish.

Before I can do that, Carter takes control again. Satisfied that no one is coming and now with even more motivation to punish me, Carter hikes up one of my legs, plants himself flush against me, and shoves his cock inside me more forcefully. This time, before I can so much as moan, he seals a hand over my mouth.

My eyes jump to his, a silent protest, but his eyes are hard now. I get the feeling I pissed him off more than I meant to, and the realization knocks some of the wind out of my sails. Instincts I don't entirely understand prompt me to seek forgiveness, to repent and make up for my bad behavior. Mental images flash to mind of him lying on his bed, me kneeling naked beside him. Bending and kissing him, running my lips over every chiseled inch of his body, letting my tongue flit out to run along the underside of his dick. When he's hard and wanting, he can take me any way he wants. He can hold me down or make love to me. He can wear a condom or come inside me.

Between my own lewd thoughts and Carter brutally pounding inside me, tension starts to build in my core. As if he can see me starting to feel too good and he wants to stop it, Carter pulls out of me.

Grasping my arm, he tugs me back over to the desk and gives me a push toward it. I require no manhandling this time. I bend myself over the desk and spread my legs as far as he had them before. I'm dripping wet now and I feel so exposed spread out here like this without him inside me.

Carter steps forward, grabbing the globes of my ass in his hands and squeezing. "Your ass is beautiful. I should take that, too."

Fear takes over and I look back at him over my shoulder, alarm clear in my expression. I want to tell him no, but I'm too worried that will seal the deal and the next thing I know he'll be forcing his too-large cock into that too-small hole.

Running a hand over my ass and smiling faintly, he says, "Maybe another time."

There won't *be* another time, but I can't tell him that. I don't know how I'll make sure of that, but I have to. Clearly, neither one of us can be trusted once he gets me alone.

Right now, he guides himself inside me, and this time, I don't fight him. I hold onto the desk for dear life, losing my grip and sliding several times while he fucks me. My insides twist and tauten as he moves inside me, hitting at just the right angle. I'm ready to climb the walls, grabbing desperately at the desk, then he shoves inside me hard and fast, hard and fast, hard and fast. I cry out again when I come. Carter is prepared this time and covers my mouth with his hand, muffling my cry of pleasure, and the helpless whimpers that follow as he continues to use my overly stimulated body to get himself off.

Finally, he groans with his own pleasure, pushing deep then pumping a few more slow times until he has emptied himself inside me.

I let my arms fall to each side of the desk. My face is smashed uncomfortably against the hard surface now, my body completely boneless as I lie here, letting the desk entirely support my weight. I know this is something I'll have to deal with later, but for right now, I just want to feel good.

Since Carter is standing and doesn't have anywhere to recover, he has to pull it together before I do. He starts moving and I don't question it until he lifts my foot and takes my panties *off* instead of pulling them back up.

I crane my head to look back at him and see my panties in his hands.

"What are you doing?" I ask.

"I'm keeping these," he tells me, dangling them briefly, then shoving them in the pocket of his jeans.

"What?" Reluctantly pushing myself up, I tell him, "You can't keep those. I'm wearing a *skirt*. You want me flashing everyone my business?"

Carter merely smirks at me. "Nope, don't want anyone seeing your business. Guess you better keep your legs closed."

I roll my eyes. "You keep *your* legs closed," I mutter, straightening my skirt around my waist. I feel naked in this skirt with no panties on, and dirty on top of it because I can feel the evidence of Carter fucking me between my legs. "I can't... Just give me my panties back."

"Nah. Gonna keep 'em. Might need visual aids when I talk to your buddy, Luke."

Panties forgotten, my eyes widen. "You better not really talk to him, Carter. I will be so pissed at you if you embarrass me like that."

Carter shrugs, then crosses his arms. "Then you better handle it yourself. If you really went out with him, end it. Feed him the same bullshit you gave me about needing to focus on your schoolwork, I don't care. Just end it. I'm not going to have some other asshole putting his hands on you. If he does, I shit you not, Zoey, I'll fucking decimate him."

I don't even have any interest in a relationship with Luke, but Carter's insistence that I remain on the shelf while he does whatever he wants really pisses me off. "You're bein' ridiculous," I tell him. "I don't need your permission to live my life."

"Of course you don't. Just to fuck someone else. You need my permission for that, and you're not going to get it."

"You are *not* my boyfriend anymore. What part of that is hard for you to grasp?"

Moving away from the wall and to the desk where he put my books down, Carter retrieves them and brings them over to me. "Here you go."

"Just gonna ignore that perfectly reasonable question?"

"You're probably hungry, huh?" He pulls out his wallet and extracts a twenty. "Better get yourself some lunch. I've gotta make an appearance in the cafeteria or I'd come with."

I do not touch the money. Instead, I take my books and look up at him. "You can't trick me back into a relationship with you. I'm not that dumb."

"I'm not trying to trick you back into a relationship," he tells me, putting the twenty on the desk since I'm not taking it. "In fact, I've gotta get to the cafeteria to give my new toy some attention. Thanks for the fuck, though," he adds, winking at me, then turning and leaving me alone to fume in the empty classroom.

CHAPTER 42

THE WEEKEND PASSES UNEVENTFULLY.

I work, study, go to church, and go out for coffee with Grace.

When I get to my locker Monday morning, I find a surprise waiting for me—though, not a mean one this time. A small shopping bag with two-toned pink stripes from Victoria's Secret is in my locker. I look around to make sure no one is glancing my way, then open the bag to find six pairs of panties, all in my size. On top of the pink tissue paper inside is a note in Carter's handwriting that reads, "To make up for the pair I stole. Wear the blue ones next time you wear that skirt."

Narrowing my eyes, I toss the note back in the bag. Does that mean he sees my skirt as some kind of sign indicating he can fuck me that day? He can fuck *off* if he thinks that. Days have passed since our last encounter, weekend days, so I'm sure he brought Blondie over to Cartwright's for a weekend group hang. I'm sure Brianna was just as welcoming to her as she was to me, and Cartwright didn't have to keep up, he could just be nice to the straightforward hot blonde on Carter's arm. The one who is supposed to be there, because she fits in like I never did.

Taking my cell phone out of my purse, I text Carter while I'm mad so I can yell at him. "If you think I dropped the girlfriend title so I could be your occasional booty call, boy, do you have another thing coming. Thanks for the panties, but you're never going to see them on me."

Since I can't very well bring a Victoria's Secret bag with me, I slam my locker door shut and leave them inside. I'll just have to try to sneak them out to my car while everyone is at lunch… which will mean lingering in the bathroom until everyone else is already in the cafeteria, which means if Carter wants to accost me, the path will be clear.

I don't know if the panties were an actual gift or just a way to get me alone again. I suppose I could throw a wrench in his plans —if they *are* his plans—and wait until I leave for the day to take them, but spending even more time in the school building and waiting for it to clear out sounds terrible and also less reliable. The last thing I need is giving anyone the visual of me hauling a bag from Victoria's Secret through the halls though.

I won't be wearing them anytime soon, anyway. Thank the Lord, I finally started my period over the weekend, so there is no Carter clone hiding out in my womb, waiting to do Daddy's bidding and ruin my whole life. The birth control I started was supposed to start working immediately, so it seems now I'm out of the woods.

I didn't want to be pregnant, so I am relieved, but there is the tiniest corner of my heart that felt a bit sad. Logically and in every sensible way, I know Carter would use a baby to manipulate me right back into his arms, to control me and ruin any relationship I tried to start with anyone else. I know he would be a nightmare to deal with, and I would probably end up waving the white flag and going back to him to try and work things out—especially with a little baby in the picture and the tempting vision of a perfect little family in my mushy heart. For all of the reasons in the world, it is good that I am not pregnant.

On an irrational, sentimental level buried deep, I'm just a pinch sad about it.

But that can easily be ignored. I'm rational most of the time, and the overwhelming majority of me is immensely relieved Carter didn't ruin my life.

Not yet, anyway. When I saw Luke at church on Sunday, I didn't get a chance to talk to him like I wanted to. At school,

Carter would be able to see me talk to Luke, but if I pull him aside at church… well, Carter isn't going to church, that's for sure.

I don't think Carter did talk to Luke though, because while I didn't get to pull him aside and talk to him, Luke didn't act weird around me. He flashed me friendly smiles from across the room, both of us gesturing that we would catch up later, we just never did.

I'm relieved Carter respected my wishes. I don't know what possessed me to lie to him in the first place, I just didn't think he would get so crazy about it. I thought he might experience the same wounded sensation of a bruised ego and a punched heart as I felt when I saw him flirting with Blondie right in front of me. I didn't think he would threaten to target my mystery boyfriend, but on reflection, I should have been prepared for the possibility. Carter is crazy and spoiled, so of course he thinks he should get his way while doing whatever the hell he wants. Of course he wants his unused toy on a shelf instead of letting it move on and find someone else to play with.

I can't even fault him for that sentiment, though. It would be severely hypocritical. I'm finding I feel the same way. I don't want to *be* with Carter, but I don't want him to be with anyone else either. It's not like I want him to be lonely or unloved, I just… don't want him to be sexually or emotionally invested in any other girls.

I think what I *actually* want is a time machine so that I could travel back to the moment Erika shoved her cell phone at me. Instead of wanting to know and looking at the phone, I would have just surprised her by punching her in the face. Would have been well worth the detention or suspension, or whatever it is they do to bad kids who punch other students. I've never actually had a detention, but it seems like I could just use it as an additional study hall and get a jumpstart on my homework. At any rate, after the detention, Carter would still be my boyfriend, and I wouldn't have to feel conflicted about anything.

Or maybe I need to set the time machine back a little more. Return to that night I left him unsatisfied and remedy the damn issue myself, then he never would have gone over to Erika's house in the first place.

When it's time for history class, I walk a little slower. Ideally, I want to arrive right before the bell rings, that way I don't have to witness the pre-class flirting of Carter and Jenna. I get there just before the bell, but Carter isn't in his seat. I frown at his absence, but figure he's just running late. I set up my study area, the bell rings, but Carter never comes.

About ten minutes into class, he finally shows up. Mr. Hassenfeld stops talking to stare Carter down disapprovingly. "So nice of you to grace us with your presence, Mr. Mahoney."

"I do what I can to please the fans," Carter assures him with an easy smile.

I roll my eyes, but a few kids chuckle. Ugh.

After class, I don't feel as terrible as I expect to. Maybe it was his late arrival or maybe he just didn't feel like torturing me today, but he doesn't spend the whole class flirting with Jenna. There is still some interaction between them, but she's clearly driving it. I wonder if she has already lost his interest, but that might be wishful thinking.

Lecture runs late and I'm a little slower about getting my stuff put away so I can leave. Carter and Jenna walk out together. I keep my head down, refusing to look at them, but I hear her talking about her cat. I bet Carter doesn't have a single fuck to give about her cat. I bet he would rather stab himself in the eyeball than listen to another word about Fluffy.

Trying to shake off the ickiness of just having overheard her speaking to him, I gather my things and make my way out of the classroom.

"There you are!"

I turn, startled, at Kasey, the photographer from the football game. She is plodding toward me with a wide smile on her face. Pointing at myself, I question, "Me?"

Nodding enthusiastically, she says, "I needed to catch you after class. Can you come sit with me at lunch? I need to talk to you about an opportunity I think you'll be interested in."

"Lunch? In the cafeteria?"

Kasey blinks. "Last I checked, that was the popular lunch location."

"Oh. Yeah. I don't eat in the cafeteria. I could catch you after school lets out instead?"

"No," she says, firmly determined. "I have stuff after school. It has to be at lunch. Come on, the lunchroom isn't so bad. It's one day. It won't kill you, I promise."

Dread consumes me at the thought of going back to that cafeteria. Sure, the "Zoey the ho" period has passed, but it's still a room populated with people I don't want to be around. I've grown accustomed to my peaceful, isolated lunch breaks.

Kasey doesn't give me much of a choice. She's a dog with a bone, and the bone is my presence at lunch. Grace might also be offended if she sees me back in the lunchroom, but sitting at a different table instead of with her. Can't sit with her anyway, though. Luke sits at that table, and if I show up in the cafeteria again all of a sudden sitting at a table with Luke… yeah, no.

With many reservations and heavy, reluctant steps, I follow Kasey to the cafeteria. I think up excuses the whole way there, but since I don't spit any of them out, I walk through the open doors and into the mouth of hell.

The cafeteria buzzes with energy and conversation. All the people I spend all day not interacting with gathered together in one place. Fantastic. I also don't have my lunch, which means I'll have to buy. Ordinarily I wouldn't even have enough cash on me to buy lunch, but I still have the twenty that Carter left me Thursday, so I guess I can use that.

Kasey chatters as we walk over and take our places in line. Even though she is literally invisible to most social sectors, Kasey is unafraid of the lunchroom. I admire that about her. I get the feeling if she had been my best friend instead of Grace during the "Zoey the ho" situation, Kasey would have ignored the stares, slut coughs, and open hostility from the football players. I bet she would have sat there with me, completely unmoved by the nonsense all around, and I bet she never would have let me flee the lunchroom in the first place.

This is a lot of betting I'm doing on someone I barely know, but she just has a very strong presence, and I really dig it. I love

Grace, but I feel like Kasey might be more on my level in regards to certain things. While I do love Grace, we really don't have that much in common.

I feel a kinship with Kasey already, and this is only my second interaction with her.

By the time I follow her to an empty section of table and sit down with her, I'm already feeling a little more comfortable. The odd look from the jocks has certainly come my way, mainly from Erika, who is glaring at me through narrowed eyes like she personally owns the cafeteria, and she's contemplating coming over to kick me out.

"Ignore her, she's a bitch," Kasey tells me, plucking a French fry off her food tray.

Glancing away from Erika and down at my own, I smile faintly. "Believe me, I know."

"So, anyway, the reason I wanted to talk to you is I wanted to see if you'd be interested in writing for the school paper. I cyber stalked you a little bit and discovered you work at a bookstore. Can I assume you like to read?"

"I do," I verify, unbothered by her admission of stalking. I probably would have stalked her to find out what her deal was, but I was too wrapped up in Carter.

"Okay, so, we've decided to add a book review column to the paper, but all of our writers have assignments. We don't have anyone who was interested in making this their regular beat, and I thought, you're smart, you read, you work at a bookstore—who better to do the column? Plus, if you're on the fence, it will look good to colleges," she adds, to entice me. "I know you have work and youth group and church, but you don't have any extracurric- ulars at school. You spend as little time here as you possibly can, and to be perfectly honest, I think being able to add book reviewer for the school paper to your resume would make you look more well-rounded."

Baffled by the amount of thought she has put into my college resume, I blink at her, searching for a response.

Reaching into the small purse she carries with her, she draws out a white envelope and passes it across the table. "And before you say anything, if you answer yes, you get this."

I pull the envelope closer and pick it up. Opening it, I find a $100 bill and two $50 bills inside. "What's this for?"

"Your stipend," she answers, sounding all proud of herself. "You can use that money to buy the books you want to review. We prefer new releases, but the section is yours to do whatever you want with. If you want to do a spotlight on older releases, that's fine, too. It's completely up to you. Just clear the book with the editor, write your review, and that's it. It's an easy gig, it'll look good to the colleges you're applying to, *and* you get $200 to spend on books."

"This is mine?" I question, skeptically. "I can spend all of it on books? I don't have to pay it back or anything?"

"Nope. You don't even have to show receipts. You take that money and don't even mention it again."

"Don't mention it?"

"Well, the movie reviewer doesn't get a stipend, so they'd probably be a little salty. I wouldn't mention it."

"Then why do I get one?" I ask.

"Don't look the gift horse in the mouth," she advises me. "So, are you in?"

"I guess I have to be," I admit, fingering the envelope. "Don't you want some proof I can do the job or something, though? I've never written a review before. Shouldn't I submit some kind of writing sample?"

"I mean, it's not rocket science. If you're at a loss for how to write a review, I can direct you to a few good ones so you can get a feel for it. But no, you don't have to try out. I had you in mind for the position, so if you want it, it's yours."

"Well, thank you," I say, sliding the envelope under my tray. "Do I have to attend the newspaper meetings?"

"Nope. You can if you want to, but it's not required. You'll be a designated book reviewer, so you won't need to be there to get assignments or any of the other stuff concerning the paper. You'll do your own column, submit it, and that's it. It really won't require much from you. I'm sure you would be reading the books anyway, now you'll just have them paid for and you'll write a little block of text about it."

"That's awesome." I flash her a smile. "Thank you for thinking of me."

Kasey smiles. "No problem."

I start eating my lunch, thinking about which book I'll read for my first review. Kasey doesn't seem to mind my preoccupation, and we eat in a companionable silence. She checks her phone from time to time and eats her own lunch, and overall, it's a pleasant trip back to the lunchroom.

At least, until the seat beside me is suddenly occupied, and I look up to see Luke sitting there. I don't mean to gape at him in horror as he flashes me a smile, but I do. My gaze jumps across the cafeteria to Carter, and he is looking right at me, a fry frozen mid-air on its way to his mouth.

Oh, my God.

"Um, I—you can't…" I shake my head, trying to clear out some of the panic. "I'm so sorry, you can't sit with me," I tell Luke.

Rather than look offended, Luke merely lifts his eyebrows in surprise. "Why not? This seat reserved for someone else?"

I don't feel like I have time to explain. Just the fact that he walked over here is going to be incriminating, but for every second that he sits here, Carter is going to be more convinced I really am dating Luke. I don't know what he can actually do to Luke, but I really don't want to find out.

My skin feels hot with the adrenaline surging through me. I try not to look at Carter, even though I'm tempted. I don't want to look even more like a kid caught with a hand in the cookie jar. "Luke, please. I'm not tryin' to be mean or rude, I swear I'm not, but you need to go back to your table right now."

He doesn't move. Instead, he picks up half of his turkey sandwich from his tray like he's going to start eating. "I might, but you haven't said why."

"Carter," I blurt. "We—we just broke up and I don't want to rub his face—I mean, not that there's anything between you and me, but he might think…." Sighing, I say, "Just please go sit with Grace."

"Ah." Luke nods, but his expression remains determined.

"Carter already told me to stay away from you. Turns out, Carter's not my boss." Looking at me more pointedly, he says, "Or yours. You broke up. Why does he have any say who you spend time with?"

"It's complicated," I tell him, stealing a glance at Carter. He's still watching, his eyes darkened with devious intent. Fuck. "Please. I don't want trouble, Luke."

"There shouldn't *be* any trouble," he insists, stubbornly. "You're not in a relationship with him—"

"It doesn't matter," I interrupt, since he's wasting time. "He has a mean streak you might not have seen, but please trust me on this. You don't want him for an enemy."

Luke doesn't move. "I can't believe you're letting him control you like this."

My jaw drops. More that Luke would actually *say* that to me than anything else. "I'm not letting him control me."

"Yes, you are. He clearly threatened you, and that's why you're trying to shoo me away. He threatened me, too, but here I sit." Unscrewing the cap on his bottled water, Luke suggests, "Maybe I'm not as boring as he thinks I am."

I cringe. I don't know what Carter actually said, and I'm too embarrassed to ask. I don't know if I'm more embarrassed over the possibility of what Carter might have said, or just for Luke in general. I don't even know how to respond to that. I don't want to verify that Carter called him boring, but it sounds like Carter said that *to* him. God, I can only imagine what Carter might have said. And he had my panties! My face flushes about ten different shades of red as I run through the possibilities.

Luke won't leave, so I don't know what to do.

I look up at Kasey to see what she thinks of all this, and she is looking at Luke with an expression I can only describe as faintly hostile. It throws me, and for a minute, I stop worrying about Carter to wonder what the hell that's about.

It takes less than five minutes for Carter to make his way over to the table. I have to admit, I didn't think he would. Our battle is usually a private thing, just between us. I figured he would keep to his side of the cafeteria and maybe message me later to remind me that I'm not allowed to talk to boys.

Instead, he comes over and stops behind me. He plants his

hands on either of my shoulders and does the strangest thing—he starts to give me a casual shoulder rub. "Didn't expect to see you in here," he tells me.

"I'm full of surprises," I offer.

"That you are," he agrees smoothly. "How are you feeling today?"

I frown and twist to look up at him suspiciously. "Fine," I say slowly.

His voice is warm, convincingly caring. "Good." Then he leans in, slides his hand down my core until it's splayed across my stomach, and says, "It's too soon for you to be causing Mommy trouble, little guy. You better be good in there."

I actually *feel* the color drain out of my face. Kasey's jaw drops, her eyes popping. I am frozen in shock. Since Carter wasn't quiet or even remotely subtle, and since he draws attention wherever he goes anyway, when I look down at the rest of the table, I see more wide eyes, friends nudging each other with telling glances, and at the table behind Kasey, people glancing back at us unsubtly while others lean in and whisper.

Carter just effectively told the whole senior class that I'm pregnant with his baby. Those who aren't sitting close enough to hear will have heard through the grapevine before school lets out today.

When I finally have enough composure to speak, I tell him, "I am going to kill you."

"Oh, don't tell anyone," he adds like an afterthought, smacking Luke on the shoulder in a casually pal-like way. "She hasn't told her mom yet, so—"

"I am *not* pregnant," I interrupt, beginning to seethe again.

This is the kind of rumor that stands a chance of lingering, even long past the point of people seeing I obviously am not pregnant. They won't know without a doubt that I was *never* pregnant. Not having a baby doesn't mean I was never pregnant, it could mean I got an abortion. Getting Jake kicked off the football team made me a prude bitch, but if people think I did *that*... Well, shit. That's not going to go over well.

"You won't rest until you've completely ruined my reputation, will you?" I demand.

"Hey, you're among friends here," Carter returns. "I'm sure they won't tell anybody."

"There's nothing to tell. I'm not pregnant," I say again, glaring up at him. "Least of all with the spawn of Satan, which is what I would be carrying if you impregnated me."

Carter smiles. "Now, that's no way to talk about our baby, Zoey. Those hormones are acting up something fierce, aren't they?"

"Murder," I say again, my eyes widening. "I'm literally going to kill you. I thought it would be you who murdered me, but no."

"Oh, shit. Before I forget…" He takes his hands off me, reaches into his pocket, and a moment later, he dangles my panties in front of my face. "You left these in my car the other night."

Kasey covers her face to hide a helpless grin.

I snatch the fabric out of his hands, turning an even deeper shade of red as my soul shrivels. "I hate you so much."

"That's all right," he says, touching my shoulder. "Makes the sex better." Before I can say anything else, he fists a hand in my hair, yanks me back, and plants a kiss on me. "See you later, babe."

Humiliation washes over me as Carter walks away. I swipe a hand across my mouth in a vain attempt to wipe away his kiss, but I can still taste him on my bottom lip, and it wasn't even a deep kiss. My stomach rolls over. I feel like I might actually vomit, but I know it's just from the immense stress he just delivered onto my shoulders.

"I'm so sorry," Kasey says, apparently ashamed of herself. "I know he just dropped you in a pot full of boiling water. I know it's not funny, but… damn. That was merciless."

The funny thing is, this is the *merciful* version of Carter. I don't bother telling her that. I can't even look at Luke. His brother's story about the girl who got pregnant by the former Longhorn and essentially ruined her life springs to mind. I wonder if Luke will run to James and tell him what Carter said. When I show up at church on Sunday, will his whole family think I've been knocked up by Carter Mahoney? Will someone say something to my mom? I don't know if she would be sad for me, or absolutely gleeful that I got a hook into Carter Mahoney for the rest of his life.

This is untenable. I can't believe Carter just did that.

I look over now that he's back at his table and stumble across the only small measure of satisfaction I can possibly get out of this. Jenna is sitting at Erika's table, her mouth hanging open as she glares daggers at me. I don't want to feel so vindictive toward another girl, but she tortured me when she flirted with Carter so much in class the other day. I have to admit, even though I'm horrified by what Carter just did, I'm not all that sad that I got to return the favor.

CHAPTER 43

TUESDAY MORNING as I approach my locker, my heart sinks at the sight of a pale blue party banner draped across my locker door announcing to the world, "It's a boy!"

I tear it down gracelessly, wad it up, and take it over to throw into the trash can.

I don't know if Carter put it there or someone else did, but I can feel eyes on me again. I'm pretty slim to begin with, but I notice myself sucking in my stomach as I turn with my books to leave the locker, all too aware of the searching gazes of people looking for a baby bump like I'm an A-list celeb and they're reporting for a sleazy gossip rag.

Forget that I haven't even *known* Carter long enough to be so pregnant I would be showing, but people don't think. They hear something semi-believable and run with it. The facts don't even matter.

On top of Carter's bullshit, I'm PMSing. I should have stayed home in bed and called myself in sick. There's a quiz in Spanish today though, and making them up is a hassle, so I guess I just have to deal with this nonsense.

I ignore my way through the first part of the day, only paying attention to my surroundings when I get to history. Carter isn't late today. He's already in class when I show up. Jenna is still seated behind him, but she's not flirting with him today. Looking a bit irritable, she plays on her cell phone while we wait for the bell. Carter does nothing to solicit her attention. Instead, he sits there and sketches.

I expected history class to be awful, so the calm lack of eventfulness is a godsend.

About halfway through history, someone from student council knocks on the door. Mr. Hassenfeld goes to the door and opens it, and she peers in, a bright smile on her face. "I need Zoey Ellis in the guidance counselor's office."

I blink in confusion. Mr. Hassenfeld looks back at me, also unprepared. "Zoey, you're needed in the office."

I hate being the center of attention so much, but everyone looks at me as I gather my things and slide out from behind my desk. When I'm walking past, a girl leaning forward whispers to the girl in front of her, "I bet it's about the baby."

At this point, I can only sigh. I'm getting so tired of all this. Maybe I need that time machine to go back to when Jake felt me up. Maybe I shouldn't have said anything, then he would still be playing ball, and I wouldn't have had a target plastered on my back in the first place. Carter Mahoney never would have noticed me. No one would talk about me or judge me because no one would know who I am.

Certainly, there would be no rumors. I'm not scandalous enough to do anything to provoke rumors, only the guys who terrorize me are.

Maybe I should stop washing my hair and start wearing baggy clothes to school. If no one wants to fuck me, no one will be interested in dragging my ass through the mud or ruining my reputation. Maybe fighting them off is just too much work, too unpleasant. Maybe I should just accept my role as their disposable plaything and let boys who don't give a damn about me do whatever they want.

On second thought, no. Fuck that. Let them talk. Let them try to ruin my life. I can take it.

God willing, I won't be stuck in this miserable town for much longer, anyway. A year from now, I'll be experiencing my first autumn in Pennsylvania. The weather will be so chilly, I'll need to wear a warm sweater. The leaves on all the trees will be the most beautiful shades of red, yellow, and orange. I wonder what the changing season will smell like?

Peace fills me at the thought. I need to keep that vision safe in my mind when this place starts to overwhelm me and get me down. None of this matters in the great scheme of things. I won't be here much longer. Freedom is only a few months away. I just have to keep my eye on the prize.

I feel calmer and more centered when I show up at the guidance counselor's office and knock on the door. Ms. Cunningham glances up, flashes me a smile, and waves toward the chair in front of her desk.

"Hi, Zoey. Come on in, have a seat."

I step inside and close the door behind me, then walk over and drop into the chair. I'm tongue-tied, unsure what to say or ask. Before I can figure it out, she grabs a blue piece of clothing wrapped in plastic and puts it on the desk in front of me.

"This is for you."

I put my books on my lap and grab the package. "What is this?"

"A Longhorn windbreaker," she announces cheerfully. "We're gifting all the honor roll students with one. A little reward for your outstanding achievement."

Relief moves through me and I sit back in my chair, putting the wrapped windbreaker on top of my books. This is just about honor roll, not the stupid pregnancy rumor. "Thank you," I tell her, even though I don't have much use for a Longhorn windbreaker.

She smiles and nods. "While I have you here, I'd also like to go over your college plans with you. I have some updates since we talked at the start of the school year." Rolling her chair back, she reaches into a file cabinet and pulls out my folder, then she wheels back to the desk. "I know we went over what you would need to do in order to get a full-ride scholarship at your first-choice college."

"Yes." I nod my head once. "I've been doing all that. My history grade slipped a little, but Mr. Hassenfeld gave me extra credit, so I was able to pull it back up."

She nods her head. "Yes, and that's wonderful. You're still

very comfortably in the top ten percent of your graduating class. In fact, your GPA is the 4th highest. Now, here's the problem," she says, slapping a palm down on the open folder and meeting my gaze.

"Problem?"

"Unfortunately, the school you want to attend had to make some budget cuts this year. They still want to make it easier for the best and the brightest to study there so they're still offering scholarships to high school students in the top ten percent of their graduating class... unfortunately, that will no longer be a full ride, but a half ride. Only valedictorians and salutatorians will be offered full rides this year. That means you're two spots below a full-ride. I know we discussed that financial aid was pretty important in order for you to be able to attend there, and with your family's income, you would also be able to get a Pell grant, so all is not lost."

She keeps talking, but I can't focus on what she's saying. All *is* lost. Half the tuition rate alone would be 18 grand a year, and that's not even factoring in the cost of housing and living expenses. A Pell grant wouldn't make up the other half of the lost scholarship. It would put a dent in it, but not a big one.

Shaking myself out of it, I ask her, "Okay, so what do I have to do to catch up?"

"Well, there's no catching up to the valedictorian. Charlie's GPA is—you're not taking enough of the right classes to compete with him, and even if we could get special permission to transfer you into the classes you'd need, you still can't catch up. He has been taking AP courses for too long. With only senior year left, it's simply not possible to catch up."

"But I only have to make salutatorian, not valedictorian," I point out. "I'm ranked 4th in my class, and I have to move up to 2nd. That's not an impossible climb. Tell me how to get there and I'll do it."

Grimacing in a way that fills me with dread, she says, "Currently, Carter Mahoney is ranked 2nd highest in your graduating class. If his grades remain on course, he will make salutatorian." Flipping a paper over, she tells me, "I believe with dedication you can move up to third, but if I'm bein' honest with you, sweetheart, I don't think you can bump Carter out of second. Don't tell anybody I said so, but that boy is obnoxiously smart. I know he doesn't try as hard as you do, but if not for Charlie, he would have valedictorian in the bag."

That doesn't even make sense. Yes, Carter is extremely intelligent, especially in a wily kind of way, but he hasn't even read *Catcher in the Rye*. Was he playing up his disinterest in schoolwork? With his friends, I might be able to make the jump that he doesn't want to come off like a nerd, but with me? *I'm* a nerd. I would never think of him as being *less cool* for doing his best in school. I would admire that, so it doesn't make sense to lie to me about it.

A suspicion clicks into place, and I look up at Ms. Cunningham. "Who is third?"

"Hm? Oh." She drags her finger down a printout and reads the name of the student between me and Carter. "Sara Knowles."

I start laughing. It's a crazy, maniacal, I'm-cracking kind of laugh, and the guidance counselor begins to look concerned.

Sara Knowles. Carter's rally girl. Accomplished not only at making cute chocolate covered strawberries, but assembling baskets, and probably doing Carter's schoolwork when he doesn't feel like doing it.

Of fucking course Carter would land the smartest rally girl in the history of fucking rally girls to do his bitchwork.

Nothing is fair. Everything is shit. Carter Mahoney is the worst. I'm laughing so hard a tear creeps out of the corner of my eye, and the moisture triggers a stinging behind my eyes like I might *actually* cry. That kills my maniacal humor and I settle down, trying to focus and grasp at the remaining straws.

"Sorry. Okay, so, you said I should be able to catch up to Sara. That means we're not that far apart."

She nods her head. "That's right. It would add a lot of stress on ya, though, and I know you've got a lot on your plate already. Even if you don't catch up to Carter, all is not lost. If you're open to Prairie View, you can attend there tuition free. You won't be able to commute that far, of course, but if you go to this one," she says, sliding a pamphlet across the desk and tapping it, "This one is in Dallas, so it's close enough that you could commute, that way you wouldn't have to pay for campus housing."

I stop listening. Staying in Texas for college is the absolute last resort. I'm not going to give up on my first-choice school. Ms. Cunningham thinks I need to jump *two* spots, but I know I only really have to jump one. Only Sara.

If I can catch up to her, I *might* be able to catch up to Carter, because Sara is probably why Carter *is* salutatorian in the first place. If it comes down to it, I might be able to play dirty and distract Carter from his schoolwork. She does some of his work, but surely not all of it. If I can get his authentic grades to suffer a little, even Sara's help won't keep him in second.

I don't like playing Carter's manipulative games, but he doesn't need this as much as I do. He's already in at Columbia because of his football talent. If he isn't salutatorian, it won't make a difference. Meanwhile, my future *depends* upon it.

CHAPTER 44

OVER THE NEXT COUPLE DAYS, I spin a dozen different plans to distract Carter and sabotage his academic standing.

I study up on Sara to see which classes she's taking so I can get an idea of how the hell I can get ahead of her. The main problem I see is that she's in AP math classes and I'm not. It's hard as hell to leapfrog someone who is acing a class that scores them more GPA points than mine. I need her to be weak in another class that I can ace. The problem is, she isn't. The dumbest thing about her seems to be that she likes Carter, and I can't very well blame her for that.

So, that's inconvenient. Why couldn't he just have a bimbo for a rally girl?

By Thursday, I feel terrible about all my plans of sabotage. This isn't me. I'm not a saboteur. I don't scheme and deceive to get my way. If I get out of this town only because I played like that, I don't even know if I'll be able to feel proud of my own accomplishments.

Thursday is also the day of a math exam that I have to ace if I stand a chance of catching up to Carter. I've been studying my ass off for it, practicing exam questions until my vision blurs, but math is my weakest subject. I tend to get vaguely anxious halfway through every exam, and by the second half, I end up missing a couple of questions that I know the answer to when I get the test back.

I bet Carter doesn't let any exam psyche him out.

As mad as I am at myself for it, I text Carter when I get to school and tell him I need to see him as soon as he has a minute. I don't know exactly what I'm going to do or say to him until the moment arrives. I go back and forth, warring with what I need and what I'm willing to do.

I'm at my locker putting books away and getting out my history book when he shows up.

"You rang?"

I sigh, closing my locker door and looking over at him. "Did you know you're on track to be the class salutatorian?"

He blinks, clearly not expecting me to say that. "I'm aware of that, yes."

I nod, my gaze dropping. I don't have math until after lunch, but it's Carter's next class. "Is that because of Sara?"

Carter frowns and pushes off the locker, appearing out of his element. Whatever he thought I summoned him for, this isn't it. "No, it's because I have a brain. I told you that before. You called me here to ask about my grades?"

"I need you to throw the math exam today," I state, without further preamble.

His eyebrows rise in surprise. "Excuse me?"

This is lower than I want to stoop, but not as low as I could go, so I try to soothe myself with that. "Remember I told you about the school I wanted to go to? Top ten percent isn't enough for a full ride anymore, only valedictorians and salutatorians get it. If I don't graduate second in our class, I can't afford to go. I'll end up at the University of North Texas in Dallas, and I'll have to commute from home. If I don't catch up to you, I'm never gettin' out of this town."

"And if I bomb the math exam, you'll catch up?"

"Not exactly. Your damn rally girl is in the spot between me and you, but the counselor thinks I can catch up to her if I work really hard."

The corners of Carter's mouth tip up in amusement. "Yeah, she's a smart cookie. *Makes* good cookies, too."

Ignoring him, I go on, "I can't catch you, though. The AP biology class you took last year puts you ahead of me if you ace all your classes this year, even if I ace mine, too. I need you to get a B in math, which means…"

"I need to bomb this test," he says, following along.

I nod, not quite able to look at him.

"And what do I get out of it?" he asks.

"The pleasure of knowing that, for once, you made a positive difference in my life?" I suggest hopefully.

Carter smiles and shakes his head. "Try again."

"I'll name the baby after you," I deadpan.

He shakes his head again. "Nah. We'll name him something else. Creeps me out to imagine you calling out my name and talking to a kid."

I sigh, exasperated. "What do you want?"

"If you have to ask that, maybe you don't deserve to be the class salutatorian," he suggests.

I narrow my eyes at him. "You want me to prostitute myself, is that it? You want to fuck me? Fine. Throw the math test, and I'll let you fuck me. Or *not* let you, if that's what you're in the mood for."

Carter shakes his head. "Once isn't enough. Twice, and you'll be my date to homecoming, which will likely mean a third time. That seems like a fair deal."

"I'm not going to homecoming," I tell him. "I'll agree to three fucks, but not homecoming. I don't have a dress, I don't have the money to buy one, and no, before you offer, I do not want you to buy me a homecoming dress." Lighting up my phone, I see we both have less than a minute to get to our next class. "I have to go or I'm going to be late. Deal, or no deal?"

Carter nods once. "Deal."

Relief trickles through me and I feel myself soften. Sure, he made me bargain for it, but I sort of can't believe he's willing to do this for me. "Thank you."

Carter smirks and takes a step forward. Bringing a hand up behind me and cupping my neck, he draws me close and bends his head to seal our deal with a kiss. "You can thank me later."

IT'S lunchtime on Friday and I am sitting in my car, eating a PB&J and reading the new book I bought to review for the school paper. My cell phone starts vibrating in my cup holder, so I glance at the screen. It's a phone number I don't recognize, so I slide a bookmark between the pages and close my book, grabbing the phone and answering it.

"Hello?"

"Hi, is this Zoey?"

It's a woman's voice, but not one I recognize. "Yes, I'm Zoey."

"Hi Zoey, this is Angela Mahoney. Carter's mom," she offers for clarification.

"Oh. Um, hello," I say, awkwardly.

"Carter gave me your number," she explains. "I was wondering if you were free tonight. Carter has an away game, as you probably know. His father and I intend to go, but Chloe gets bored of going to every game. She wants to stay home tonight. Normally I'd just stay with her, but Carter suggested you might be interested in babysitting to make a little extra money. I pay very well."

I'm floored that she's calling me in the first place, but to babysit Chloe? I would find it hard to say no to that even without the enticement of good pay. Chloe is adorable, and now that I know she's technically Carter's daughter... well, I'm still not sure I've wrapped my mind all the way around that, but it makes the offer even more compelling.

"Sure, I could probably do that," I tell her.

"Wonderful. I'm so happy to hear that. I was afraid you might hold a grudge for the way Kevin behaved when you were here before."

I don't know what to say to that, so I merely offer a half-hearted, "Oh, no."

"He's a bit of a grump sometimes and he doesn't always approve of Carter's promiscuous ways, but I think my husband will be much nicer to you now that he realizes you're not one of those girls. That Carter trusts you to watch Chloe speaks volumes. Carter doesn't trust anybody, but he clearly trusts you. I'm so sorry your first impression of us was what it was. I hope you'll give us a chance to make a better one."

I don't have the heart to tell her that Carter and I broke up, so my impression of them no longer matters. Instead, I finish the conversation as politely as possible, go over the details of the babysitting job, and tell her my lunch is nearly over, so I have to go, but I'll see her then.

CHLOE IS ALREADY EATING dinner when I arrive at the palatial residence Carter calls home. Angela gives me a tour of the house, showing me Chloe's bedroom and going over her routine. She assures me I don't need to give Chloe a bath tonight, just help her change into her pajamas and read her a story before she goes to sleep. She shows me to the media room, in case we want to watch a movie. Apparently, Chloe is on a *Sing* kick right now. If we want to play video games, she redirects me to the living room. I get acquainted with the board game closet and Chloe's designated playroom.

As we head back into the kitchen, Angela tells me, "We pretty much let her eat whatever she wants for snacks. We have plenty of stuff in the refrigerator and cupboards. If you're feeling ambitious, you could bake some cookies or cupcakes."

"Yeah, yeah, yeah," Chloe says, bouncing in her seat. "I wanna make cookies!"

Angela smiles at her, then looks back at me. "She has crackers and fruit snacks and all sorts of things in the cupboard. She likes to snack on pretzel sticks. Whatever she wants, she'll tell you. She's far from shy about expressing her desires."

I crack a smile, thinking she must get that from Carter. Since I obviously can't say that to his mother, I nod my head and say, "Yeah, I've noticed that."

Clasping her hands together, she looks around and says, "I guess that's it. You girls have fun. Can we get a good luck cheer from Carter's favorite cheerleader?"

Chloe throws her hands in the air and calls out, "Go Longhorns!"

Angela smiles. "There we go. I'll pass it along. I'm sure they'll win now."

Chloe nods, looking at me seriously. "My brother's really good at football. He wins a lot."

I offer a smile back. "I know he is. I went to one of his games."

"There's too many of them," she informs me.

"That's a true story. There are an awful lot of them. You can take a break tonight and hang out with me."

Nodding her head, Chloe grabs her juice box and takes a drink. "We can make Carter cookies for when he gets home. And I'll eat some of them, too."

"Naturally. Gotta give 'em a taste test and make sure they're delicious."

"Exactly. See, she knows," Chloe says.

Angela walks over to the counter and grabs her purse. "I do believe you ladies will fare just fine." To me, she adds, "Thanks so much for watching her."

"No problem," I assure her, heading over to the table to keep Chloe company while she finishes eating.

AFTER A LONG NIGHT of playing and baking cookies, it's time to read Chloe a story and put her to bed. She informs me no one but her family has ever put her to bed before and I'm doing it "weird," and I don't know what that means.

Sitting on the edge of her bed with the finished storybook in my lap, I inquire, "How am I supposed to do it? I'm new to this. I don't know the drill."

"Don't you have a little brother or sister?"

I nod my head. "I do. I have a younger brother, but I don't put him to bed. I did a couple times when my mom was sick, but usually older siblings don't do that. Not in my house, anyway. Maybe you do things differently at your house."

Chloe nods. "Carter puts me to bed a lot. Our mom gets sleepy sometimes, and she stays in bed a long time."

Absently reaching out and smoothing a long, dark strand of hair out of her face, I murmur, "That must be kind of tough, huh?"

"Yeah. I don't like when she's sad. I like when Carter puts me to bed though. He does funny voices when he reads stories."

"I didn't think of funny voices. My bad. If I ever babysit you again, I'll make a note."

"You should ask him for some tips," she advises.

Biting back a smile, I assure her, "I'll do that." Pushing off the bed, I cross the room and return her storybook to the book-shelf, then walk back over to tuck her in. "I don't know the correct protocol. Should I give you a forehead kiss?"

Chloe pulls the covers up to her chest and nods. "Sure."

"Okay." I smile and lean down, kissing her little forehead. "Have sweet dreams. If you need anything, I'll be downstairs in the living room until someone gets home."

"G'night, bookstore lady."

"Good night, Chloe." I pause to turn out her light, steal one last glance at her and her nightstand to make sure she has her water bottle, then I pull the door shut behind me.

I intend to go directly downstairs so I can start studying, but I can't help a faint stirring of curiosity when I go to walk past Carter's bedroom. His door is closed, but my hand finds its way to the knob and it twists easily. I don't know why I imagined he might have his bedroom door locked, but I'm surprised when it easily unlatches and drifts open. It shouldn't be so easy to pene-trate his sanctuary, when in so many ways, he is so well-guarded.

I shouldn't be in here when he isn't home, when he hasn't invited me, but as I look at his bed, I can't help thinking about when I slept here with him and missing it. Since he isn't here to witness it, I climb onto his unmade bed and crawl under the covers, pulling them up around me. His bed smells like him. I close my eyes and breathe it in, memories stirring of his arms around me. His lips on my skin.

God, I hope he hasn't brought anyone else in this bed since me. My heart aches at the thought, even though I know he can now and he wouldn't be doing anything wrong. Since he went to Erika's when we were on the brink of a relationship, it's probably unreasonable to imagine he hasn't slept with anyone now that he's completely single again.

I relax in Carter's bed for a few more minutes, thinking about him, then I drag myself out of the bed and wander around. I don't want to invade his privacy by outright snooping, going through drawers or anything, but I glance at the surfaces to see what he's left out, unguarded. His history book is sitting out on top of his desk. There's a little desk lamp and some scattered folders and notebooks. His school things.

I see a paper sideways and hanging out of his history book and I can't resist opening it up to see what it is. Probably just notes, nothing exciting.

But when I open it, it's not notes. It's one of his sketches. And it's a sketch of *me*. In the picture, I'm sitting at my desk with my elbow propped on the surface, my face propped on my palm, gazing out the window. He's clearly got some skill, because this is just lead spread across a sheet of paper, but looking at it, I can feel the girl's longing to be somewhere else. Maybe it's because I know it's me, but I don't think so. I think he really captured me and committed me to paper. This is amazing.

I wish I could tell him it's amazing, but then he'd think I went snooping around his room. Since I can't keep the sketch, I pull my phone out of the pocket of my jeans and snap a picture of it. After sliding my phone back into my pocket, I tuck the sketch between the pages and close the heavy history book.

No point looking around at more stuff I can't ask about. I'd rather explore his room with him on the bed watching me, not alone, feeling like I'm being sneaky.

I go downstairs instead. His mom told me earlier Chloe would go to bed long before they got home, so I take advantage of the quiet to get out my own school stuff and do a little studying. Actually, a lot of studying. I study and study and study until the words stop making sense and I can't stop yawning. I didn't sleep well last night, and I woke up before my alarm today, so I'm exhausted.

Deciding to take a short study break, I mark my page and

leave my study materials on the coffee table, then I lie down on the couch, pulling one of the decorative pillows under my head.

I just need five minutes to rest my eyes, then I'll get back to studying.

CHAPTER 45

MY FIVE MINUTES must run a little long, because the next thing I know I'm roused from sleep by a hand cradling my face. My heavy eyelids drift open, and I see Carter sitting on the edge of the couch with me.

Offering him a sleepy little smile, I say, "Hey, you."

Carter's lips curve up and he brushes my hair off the side of my face. "Long night?"

"All the playing. Chloe has many toys, and she thought we should try every single one of them out, just in case I never come back." Turning my head to look at the coffee table where I left a plate of them, I add, "We also made you cookies."

"How thoughtful," he remarks.

"It was Chloe's idea."

He leans forward and grabs a cookie, then turns it over and inspects it. "Chocolate chip, huh?"

"She said they were your favorite."

"She knows what she's talking about," he says before taking a bite.

I give him a minute to taste it, then I ask, "Good?"

"Delicious."

Cocking an eyebrow, I ask, "Better than your rally girl's cookies?"

Grinning, he puts the cookie down on the plate and then

looks back at me. "Much better. A million times better. I don't think it's an exaggeration to say these are the best cookies I've ever tasted."

"Hmph, that's right," I mutter, satisfied. "How'd the game go?"

"Good. We won. It was a close one, though. Looked like we were going to tie, but we pulled it out in the end."

Carter shifts positions, kicking off his shoes and nudging them under the table. Then he peels off his letter jacket and drapes it across the empty side of the coffee table. Once he's down to a gray tee and jeans, he braces his weight on the couch and climbs on top of me.

"How are you and the baby doing tonight?" he inquires.

I roll my eyes, but I'm feeling more indulgent than annoyed about it at the moment. "I'm not pregnant."

"That's not what I heard," he informs me.

"Because *you* started the rumor."

"Would I ever do something like that?" he asks with feigned innocence, before bending his head to kiss my neck.

"Yes, you most certainly would," I mutter, bracing a hand on his back regardless and closing my eyes, giving myself up to a moment of pleasure to soak up his perfect kisses.

"Would you tell me if you were?"

I can't tell if he's serious or not, but I pull my neck away so he'll look at me, just in case. "Of course I would tell you."

His tone is light and teasing, but his words make me feel protective, anyway. "Even though you hate me?"

"Don't be ridiculous," I chide, reaching up to caress his face. "I don't hate you."

I don't know if it's my unguardedness due to the fact that he woke me out of a dead sleep, or something else, but there's a tenderness between us right now that has been lacking since the nights we spent together, before it all went to hell. My tummy flutters as his hand moves down my torso and stops to unbutton my jeans.

I don't balk as he unzips them and slides his hand down inside to touch me. It feels too good, and technically speaking, I owe him three rounds, anyway.

It should feel cheap and sordid, I suppose, but there's a freedom in letting him push me into corners, especially now. I can't bring myself to get back together with him, but doing it his way, we still get stolen moments like these—just without the commitment of a relationship.

Carter breaks away from kissing my neck so he can sit back and drag his shirt off. My gaze drops to admire his beautiful physique. I reach up to drag my hands along the chiseled ridges of his abdomen. My index finger follows the start of the V-shape that starts at his lower abdomen, then I unbutton and unzip *his* jeans so I can see the rest.

"I like this," I tell him.

Faintly amused, he watches me trace the line. "Yeah?"

I nod. "I'm a fan. You should keep this."

"You should probably be careful about making me cookies then," he jokes.

I let my hands drop and he scoots back. "Well, not at the expense of cookies. I'm not a *monster.*"

Carter cocks an eyebrow at me, dragging down my jeans. "No, I get to be the monster in this relationship. You've gotta be the good one."

"If I'm not, you can just tell people I'm pregnant so all the other guys will stay away from me."

"Or I can spank you," he counters. When he sees what's underneath my clothes, he smirks at me. "You wore the blue panties I bought you."

"I thought you might take advantage of my presence at your house tonight and cash in on the math test sex I owe you," I explain.

"Math test sex," he repeats, shaking his head as he drags the panties down. "Only you would be so casually forthright about that."

He tugs my jeans and panties all the way off and tosses them on the floor with his shirt. He doesn't bother removing my shirt though, merely shucks his pants and climbs between my legs. Pushing a finger inside me, he meets my gaze.

I want to kiss him again, but he's too far away. Suddenly

impatient to get his lips on mine again, I reach down and grab his wrist to tug it away. "I want you inside me."

"You're not ready yet," he tells me.

"That's okay," I assure him, reaching for his sides to urge him closer.

Carter shakes his head, but withdraws his finger anyway. "Of course, the night I'm in the mood to make love to you, you're like, 'just force it inside me.'"

I bite down on my bottom lip to slightly suppress my smile. "Hey, you can make love to me all you want, just get to it. Chop chop, I'm waiting."

Just for my sass, he pushes inside me hard. I wrap my arms around him and draw him closer, closing my eyes as his lips brush mine.

"A little demanding tonight, huh?" he murmurs, between kisses to the corner of my mouth. "You must've missed me."

I move my hips and try to accommodate him better, but he's not fully inside me yet. "My body has other ideas, apparently."

"Doesn't want to let me in," he agrees, pulling back and pushing in a little slower. "What have you been telling it about me?" he asks lightly.

"The truth," I tell him, cocking an eyebrow.

Now he nods. "It all makes sense now. I needed you to lie and cover my ass. God, Zoey. Way to drop the ball."

I crack a smile, which is mildly annoying. It's impossible to hold the grudges he deserves to have held against him when he's making me smile. My stupid body even gives in; I feel him push all the way inside me and I gasp a little at the sudden fullness.

"There we go," he murmurs, satisfied. "Your body says it's willing to give me another chance."

"Oh, does it?"

He nods, then bends to kiss the corner of my mouth again. "Insists it's the mature thing to do."

"My body just likes your dick," I inform him. "It's hypnotized and its judgment can't be trusted. I assure you, my mind is not so easily swayed."

"Well, yeah, because I can't fuck your mind."

"You probably could, but it sure wouldn't help your case," I toss back.

Carter grins before kissing me square on the mouth. "Have I mentioned lately that I miss you? Because I do. Very much."

"That won't work," I advise him, closing my eyes as he trails kisses across my jawline to my neck.

"What won't work? Honesty?"

"Sweet talkin' me. You said yourself, I know you better than anyone else. That works against you as well as it worked for you. I know when you're tryin' to play me. I know what you want, so I know you'll say anything to get there. Nothing you do will work. I won't even believe you if you're sincere. Let's just do what we came for and not make it complicated, all right?"

Carter comes up to meet my gaze and watches for a moment, his movements paused. When he finishes studying my features, his jaw furrows. He must not like what he sees. Determination. I took the gamble once, but I won't make the same bad bet twice, and he knows it.

"Fine," he finally says, pulling back and then pushing inside me slowly. "If I can't tell you, I'll show you. I *will* make this up to you, Zoey. One way or another. I won't stop trying until you forgive me, so if at any point you want me to? That's the only way. We are at a stalemate until someone swerves, and I think you know it won't be me."

"It won't be me either," I assure him honestly, holding his gaze. "I appreciate the effort, Carter, I really do, but I'm not gonna change my mind. Even if I want to, I won't. I can forgive myself for betting on you the first time, even after all the red flags. But how do you expect me to sell myself on doing that a second time? I can't be convinced that's a good idea. It can't be done."

His eyes narrow, momentarily calculating. "Sure it can. I'm just using the wrong method."

I don't like the sound of that, or the look on his face. "What does that mean?"

His expression clears, and he offers me a smile, his eyes glimmering with mischief. "Don't you worry about it, princess."

I want to worry about it. I feel like I *need* to worry about it.

But then he stops talking and starts using his body against me. Before I know it, I'm too busy being driven out of my mind with pleasure to worry about anything.

WHEN MOST BOYS SCREW UP, they send flowers.

Carter sends chaos.

I try to ignore the reality at first. Sunday morning at church when everyone is talking about the terrible vandalizing of Luke's car last night, I pray with every ounce of faith inside me that Carter wasn't involved. I'm sure he wasn't out there using a bat to bust out the windows and slashing all four tires himself, but he very well could have sent someone to do his dirty work for him.

He wouldn't, though. He *wouldn't*. It's an uncomfortable coincidence, that's all.

Still, I can't help feeling responsible.

When church lets out, I head to work. It's a slow night, being a Sunday, but that gives me a chance to check up on Carter. I probably shouldn't persist in cyber stalking him now that we're over and I'm the one insisting we are never getting back together, but I tell myself I'm looking for any sign of incriminating evidence. I don't actually expect to find anything, but my heart stalls when the most recent update reads, "Oops. I broke it."

My heart thuds and my gaze jumps to the accompanying picture. It's a picture of a pink Barbie doll car in Chloe's playroom. The door is crooked and falling off, and Chloe has a hand propped on her hip, mean-mugging the hell out of the camera.

My jaw drops open and I close the app, pulling up my messages so I can yell at him. I don't know if I want to yell at him for breaking Chloe's toy first, or for Luke.

"You are a psycho!"

I push send before I can overthink it. He must have his phone close by, because he's texting me back a few seconds later. "Me? No. You must have the wrong number."

"Did you break Chloe's car?" I demand.

"Yeah, but I bought her a new, better car. It's all good now."

He sends an accompanying photo of Chloe grinning with her stylish new Barbie car to prove it.

"And Luke? Are you buying him a new car?" I ask, my hands shaking with anger.

"Why would I buy Luke a new car?" he returns.

"This is NOT the way to get me back," I tell him.

"You sure?" he replies.

I'm too angry to talk to him and a customer is approaching the counter anyway, so I put the phone away. I ring that person out as quickly and politely as I can, but I can't stop thinking about Carter. I pull my phone out as soon as the customer walks away and read Carter's message.

"Maybe Luke shouldn't touch other people's toys, then they wouldn't touch his."

My eyes all but bulge out of my head. I send back in all caps, "Luke never touched me! He is a friend, nothing more. But you're less than that, so stop terrorizing him and leave me alone."

"You wound me, princess."

"I wish," I shoot back. "I wish I could wound you, Carter."

CHAPTER 46

VENGEANCE NORMALLY IS NOT my thing, but after tossing and turning all night long, wracked with guilt, I have the perfectly crafted "fuck you" to Carter by the time I get to school on Monday.

I buzz through all my morning classes, waiting for the moment when I'll be able to irritate Carter. I've gone back and forth, afraid that giving him a response will cause the behavior to worsen, but at the end of the day, I think I can control the fire. I have zero doubt that I will piss Carter off, but if he tries to take it out on Luke again, I will stand up to him. I will redirect his wrath to me and deal with his temper myself—I am the one it should be directed at, anyway. I'm the idiot who made up a fake boyfriend on impulse to begin with, I just never expected Carter to believe it so vehemently.

When history rolls around, the sight of Carter gets me jittery, ramps up my pulse. It's strange how the sight of him excites all my senses even now, when he's being so awful, I want to punch him in the face.

Friday night after he made love to me, we cuddled on the couch for a little while. Afterward, he took $200 out of his wallet and gave it to me for the babysitting. I stared at the excess of cash for a moment, wondering if I should change my career plans and become a full-time babysitter, then his ulterior motive presented itself. He told me now that I have some extra cash I didn't plan on having, I could buy myself that homecoming dress and be his date, after all.

How convenient.

It was sneaky and Carter-like enough that it made me smile. As much as I hate the idea of spending all that money on a dress I will wear one time to a dance I don't even want to go to, I couldn't bring myself to tell him no.

Now I can.

I expect him to linger and hassle me on our way out of class, but Carter only shoots me a wink as he walks past and heads out by himself.

The dumb part of me is disappointed by his lack of attention, but the overwhelming majority of me is relieved. It's harder to try to hurt his feelings when I'm exposed to him at all. He has a way of melting away my defenses, no matter how angry I am at him, no matter how justified that anger is.

It's a daunting walk from my locker to the cafeteria, but after dumping my books in my locker, that's where I head. Dread fills me at the mere sight of the open double doors, at the buzz of chatter coming from within.

I don't want to go in there. Stopping just short of entering, I take one more fortifying breath, then I square my shoulders, lift my chin, and march through the doors.

I guess the nice thing about the cafeteria is nothing much ever changes. Even being absent from lunch for so many weeks, everything is more or less the same. The same groups of kids sitting at the same tables—especially the popular tables. The jocks and the cheerleaders. They may as well have their names stamped on the tables and their accompanying benches, because even if they were all absent one day, no one would dare sit in their places.

Some of the other kids are at different tables, but in the same groups as usual.

My perusal of the room stops short when I feel Carter's eyes on me. I turn my head to meet his gaze and he frowns, cocking his head in confusion. I avoid the cafeteria like the plague, so he must wonder what brought me here.

I smile blandly, holding his gaze as I reach into the small school purse dangling by my hip. His gaze follows the movement, then darts back to my face, still confused. I pull out the cash he gave me Friday night and hold it up for him to see. His scowl deepens. My smile widens, then I break eye contact altogether and make my way over to the table where several members of my youth group sit, eating their lunch.

Luke looks up as I approach. His sandwich is frozen halfway to his mouth. Since I'm looking right at him with a look of determination on my face, he puts it down and offers up a pleasant smile and scoots down to make room for me.

"Finally comin' back to our table?" he surmises.

I shake my head. "No, I'm not staying. I just wanted to give you this," I tell him, holding out my babysitting earnings.

He looks at the money with a frown, then looks back up at me. "What…?"

"I heard what happened to your car, and I felt terrible about it," I explain, dropping my gaze, not quite able to meet his gaze.

"Yeah," he mumbles.

"I recently came into a little extra cash, though. I was plannin' to waste it on something I didn't need, but it feels right to use it to help a friend instead."

Beaming up at me, then over at Luke, Grace says, "What a blessing."

I nod and look back at Luke. "I know this doesn't cover all the damage that was done, but… I just wanted to…"

He doesn't make me finish. Nodding his head as the money transfers from my hands to his, he says, "Thank you, Zoey. You really don't have to do this."

"I feel…" *Responsible.* I can't say that though, because it implicates Carter.

As much as I probably should be ready and willing to turn Carter over for his crimes, I'm not. I don't even think they would stick. This town would let Carter out of a rape accusation, so really, what's a little vandalism as long as he takes the team to the championships?

Ugh. Gross.

Shaking it off, I clear my throat and offer up a weak smile. "I want to. Please let me know if there's anything else I can do."

Now that my mission has been accomplished, I excuse myself from my old table as quickly as possible and turn back around. Before I head for the exit, I decide to walk over to Carter's table. Clearly understanding what I have just done, he does not look remotely amused. He looks pretty pissed, and just being so close to his temper turns my blood hot. A mental image floats across my mind of him grabbing me, pushing me down on the table, and taking me right here in front of everyone. My body throbs in response, but I try to shake it off and stay focused.

He really has broken me, hasn't he?

Ignoring the heat, I walk around the table and stop behind him. Wrapping an arm around him from behind, I lean down and whisper in his ear, "Turns out I don't have money for that dress, after all. Guess you're gonna have to find another date to homecoming."

Carter faintly shakes his head, but he doesn't respond verbally. All of his friends are sitting at the table. None of them know what just happened, but they're all casting looks at me— some confused, some guessing and getting it dead-wrong, others who missed that Carter and I even broke up in the first place. In any case, Carter isn't going to let me embarrass him in front of his friends, so he can't say shit to me about what I just did.

I knew he wouldn't, so I'm feeling pretty smug. I stand and let my arm fall from around him. Then I flash him a little smile and wink like he did in history class, make my way around the table, and walk right out of the cafeteria.

<hr />

NOTHING HORRIBLE HAPPENS over the rest of the week. I go to school, study, and work. Carter doesn't commit any additional crimes, as far as I can see. I don't think I won the war that easily, though, so even his silence makes me worry about what he's planning.

He hasn't cashed in his second booty call yet, either. I know he planned to save the third for homecoming, but now I'm not *going* to homecoming with him, so he had better pick a different time and place.

It occurs to me I should have given him a strict window when I made this deal. Like, three times within the next four weeks. I hadn't been in a position to negotiate terms—or even think about terms—but now that circumstances are what they are, I'm wondering how long Carter could string me along with time two and time three. I suppose it wasn't a very honorable agreement to begin with, so maybe I don't *have* to keep up my end of the bargain... but even if it was a sex agreement, that doesn't sit right with me. I don't like to renege on my obligations, and I *know* Carter wouldn't like it.

I'm not going to like if I'm in Pennsylvania settling in for my first semester of college and I get a text from Carter in New York telling me I better take a weekend road trip, because it's time for our second round of math test sex.

If I ever make another deal with him, I need to set clearer terms. I gave him way too much leeway on this one. It could be a real headache, if he wants it to be.

By the time Friday rolls around, I think maybe it's all over. Maybe he realized this was also the wrong method for getting me back and he is concocting a new idea...

Or maybe he'll just give up altogether. I'm not proud of the fact that it makes me a little sad to consider. I know I won't like when he moves on. Considering he went so long without a girlfriend before and he's not fond of girlfriends to begin with, I'm hoping it will remain that way for the rest of the school year. Then he can go off to college and I won't have to witness it. As long as we're in school together, I have to live in fear of the day I see him with someone else, see him looking at her the way he looked at me, and know he's not just doing it to piss me off, like the Jenna situation.

I'm kept awake a good part of Thursday night worrying about that and my math test, so I make sure to stop and grab myself an iced coffee on my way to school. I'm early this morning anyway, so I have time for a caffeine fix. I text Grace on my way and ask if she wants me to pick one up for her, but she doesn't respond. Just in case she is watching her sugar intake today, I don't bring her one.

When I get to school, I feel naively good about the day. It's Friday, so I only have to make it through a few hours, then it's the weekend. Even better, I don't have to work tonight, so I actually get to go home after school, and since there's no school tomorrow, I can have some down time tonight. Tomorrow I study, since I still have to kick Carter's rally girl's ass, academically speaking.

I spot Grace's car in the parking lot with an empty spot next to it, so I nab it before anyone else does. Close to the building—another win. I can't help smiling as I get out of the car… at least, until I see Grace crying in hers.

My heart drops and I slam my door shut, hoping the noise will get her attention. She looks up and meets my eyes. Even from the distance and through the window, I can see her eyes are red and puffy and her nose is red.

I hustle over to the car and open the driver's side door. She doesn't even have the car running, so the air isn't blowing and her car is an oven. "Grace, what's wrong?"

Sniffling into a Kleenex, she looks up at me. "I'm sorry. I'm having a really bad couple of days."

Leaning down so I'm closer to her level, I ask, "Why? What's going on?"

"Scout got out of the yard last night. We never let him out of the fenced area. He's too little, and he runs after cars."

Gasping, putting the pieces together, I try to think how delicately to ask. "Did he… get hit?"

She sniffles and brushes tears from her already red cheeks. "I don't know. We couldn't find him. We were out looking everywhere for him last night. My dad said maybe he would find his way home, but when we woke up this morning, still nothing. He could be anywhere, and he's probably so scared and hungry…" The image of him hungry and scared must break her, because she bursts into fresh tears.

"Oh, Grace." I bend down and hug her. "You should have texted me, I would've come over and helped you look. I'll help today, after school. Don't worry, we'll find your puppy."

"What if he did get hit?" she wails into my shoulder.

"I'm sure he didn't get hit. Someone would have seen him in the road."

"I don't understand how he got out in the first place. Before I left him out there, I walked the fence and made sure he hadn't dug any holes I missed. The gate was shut and there are no loose boards. I was so careful."

Dread fills me because this is a bad situation either way, but the party at Erika's house surfaces in my mind. Carter knew he wanted me at the party that night, but no matter how much he asked, I declined. Eventually, he used Grace and my protectiveness of her to get me there, threatening Grace if I didn't show.

He wouldn't hurt a dog, right? I don't think he would, he's not a *monster*, but kidnap a dog? He might do that. Keep it—and Grace's emotional well-being—hostage until I give in and come riding to her rescue.

Dammit, Carter. It's not fair that he has all these ways of defeating me. He plays so dirty, and he knows I can't match him. He knows I won't stoop, so he knows he will win every damn time as long as he does.

Once I'm done comforting Grace and calming her down with assurances that we'll get Scout back tonight, I give her a minute to get it together and walk by myself up to the entrance of the school.

My blood heats when I see Carter standing against his wall, arms crossed, watching me as I approach. This time, it's anger heating my blood, not arousal. Unluckily for the people in my life, I only really have a few relationships, so if he wants to terrorize me into getting back together with him, he can only target those same people over and over again.

"Good morning, Ellis."

I glare, ignoring his jock buddies who part like the Red Sea as I storm up to him. "Did you steal Grace's puppy?"

Pulling a look of exaggerated innocence, Carter points to himself. "Why would *I* steal a dog?"

"Because you're fucking crazy," I snap.

"Whoa, shit," Cartwright drawls, laughing a little. "Carter's drivin' Zoey Ellis to curse. This must be bad."

"Baby girl, bring that dirty mouth over here," Shayne says.

"Fuck off, Sutton," I snap, before looking back at Carter. "The puppy is too far. You give that puppy back to her, or I swear to God, I'll never speak to you again."

Carter keeps his tone level, but the warning behind the words is real when he tells me, "Don't threaten me, princess."

I *know* I would get better results if I had waited to confront him until we could be alone, but when I saw him, I was too angry to wait. As much as I want to escalate things and fight him to the death, I know I'm outmatched. He knows, too, so if I want to be smart, I need to heed his warning and rein myself in a bit.

When a few seconds pass and I haven't continued to rage despite the clear fury in my eyes, Carter nods once and says, "Now, go ahead and try again. I'll give you a do-over."

I grit my teeth, wanting to hit him for being such a jerk, but I keep my eye on the prize. It doesn't matter that his friends are snickering. Only he cares what they think, I sure as hell don't. Swallowing down a lump of anger and meeting his gaze, I ask, "Can we talk privately, please?"

Carter reaches out and caresses the side of my face, an intentionally condescending move. "Since you said please."

Murder, murder, murder. Stab, stab, stab.

Thinking happy thoughts, I turn on my heel and head for the school entrance.

"I'll catch up to you fellas later," Carter tells the guys as he follows after me.

"Have fun," Cartwright calls.

"He's goin' off with Zoey Ellis, you know he will," Shayne says with a snicker.

"Hey," Carter barks more sharply. A little more civilly, he reminds Shayne, "Show a little respect unless you want to lose your place again, Sutton."

Yeah, asshole. At least Carter isn't being a *complete* toolbag. Just *mostly* a toolbag.

I don't know where I'm going as I walk through the doors. This isn't our normal meeting time. When we encounter each other after history, everyone else is heading to lunch and there are empty classrooms in every hall. Right now, everyone is just getting to school, making their ways through halls, chatting up friends, opening lockers. There's nowhere for us to be alone.

Apparently unconcerned, Carter picks up the pace until he's ahead of me, then his arm shoots out. He grabs me and backs up, pulling me with him against an empty stretch of wall. There are still lockers and students everywhere, we have no actual privacy, but as if he sealed us inside a bubble, Carter looks at me like we do.

"Now, what can I do for you?"

"Give Grace her dog back."

Cocking his head slightly to the side, Carter asks, "Why did you just find out about this today?"

"What? I... I don't know."

"The dog went missing last night. This wasn't today's scheduled hissy fit, it was yesterday's. Did she tell you, and you just didn't connect it to me until today, or did you just find out?"

Given that also briefly crossed my mind when I first found out, I frown. "She didn't tell me last night. She was probably too busy looking for Scout. She didn't think to text me."

"That doesn't make sense," he points out. "If she wanted to find the dog, the more eyes looking for it, the better."

"I don't know," I say, shaking my head. "It doesn't matter. Where is her dog?"

"Hmm, Grace must be mad at you," he says, ignoring me. "Did you do something to piss her off? Maybe I did. Maybe she blames you for Choir Boy's car. Yeah, that makes sense. It's probably that. She's got a point, too. Maybe you should stop fighting and come back to me now, so nothing else bad happens to your friends."

"Maybe I should stop talking to you and see what happens if I ignore you completely," I suggest.

Carter grimaces. "I wouldn't recommend it. If I get much more destructive, I'm bound to start attracting notice. It's gonna get more complicated. I'll have to frame someone else for my wrongdoing. I haven't pinned anything on Jake lately," he muses, theatrically rubbing his chin and glancing up in thought.

Reaching out and grabbing his hand, I pull it away from his chin. "Stop it, Carter. No more destruction. The sweet talk may not have worked, but this… I hate this. You know I hate this. You know I hate you hurting other people, period, but especially my friends."

Carter smiles faintly, catching my other arm and tugging me closer until my breasts touch his chest. "Yes, I know. That's the point. Only you can stop it, Zoey. Better go grab your red cape. You can wait in my bed wearing nothing else. Fucking me is morally upright if you're doing it to save the world, right?"

"Or I could just call the cops and tell them what I know," I suggest innocently, looking up at him.

"Go for it," he says, unconcerned. "You don't really *know* anything, you just suspect. Surely you don't think there's any actual evidence that I've done anything wrong, right? Tell me you don't think I'm that sloppy."

"Maybe I'm recording this conversation," I offer.

"Maybe you are." His gaze moves over my body, lingering on my breasts, then dropping lower. "Maybe I should do a strip search, just to be safe."

Arousal stirs at the mental image of his hands running down my sides, moving over every inch of my bare body. Languidness follows, making me wish for a bed so we could work out all these frustrations.

It's entirely off-topic, but since my mind has gone there, I ask, "When are you planning to cash in on round two?"

Carter smirks at me. "I'll get around to it. Getting impatient? I can buy you a toy to tide you over until I fuck you again."

"I think for simplicity's sake, we should establish a time frame. An expiration date of sorts. If you don't use your two remaining passes before a certain date, they expire."

"Coupon prostitution, huh? That sounds cheap."

Ignoring him, I plod on. "I suggest fall break. If you haven't cashed in by fall break, you don't get to."

"Hmm." Carter pretends to consider for a moment, then says, "No."

"Winter break, then. That's *plenty* of time."

"No expiration date. That's not what we agreed to, and I'm not amenable to changing the terms. Sorry, princess."

"I don't like being on your hook indefinitely," I tell him honestly.

"Too bad. Back to the dog. I can't imagine you showed up to a hostage negotiation without an offer to put on the table? Don't you know how this works?"

Narrowing my eyes at him, I mutter, "You already have me on the hook for two more rounds. What do you want this time?"

"Your mouth around my cock. I might end up fucking you, too, but it doesn't count toward the first debt if I do."

I try to ignore the throbbing in my core, try to stabilize the rise and fall of my chest as I breathe, but judging by the warmth in Carter's eyes, he recognizes that he's turning me on. More because I actually want it than because I want Grace's puppy returned to her, I say, "All right. Lunchtime today?"

Regretfully, he shakes his head. "Can't do it today. Can't do it tonight. How 'bout tomorrow? We can grab some dinner or catch a movie."

"You don't get a date," I inform him, keeping my voice low, given the occupancy of the hall. Leaning in a little to remain unheard by passersby (and a little to torture him), I murmur, "You get your dick sucked. Nothing more."

His grip on my arm tightens, and he pulls me harder against him. "Then I'll take more, whether you want to give it to me or not."

Since I only have so many tools at my disposal, and my version of playing dirty is much more limited than his, I lean in and whisper in his ear, "Promise?"

"You're making it difficult not to fuck you right here, right now."

Biting back a little smile, I point out, "Even you can't get away with that."

Lust burns in his dark eyes when I pull back and meet his gaze. I can *feel* how much he wants me, and as menacing as he is, as angry as I've been at him, being wanted by him this much sends a spike of excitement straight through me. My breasts feel heavy and restrained inside my top. I want to rip it off and let him feast on them. I want him to turn me around, push me up against that wall he's leaning on, and fucking devour me.

I want him, period.

I need to get away from him before I do something incredibly stupid. Before I toss my principles out the window and agree to be with him again, just so he'll stop playing these senseless games and fuck me already.

I take a step back, since distance is the only thing that can help me now.

Carter sees me trying to retreat, but he doesn't stop me. "Tomorrow," he says, simply. Pushing off the wall, he touches my face one more time before walking away.

CHAPTER 47

GIVEN the peace accord I felt like we struck this morning, I did not expect any additional Carter drama for the rest of my Friday. I figured I would go to Grace's house after work, "help her find" Scout, and then go home. Nice and simple, no more surprises.

Then Kasey texts me a picture from the hallway, freaking out about something going on with Erika Martin. I couldn't give fewer fucks about Erika Martin, but curiosity gets the best of me and I check the picture Kasey sent. It was a sneaky photo taken while she walked past, so it's not a great picture, but it shows Erika standing at her locker in her cheer uniform, the principal and guidance counselor both standing beside her at her open locker.

"What is that?" I text back, unsure why she's sending me this picture.

"Shit is going DOWN," she tells me. "Idk, I've gotta get details."

Feeling unsettled, I put my phone back on my desk before the teacher sees me messing with it and turn my mind off Erika for the rest of class.

My next class is history. Mr. Hassenfeld doesn't suffer fools, and he's already given me my free pass for the year, so I don't worry about Erika's ordeal while he's teaching. When history lets out, I check my texts, but Kasey still hasn't sent anything back. I hate even *thinking* about Erika Martin at this point, since thinking of her just brings back mental flashes of her in bed with Carter. By the time I get to history, I'm thinking less of ripping Carter's clothes off and more of burning them.

Perhaps because I didn't cast him any longing or lustful looks, Carter catches up to me in the hall after class.

"You look grumpy. Sexually frustrated?"

I slide him an unamused look. "Just the 'frustrated' part. Do you know anything about what's goin' on with Erika today?"

"I no longer associate with Erika," he informs me.

"Uh-huh."

"I don't." He draws an ex over the left side of his chest. "Cross my heart."

"She's a cheerleader. You're the quarterback. You can't be strangers, even if you tried."

Carter shrugs, but strangely offers no further argument. "You should come to lunch today. You can sit with us."

"I don't want to sit with your friends. Besides, your table is all guys. Segregated lunch seems to be your thing."

"Usually, but exceptions can be made. Come on, I'll buy you lunch. Cafeteria lunch is admittedly not as appealing as outside lunch, but I work with what I'm given."

"No."

Sighing, he says, "All right, how about this? Out of the kindness of my heart, I'll offer your buddy Luke a killer discount on new tires if he buys them at my dad's dealership."

"I'm listening."

"That's it, that's the whole offer. You sit with me at lunch today, I'll make sure Luke gets new tires. It's not a big ask, so the reward can't be too extravagant."

I mull it over for a few seconds, adding in the peanut butter and jelly sandwich with borderline-stale chips waiting for me in my locker, then nod my head. "All right, I'll make that deal."

"Now, if you wanna sit in my lap, we can talk about those windows."

I crack a smile. "The lunch lady would never allow that." Looking over at him, I cock an eyebrow. "And I never told you his windows were busted out. Way to incriminate yourself."

"I heard it through the grapevine, otherwise I would have no idea," he assures me.

"Mm-hmm." I know he's not even trying to convince me, but I shoot him a look, anyway.

Deflecting my look entirely, he wraps an arm around my waist and draws me close. "Let's go put those books away and get you some food."

Since I don't usually go to lunch, I don't keep track of what they're having which day, but I'm pleasantly surprised to find that today is Mexican burrito bar day. Carter buys us both chicken fajitas and a cup of diced peaches for dessert.

"I don't know if I should let you spend this kind of money on me," I tease as we move forward in line.

"I know. I might have certain expectations about what you owe me after a feast like this one," he replies.

"I mean, a plastic cup of diced peaches for dessert? What am I, the queen?"

"What can I say? I like to spoil my woman."

I bite back a grin, attempting to cast him a severe look over my shoulder. "I am not your woman, Mahoney."

Ignoring my rebuff, he says, "This reminds me, when we go to New York in a couple months, there's a Mexican place I'm gonna take you to not far from the apartment. Great enchiladas. When we're tired after a long day of classes next fall, I can see us getting dinner there and bitching about the professors we don't like."

I nod my head. "Yep, that's definitely going to happen. I always go on trips to New York with all of my ex-boyfriends. I *definitely* drive six hours after my classes so I can eat dinner with them in another state, too."

"You won't have to drive. You're going to live there with me," he informs me.

"Oh, am I?"

Carter nods confidently, giving me a nudge to let me know I need to move forward in line. "Yep. I know you're not completely sold on *me* right now, but wait until you see the apartment. You'll be sold on the apartment."

"I don't doubt that. It's more the skipping college to live with my ex-boyfriend part I'm not so sure about. I don't think I can live with you in New York and commute to my school six hours away, either. All of this seems pretty unlikely."

Carter hands over his card to the cashier. "Hers, too."

The cashier nods and adds up the total for both of our lunches, then swipes his card and hands it back. Once he has paid for our food, we each grab our trays and Carter leads the way to the jock table. Naturally, my gaze drifts to the table I would sit at if I played the role of Carter's girlfriend the way he would probably want me to. Cheerleaders and girls' volleyball players mostly fill the table, but I notice Erika isn't there yet.

I can't believe I'm going to sit at Carter's table with Erika this close. She's going to shoot me snide looks, and while normally her opinion of my decisions wouldn't matter, since I agree with her on this one, I'm going to feel like an idiot.

The more time I spend with Carter like this, the more damned I am. When I start missing him and wanting him back in weak moments, if I'm around him all the time, I'm much more likely to fall back in. Since I am determined not to, I need to make sure when I'm having those moments, I am safely away from Carter and unable to act on them.

I take a seat right next to him as I have that thought. Clearly, I am failing all over the place today, but I have high hopes for myself once all my debts have been settled.

"Look who's back," Cartwright says, offering a nod of acknowledgement. "'Sup, Ellis?"

"I'm pretty excited to eat this chicken fajita, Cartwright. What's up with you?"

"Hell yeah, burrito bar day is my shit," he agrees, grabbing his own fajita and taking a bite. "You like this, you should go to this place we went to in Dallas. I don't remember what it's called," he says, glancing to Carter for help. "You know the place with that massive burrito that was just fuckin' *smothered* in queso? Dear lord. The waitress was hot as hell, too."

"Oh, well, I wasn't entirely sold on the food, but if the waitress is hot," I murmur, opening my drink.

Cartwright grins and nods. "That's what I'm talkin' about. See, Ellis is cool. She knows."

I crack a smile and shake my head. I can't decide from one moment to the next whether or not I actually like Cartwright, but his ability to go with the flow and jump tracks so comfortably amuses me. I think for today at least, I will like him.

"I'm all about the babes," I comment inanely, picking up my fajita so I can start eating. Before I do, I lean into Carter, "Hey, you didn't actually take that puppy back to your house, did you?"

"No way. Chloe would demand a puppy when we had to return it. Brianna has him. She's a dog person."

I nod my head, then turn my attention back to the burrito. "Then I'm going to tell Grace, that way she knows Scout is safe and she won't be upset."

"You can't *tell* her," he says, frowning at me.

"I won't get any of you deviants in trouble, don't worry. I've already thought it through, I just had to find out where the dog was. Now that I know he's at Brianna's, we can just pretend Scout did somehow get out of the yard and Brianna happened to find him. While I was over here having lunch with you, I mentioned that Grace's puppy was missing. Brianna overheard and asked what the dog looked like. I showed her on my phone, and what do you know? Same puppy Brianna found running around last night. Obviously, she took the puppy home so it wouldn't get hit by a car, but now he can be safely returned to his owner. Boom, your ass is covered, but Grace still knows she's going to get her well-loved puppy back as soon as school is over. It even saves me the step of having to go through the motions of searching for the puppy and getting very lucky finding him. Just had to make sure it wasn't at your house, as you obviously do not live in the same part of the neighborhood, and that story wouldn't have made any sense."

Cartwright is staring at me across the table, his fajita dripping toppings onto his plate. "Damn, will you come up with all my alibis, too? That's fuckin' thorough."

I point at him with the corner of my fajita and lift a severe eyebrow. "You'll say nothing."

"I always say nothing," he assures me, before taking a bite. "I can see why Carter likes you so much now, though. You got a brain in that pretty little head too, don't ya?"

"The Zoey Ellis package is a pretty good one, I won't lie," I tell him, flashing him a playfully boastful smirk.

"Sure is," Carter says, wrapping an arm around me, not appearing to like Cartwright's praise. "And all mine."

"Nope. Not yours," I remind him, but don't bother shrugging off his arm. I like it where it is.

"It's all mine," he assures the guys, who nod like they understand, and my word means nothing.

I roll my eyes, but I'm too worried about getting this fajita in my belly to argue.

A short time later, a decidedly less enjoyable event occurs. Erika comes walking over to the table she has sat at since the first day of freshman year. The table where the cheerleaders and select volleyball girls are gathered, the table where I would sit, as Carter's girlfriend, if I so chose. I can't help noticing she changed out of her cheer uniform, which is odd. It's a game day, and the cheerleaders often wear their uniforms to school on game day. She was wearing it earlier in the picture Kasey sent me.

When she stops at the head of the table, I notice no one moves down to make room for her.

"What are you doing? Move down, you're in my seat," she tells Brianna.

Grimacing, Brianna darts a look directly at Carter, then quickly looks away when she sees I caught her. "Um, there's no room," Brianna says, a bit awkwardly.

A startled laugh slips out of Erika. "What? Of course there's room. Move your fat ass and there will be plenty of room."

One of the other cheerleaders speaks up. "Come on, Erika, don't make this weird. Just go sit somewhere else."

Erika's eyes nearly bug out of her head. "No, I'm not going to sit somewhere else. *Move.*"

"You can't sit with us," Brianna snaps, then shakes her head in frustration. "I can't believe you actually just made me say that."

Her blue eyes alight with fury, Erika demands, "You're *seriously* not going to let me sit at my own table? This is *my* table. I established it. I'm a fucking—"

"You're not on the squad anymore," Brianna states. "You

don't hang out with us anymore, so why would you sit with us? Just find another damn table, Erika. Go away."

Erika clutches the ends of her tray, holding onto it the way she's trying to hold on to her status. "This is all a mistake. I'm goin' for a damn drug test after school to prove it. I'll be back on the squad tomorrow, and if you seriously try to squeeze me out of my own seat at lunch, boy, are you gonna regret it tomorrow, bitch."

Finally, Carter intervenes. "Erika. Go sit somewhere else."

Her gaze snaps to him now, her eyes cold little chips of blue ice. Walking over here to redirect her anger, she says, "This is some way to treat a person you've fucked, Carter. You put that shit in my locker, didn't you?" Not even waiting for him to answer, she shakes her head. "I know you did. Well, you probably had one of your grunts do the dirty work. I damn sure never touched those drugs myself."

Drugs?

Erika's gaze whips to me next, and she must see the look of confusion plastered all over my face. "Don't play innocent. This is all your fault, you little whore. I hope all y'all are payin' close attention, too, 'cause this is how Carter treats a person he no longer has any use for. Y'all think this can't happen to you?" She gives a short, bitter little laugh. "Not hardly. You're all as disposable to him as I am."

There's steel in Carter's voice as he cuts her off. "That's enough, Erika. Do you think you can afford to piss me off more than you already have?" he asks. "Because let me assure you, I haven't done my worst yet. Keep fucking pushing and you'll see what I can do."

Brianna speaks up. "Erika, please just… stop fighting and go."

Turning to Carter, my brow furrowed in confusion, I ask quietly, "What is she talking about?"

"Don't worry about it," he says to me, but he's still looking at her. "Last fucking warning, Erika. Walk away while you still can."

"Don't threaten me, Carter."

"Don't mistake that warning for a threat," he says simply.

"You can't take things farther than this," she says, shaking her head.

"Wanna bet?" he asks, the menace in his voice plain for all to hear.

Whether she does or not, *I* don't. On instinct, I place a calming hand on Carter's thigh, trying to rein him in without words. Just hearing the edge in his voice, imagining the same dark horrors that flitted across my mind in that classroom the first time he got me alone, I'm shaken. Erika isn't taking him seriously enough, and she probably should be. I don't know what she's talking about, I don't know what happened today, and I don't know if Carter had anything to do with it, but I *do* know that provoking Carter is a bad idea for both of them.

I don't know how to halt her, though. Carter, I might be able to manage to a certain degree because he cares for me, but Erika... she hates me.

An idea pops into my head, perhaps a way to hit both birds with the same stone. In an attempt to calm Carter and piss Erika off enough that she does herself a favor and goes away, I grab Carter's face, pull him close, and kiss the hell out of him. I can feel him jerk in surprise, but he's not about to turn down a kiss in the current climate of our relationship. Being pissed off doesn't make him want to kiss me less, it just makes him rougher. His arm curls around my waist and he yanks me against him. His other hand moves, and he pushes his fingers through my hair, cradling my head while he kisses me.

I didn't mean anything by the kiss, I certainly didn't mean to fall into it myself, but when he cradles my head this way, rough in a sense, but at the same time like he's holding something precious... well, I just melt. None of the reasons around us matter anymore, the only thing I can focus on is one single truth: I miss him. I miss his kisses, his touches. I miss being his.

Cards on the table, I wish I could put aside my fears and my pride, I wish I could stop resisting and just go back to him. I really don't think he would mess up like that inside a relationship with me, but I'm too afraid I'm wrong. Maybe it's wishful thinking. It's not uncommon for people to disdain something in someone else that they recognize in themselves, so maybe his disdain for his father isn't the good sign I took it as, but a bad sign. A bright red flag, waving in the wind. Maybe…

Carter breaks the kiss, and I realize I let it go on for too long. I was supposed to be the one to pull back, but I got pulled in instead.

Swallowing and avoiding his gaze, I turn back to my food and glance up to see if Erika is gone. She is. If I were her, I wouldn't have stood there and watched that either, which was my original thought. Now my mind is too fuzzy for thoughts, too entranced by Carter and his magical mouth.

Get it together, mind.

Carter's arm curls around my waist, casually possessive. With his other hand, he lifts his own fajita. "Good thinking, babe," he remarks.

"It was a stage kiss," I assure him. "Nothing more."

"Uh-huh," he says, unconvinced. "Why are you flustered, then?"

"I'm not flustered," I mutter.

"Aw, are you blushing?" Cartwright asks, smirking at me. "She's blushing."

I look up at him across the table. "*Et tu*, Brute?"

Cartwright frowns. "Huh?"

"I'm gonna buy you a book for Christmas," I tell him. "Even in the likely event that we have nothing to do with one another by then. If you get a random copy of *Julius Caesar* slipped into your locker, know it was from me."

"Nicer than what he's slipped inside *your* locker," Carter murmurs.

I cock an eyebrow and look up at Cartwright, remembering the lube someone put into my locker all those weeks ago. "Really?" I ask him.

He has the good grace to look bashful about it, but I know it's only because I'm in Carter's good graces today. As much as I might like to write Erika off, more than anyone else at either of these tables, I know she's not entirely wrong about Carter. Right now, she might be between his crosshairs, but he could turn on a dime and treat any one of us the exact same way. He could tire of chasing me tomorrow, and by this time next week, have Cartwright lubing up my locker again without remorse.

It's a shallow, unreliable world, this world of Carter's. One might think it would be a comforting thing to have friends like these who do his bidding without question, but I can see why it isn't. Because something Carter said to me a long time ago is so very true. These people don't like *him*, they like what their closeness to him does for them. They don't follow his orders out of loyalty or a genuine desire to support him, but out of fear—fear that if they step out of line, he will banish them, and all the benefits of his friendship will disappear in a puff of smoke.

Erika was wrong. None of Carter's friends think they're safe. They just make sure not to cross him so that he never has a reason to throw them to the wolves.

Looking over at him, I feel a strange stab of sadness for him. In so many ways, he is so spoiled, but in the most basic ways, I think he might be starving. Like he said to me once before, I am the first real thing Carter has ever encountered. To have gone this many years never believing a single person likes who he is... I can't imagine how lonely he must be, despite his superficial fans and his army of minions.

My own thoughts make it even harder to stick to my guns. I yearn to wrap my arms around Carter and give him a big hug. To tell him even when I'm so angry at him I want to scream, I still like him. I always like him—and not the shiny, perfect side of him, either. I like the filth and the sadness and the darkness. I *do* crave his depravity, because I know it's inside him whether he has somewhere to put it or not.

I love being the place he puts his darkness. I love being the keeper of the secret of who Carter really is.

I love him, dammit. I didn't entirely mean it when the words slipped out that night in a post-orgasmic bliss bubble, but God help me, I do.

I love Carter Mahoney, and that means I am well and truly fucked.

CHAPTER 48

"CARTER, NO!"

His hand roughly covers my mouth, cutting off anything else I intended to say as he drives his cock inside me. I close my eyes and groan, relieved that he stole my ability to speak. It's getting harder and harder to beg him to stop when all I want is for him to keep going.

"Not another fucking word out of you," he says roughly, his fist tightening as he yanks my hair.

God, yes.

I shake my head and try to utter a muffled no, but his hand is closed over my mouth too tightly. He draws back and pistons into the tight, hot wetness between my shaking legs and I cry out against his hand. My whole body *needs* release more than it needs even the most basic necessities. I'll give up oxygen for the next two minutes and take my chances if he'll just let me come.

Carter moves his hand from my mouth after only a minute, telling me, "I hear your voice, I smack your ass. Keep your mouth shut."

"Fuck you," I spit back.

His low growl sends a thrill down my spine, then Carter's hand comes down across my ass and I let out a little yelp, clutching his bed sheets and holding on for dear life as he fucks me harder. I'm too close to the edge of the bed for him to be thrusting this hard. It's hard to think straight when he takes me like this, but a sudden awareness of how much closer I'm moving to the edge with every thrust has me grabbing for purchase and trying to stop him, for real.

"Carter, wait."

He ignores me, pounding into me even harder.

"Carter, stop," I call out, unsure how to get his attention. "I'm serious, I need to—"

With one more brutal drive, he sends me right off the edge of the bed. My arms shoot out and I catch myself on the ground a split second after our bodies disconnect. I roll to a sitting position and start to laugh, feeling stupid for literally falling off his bed, but Carter cuts off my laughter, grabbing me and shoving me down on the floor.

Oh, shit.

I'm not sure how it's possible, but I feel myself get even wetter. Before I can utter a sound, he grabs my hips, positions me, and shoves his cock back inside me. My insides explode with sensation. I try to put my palms on the floor to brace myself, but as soon as I try, he knocks my hand out from under me and pushes me down face first.

"Ass up."

Lust coils through me, even as he moves inside me. I don't know what he's doing to me, but I can't get enough tonight. Maybe he needs it more than usual and my body is responding to that. I love to give him what he needs. I love to *be* what he needs. He's the one with two rounds left, and I'm the one dreading the last time this happens.

The last time.

Sadness lands like a boulder in my gut. Even if I let him keep playing these games with me for the rest of senior year, it has to end when he goes off to college. We're going to school too far apart, and I know firsthand now, Carter will not go without sex. If he can't get it from me, he'll get it elsewhere. Long distance won't work with him. No way.

My own thoughts screw me over, dampening the arousal that has been building since Carter got me back to his house after the movie I swore I wouldn't go to with him. We were barely inside his bedroom when he told me to get on my knees and pay my debt. As expected, a blow job turned into sex, and the sex got dirty. It's hard to build to a climax when you're dousing yourself in sadness though, and Carter isn't in a giving mood tonight to begin with.

I can tell by his increased speed and the guttural noises as he takes my pussy that he's getting close. Shit. I missed my chance. Stupid brain, wandering too far off base.

Sure enough, a moment later, Carter drives deep and groans as he shoots his release inside me. I clench my feminine muscles, squeezing him as he does, trying to maximize his pleasure.

When he finishes, he collapses beside me on the floor and pulls me into his arms. I snuggle close and rest my head on his bicep. It's not a comfy pillow, and the floor certainly isn't as welcoming as the bed, but I know he just came, so he's probably not eager to stand up and relocate right now. I'm feeling cuddly anyway, so I wrap my arms around him and hold him close.

Once he catches his breath and his heartbeat returns to a steady pace, he looks over and asks me, "You all right?"

With a little smile, I nod my head. "Yeah."

"I couldn't tell if you meant it this time," he admits, looking up at the ceiling. "When you were asking me to stop."

"Oh. Well, I did, but only because I could feel myself about to fall off the bed. If I'm going to have bruises from you fucking me, I'd prefer it not be because I fell off the bed."

That catches his attention, and he looks over at me, slightly alarmed. "Have I bruised you?"

"Just a little. Barely worth mentioning. Sometimes you grab a little harder than I think you mean to, and you have the strong hands of an athlete, go figure. I get the occasional thumb print."

"Shit. I'm sorry."

I smile faintly. "It's not a big deal. It's usually not anywhere someone would see it, anyway. Maybe if I'm wearin' a bikini, but oddly enough, I don't spend a lot of time in a bikini."

"You should," he advises. "We do have a pool, you know."

"Chlorine does unpleasant things to my hair," I inform him. Then, dragging a finger saucily down his chest, I add, "Besides, if we went swimming alone, I'm sure we would both be naked."

Carter smiles, curling his arm to drag me closer so he can give me a kiss. "Good point. You don't need a bikini. The fewer clothes on you, the better."

I sigh with pleasure as he bends his head and starts kissing my neck again.

"Want to hear something funny?" he asks.

"Sure," I answer.

"My mom asked me this morning if you were pregnant. Heard it around town."

I sigh heavily. "Hilarious. Did she tell your dad? Should I be on the lookout for a hitman now?"

"Nah. They don't handle unwanted teen moms with hitmen. A checkbook is their weapon of choice. You wouldn't be unwanted anyway, though. If we had a baby, it would be different. We're more or less old enough for that now."

"Okay. I'm gonna reiterate one more time that I am not pregnant."

"I know, I just thought it was funny hearing my own rumor echoed back to me."

"I'm just tickled, let me tell you."

Shrugging unrepentantly, he says, "Shouldn't have told me you were fucking someone else."

"I didn't. I told you I went out with someone else, and I'm not you. A date doesn't necessarily lead to sex with me."

"No kidding," he says, as if I made him wait an eternity. "Sex doesn't always lead to dates, either. You're a weird girl."

Since he has given me an opening to ask a question I've been tempted to ask, I set aside my wariness of the answer and take the plunge. "Anyway, you're the one who actually went out with someone else," I begin, lightly enough considering how hard my heart pounds as those words tumble out of my mouth.

"'Went out with' might be an overstatement. We didn't go anywhere, I just used her to fuck with you."

He's so fucking mean sometimes, I swear. Not even to me in this instance, but to stupid Jenna. "You didn't like her at all?" I question, heart in my throat. Despite being grounded in reason much of the time, my heart thuds like its continuing function depends upon his answer. Stupid, stupid heart.

His dark gaze locks with mine and he shakes his head in such a way that I feel foolish for asking. Even though it's completely possible he could have liked that girl, the look on his face tells me otherwise. "I like *you*," Carter answers, simply.

"Have you slept with her or anyone else since me?"

"Not yet."

My heart soars and then stalls at his answer. Such a bittersweet reminder that he could, if he wanted to, but he doesn't —*yet*.

In a sense, for me at least, it feels like *that* is when it will really be over between us. That is when whatever ties us together will dissolve, when I will actually be free to move on with my life and veer in a direction that leads entirely away from him.

It's hard to imagine grasping that any other way. It will happen when he sleeps with another girl, because I sure as hell won't be the one jumping into bed with anyone else right on the heels of whatever this is.

He will, though. He did already when I didn't put out expediently enough to satisfy his baser needs.

"You know me. If I had wanted to get off, I would've made you do it, not called in a sub."

His words that night come back to mind. I'm mulling them over, trying to put together an impossible puzzle. How do I have Carter and also some semblance of safety? How do I ask him not to sleep with anyone else, without promising to meet his needs myself? For that matter, how do I ask him not to see anyone else —period—if I'm not ready to jump back into being his girlfriend? I can't. It wouldn't be fair.

My head and my heart couldn't be further apart on this issue, though, and before I can stop it, my heart recklessly throws a hand on the wheel and hurls us around a scary corner. "I don't want you to."

His eyebrows rise in surprise at my frankness, while my formerly ballsy heart drops right down into my stomach. "Then you want to get back together."

No. That's too scary. I shake my head, dropping my gaze to his chest so I don't have to look him in the eye.

"You're gonna have to help me out here, babe. I don't know what you want," he tells me.

I want a time machine that can travel back to the night he told me nothing happened between him and Erika, and I want him to tell me the truth instead. Or a trip ahead in time, so I can see if giving him another chance would lead to a much deeper heartache down the road.

I don't always need to be comfortable, but I really hate feeling stupid, and if I give him another chance and he ends up cheating on me, there are not words for how unbelievably foolish I will feel.

"I don't have anything new to offer you, Carter. I was just being honest," I explain. "I like that you and I can always be honest with one another, even if the truth isn't pretty. I like that we're not afraid to talk about anything, no matter how messed up, and I feel like that's a large part of what I lost. That's why our relationship stopped working for me. Maybe you need sex more, but I need openness and an unshakeable mutual trust. I don't need you to be that way with anyone else, but I do need you to trust *me*, and to know I can trust *you*. You never lost your supply, but I did. I stopped getting what I needed out of us, so... yeah, I still have conflicted feelings, and I still care about you, but that's where we are. Nothing you've done since has given me back that feeling I had before, that... awe. I don't want you to be with anyone else. I don't want to watch you move on, but I don't want to take another chance on you, either. That means it's over, and at the end of the day, you will move on. Maybe then it will be easier for me to move past this."

"Okay, that's not entirely true. Most of it is," he amends, before I get defensive. "I know I'm going to sound like an asshole saying this, but you claim my supply was never interrupted, that I got everything I needed from you, but..." He trails off, uncharacteristically hesitant.

I brace myself, knowing something unpleasant is coming my way.

"I didn't know we were going to have sex that weekend, Zoey. When I went to her house, I had no idea where you and I were heading. Don't get me wrong, I like the occasional blow job as much as the next guy, but I didn't know I'd get you into bed so fast. You have the reputation of being a stuck-up virgin who spends her free time at *church*, for Christ's sake. I figured it would take a little longer to wear you down, and I didn't really want to go without while I was waiting. That's the truth. It's selfish and ugly, but yeah, I do have needs, Zoey. I'm not a slave to them, I wouldn't have cheated on you once we were together, but we weren't quite together yet. The timing was shit, and if I had known I could have you if I just waited another couple of days, obviously I would take it all back. I wouldn't have gone to her house. I wouldn't make that mistake again. I should've been honest with you. I should've known that you could take it, and I'm really sorry I lied instead. I know better now."

"Did you sleep with her?" I ask.

"No," he answers, seriously.

"Did she go down on you? Or get you off another way? Any variation of sex acts between you two?"

"Nothing happened beyond kissing. I got a copy of the video, I can show you the proof if you want to finish watching it. Well, listening to it."

I shake my head. "No, I never want to see that again."

Grabbing my hand and interlocking our fingers, he says, "Nothing happened, Zoey."

"She said she got you off," I remind him.

"She was lying to rile you up. That part was not true. Even showing you the video was a calculated bluff, because if you had kept watching, you would have heard me come around to my senses and leave."

I want to fire more questions at him while he's being open again, but I don't really know what to do with the answers. After the scene at lunch, Kasey filled in all the gaps in my knowledge. Apparently, someone confessed to the principal that they saw drugs in Erika's locker when she had it open. An unannounced locker search—which Kasey sent me the picture of some part of—turned up a plastic bag filled with narcotics. Erika swore she was innocent, that she didn't do drugs and had no idea where those had come from.

She was suspended from the cheer squad, pending a drug

test. If it comes back clean, she will be reinstated. If it doesn't, she will be kicked off the squad permanently, possibly suspended from school, and she could even face criminal charges.

"Did Erika do drugs?" I ask.

"Has she ever? Sure."

I give him a droll look. "No, not has she ever. Are you responsible for what's going on with her right now? The drugs in her locker? Getting kicked off the squad?"

He shrugs. "She should have known better than to fuck with me. I warned her more than once. At a certain point, you have to act or no one believes you anymore."

"So, you framed her. Just to scare her? What happens when the drug test comes back clean and she's back on the squad this week? She's gonna be pissed."

"Who says she's going to pass the drug test?" he asks rhetorically.

"She's not doing drugs. Your rewording of my question said as much."

"She won't be back on the cheer squad," he says, simply. "She's done. Suspended for the rest of the season, just like her buddy Jake."

"I got Jake suspended because he was sexually inappropriate with me. He violated actual codes of conduct. That's not the same thing," I tell him.

"Erika cost me you," he states. "That's a good enough reason for me."

In a twisted way, that's kind of sweet. Still, my better intentions win out and I tell him, "I don't want this. I appreciate the gesture, I think, but I don't want or need you to take her down to punish her for showing me the video. It was a bitchy thing to do, but—"

"It's too late now," he assures me. "She's off the squad. She's done." His arms tighten around my waist. "I don't want to talk about her anymore."

"Don't go after anyone else. Please," I add, shooting him my best puppy dog eyes. "Stop being destructive."

Gazing at me with a gleam of mischief in his eyes, he asks, "What'll you give me for it?"

"Why do I have to give you anything for it? It's not for me."

"You want to be a defender of the people, you pay the piper."

"Fine. I'll go to homecoming with you," I offer. I gave away my dress money, but I could probably find something at a thrift shop, or maybe borrow a dress from Grace. I know she doesn't want to wear the dress she wore last year, but I kind of liked it. Maybe I could give her some money for that one, then she could use the money toward a new gown for this year.

Carter shakes his head. "A big ask demands a bigger payment than that. Homecoming, stay the night with me tonight, and promise you'll still go to New York with me after state, no matter what happens between now and then."

Immediately suspicious, I narrow my eyes. "You mean no matter how many other girls you sleep with. No, I won't agree to that."

Giving my side a light squeeze, Carter remarks, "For someone who supposedly doesn't want to be part of it, you are very concerned with my sex life."

"I'm prepared to do homecoming and I can probably stay the night tonight, but that's it. New York is not on the table."

"Then I don't stop terrorizing your friends," he says, simply. "New York is non-negotiable to me. It's what I was working toward all along. If New York is a no, it's open season. I can do whatever, because I'm not going to get what I want at the end of the day, anyway."

"Why are you so set on me going to New York with you?" I ask, shaking my head.

"I told you I'd take you there. I know you want to go. When will you go, if not with me?"

I have no answer to that. "I can't afford to go on an impromptu trip to New York, and it's not right to expect you to pay my way when I'm not even your girlfriend."

"Money is not your issue," Carter states, dismissing my smoke screen. "Sex is your issue. You immediately dumped me when you thought I might've been with someone else, and now you've decided your feelings for me dissolve if I sleep with anyone else, even though we're not together. You don't want me if my dick gets hard for anyone but you. This is your possessive side coming out, doesn't have a damn thing to do with money."

"Fine, maybe it is," I admit. "You don't want anyone else touching me either, do you? I'm not alone in feeling that way."

"The difference is, I'm not asking you to be celibate. I am happy to fuck you any time you want it. The road doesn't go both ways. You make me bargain for sex. I have to wreak havoc in order to get you into bed, and then I have to budget our encounters so I don't use them all up at once. All you have to do is shoot me a text. That doesn't work for me. You *are* the only one I want to fuck, but if you're not on the table, you can't expect me to turn into a monk. That's not going to happen."

An ugly kind of fury burns through me at the thought of another girl in my place, of him kissing, touching, burying himself inside anyone but me. I don't know what to do about it, but I don't want that to happen. I especially don't want it to happen unexpectedly and then be something I find out about later.

An idea bursts open inside of me, unsettling my tummy, but I open my mouth and let the words tumble out before I can stop myself. "Since when has me not wanting it ever stopped you? If you need to fuck someone and you're not willing to wait any longer..." I trail off, swallowing, unsure what exactly I'm suggesting or how he'll receive it. Part of me thinks he might tire of working so hard for me, but hell, it's not like *he's* a piece of cake, either.

His predatory instincts surface and he rolls me onto my back, moving on top of me. "Go ahead and finish that thought, princess. If I'm at a party with some girl who's ready to go, I should, what? Leave her there and come see you? What if once I'm there, you tell me no?"

"Take it anyway."

My heart gallops, giving him permission like that. We don't have any kind of system set up where I can interrupt if no really does mean no that time, no safe escape if I want out of the moment. There is none of that with him, so it's more dangerous to set him loose. He could potentially end up forcing me to do something I really don't want to do, and even if I want it now, there's no way of stopping him later if I change my mind. I have a feeling he only needs one yes, and telling him "no" ten thousand times after that would fall on deaf ears.

His voice is low, but so intimate, my bones turn to jelly as he murmurs, "Yeah? Even if I think you mean it?"

It was a terrifying ledge to tiptoe up to, a deeply buried truth I didn't want to confess, but now that we're here and I've already taken the leap, I feel bolder, freer in telling him the twisted truth. "Even if I mean it. I would rather you force me than sleep with someone else. I know you'd take care of me after, if something went wrong. Whatever happens between you and me, I can handle. I just don't want you with anyone else."

His fingers burrow into my hair as he cradles my head, pulling me in for a soft, tender kiss. I'm vulnerable in the wake of such an admission, so I drink in the affection like it's the drug I need to live. When he ends the kiss, he stays close and murmurs huskily against my lips. "Do you know what you've done, princess? You just gave me the keys to the kingdom. There's no stopping me now."

I swallow, so aware of the truth of that statement. I knew that when I said it, though. I may not be ready to trust him with my heart again, but I do trust him with my body. I'm not afraid he'll break that.

"I know," I answer softly, meeting his gaze. "I don't want you to stop."

For a moment, he just looks at me. As he does, he soaks up every last doubt I might have about the choice I just made, the big and the small. He might like to call me his plaything, but he doesn't look at me like a toy. He looks at me like a treasure. Like the heavens opened up and dropped me into his lap, and he's forever grateful for the gift, even if he doesn't express it with words. Even if his way of loving is sometimes brutal and scarring, even if he is more predator than prince, somehow, he is the perfect fit for me.

I don't know what that says about me, but I don't really care, either.

"I love you, Zoey."

My heart gives, then flies high in my chest. I've never really expected to hear those words from his lips, and certainly not on this fucked up timetable where we're not even together. It doesn't matter, though. We don't have to be together to love each other. I have a feeling none of the rules of ordinary relationships will ever apply to us, unless we want them to. Whatever cloth he's cut from, it's not a normal one, and that's fine with me. I love his abnormality. I love him just the way he is.

Smiling softly, I reach out and push a hand through his hair, guiding his face close to mine again. I kiss his lips tenderly a few times, then I tell him, "I love you, too."

CHAPTER 49

EVERYTHING CALMS DOWN after I give Carter the keys to the kingdom. He no longer has a reason to storm the castle gates, so he lets my life return to normal. No more terrorizing the people in my life to force me to come to him and bargain, no more insane rumors to try to force me into isolation. He treats my admission like a victory, and maybe it is, but it's one I can live with.

No longer fearing the possibility of him with anyone else makes it all worth it, to be honest. I tried to ignore how stressful that was when it was happening, but now that it's over, it's as if a fifty-pound weight has been pushed right off my shoulders.

I couldn't save Erika. Not that I would have expended much effort trying, but by the time Monday rolls around, the hottest gossip around school is that she failed her drug test and is no longer a cheerleader. I don't know how Carter managed that, and I decided not to ask. I decided not to let her into our relationship any longer, because she has no place there. Sure, I feel bad about what happened, but Carter did warn her, and she chose to treat him like he wasn't a threat. I don't think all is fair in love and war, but Carter clearly does, and she has known him longer than I have. Shouldn't she have known that?

In any case, she does now. After hearing the rumors, I expected her to be out for blood, but to my surprise, she seems to finally accept defeat. She doesn't show up to lunch Monday or Tuesday, but Wednesday she does. She doesn't even look at her old table. She walks across the cafeteria and finds an empty spot somewhere else.

I don't skip lunch in the cafeteria anymore. I don't sit at the popular girls' table where Carter's girlfriend should sit, either; I sit right next to him at the guys' table—the sole girl among them. Perhaps because of that, the message is clear that I'm with Carter, whether I say I am or not.

Now that we've come to our own arrangement, I'm less concerned about titles. Carter never much liked them, anyway, and all it did was make me feel pressured. Other people can be boyfriend and girlfriend; we will be Carter and Zoey.

By Wednesday night, Carter has already blown through his two remaining rounds of math test sex. Not that it matters now. He shows up at my house Thursday evening when the rest of my family is out and fucks me right in my own bed. It's a brutal, noisy fuck, the kind of convincingly hateful fuck most people who like each other so much probably aren't capable of. When my body is blissfully spent and drained of energy, I curl up next to him, wrap my arms around him, and nearly drift off to sleep.

His voice draws me out of it and my heavy eyelids drift open so I can look up at him.

"When I was younger, I had this babysitter. From the time I was eight until I was thirteen. Didn't really need a babysitter by that age, but I liked hanging out with her. She was only six years older than me, so it was more like having a friend over than a babysitter, just a smart friend who could help with my homework when my parents didn't want to."

I push myself up in bed a little, trying to shake the bleariness. "Okay," I murmur, not quite sure where he's going with this.

"When I was 12, she started playing this game with me. Sometimes she would bring stuff with her, sometimes we would use stuff around the house, but... she wanted me to put things inside her. She would wear a skirt with no panties, or a top with no bra. I always knew which game we would play by what she would show up in. No panties, I would put stuff inside her until she came. No bra, she'd want me to use my mouth."

My stomach drops as I start to piece together what he's saying.

Glancing at me a little uncertainly, he says, "It was kind of like a signal, so I guess I knew what was coming, but I couldn't tell anyone. Wasn't even sure what I would tell them, you know?"

I nod, my heart in my throat. I can't get any words out past the lump, so I just nod like a broken bobble-head doll.

"It went on for a while, then the game changed. Then it wasn't enough for me to use stuff on her, she wanted *me* inside her. I didn't even feel comfortable with the game. I didn't want to do those things I wasn't allowed to tell anyone about. It all felt wrong, and not in a remotely sexy way."

"Oh, God, Carter," I murmur, knowing where this is going.

Clearing his throat, he says, "Anyway, so, that was Chloe's mom. When she got pregnant, everything kind of went to shit. She freaked out because she knew what she had done was illegal, even though she told my parents I was the one to come onto her. I wasn't," he says, looking me straight in the eye almost defensively.

"I know," I assure him.

"They either didn't believe me, or didn't want to. My father wanted to sweep it under the rug. He thought of it as something I had done wrong, something *I* had screwed up. He just wanted her to get an abortion and go away. My mom, though. She wouldn't have it. According to her, it would be wrong, and two wrongs didn't make a right. My mom decided she would keep Chloe and raise her as my sister. Pay the babysitter off, make her sign an NDA." He cracks a cynical smile. "She made me do shit I didn't want to do, and she got paid for it twice. It was a nice fucking pay-off, let me tell you."

"I'm so sorry, Carter," I say, wrapping my arms around his bare torso and burying my face in his chest. This is so unexpected, I have no idea what to say to him.

"Anyway, that's why we moved here. My father did have an affair, but that wasn't the main reason, it was just the final straw. We moved here to start fresh, to leave behind all our skeletons. Sometimes they follow you, though, even if you never see the person again. I don't know if all this shit is why I am the way I am, but I do know how I was introduced to sex, and I still like it the same way. Now I just like to be the aggressor." He shrugs. "Maybe a coincidence, maybe not. I don't know."

My introduction to intimacy was a bit violent, too, and now I crave all the things he does to me. At this point, I have no better idea than him where these cravings originate, but I nod my head in understanding, anyway. I don't need for there to be a reason for the way Carter is anymore, but I can tell he's trying to explain himself to me. He's opening up and sharing with me the one thing he wouldn't share before.

He's letting me in, deep into depths maybe he doesn't even entirely understand. Places maybe he hasn't even fully explored. I squeeze him tighter, wanting to express my appreciation, but unsure how. Normally I would kiss him or do something physical, but that feels wrong in the wake of what he just revealed.

Judging by his tone, he's ready to wrap it up, but he says, "Anyway, you wanted to know about Chloe's mom. Now you know."

Socked by a sudden memory of me asking *him* if he raped some girl and got her pregnant, I want the floor to open up and swallow me whole. I want to apologize for even asking that, but I also don't want to bring it up again.

"Thank you for telling me," I offer softly, meeting his gaze. "I'm so sorry that happened. I honestly… I don't even know what to say."

"Don't need you to say anything." He flashes me a half-hearted smile to let me know it's okay. "You asked, I answered. That's all."

Cringing, I remember, "I asked you if you loved Chloe's mom."

"It was a reasonable question. You didn't know. Anyway, I don't like talking about it, so I'd rather we didn't. I just figured since you're stuck with me, I should give you some of that openness you're so fond of."

It feels wrong to crack a smile, but I don't want to make him even more uncomfortable than he already is, either. "I appreciate that, thank you. And if you ever *do* need to talk about it, you know I'm here."

"I know," he assures me, tightening his arm around me and leaning forward to kiss my forehead.

I don't know if it's the right thing to do, but I tip my head back so my lips meet his. His response is immediate; he pushes his fingers through my hair and cradles my head, closing his eyes and kissing me back. I want to offer comfort and support he swears he doesn't need, but I have a feeling he will be more receptive to it coming physically than with discomfiting words. Usually there's nothing tentative or uncomfortable about it when our bodies communicate, and while at first I wonder if this time will be an exception after what he just told me, he quickly disabuses me of that notion.

I GO to his game Friday night, but I bring a spiral notebook from history class so I can study between plays. I also bring a hard copy of my book review, that way I can read through it again and make any necessary changes before I turn it in on Monday.

"Workin' through the game. I see your team spirit's in full swing."

I look up at Jake, standing there towering over me with a little smirk on his face. I wouldn't look so smug if I were him, but I don't want to get into it with him again, either. "Can I help you with something?"

He gestures to the bench beside me, occupied by the school stuff I've spread out there. "Mind if I sit?"

"I think Carter might," I offer, since Carter's word holds more weight with Jake than mine.

A cynical smile tugs at his lips. "I think Carter knows he's the only asshole you're interested in." Gesturing to the full stadium, he says, "Place is full. I just wanna watch the game."

Sighing heavily, I begin gathering my things to make room. "Fine."

Once I've gathered my things in my lap, Jake scoots down the aisle in front of me and takes a seat beside me. It's more awkward now, but I situate my stuff in my lap and look down at the field. I don't know what's going on, but I spot Carter in his blue and white jersey. Even from this distance, I can't help noticing how much more imposing he looks with all his gear on. Mm, he's so sexy. He glances my way, and on impulse, I wave at him.

I can't tell from here if he cracks a smile, but he lifts his hand in a brief wave back.

"Don't fuckin' distract the guy," Jake snaps. "We've got a lot ridin' on this game."

"I wasn't distracting him," I say, scowling at Jake. "They're just standin' on the field. Obviously, I wouldn't wave in the middle of a play."

Shaking his head, Jake takes a swig from his Longhorn water bottle. Judging from the strong smell that wafts my way, it's not water inside this week, either. "Just let him focus, fuck."

I huff, returning to my notes. "You're the distraction," I inform him as I turn the page. "Now he looked up here and saw you sittin' next to me. If he gets distracted, that will be why, not because I waved."

"Yeah, I'm sure Carter Mahoney feels real fuckin' threatened by me," Jake mutters dryly. "Bet he cries about it in his marble-floored money pit every damn night."

"I didn't say he feels threatened, but he is protective, so I doubt he would want you sitting by me."

"Why? Afraid I might pin you down on the bleachers and take you for myself? Actually, maybe he should be. Apparently, you're into that sort of thing."

He's such a dick. I'm just going to ignore him.

After a minute, he asks, "What are you studyin' for, anyway?"

"History," I murmur, dragging my finger down the page of my neatly written notes to find the answer I'm looking for.

"No, I mean, didn't Mahoney knock you up? What do you need to study for? You're set for life."

Looking over at him, I remark, "You are obsessed with Carter's money, aren't you? No, I'm not pregnant. That's just a rumor."

Jake cocks a skeptical eyebrow. "It came directly from Carter. He started a rumor about himself?"

"It's a long story. I wasn't pregnant, he was just pissing on a tree. Telling a bunch of teenage guys I'm knocked up was an effective way of makin' me unappealing."

"Nice guy, that Carter," he deadpans.

"The nicest."

"Not controlling at all," he adds.

"Doesn't even know the meaning of the word," I volley back.

"Well, my whole congregation prayed for your soul last weekend," he tells me.

"Their efforts are much appreciated," I offer back, wishing he would stop talking. It's hard to study with him being so noisy.

A moment of blessed silence passes, then he ruins it by saying, "Bet you liked watchin' Erika fall, huh?"

I flip a page more violently, even though I think I already passed the information I needed. "Not especially, no."

Jake laughs. "Bullshit. Any girl would get a charge out of watchin' their cheating ass boyfriend take out a social hit on the other girl."

"He didn't cheat, and it wasn't—" Cutting myself off, I tell him, "You know what? I need to study. It's been a lovely chat, but I need to get back to it."

"Why won't you just admit it? He cheated, but you took him back anyway because he's fuckin' Carter Mahoney. You did the same shit Erika did. You drive me crazy with that shit. If you'd just admit why you do things, you'd annoy me a whole hell of a lot less. This nice girl routine is bullshit."

"I don't actually care about being a nice girl, Jake," I tell him. "I am who I am, and if people like it, cool. If they don't, fuck 'em. You want me to be someone I'm not, that's the problem. You want to vilify me. You *want* to see me as shallow and meaner than I am, you want me to like Carter for his money, and you *want* him to have cheated, because wouldn't that just serve me right? You wish ill on me, but it's not for anything *I've* done, it's just what you need to see in order to be the good guy in your own narrative. Here's the problem. You're not the good guy. You'd be a much better guy if you just admitted to your fuckups and imperfections. If you want to be the good guy, act like one, don't try to warp everyone else to make yourself look better. That's not just lazy, it's cowardly and pathetic."

Since clearly I'm not going to get any studying done and Jake is only going to further annoy me if I stay here, I gather my things, grab my purse, and prepare to leave the aisle. Before I can, his hand shoots out and he grabs my arm. "Not so fuckin' fast, sweetheart."

"Get your hand off me," I tell him, glancing back over my shoulder. "How many fucking times do I have to say that to you before it sinks in? I don't like when you touch me, even casually. Keep your hands to yourself."

I have to yank hard on my hand to get it free, then I make my way down the steps of the stadium. I don't know where to go, I just need to get away from him. Looking down the aisles as I move lower and lower, I look for a spot, but there really aren't any. It's close to championships, homecoming is next week—people aren't missing games right now, they're bringing more people to cheer.

By the time I've made it to the ground, all I feel like doing is going home. I wonder how disappointed Carter would be if I left. We're all supposed to go to the café after the game, but I don't feel like scouring the stadium for a place to sit, either.

Making matters much worse, when I turn around, I see Jake heading toward me down the steps.

"You've gotta be kidding," I mutter to myself. I start to round the corner to leave the stadium, but then it occurs to me, he could follow me. I don't think he would take things as far as Carter has, but having seen the way Carter fights, I know Jake will be his next "social hit" if he hears about Jake so much as touching my wrist.

"Look, I'm sorry," Jake says, surprising the hell out of me.

I can't help turning to face him, wide-eyed. "What did you just say to me?"

"I didn't intend to piss you off, you just...." He trails off, shaking his head. "I don't think Carter's good for you. I don't understand why he did worse to you than I did, but you like him. You say it's not the money, but what else could it be? What does he have that I don't?"

I don't know whether to feel bad for Jake because he is so unaccustomed to rejection that he literally can't process it, or aggravated by his entitlement. I understand that he doesn't understand, but I can't explain it in a way that would ever help him accept it, either. The better question to me is, why the hell does he like me? I've never spent time with Jake like I have with Carter. At this point, I feel like Jake only likes me because Carter wants me. If I can hold the attention of Carter Mahoney, I must be something special.

"Look, what do you and I have in common, Jake? What do I like to do in my free time? What's my favorite subject in school? Why is it my favorite? What do I want more than anything else in the world? What is it about a guy that really turns me on? Why do I come to my boyfriend's football game, then spend half the time studying? Am I just an asshole? What matters to me? For that matter, what is your favorite thing about me? Not physical, something else."

He blinks vacantly, completely unprepared for any of those questions.

I nod my head knowingly. "Exactly. You don't know. Carter does. He knows the answers to all those questions and more. He gives me answers to questions I didn't even have. Carter *gets me*, and he likes what's really there. I'm an idea to you, that's all. Being infatuated with an idea might feel nice, but it isn't *real*. I am not the girl you have in your mind. If I were, you wouldn't be so constantly agitated by my reality. Carter and I see each other, the real shit, the dark and dirty stuff, not just the nice stuff. We know each other well, and the more we learn, the more we like. We just fit better. That is the explanation. That is why he and I are good together, and you and I never could be."

He's scowling at the end of my speech, but before he has a chance to respond, Brianna comes bouncing over from the line-up of cheerleaders.

"What's goin' on over here?" she asks, glancing between us.

"Nothing, he was just leaving," I tell her. To Jake, I nod pointedly back up the stadium steps. "You better go get that seat before someone takes it."

He doesn't immediately move, so Brianna props a hand on her hip and looks at him expectantly. "Go on, Jake."

His lips curve up cynically. "You know, Brianna, I think this is the first time you've spoken to me since Carter banished me."

"He's gonna banish you even further if you keep botherin' his girlfriend," Brianna states. "What is wrong with you people? Just leave Zoey alone and Carter will leave you alone. It's not that hard!"

"Yeah, well, we don't all enjoy bein' Carter's bitch as much as you do, Bri," Jake tells her. Then to me, he nods. "You better watch this one. Anyone this eager to do Carter's bidding sure wouldn't say no to his dick—*again*."

Brianna flushes, glaring at Jake. "Stop tryin' to cause trouble and go away."

"Is there a problem over here?"

My eyes widen and I look up as Carter's father makes his way down the aisle, his stern gaze locked on us.

"Nah, Mr. Mahoney, no problem over here," Jake tells him.

"Good," Carter's father clips, giving Jake a stern look. "Why don't you go find a seat before you miss the game," he suggests. Ignoring Brianna entirely, Mr. Mahoney puts a hand at the top of my back and nudges me toward the row he just exited. "Come on over here, honey. You can sit with us."

Honey? I wasn't entirely convinced by Carter's mom's assurance that Mr. Mahoney would be more accepting of me, but he went from "She's going to drag you through the mud, just like she did Jake" to "honey" pretty damn quickly.

"Hi Zoey," Chloe greets brightly as I approach.

"Hi, honey," I offer back, looking at the row where they're sitting.

There's really not room for me, but Carter's mom notices they need to make room and grabs Chloe, pulling her on her lap. Flashing me a smile, she pats the now empty bench and tells me, "You can sit here."

I settle my things on my lap, but now that I'm not sitting alone, I would feel too awkward ignoring them to study. The view from this row is a lot better than my seats before, too. The cheerleaders are right in front of us. Carter is too far down the field to get a good view of now, but when they move back this way, I'll get an eyeful of his butt in those football pants. Carter has such a nice butt.

"Want some of my popcorn?"

I pull myself out of lusty thoughts to glance over at Chloe, holding out a paper cone full of popcorn. "No, you can have it, but thank you for the offer."

Shrugging, she tips the cone back toward herself and grabs some popcorn to shove into her mouth. Her attention returns to the field, but mine lingers on her.

This is the first time I've seen her since Carter told me the truth about her shitty mother. I've never heard of something like that happening to anyone I've known before, but I guess it's not the kind of thing most people would share openly.

I wonder if he will ever tell her the truth. If not the traumatizing part, at least that she is actually his daughter, not his sister. I wonder if she'll go to live with him in New York, although without me or a babysitter—which apparently, he won't allow—I don't see how she could. Social life aside, he'll have classes, and they may not all coincide with kindergarten hours. Or maybe they would, I don't know.

I wish our schools were closer together. I wish the only considerations were what we want, and not what is possible.

"Did you bring a coloring book?" Chloe asks me.

"A coloring book?" I ask, confused. "No. Was I supposed to?"

She points at the notebook in my lap. "What's that?"

I place a palm on the cover. "Oh, this is schoolwork. I'm trying to cram as much information into my brain as humanly possible, so I keep these with me pretty much everywhere I go."

Carter's dad pipes in with, "Carter tells us you're on track to be class salutatorian. That's quite the accomplishment."

He must *not* have told them *he* was the one on track to be salutatorian, and he blew it so I could have the spot. I still feel a little guilty about that, but I keep telling myself Carter doesn't need it like I do. Besides, it was his choice.

Over the course of the game, both of Carter's parents chat with me. Chloe gets bored by half time and asks if she can use my highlighters to color pictures in my notebook. She winds up in my lap, drawing blue stick people with yellow hair and green clothes. Thankfully, I keep a multitude of colored highlighters and pens in my purse for note-taking purposes.

When the game is over, despite Chloe's numerous requests to leave, Carter's parents remain behind with me until Carter comes out to claim me. I get the feeling they don't want to leave me alone in case anyone else tries to cause trouble. They certainly never bothered protecting me before, but after tonight, I feel more officially Carter's girlfriend than I ever have before.

I'm not sure funny is the word, but it's certainly remarkable how different things are from how they were before Carter. When I was nobody, when I reported Jake's behavior, not a single person sprang to my defense. Not even my own parents. Now, Jake is a little unpleasant to me and I have cheerleaders and parents running to my rescue, all because now that I'm Carter's, I matter. Now, I have a voice worth listening to—because I belong to Carter.

It's kind of annoying, but I guess I'm not going to change the world all at once. I'll take the reprieve, and maybe someday my voice will matter, even when he's no longer around to make it count.

Or maybe not. Who knows?

At least I've survived the worst of senior year. From now until graduation, aside from jealous jerks trying to shake my trust in Carter for no reason, I have a hunch things will be calm. By the time I get used to it, it will be time for college to separate us, and I'll begin a whole new adventure by myself.

My heart feels emptier just thinking about it. There's no reason to let concerns about the future dull the present, though. Shoving them aside, I enjoy the feeling of Carter's strong arms locking around my waist, his kisses peppering my mouth before he claims it in a deep, possessive kiss.

The first words out of his mouth when he breaks away are, "Why was Jake bothering you?"

"Because he has a crush on an imaginary girl who looks like me," I inform him, winding my arms around his neck.

"Damned doppelgänger," he says lightly, shaking his head.

"Always causing trouble," I murmur, before stealing another kiss.

"Need me to take care of it?"

"I do not," I tell him, firmly. "Your dad was nice to me today."

I expect at least a hint of pleased surprise, but he merely nods confidently. "I know. I told you I'd take care of that. I got him on team Zoey."

"Last time he was team 'Zoey the ho,' so good job on that turnaround."

Smiling faintly, he kisses the end of my nose. "I have my ways." Releasing my waist, he takes a step back and fishes his keys out of his bag. "Come on, let's go get something to eat. I'm starving."

CHAPTER 50

SATURDAY AFTERNOON, I'm sitting on my front porch doing some more studying and enjoying some fresh air when a shiny black limousine pulls to a stop in front of my house. It's odd enough to *see* a shiny black limousine prior to prom, but to see one stopping in front of my house? No idea.

The door opens and a familiar sandal emerges. Grace has these brown sandals that are the ugliest thing anyone has ever seen, but she absolutely loves the things. She's had them since we were 15, and ugly or not, they're not going anywhere.

What is Grace doing in a limo, though?

With a big grin on her face, she pops out, iced coffee in hand. "Look at this!"

"I'm looking," I say, setting my textbook aside. "What, exactly, am I looking at?"

Next out of the limo is Kasey. I have to do a double take because, while they are both my friends, I have never seen Grace and Kasey interact at all, let alone hang out together.

Before I have time to question this odd occurrence, a third head pops out of the limousine. Raven hair and good looks to spare—Carter's older sister, Caroline.

"Hey, Zoey," she greets.

I am *so* confused. Tentatively standing, I call back, "Hi…"

"Carter didn't tell you we were coming, did he?" she realizes.

"He didn't. He likes to surprise me," I offer.

Grinning, she says, "I'll bet he does. This is a good one, though." Reaching into the front pocket of her tiny, stylish hand-bag, she holds up a credit card. "We're going shopping."

"Why?"

Caroline opens her mouth to answer me, but Grace is bursting with excitement and can't help shrieking, "Homecoming! Carter's buying us all dresses."

Caroline nods and comes closer. I'm at the foot of the stairs at this point, so she leans in to tell me, "He said you might say no. If so, he said to tell you if you let him buy your dress, he'd buy their dresses, too. Your enthusiastic friend got me all discombobulated, and I ended up telling her in the car, so... if he asks, you said no, then I had to bring the dress offer to the table. I'm a terrible negotiator," she states.

Biting back a grin, I tell her, "Don't worry, so am I."

"Since he was open to blackmailing you into letting him buy your homecoming dress, I assume he did something terrible and deserves to buy their dresses, anyway."

I nod my head and whisper, "He kidnapped Grace's dog."

Caroline frowns. "Do I even want to know?"

Now I shake my head. "You don't. The dog is home now, but yeah. Just Carter being Carter. Manipulating everyone in his life to get what he wants."

"That sounds right," she admits. Without missing a beat, she flashes me a grin. "Now, put your books away and grab your purse. We have shopping to do!"

ONE INCREDIBLE GOWN LATER, I am ready for homecoming. Or, I think I am, until we drop off half of our girl gang and then Caroline tells the driver to take us to the mall.

"I thought you were taking me home," I tell her.

Sipping on her smoothie straw, she shakes her head. "Just taking them home. We've gotta get you some shoes to go with that dress."

"We don't have to go to the mall for shoes," I reason. "I'm sure we could find something suitable at the thrift store. They have tons of shoes."

Judging by the alarmed widening of her eyes, I get the idea Caroline has never once stepped foot inside of a thrift store. "We're going to the mall," she states.

Depending on how far you want to drive, there are several malls we could go to, but Caroline opts for the closest—and the cutest, in my opinion. It's the same shopping center that houses the bookstore I work at, so I'm very familiar with the place, I just don't make much time to shop there. It's a cute shopping center with cute little outdoor areas for the kids and tons of places to shop if you have money to spend. Today we do, and shoe shopping is not my area of expertise, so I let Caroline take the lead.

"Oh, my God, try these. They're so pretty," she says, handing me a pair of black mules with an asymmetrical strap.

"Um, I'm no style expert, admittedly, but… these are black."

She blinks at me. "What's wrong with black?"

"Well, nothing. It's just that my dress is gold. Wouldn't this clash?"

Sudden comprehension lands, but she waves me off. "Oh, honey, these aren't for homecoming. These are for New York. Carter said you need some new things for the trip. These don't look super comfortable, but if you're not used to walking in heels, here's a tip. Wear comfortable shoes for walking if you won't be talking a cab, but bring a big purse. Put your heels in your purse, then change into them right before you get to wherever it is you're going. Saves your feet, but you still get to wear the pretty shoes." Waving her hand at the shoes, as if to urge them closer, she says, "Go ahead, try them on."

I push back the thin white tissue around the shoe and pull it out of the box, eyeing up the heel. "These look high."

"They are, hence the advice. They're so cute though. Imagine all the outfits they would go with."

While I wrestle with this heel, she goes back to the shoes to browse some more. I no more than get this one on the ground and she comes over with a big smile and another pair of heels.

"These," she enthuses, holding them out like an offering. "I don't even care if these are uncomfortable, we're buying these. Try them on anyway," she orders.

These shoes are much bolder than I would wear. A black base with fire engine red pointy toes, I can see them on her, but I think they might be a little much for me. "I don't know where I would wear these," I tell her.

"I do," she says, firmly. "You're getting them. They're perfect for something Carter has planned for you that I can't tell you about. Just trust me. Those shoes say all the right things. You'll thank me later." Already onto the next thing, she murmurs, "Now to find you an outfit," and wanders off, presumably to find an outfit.

We end up leaving with 3 pairs of shoes for New York and a pair of apparently boring nude strappy sandals that I picked out myself. Once Caroline got distracted buying my wardrobe for New York, she completely forgot about the homecoming shoes and left me to fend for myself. I was more interested in the comfort of the shoes I would be dancing in all night—especially since my gown is floor-length, and no one will even *see* the damn things—than the look of them, so I picked out a pair of basic-looking shoes that didn't kill my feet when I walked around in them.

Meanwhile, Caroline picked out some dressy-casual clothes, a long belted coat for the cold weather, and a big white handbag to smuggle my pretty shoes in for the 90% of the time when I prefer comfort over elegance. It's definitely someone else's wardrobe, but someone who dresses very fashionably, so I can't complain. It's crazy to think about going to New York, and even crazier that I haven't even asked my mom if I could go yet. It was one of those pipe dreams that didn't seem like it would ever happen, but now that I have a wardrobe for the trip, I decide it's probably time to ask.

She has been permissive about letting me stay the night with him, but I don't know how she'll feel about a whole weekend 1,500 miles away.

It's slow cooker BBQ sandwiches for dinner tonight so there's not much help needed, but that's my in to start a conversation, so

I make my way into the kitchen when she's taking the lid off the Crock-Pot and stirring the meat inside.

"Need help with anything?" I ask her.

Glancing curiously over her shoulder, she says, "Not really. I suppose you can take the macaroni salad out of the refrigerator, if you want to."

"On it," I say, heading to the refrigerator. I grab the bowl, pop the lid off, and tell her, "Mm, looks delicious."

"Oh God," she says, putting the lid back on and spinning around to face me, her eyes wide. "It's true. You *are* pregnant."

I frown back at her as I put the bowl down on the counter. "What? No, I'm not. I was just saying the macaroni salad looks good. Am I not allowed to compliment your cooking for no reason?"

"How far along are you? Have you told Carter yet? It is Carter's, right?"

Rolling my eyes, I open a drawer and grab a serving spoon. "Mom, I'm not pregnant."

"Everyone is sayin' you are. I couldn't believe you wouldn't tell me first, but—"

"Mom," I interrupt, shooting her a look. "Relax."

"I'm not mad if you're pregnant, you just need to tell me. It's not the end of the world. Carter certainly has the means—"

"If I hear one more word about Carter's financial means, I'm going to scream, I swear to God. Can't anyone in this town see past his money?"

Frowning, Mom asks, "Well, if you're not pregnant, what's wrong, then?"

"Nothing is *wrong*, I just had something I needed to ask you." I don't know why I feel so awkward asking her about college. Maybe it's because she never went and she seems a little defensive about it, maybe it's because I know she thinks of college as something that's not that important, while for me it's a crucial life goal. Whatever the reason, I would actually rather tell her I'm going to be a teen mom than talk to her about college.

"All right," she says tentatively, watching me. "What is it?"

"Okay, so, you know how college visits are coming up, and students will be visiting the colleges they're hoping to attend?"

Grabbing a hand towel off the sink and absently wringing it, she murmurs, "You said something about that. We can't afford to take some vacation to look at some fancy college out of state, if that's what you're thinkin' about."

"I'm not. Well, sort of. It's not really my college visit." I'm getting nervous and tripping over my words, so I focus and blurt. "Carter is going to Columbia next fall. He's already in. They're giving him some football scholarship."

"Where's that?"

I blink, momentarily taken off-guard by that question. "Columbia? It's... in New York City. I guess Carter is from there. Anyway, he's going there for school, and his dad bought him an apartment near campus. After the state championships, he has to fly out there to visit the campus and sign some papers on the apartment. He wanted to take me with him and show me around, since he knows I've always wanted to go there."

"Oh, how nice," she says, instantly warmer.

"We wouldn't have to pay for anything. Carter even sent me out with his sister to buy me some warmer clothes for the trip. We'll take a plane Friday after school is out and come back Sunday night, so I won't miss anything. I might need money for food, but I'll use my own money for that. Anyway, Carter is really looking forward to it. I figured it wouldn't be a big deal, but I told him I needed to ask you before he booked the plane tickets."

"Well, I think that sounds wonderful. How romantic," she says, flashing me a soft little smile. "New York at Christmastime. Do you think he'll propose?"

"Do I—?" A bubble of nervous laughter slips out of me. "No, Mom, I don't think he'll propose. God, I don't even think we'll date past high school."

Her smile falls. "Why not?"

"Because we're just starting our adult lives and we won't even live in the same state."

"Well, why won't you? You've always wanted to move up north, you've always had that idea bouncin' around your head. If his father bought him an apartment up there and he's taking you to see it, that sounds to me like he's hoping you'll move there with him."

Sighing, I tell her, "Trust me, I've already thought about that, but I can't. There aren't any schools in the city that are afford-able *and* offer the programs I'm interested in. None of them are even affordable, but livin' with Carter would obviously cut down on living expenses, so I thought maybe with a small loan… But at the end of the day, I would have to sacrifice too much to move to New York with him. My future starts in Pennsylvania and his is in New York. Four years is too long to attempt long distance. It just won't work."

"Of course it won't work if you decide it won't work," my mother says, firmly. "It's a matter of priorities, Zoey. If you've got a good man on the hook, I'm not afraid to tell you those don't come around all that often. You can read your books anywhere, they even have those online classes you can take now. If Carter wants you to move to New York and start a life with him, I think you'd be crazy to turn him down."

Frustration rolls through me like a slow train about to putter to a stop at the railroad crossing. I can already tell this conver-sation is going to go south and end up in a clash of personali-ties, so rather than sit at the tracks and endure the pointless frustration, I steer into the nearest open parking lot and turn around.

Pulling my phone from the pocket of my jeans like it just vibrated, I flash my phone a smile. "Oh, what do you know? That's him now." I slide a finger across the screen and glance up at her. "I'm allowed to go to New York for the weekend, right?"

"Yes, of course," she tells me, glancing anxiously at the phone. "You haven't told him you won't move there with him yet, have you?"

"No," I murmur, opening the message to Carter. Since I have the phone out, I may as well share the news. It goes with my excuse to exit this conversation, anyway. "He hasn't asked, so I haven't had to."

"Well, do yourself a favor and don't tell him no just yet. Think it over, Zoey. Think long and hard. If you love him, maybe the small sacrifice is worth it. He can give you a beautiful life. Chances like this don't come around a lot in one lifetime."

Neither does the chance to go to college, I want to tell her, but I don't want to fight, so I keep my mouth shut and flash her a faint smile. "I'm gonna go upstairs so I can call him."

"All right. Don't be too long. Dinner's just about ready."

CHAPTER 51

"HONEY, CARTER'S HERE!"

I hear Mom calling up the stairs, announcing Carter's arrival. My tummy flutters with nerves as I spin sideways, watching the swish of my dress.

"Diamonds are forever" is the homecoming theme. I don't have any diamonds, but I bought a pretty pair of cubic zirconia earrings that glimmer prettily in the light.

My *dress* glitters in the light. I love this dress so much, I would get married in it. It's not white, it's champagne with a glittery gold overlay that sparkles every time I move, but it's the prettiest dress I've ever worn. It was embarrassingly expensive for just a homecoming dress, but Carter was paying, and after all he's put me through this year, I figured I deserved a gorgeous home-coming dress. I'll wear it to prom, too, and get a little more value out of it. Hell, I would wear this dress to buy groceries if I wouldn't get funny looks.

I can't help smiling at my reflection one more time, spinning so I can watch my gown glitter in the light. I sigh happily, then grab the small purse Caroline picked out to go with my dress. I slide it on my shoulder and walk over to the mirror for one last check.

Caroline booked me an appointment at her salon in the city earlier today, so I look fancier than I ever have. I got a manicure with white French tips, and my blonde hair is pulled half-back and gathered at the crown of my head, long, shiny curls cascading down the back and sides. Caroline had them do my make-up to compliment my gown, too, so that all I had to do when I got home was put on the dress.

I look like a princess. I probably won't look this good *on* my wedding day, so I might as well enjoy it.

Carter is waiting for me at the foot of the stairs. He looks incredible in a black tux with gold accent pieces to match my dress. The way he looks at me as I descend the stairs is everything. There's a gleam of softness in his eyes, a sense of awe that makes my stomach sink and my heart soar.

My foot barely touches the living room floor and Carter is already reaching his hand out to grab my waist and pull me close. I feel his breath on my neck as he leans in to tell me, "You look amazing."

I want to touch him, too, so I brace one hand on his shoulder and run the other down the length of his gold tie. "So do you." I lower my voice, since my parents are in the room, and lean in to whisper, "I wore those panties you bought me, but if I'd known you'd look like this, I wouldn't have bothered."

Carter chuckles, his hand around my waist tightening ever so slightly. "Don't worry, I'll take them off you later."

"Too late, they already disintegrated," I tell him, cheekily.

He pulls back to smile at me, then leans in to kiss me, like he can't quite make up his mind what he wants to do with me. I'm not used to seeing indecision on him, but that alone tells me he *really* is impressed. I already felt beautiful tonight, but now I'm glowing.

"Oh, don't you two look so perfect," my mom croons, walking over to us with her camera. "Let me get a picture of you in front of the stairs."

Carter turns to her. "Just one second." Turning back to me, he says, "I know you said you didn't want a corsage, but I figured I shouldn't show up empty-handed." He draws a thin, square box out of his jacket pocket and informs me, "Now, my mom says you can't *have* this unless I marry you, but you can borrow it for tonight."

"This must really be something, if it requires marriage," I comment.

Carter nods, cracking open the case. "Family jewels. Passed down a couple of generations. It's worth about the cost of a new car, so, you know, don't take it off anywhere."

"Whoa, wait, what?" I blink a couple times, then look down at the necklace nestled in velvet in the box. When I do, I can't stifle a gasp. This is *exactly* the image that would pop up in my head if someone referred to *family jewels.* An incredible diamond and gold necklace set in gold sparkles up at me. It belongs on the neck of a queen, not me. It's incredibly elegant without being too much.

I wish I had the story of the woman who was originally given this necklace. I picture a French courtesan, worshipped by a man in a much higher station. In a scandalous gesture, I picture him handing over his prized family jewels since he can't offer her marriage, living his life with her, regardless of the rules.

It's all terribly romantic in my head, and then Carter takes the necklace out of the box, carefully moves my hair over my shoulder, and fastens the elegant necklace around my neck.

I walk over to the large mirror on the wall so I can see how it looks, and it's absolutely stunning. Carter looking so handsome standing beside me, me wearing his mother's necklace and this gorgeous dress. We haven't even left the house, and this night is already perfect.

Gazing at me in the mirror, Carter asks, "Like it?"

I touch the lovely piece, shaking my head. "Love it. I'm afraid you're gonna have to marry me now."

Carter chuckles, taking my hand and tugging me back toward the staircase. "Let's get these pictures taken so I can maul you in the car."

Carter and I pose in front of the staircase and let my mom take her pictures. Then she tells me she needs to get one of us in front of the door, and then the front porch, and then in front of the limo Carter is picking me up in. I finally cut her off before she tries to climb into the car with us.

I try not to fiddle with the necklace, but I've never worn something so expensive, so I feel like I'll be checking on it all night long. My earrings feel too cheap to wear with something so grand, though, so before we get to the dance, I take them out and put them in my purse.

The dance is held in the ballroom of the nicest hotel in town. Originally, it was going to be held at the high school, but the senior class made a big push for the hotel instead. The darkened ballroom is decked out with colored lights and strings of faux diamonds hanging like waterfalls around the room. Tables are set up around the room with black and white linens, a handful of fake plastic diamonds sprinkled across the center of each table. A lot of girls are wearing shorter dresses, but I expected as much. Grace got a long gown like I did, but Kasey's red dress barely hits mid-thigh.

I don't really care what anyone else is wearing. I feel like I'm in my own little world with Carter, and I like it that way. Of course, our own little world gets immediately more populated when we get to the dance. Carter gravitates to the table where his friends have set up camp. The music is playing already, but no one is dancing yet. The way our school does things is sort of like a wedding—no one dances until the king and queen have had their first dance, then the floor opens up to everyone else.

"Everyone bow, the king has arrived," Sutton announces, bowing sarcastically as Carter approaches.

"Damn right," Carter says, his hand still at my hip.

"Damn, Ellis, you brought it tonight," Cartwright says, openly checking me out.

"I love your dress," Brianna tells me, flashing me a bright smile. She went with a short one that boldly flouts the "no excessive cleavage" rule of the homecoming dress code. My dress is strapless, and I have some cleavage over here too, but the necklace is such an attention-stealer, I hardly expect anyone to notice my breasts. When Brianna's eyes land on it, her eyes widen. "Holy shit, is that real?"

I nod, absently touching it again as she comes over to peer at the pearls hanging from the necklace.

"This is, like, royal wedding jewelry right here," she informs me.

"Isn't it? Carter's mom let me borrow it for the night."

She fusses over my dress, hair, and necklace for a minute while Carter visits with the guys. We got here a few minutes early, but they wait for the people who got here a few minutes late to wander in before the principal takes the stage and starts yammering about what a wonderful start we've had to the school year and the football season.

Carter comes over and grabs my waist, nodding toward the stage. "We should probably head over there."

Somehow, I managed to forget that—to the surprise of exactly no one—Carter was announced homecoming king at the football game last night. Cartwright is on the homecoming court, too, so he wanders up by Carter.

"Yeah, we probably should," he agrees.

Brianna comes up beside Cartwright, glancing up at him hopefully. "You're picking me for princess, right?"

"Eh, I don't know. I might pick Erika."

Carter slides a dry look his way. "Not funny."

Cartwright grins. "Come on, it's kinda funny."

"If you pick anyone but me, you better be sure they're sucking your dick tonight, because if I don't get that damn sash, I'm sure as hell not," Brianna informs Cartwright.

"Well, shit, I guess you get a sash then."

Smiling victoriously, she mutters, "Damn right, I get a sash."

It *also* slipped my mind that at our school, only the guys get voted to homecoming court. Then the guys pick their own counterparts. Blinking in sudden realization, I look up at Carter. "Oh, God. Does this mean I'm…?"

Carter's attention is on the stage, not on me. The junior class court has already been called to stage, and now it must be our turn. Carter flashes the principal a smile, nods, and grabs my hand to drag me closer to the stage. He stops at the stairs, drops my hand, and heads up on stage.

My heart beats irregularly. I don't like being the center of attention, but unless this is the long con from Hell, I don't see Carter picking anyone else to be his queen.

Everyone on the floor claps as Carter takes the stage. Last year's homecoming queen is up there with his crown and sash. Other than the sizeable baby bump she's rocking, she looks like a retiring pageant queen, all smiles as she stands on her tiptoes to reach the sash over Carter's head, then she puts the crown on him. Carter doffs the crown and winks at the crowd, causing a few chuckles and more than a few dreamy sighs.

I crack a smile at the reaction and look back up at him under the spotlight. Cartwright is called up next. He doesn't get a crown, but he does get a sash, then the former queen hands him a tiara and the "homecoming princess" sash.

He knows what's good for him, so when the principal asks who his princess is, Brianna is called to the stage. She grins and waves as she ascends the steps, then pleasantly thanks him and grabs the sash, putting it on herself. He tries to put the crown on her, but it gets caught in her hair and she ends up doing that herself, too. I can't help laughing a little. Poor Cartwright.

When the focus is back on Carter, the principal can't help praising him some more for the incredible football season we all know he's largely responsible for. Finally, the principal is done kissing Carter's ass.

"Well, son, don't keep us all in suspense. Who is going to be your homecoming queen tonight?"

Carter leans in to the mic, flashes me a smile, and says lightly, "She's my queen every day, Mr. Cousins. Zoey Ellis, get up here."

Even though I knew it had to be me, my heart plummets. Everyone claps and I gather my dress, heading up the steps onto the stage.

After watching Cartwright fumble with the sash, the former queen decides to drape that on me herself. It's a gold satin sash with black font, while Carter's is black with gold font. I'm not sure if it's by coincidence or design, but they match our outfits like they were made specifically for us. Carter takes the crown before she can put that on my head, then he meets my gaze, smiles at me, and puts it on me himself.

"Perfect," he murmurs.

Last year's queen turned away to retrieve a big bouquet of roses from the table. She hands them to me now and I'm struck by their beauty. Ordinarily, I believe the homecoming queen gets red roses, but these are white with gold glitter lining each petal.

"Wow, these are beautiful. Thank you," I tell her, though I'm not sure who I'm supposed to thank. Never in a billion years would I have expected to be homecoming queen at this high school or any other.

The former queen leans in to confide, "Your boyfriend ordered 'em special for you."

Carter leans in to whisper jokingly, "Why are you giving away all my secrets?"

She smiles at me. "You're a lucky girl."

I do feel like a pretty lucky girl tonight. Even luckier, since my class didn't pick me, I don't have to touch the microphone or give any kind of "thank you" speech. Since I'm going to be dancing, I give the girl the flowers back and she tells me to make sure I come get them before we leave the dance. I assure her I will, and turn back to watch the principal finish up the crowning ceremony.

"Now, ladies and gentlemen, the king and queen will have their first dance. After that, everyone is welcome to join them on the dance floor and dance the night away! Have fun, be safe, and don't do anything your parents wouldn't approve of," he tells them, shaking a finger at the assembled audience. He gets a few polite chuckles, but there are a lot of blank stares, too.

Carter takes my hand and leads me down the steps. The spotlight follows us out onto the dance floor. Carter takes me in his arms, heedless of the rule about distance between dance partners. Ben E. King starts crooning *Stand by Me* from the speakers and Carter pulls me closer.

"She's my queen every day, huh?" I murmur playfully.

Carter shoots me a mischievous smile. "You liked that line, huh?"

"Your audience sure did. You tryin' to make all the other girls wanna steal you away from me?"

"Nah, I'm not a necklace; I can't be stolen."

"I can't believe I'm homecoming queen," I tell him.

"Perks of dating the king. Better get ready, come prom you'll sweep up that crown, too."

"I doubt that. Senior class picks that one, not you."

Cocking a disbelieving eyebrow, he says, "You cannot

honestly doubt my ability to get shit done at this point. Come on now, Zoey. I'll make sure you win."

I shake my head indulgently. "I don't want you to fix it."

"You want me to dance this close with some other girl, then?"

I pause to consider, then tell him, "Fine, you can fix it." It's not like he'll need to break any rules, just wield his considerable influence and tell people what he wants them to do. I'm sure his minions will help him out. "What are you gonna do when high school ends and you have to start over at Columbia? You won't have any minions to do your bidding."

"Not right away, but it won't take long to break some new ones in," he says, confident in his leadership skills. "Besides, New York is home. I have plenty of friends there."

"Any I'll like?"

His lips curve up faintly. "One you might like a little too much. I'll have to keep you away from him so he doesn't try to snatch you up."

"Impossible," I declare. "I am also not a necklace."

"Can't be stolen, huh?"

I shake my head. "I'm all yours."

"I'm gonna hold you to that," he tells me.

"Well, until we live too far apart to be together, at least," I amend, knowing he *will* hold me to that. "Will we see your friends on the visit?"

Carter shakes his head. "Doubt it. Only staying the weekend doesn't give us much time, and I want to show you the city."

Smiling at the mental image of us walking the sidewalks in a crowded Times Square, I tell him, "I can't wait. I think we'll have fun."

"You know when *I* think we'll have fun? When this stupid dance is over," he murmurs, bending his head to kiss my bare shoulder. "When I can haul you out of here and get you the hell out of this dress."

"I love this dress," I tell him.

"I love it, too. I'll love it more when it's on the floor and you're naked in bed with me."

"What kind of animal would put this gorgeous dress on the

floor?" I demand, wide-eyed. "Surely there's at least a chair we can lay it out across."

"You're focusing on the wrong part of this story," he states.

"I'm aghast at your rough handling of my beautiful gown. You're allowed to handle my body that way, but my dress? Over the line."

Carter rolls his eyes. "Fine, we'll throw the dress on a chair. As long as you're naked, I don't care where your discarded clothes are."

With a perfunctory nod, I say, "Much better." Barely missing a beat, I ask, "Now, where is your mouth in this scenario?"

The beautiful mouth in question curves up in a smile. "Oh, my mouth is doing good work. You're tummy down on the soft bed, I'm kissing my way down the small of your back, palming that beautiful, bare ass."

"Mm, that does sound nice. I wonder where your mouth is heading…"

"Well, see, you have a wet pussy just begging for its attention."

I bite down on my bottom lip, leaning in to murmur, "Keep talking like that and I'll drag you out of here before the dance even gets going."

"Don't threaten me with a good time," he returns.

I grin and lean up on my tiptoes to give him a kiss. "We're not going to be here for very long, are we?"

"Not a chance," he verifies.

CHAPTER 52

I'M antsy as we stand in the hallway outside the locked door, waiting to go inside. Carter's head is bent in concentration as he taps numbers into an app on his phone, supposedly to disarm the alarm before we've even stepped foot inside.

"That should do it," he murmurs, sliding his phone back into his pocket and pushing a key into the lock.

He pushes the door open and peeks inside. When there is no shrieking sound coming from the alarm, I assume the app worked.

Carter turns back to flash me a victorious smile, then grabs my suitcase and wheels it inside. I follow him more tentatively, watching his confident stride as he makes his way inside his new apartment.

It's crazy to think he's going to *live* here. Not only will he be living all by himself, but in the city. Well, I guess it's not as big a deal to him seeing as he's from here, but… God, what a life he leads.

Carter parks both our suitcases behind a charcoal gray couch in the living room. I'm overwhelmed by how nice this place is. It's nothing like you would envision someone starting out in during college. The whole place has already been decorated by an expert, judging by the look of it.

To the right is a full kitchen with a compact island and three chairs on one side of it. There's a dining table with bold red chairs in front of a huge window with a city view, and just past that is the study area. There's a bookshelf with only a few books and some accent pieces to fill the empty space—clearly place-holders until Carter makes the place his own. A desk is set up there, somewhere for him to do his homework after a long day of classes.

The living room is just beautiful. A big area rug covers the stunning hardwood floor, there's a massive, gray, industrial-looking coffee table in front of the couch and a huge television mounted to the wall in front of it. There are end tables with stylish lamps that I love, but that a bachelor would never pick out for his home.

His home. This is going to be Carter's home.

"Want to see the bedrooms?" Carter asks once I've finished taking it all in.

I nod and follow him. When I was assigning the study area downstairs, I completely forgot he has an extra bedroom that has been turned into an *actual* study. Even more bookcases line one wall and there's a gleaming mahogany desk set up in front of them.

"You can study in here," he tells me, nodding toward the corner on his left-hand side. "We can put your fish over here in a big aquarium so you'll have your reading buddy close."

I know he's joking, but the sight of this place, the excitement and energy of this city in the couple hours we've been here... it's just mean to make me imagine a version of life where I could live here with him. Where this could be *my* study, these shelves could be full of *my* books... this could be *our* life.

Trying to keep things light, I tell him, "I hope the wife you meet at Columbia enjoys it as much as I would."

"Want me to fuck you on her desk?" he offers.

"Maybe later," I murmur, backing out of that room and heading down the hall to the next white door. It's just a bath-room, but for all I've heard about New York being incredibly cramped, it's a nice sized bathroom. It has two sinks, two closets, and a bathtub where Chloe can take baths when she comes to visit.

Speaking of Chloe, the next room is hers. The pink walls are the first hint, but the interior decorator has already put some things in here, too. A nice white dresser with a huge mirror behind it and a ballerina lamp on top is at the front of the room. A full-sized bed is already made, complete with decorative pillows and pale pink bedding. There's a white end table that matches the dresser and a princess lamp on top of that one. In the corner is a white bookshelf in the same style. A few kids' books are already placed on the shelves along with a stuffed bear and a white unicorn, but like the living room shelves, it's mostly placeholder stuff until Chloe makes it her own.

"This place is gorgeous, Carter. Truly."

Taking my hand, he leads me to the next door. "Let's check out our room."

"Your future wife is going to be miffed when she finds out you had sex with someone else on all her things," I inform him.

"Get in here," he says, unconcerned about our impossible future as only Carter can be. He's so accustomed to things working out the way he wants them to, maybe it really hasn't hit him yet that we have a few more months, but when he comes to this city, he'll have to come without me.

There have been moments where I thought about suggesting we extend things a little longer. After graduation, technically I could move to New York with him just for the summer, just until I have to start school in PA. The problem is, I think that will make it a million times harder. Even now I can tell these couple of days we're visiting will haunt me, give me ideas of what could have been that I could have lived without, if only I hadn't come on this trip.

I had to, though. If someone is going to take me to New York for the first time, it should be Carter.

Living here for the summer would be different, though. It wouldn't feel like a weekend trip, it would feel like the start to a life I can't keep living. It would make leaving much too hard, and undoubtedly cast a pall over what should be an exciting milestone in my life when I move to PA to start college.

The master bedroom door swings open and Carter steps inside. I follow him, a bit awed. This is the biggest room, and I have no doubt there are studio apartments in this city with less space. A king-sized bed is already made up in Longhorn colors— a coincidence, I hope, but I don't know who gave these decorating orders. On the opposite side of the room is a couch, a coffee table, an end table with a lamp, and a television mounted to the wall in front of it. It's basically a second living room *in the bedroom.*

That's not even all there is. Once we're in the door, I see the wall to my right has a dresser set up with an enormous mirror over it and a silver serving tray with a trio of candles as a centerpiece. There's art on the walls in this room, and past the dresser is another door. I think it's going to be the master bathroom, but when I step inside, I see it's a walk-in closet.

"This place is bonkers," I say, feeling Carter walking in behind me.

He passes me and keeps walking, running his hand across the smooth surface of the counter in the middle of the room. "I like it. When you're taking too long getting ready for a date, I'll come in, bend you over right here, and give you a good, hard fuck."

"That'll sure hurry me up," I offer dryly. "Good thinking."

He keeps walking, gesturing to the left side. "Your clothes can go over here." At the end of the closet is a built-in with doors that close as well as some pull-out drawers. He checks out a few of them, then walks around the counter and glances at the racks on that side. "My stuff can go on this side."

Mean, mean, mean.

Ignoring him, I turn on my heel and quit the closet. I check out the master bath next, trying not to let his commentary pollute my mind, but it's hard. When he shows me where he's going to fuck me in the large tiled shower, I'm tempted to take all my clothes off and hop in so we can try it out. When he runs his hands along the 'his and hers' sinks where I'll get ready to go out with him on weekend nights, my mood sinks, because I can see that, too.

After the tour is finished, I return to the bedroom and climb up on the Longhorn blue bedspread. It's so soft, I just want to lie down and get comfy. We need to unpack my clothes before they wrinkle, but for a moment, I lie back and stare up at the ceiling

Carter will look at every night before he falls asleep. Every night when he's living his life without me.

Carter lies back on the bed with me. Looking over at me and folding his hands over his abdomen, he asks, "What do you think?"

"I think it's amazing," I tell him, honestly. "You're going to love living here. I'm so happy for you."

"You could move here with me, you know."

This is not the first time he has mentioned me moving here with him. It's not the first time he has made the joke that my mom's right, what do I need college for when I have him to foot the bill? I know he's only joking and I know he probably really does wish I could move here with him, but after many hours online trying to imagine a new college into existence, I finally accepted that everything in this city is so far outside of my budget, I can't even afford to *think* about it.

I know if I asked, Carter would try to find a way to help me pay for it, but that's over the line. I'll let him buy me a homecoming dress or even a plane ticket to New York, but he has offered those things, I have never asked. It's too presumptuous to assume we *will* end up married, that the debt for enormous school loans would inevitably be *ours*, not just mine.

I may hope for the best, but I plan for the worst, and the worst-case scenario is I give up a free ride at a great school to follow Carter to New York. Fast forward six months, I catch him with some vicious pre-law brunette who doesn't even bother to cover up her perfect breasts when I walk in on them in our bed. Instead, she smirks at me, knowing she's won the game and the prize is all hers now.

I trust Carter, but I also know I'll always have to deal with other women chasing him. He's too much of a catch, especially on the surface. The average woman won't know his dark side or his baggage, but she'll see his money in the clothes he wears, his intelligence in the classes they take together, how handsome he is because she will inevitably have eyeballs. Even if he's never interested in anyone but me, there will be women who think they can steal him away from me—who will actively try. And while I do have faith in Carter, the reality is if the worst happened and I'd already given everything up for him, I would absolutely hate myself.

I can't take that risk. I won't.

I also can't look at him when I'm thinking such awful things, so I sigh and look up at the ceiling instead.

"What's wrong?" Carter asks.

"Nothing. Just thinking about the future."

"You have your defensive, daddy issue face on," he informs me. "Are you thinking about me on a beach with a super model again?"

Even though it's hardly funny, I can't help smiling faintly as this little game of *Infidelity Clue* he has gotten used to. It's not the professor with the candlestick in the kitchen, but in my own personal hell, it's some pretty girl in some location with the guy who's supposed to be mine. He's remarkably tolerant about my worries. Poking fun at them instead of getting annoyed seems to work for him, so I go with it.

"In this bed with a gorgeous but vicious future lawyer. She seduces you and ruins my life, then I hate myself because in this scenario, I gave up college in PA to move here and go to City College instead. Now my pride demands that I leave you, but I'm broke, so I end up in a shared studio apartment with a crazy, loud roommate, living on Ramen noodles and cursing your name."

"A lot of scenarios end up with you cursing my name," he points out.

"There are a lot of ways you could be a disappointing jerk," I tell him.

"Maybe by the time I retire, you can tell me every last one of them," he suggests.

"I think we'd need a couple of lifetimes for that. The doubtful side of my mind is very prolific."

Even though we're just playing, he looks over at me seriously for a moment. "You know I love you, right?"

Guilt pinches me because I know these are my issues, not his. Since everything happened with Erika, Carter has been 100 percent trustworthy, and when I think about it logically, I really don't believe he would do anything to jeopardize our relationship. It's just that sometimes fear takes hold, a fear he isn't even entirely responsible for putting there, and it makes me go to crazy places in my mind, places that convince me I need to protect myself from the one person in the world I want to give every bit of my trust to.

Trust is scary by nature, but I tell myself if Carter can trust me with his baggage, I can certainly trust him with mine. My baggage might be a nuisance sometimes, but his is next level, and I deal with all of it without complaint.

Being here like this, though, seeing the life I can't have... it does kind of make me want to push him away. He's giving me more to miss, and I had enough already.

As if he can read my mind and he wants to drive it home even more, he reaches over, snakes an arm beneath me, and tugs me against his side.

"Get over here, you."

I wrap my arms around him and snuggle up close, but my mind won't stop wandering to unpleasant places. Even things I was looking forward to are starting to wilt into unpleasantness. Conjuring an image of the twin-sized bunk bed in the dorm room I'll share with three other girls... while Carter, bless his heart, is living like a king in New York, single and eligible, attending what would have been my dream school if my dreams weren't grounded in reality. Even in the wildest of my dreams, I can't go to Columbia, and he fell right into it. I hope he appreciates all of this, because Carter Mahoney is the luckiest person I have ever met.

"What are you thinking now?" he asks.

I sigh. "Impossible things. I wish long-distance wouldn't be so hard."

"Might not be as hard as you think," he tells me. His tone is too blasé though, so I don't believe him. He hasn't considered how lonely he will be with a girlfriend too far away to ever spend the night with him. I have, and I have many rounds of *Infidelity Clue* to show for it.

"It wouldn't be fair to either of us," I tell him.

Carter is quiet for a moment, then he says words that turn

my beating heart into an ice sculpture. "Yeah, you're probably right."

He's never agreed with me before.

I'm the one trying to keep us rooted in reality, and Carter is the one blissfully positive that even if we only saw each other every other weekend for a single day, our relationship is worth hanging onto. Carter is the one who refuses to accept defeat, so if *he* is finally agreeing…

Well, it's inconvenient that he finally came around on day one of this trip. It will probably be a little awkward now, walking around with someone I am 100 percent positive is my future ex-boyfriend.

The vicious brunette appears in my mind again, smirking because her family could afford to send her to Columbia, because she runs in Carter's circles and is exactly the kind of girl he was meant to end up with.

Me, I'm just the girl he was supposed to leave behind in Texas, and boy would she not shy away from telling me that.

"Your future wife's a bitch," I inform him, scooting out of his embrace so I can sit up.

Carter cracks a smile. "Hey, no one talks about my future wife like that."

I wrinkle up my nose with displeasure and go to climb off the bed.

"Hey, where are you going?" he asks, grabbing my wrist and tugging me backward.

"We need to unpack. Everything your sister picked out for me is highly prone to wrinkling. Unless you want the first item on our itinerary to be a trip to an authentic New York dry cleaner, I need to hang up my clothes."

Reluctantly, he lets me go. I leave him alone in the bedroom, coaching myself to get it together as I head toward the luggage. There is no reason to let our doomed future dull our enjoyment of this weekend. Knowing it will end doesn't mean I can't enjoy it while it's happening, and Carter has really been looking forward to this trip. For that matter, so have I.

By the time I make it back to the bedroom, I am in better spirits. I hoist the suitcase up on the bed and unzip it, then

Carter watches me unpack. He hasn't told me any of the things we'll be doing this weekend, but I trust him to take care of the planning. He knows New York much better from living here than I possibly could from hours of looking online.

I hope he takes me to see the tree at Rockefeller Center, though. I'd love to lace up some skates and stumble around on the ice with him. Afterward, we could warm up with some hot chocolate while we stroll through the lively city streets.

Carter is still on the bed, his weight propped up on his elbow. "What's that smile for?" he asks.

"Just thinkin' about touristy things. I hope you're not opposed to doing touristy things just because you used to live here, because I am, in fact, a tourist."

"There are touristy activities on the docket, don't worry."

I nod once. "Good. Also, I have decided to look on the bright side of all this. You and I are about to dive into a super exciting time in both our lives, and there's no reason to let the inevitability of your bitchy future wife ruin it."

He rolls on his back and props his hands behind his head. "Go on."

"Until one of us isn't single anymore, maybe I could still come visit you here during the school year. Obviously, we would have to stop once one of us moves on, but..." I trail off, shrugging as I hang the last blouse on a hanger. "I don't know, just something to think about."

"You'll do periodic booty calls, but not a long-distance relationship?"

"Correct," I tell him, crossing to the closet. The small amount of space my clothes take up in this closet is a bit pitiful, even though I only packed for the weekend. If I actually lived here, I probably wouldn't fill much more space than this since I don't have a large wardrobe. Closing the closet door, I tell him, "If we keep it casual, we don't owe each other anything but honesty. You won't be required to spend every night alone after a phone call with a girlfriend who lives in another state, and I won't have to worry about all the sexy New York ladies who will inevitably throw themselves at you. When I'm not here, you can do whatever you want with whomever you want."

"And you can do whatever you want with whomever you want."

"Obviously."

Carter shakes his head. "Nope."

"Don't shoot it down without consideration," I tell him, taking a seat on the edge of the bed. "I know it's not ideal, but it's a way for us to still enjoy each other for a little longer without ripping my heart out."

Without warning, Carter crawls over, pushes me back on the bed, and climbs on top of me. Cocking an eyebrow as he looks down at me, he reminds me, "Remember what I did last time I thought you were seeing another guy? It may not be easy to ruin some asshole's life when he's in PA and I'm here, but you better believe I'll find a way."

I crack a smile, grabbing his sides and rubbing affectionately. "No, it wouldn't be like that. You and I would essentially have to evolve into friends with benefits. We couldn't be possessive or we'd both be miserable."

"I reject this proposition. I don't want you to be my friend with benefits. I want you to be mine, period."

Sighing and dropping my hands from his sides, I tell him, "I want that, too, but it's not an option. I'm just trying to find a way to salvage things between us without ruining them."

Carter takes my wrists and pins them over my head, then leans down so that his handsome face is much closer to mine. "As usual, Ellis, you're thinking too small. Haven't you learned by now you've gotta go big or go home? Sometimes compromise is not the answer. Sometimes taking what you want is the answer."

I open my mouth to offer the same cautious excuses he has already heard before, but instead of letting me utter them again, he covers my mouth with one hand.

"No. I wasn't done talking," he tells me. "I don't want to hear how hard it would be. I don't want to hear how I could potentially let you down and ruin your life. I've told you again and again, I am not going to ruin your life, only change it. When are you going to start believing me?"

He uncovers my mouth so I can answer. "Our fiftieth wedding anniversary?" I suggest.

"That's a pretty long wait. How about our first wedding anniversary?"

"Are we getting married when we're 69?"

Carter chuckles. "No, you psycho."

"Then that's too fast. I don't see how I could possibly be sure you wouldn't ruin my life by then."

Suddenly cocky, Carter says, "Oh, I don't know. I think you'll be convinced a lot sooner than you think. Like, before the new year."

Choking on a stifled laugh, I tell him, "You know December is nearly over, right?"

"Yep. I still have a couple tricks up my sleeve."

Now it's my turn to cock an eyebrow. "You think you can convince me with tricks?"

"I'm pretty sure. They're really cool tricks."

"You are unreasonably confident."

"Usually. But it all ends up working out," he says.

I don't feel like wasting my energy—or more time in the city—arguing about it, so I settle with a simple, "We'll see."

Carter shakes his head at me. "I can't decide if it's me or you that you're so intent on underestimating."

That brings an immediate scowl to my face. "Excuse me? I don't underestimate myself. I'm quite confident in my own abilities, thank you very much."

"You are," he says with a faint nod of acknowledgement. "When it comes to certain things, absolutely. But you have these blind spots, these bizarre specks of inferiority when it comes to just a few things. You keep trying to sell yourself on this narrative that I'm not serious about you, Zoey, but it's wrong. I *am* serious about you, more serious than I've ever been about anything else in my life."

"It's not that I don't think you're serious about me," I deny, but I don't expand because I'm not sure how to refute his claim.

"College is another thing. It's like you're afraid to set your sights above a certain level, but you should. Maybe if you did, maybe if you aimed higher, you'd land there. How do you know if you're afraid to try?"

"I'm not *afraid*. I'm realistic."

"I think you're slapping a label on fear and calling it realism," he tells me. "You weren't afraid to take a gamble on me, but now that college and the future are calling, all of a sudden, you're playing it safe." Holding my gaze, he shakes his head. "We don't play it safe, Ellis. We don't turn away from what we want because it might end up hurting a little if it goes sideways. We trust each other to be there to pick up the pieces if it does. So, either you're being a chickenshit, or you're not trusting me. Tell me which one it is."

I wrinkle up my nose and whack him in the stomach, not appreciating being called out on my own bullshit. "It is not being a chicken shit not to throw caution to the wind and trash my life plans so I can join you chasing yours."

"What if mine are better?" he suggests. "Don't take this the wrong way, but your life plans are mediocre. A mediocre school, a mediocre setting. I know you've worked your ass off to achieve it, and maybe that was the ceiling for you before you met me, but it isn't now. Don't you get that? I can take you higher. You let me use you all the damn time. Use me."

I feel like my heart is in my throat, him lecturing me this way. It's not unheard of for him to call me out, but normally, he doesn't need to. Normally, I'm not acting like a chicken shit.

I shake off his words and pull up my facts. "If I went to City College, it would cost me $20,000 a year more than the private school in Pennsylvania, Carter. Over the course of a bachelor's degree, that's a lot of money. And I don't want to *go* to City College, I want to go to the one where I earned a free ride. I *like* the school in PA, I like the campus—"

"Like, like, like. Do you *like* me, or do you *love* me?"

Huffing, I tell him, "That's not fair. You're not a college."

"You love me," he states. "And I love you. Even aside from wanting to be with you, I want more for you than mediocrity. More than anyone else I have ever met, you deserve it."

Folding my arms across my chest, I echo his own sentiment right back at him. "People don't always get what they deserve, remember?"

"Not always, but in this instance, you can. Just let me give it to you."

I should feel better about the offer I know is coming, but with him offering to help me pay for school if I go here, I have one less excuse. Clearly, whether or not I actually *like* the school I attend is lower on his priority list than location. "Do you want me to have regrets? You're askin' me to go all-in on the success of our relationship, because if I make this compromise, if I go to the school I *don't want to go to* and then we break up? I will regret making this decision."

Apparently unconcerned, Carter shakes his head. "I'm not asking you to make that kind of compromise. I'm not asking you to do anything you would regret in the *unlikely* event that it doesn't work out between us."

"But you are."

He's quiet for a moment, holding my gaze, then he says, "I'm not talking about City College, Zoey."

"That's the only college in the city that—"

He doesn't let me finish. He cuts me off and steals all of my words by saying, "I got you an interview at Columbia."

Everything stops for a moment. I stare up at him, afraid to breathe. He stares down at me, awaiting a response. His words play in my head again, but I can't entirely absorb them. They don't make sense—the words are too incredible to be true, aren't they? I know Carter gets shit done when he wants to, but there's no way…

He got *me* an interview at *Columbia*?

Finally, I manage to ask, "What—what do you mean? What kind of interview?"

"An *interview*," he says, meaningfully. "An admissions interview."

My stomach drops and my head shakes of its own volition. "That's impossible. I didn't even apply to Columbia, and they—"

"It's not impossible, because it's done," he says, not bothering to let me argue. Reaching down and tenderly pushing his fingers through my hair, he says, "I couldn't say anything to you until I knew for sure I could pull it off because I didn't want to risk you being disappointed, but I've been working on it like a pet project. Padded your resume a bit, had Kasey offer you the book reviews so you can list the school paper. Bought you all those ACT books and left you to your studying so you'd hopefully do well enough to meet their general admissions criteria. Letting you have salutatorian can't hurt. I figured it would help if you met their standards on your own, but I've been talking to my Columbia contact about you, stressing that in order to perform as well as I want to for them, it would *really* help me if I could bring my brilliant girlfriend with me."

Covering my face with my hands, I tell him, "You probably oversold me. They'll meet me and be expecting Einstein with boobs."

"Nah. They know the score. Unless you drool your way through the interview and can't string a sentence together, they'll make sure you get in. When there's a student they *want* to let in, they search their admissions materials for reasons to justify their admission, and you have plenty."

"But I'm nobody," I say, shaking my head in disbelief. "I mean, yeah, I have the grades, but… I can't believe they *want* to let me in. Just because you asked them to?"

"Asked? I've fucking *campaigned*," he says lightly. "I knew getting you into Columbia was the only nice way to get you to move here with me, so I did what I had to do. Usually, for special admissions like this, they would look at a prospective student's family to see if they're worth letting in. Obviously, your family isn't worth bending admission standards for, but mine?" None too modestly, he shrugs. "In addition to all of your hard work and all my campaigning, my dad is making a sizable donation to the university on your behalf."

That admission warms my heart and blows my mind. I don't know how to process what he just said. "For me?"

"For you. For us," he amends.

This is too much. I don't even know what to say, how to express my confusion or my gratitude. "But why? Why would he do that for me?"

Cocking his head to the side in a guilty fashion, Carter says, "I may have told him some things to give him incentive. Things I've done to you. Things you could potentially tell people about down the road if you didn't like me so much. Things that might derail that career in law I'm planning to pursue. Wouldn't make the family look too good, either."

My eyes widen as I take his meaning. "You *told* him about that?"

Shameless as he is, Carter smirks. "Even embellished a little to really drive home the point of how much damage you're capable of inflicting, if we didn't make some gesture to keep you on our good side."

I'm glad he finds this so amusing because I'm starting to sweat. "Are you crazy, Carter? He really *will* send a hitman after me!"

Carter shakes his head dismissively. "I told you, my dad fights potential scandal with his checkbook, not hitmen. He wasn't too thrilled that he had to pay off another girl, but I assured him you'll be the last. I'm keeping you, and that'll keep me in line."

He's completely crazy, but as he bends down to kiss me, I can't help wrapping my arms and legs around him and pulling him down on top of me so I can properly kiss him back. "I can't believe you told your father about that. You are absolutely insane, but you're wonderful. Your father must think *I'm* crazy to be in a relationship with you after all that."

Brushing my hair back, Carter shakes his head. "Nah. He knows there are a lot of behaviors women will tolerate if it comes with a comfortable living."

I lose my smile, reaching up to caress his face. "You know it has absolutely nothing to do with that for me, right?"

Touching my hand on his face, he offers me a little smile. "Of course I do. That's none of his business, though. Let him believe whatever makes sense to him. As long as you get to go to Columbia and I get to keep you with me, I don't care what he thinks."

"I can't believe you did all this for me, Carter. This is huge. This is… life-changing."

Capturing my hand and bringing it to his lips, he presses a soft kiss there. "I'd do anything for you."

And there it is. Not just his words or his enormous gesture, but that look in his eyes, the one that communicates all the love he has for me. That's the reason I believe his promises. The reason I believe in *him*, period. Whatever wickedness he's capable of, Carter doesn't want to lose me. He may be hell on wheels sometimes, he may be a challenging, difficult guy with as many issues as he has privileges, but when he looks me in the eye after all this and tells me he would do anything for me, no part of me doubts that he means it. Scary as it can be sometimes, Carter *would* do anything for me.

"Someday, you're not going to get something you want," I inform him. "But today is not that day."

Grinning, he pecks me on the lips. "Finally convinced being with me won't ruin your life?"

I nod my head. "This may have done it. There's no way I can afford the tuition, but for Columbia, I'll take on some debt. Hopefully, I can get the loans I need to pay for it."

"No need. My dad's paying your tuition. Part of your pay-off deal."

Pumping my fist in the air, I say, "Yes!" Grabbing his face, I demand, "Do you know what this means? We're going to Columbia together. I can save you from your bitchy future wife!"

"And warm my bed every night," he adds.

"This is why you weren't worried about long-distance," I realize. "You knew we wouldn't have to do it. You knew I was moving here with you all along and you've just been torturing me."

"I had to. Just in case I couldn't get everybody on board. Imagine how much more disappointed you would have been if I told you I'd try to get you in, and then I couldn't. It was much better as a surprise."

"Did Caroline know?"

"Yes. She knew she had to help you pick out an outfit for your Columbia interview, but I told her not to say anything."

"And Kasey? Did she know you were trying to pad my resume?"

"I told her for college, but I didn't specify which one. I knew Caroline would keep my secrets. I didn't trust your friends to."

"You're amazing," I tell him, kissing the side of his face. "And wonderful," I add, dropping a kiss at the corner of his mouth. "And incredible." Another kiss. "Thank you so much for doing this, Carter. This is above and beyond anything I've ever hoped for."

His tone is light, but his eyes are solemn as he tells me, "I'm the one who should be thanking you. *You're* above and beyond anything I've ever hoped for. I never even knew to look for you, but I sure am glad I stumbled across you."

I feel a pang of affection as my heart fills up. I wrap my arms around him to draw him as close to me as possible.

It sure has been a hell of a ride. I haven't always been thrilled to have encountered Carter Mahoney, but at the end of the day, despite pushing past—and sometimes exploding—my comfort zones, he has opened up parts of me I didn't even know were closed, and I think it's for the best. In all honesty, I don't want to be the kind of person who is so afraid of leaving my comfort zone, I become imprisoned by it. I don't want to be a person who is afraid to be challenged.

Truthfully, I'd rather be captivated by Carter than be comfortable any day.

In all the ways that matter, I make Carter better, and I think he makes me better, too. He needs a little taming, and I need a little shove sometimes. Carter can love me and challenge me at the same time, and I can keep him from being too catastrophic. Oh, and keep him happy. I'm pretty proud of that.

I know life with Carter won't always be easy. Sometimes he'll be mean and pushy, and I'll have to stand my ground until he finds a way around it. He probably will, too. He'll always try to outsmart me, try to find alternative paths to getting his way, even when I don't want to give it to him. That doesn't annoy me, though. That has been our dynamic since day one; I'm almost looking forward to taking him on again and again.

Whatever life with Carter will be like, it will *never* be boring.

EPILOGUE
ONE YEAR LATER

"WHAT I'M SAYING IS, you can't blame the psychiatrist in the study for incorrectly diagnosing. The pseudo-patients *made up* a schizophrenic episode in order to get admitted to the hospital. Just because they didn't exhibit symptoms when—"

"Psychiatrists, *plural*. Are you really going to tell me there's not one competent person in that hospital who would have noticed, hey, wait, this person seems totally healthy and not schizophrenic at all?"

Gaping, Max rears back dramatically in his chair. "Except for the *schizophrenic episode* that got them admitted, you mean? So, what, we're supposed to completely throw out the behavior if they act normal tomorrow? Should we just go on a day-by-day basis? Hey, I know you committed a mass murder yesterday, but today you dropped a dollar in the Salvation Army bell ringer's shiny red pail, so now you're a-okay."

I grin as Cadence grabs her head like it might explode from the mounting frustration of conversing with him. The study sessions for my psychology class are always intense, and Max and Cadence are *always* at each other's throats. They've never met an issue they could agree on, and it's so entertaining to watch them fight to the death, we've literally started bringing popcorn.

While they continue to go at it, Lucis moves the bowl toward me invitingly. Flashing him a conspiratorial smile, I grab a handful of popcorn and reach for my phone to check the time. My smile drops along with my heart when it lights up and I see the time.

I was supposed to leave 16 minutes ago.

"Shit." Shoving the popcorn in my mouth and slamming my notebook shut, I start to gather my things.

Noticing movement, Max tears his attention away from Cadence and glances my way. "What do you think, Zoey?"

"I can see both sides of the issue, honestly, but I don't have time to debate. I did not realize what time it was. I have to go."

"What?" Cadence demands, wide-eyed. "But we're right in the middle of this, and we haven't even finished reviewing the material. We've got finals this week, you can't *leave.*"

"I have to," I tell them, shoving the last of my things into my messenger bag and dragging it over my head. "It's date night."

"Date night? Isn't that something middle-aged, married women have once they've stopped having regular sex?" Lucis demands, cocking a dark eyebrow at me as I pull on my coat.

I slant him a look as I button up my coat. "Trust me, I have not stopped having regular sex."

Cadence snickers while Lucis rolls his eyes. "Come on, stay," he implores. "Carter won't actually die if he has to entertain himself for one evening. I promise."

"Seriously, you can't ditch us for *date night*," Max mocks. "Just text him and tell him you'll be another hour."

Cadence grabs a fistful of popcorn and comments to Max, "I love that movie, though. Have you ever seen it? With Tina Fey. So funny."

I don't bother telling them if I text Carter and try to put him off, he'll show up at our study group and haul me out of here over his shoulder like an uncivilized caveman. Instead, I flash them a smile, let them think date nights are a lame establishment for stale relationships, and leave them with a wave, knowing otherwise.

To make matters even worse, my walk home takes a few minutes longer than usual. It has been snowing all day, light fluffy flakes, but all those flakes add up. A few inches cover the slick sidewalk with more coming down, catching in my hair and all over my coat.

It may take a little longer, but I *love* when it snows in the city. Big snow, little snow, I'm still so enchanted by the chill in the air and the sight of the white flakes against the backdrop of skyscrapers and the dark night sky… there's nothing better. I can't decide if I like fall or winter up here better, but I was definitely right when I thought how nice it would be to have both.

The door is unlocked when I make it back to the apartment. We usually keep it locked even if we are at home. Our building is safe, but just as an added precaution. Carter must have unlocked it to save me an extra minute fiddling with the key. That means he has definitely noticed I am running late.

I kick off my boots and pluck off my hat as soon as I get in the door. Lisa, our nanny, stands at the sink, cleaning up from dinner and post-dinner snacks.

"Hey, Lisa," I say warmly.

It was quite a feat convincing Carter to hire a nanny, but I told him we would take every precaution to make sure we didn't hire anyone unsafe. I put this poor woman through extensive interviews myself, contacted every single reference she could scrounge up, and even interviewed the now-grown children she nannied for early in her career. Lisa is a grandmother, a retired teacher, and a lovely addition to our family. Chloe just loves her, and I know the feeling is mutual.

"Oooh, you're late," Lisa jokes, flashing me a smile over her shoulder as I peel off my coat.

"I know," I say on a sigh. "I got caught up and lost track of time. Thank you for doin' the dishes," I add, before hustling toward the bedroom.

As I approach the bedrooms, I hear Chloe's voice, haltingly sounding out words as she helps Carter read her bedtime story. She's in kindergarten now and she's got all the words on her kindergarten word sheet memorized, but her level readers like to throw her a curve ball every now and then, depending on the story.

"What?" Carter demands playfully when she gets it completely wrong. "That word doesn't start with a B."

I peek my head in just in time to see Chloe throw her hands down on the book and sigh. "I get confused sometimes!"

Carter leans in and rubs her back, then leans over the book. "It's all right, just slow down." Pointing at a spot on the page, he asks, "What letter is that?"

"That one's a D. Sometimes I get the B and D mixed up when they're lower case."

"No big deal. I did too, when I was your age. So, what's the D sound?"

I sigh quietly to myself, then leave them to finish their story so I can go get ready for our date. I wanted to take a shower before we left since the snow did a number on my hair, but I don't have time now. We can always take a nice, hot shower together when we get back home.

By the time Carter makes it in, I'm standing at my sink in the master bath, putting my earrings in. I catch his gaze in the mirror and smile at him.

"How did the bedtime story go?"

"She's just about got all these level readers memorized, we're gonna have to get her some new ones."

"Pretty sure Santa has that taken care of," I tell him.

"Mm," he murmurs, wrapping his arms around me from behind. "You're the sexiest Santa I've ever seen."

Winking at him in the mirror, I tell him, "Wait until you see my Christmas lingerie."

"I thought it might *be* Christmas before you got here," he informs me. "Study session run long again tonight?"

"Yeah. It's still going," I tell him, bumping my butt against him to move him back so I can open my drawer and grab some Chapstick to run over my lips. "I told them I had to bail early for date night and they made fun of me."

Cocking an eyebrow, he points out, "It wasn't early. You said it would be over an hour ago."

"I know," I say on a sigh, capping my Chapstick and putting it back. "Max and Candace started fighting about the case study and… it just became a whole thing. You should just let me study with Lucis and leave the other two out of it, then there'd be fewer distractions and I'd get home a lot sooner."

"Yeah, right. Lucis would keep you out just as late flirting with you," he states.

"He doesn't flirt with me," I murmur.

"He wants to fuck you."

"You always think someone wants to fuck me. You're biased by your own personal interest in fucking me."

His arms tighten and he smiles, kissing my neck and sending a thrill down my spine. "Damn right, I want to fuck you. I would right now if we weren't already running late." Releasing me and disappearing into the other room, Carter lets me finish getting ready.

Or, I think he's leaving to let me finish getting ready, but then he comes back holding a small black case. He cracks it open, draws out a little black and silver bullet vibrator, and hands it to me.

"What is this?" I ask, inspecting the toy since I've never seen it before.

"Early Christmas present. Put it in."

"Right now? We're already late."

In response, he grabs the soft fabric of my little black dress and draws it up over my ass and around my waist. My body throbs with interest as he bunches the fabric in one hand and runs his palm over my ass. "Right now."

Well, all right, then. I push down my panties and push the little bullet vibrator inside me. Once I've finished, I hit the light and join Carter in the bedroom, but frown when I see him slipping on his coat.

"What are you doing?"

He glances back at me and cocks an eyebrow. "Putting my coat on. If you want to see the Rockettes, we need to get the hell out of here."

"But... I have the..." I glance toward the hall, even though I know Chloe can't hear us. "I have the *thing* in."

Carter smirks at me. "I know."

I widen my eyes pointedly, but before I have to ask, he reaches into his pocket and draws out a matching black and silver circular object.

"Wireless remote," he explains. "We're going to have a little fun tonight."

My heart skips a beat as I follow him out of the bedroom. "In public?"

"Wherever, whenever I want," he says.

Mm, that sounds intriguing. "You're tryin' to get me put on the naughty list, aren't you?" I ask, following after him. "Santa isn't gonna bring me anything but a lump of coal this year."

"That's okay, I give better presents than he does, anyway." Glancing back over his shoulder, he says, "You're lucky it has limited range, I'd make you wear it to study sessions. Every time I have a hunch Lucis is doing something that would irritate me..." He reaches into his pocket, and a moment later I jump, startled by the jolt of vibration inside me. Damn, for a little bullet massager, this thing has oomph.

"Scandalous," I tell him, breathing a sigh of relief when he turns it off just before we approach Lisa. "Hey, I could always invite Lucis to study here sometime," I tease. "He and I could study in the privacy of the bedroom, while you—"

"Keep it up," Carter says.

I grin, speeding up so I can hug him from behind. "You know I'm just teasin' you."

"It's all fun and games until I fuck up someone's life," he half-jokes.

"Don't you dare. He's my TA, he might revenge-grade my papers."

He turns, catching me around the waist and drawing me against him. "Plus, you only want me."

"Naturally," I say, winding my arms around his neck and gazing up at him. "How could I ever want anyone else?"

He smiles faintly and pecks me on the lips, then with much more force, he smacks me on the ass. "Get your coat so we can leave."

I THINK New York is wonderful all year, but it's especially lovely during the Christmas season. Since we have tickets for an eight o'clock show and we're clear across town, Carter gets us a cab when we leave the apartment. When we leave Radio City after the show, though, we're close enough to walk to our dinner reservations.

Tucking my arm through Carter's as we stroll down the street, I lean my head on his shoulder and muse, "We should go ice skating in front of the tree like we did last year."

"We will," he assures me. "I have a whole anniversary date planned. I'm just waiting for finals to be over so you won't be as stressed."

"I'm not stressed," I deny. "There's just so much information to remember. I want to finish my first semester strong so they don't regret lettin' me in."

Wrapping an arm around my shoulders and pulling me into his side, he says, "No one's going to regret letting you in. You're smart enough to be here even without the nudging we did on your behalf; you don't have to kill yourself studying now that you're here. The world won't end if you don't have a perfect GPA. Once you graduate and you're in the field, it won't even matter what your GPA was."

"It's not all about my GPA. It's important information I'll need to know later, in med school and when I'm practicing."

"Some of it is. Other stuff is filler. How often do you think you'll need to be able to quote Socrates? Yet, you spent all last night jamming ancient Greek philosophy into your head. It's crowded up there, save space for what matters and give yourself a break."

"Maybe I'll have a patient who is obsessed with the Socratic method, and my in-depth knowledge will be the key to figuring out his problems," I suggest primly.

Carter smiles and tugs me closer so he can kiss the crown of my head. "If that ever happens, I'll eat my words. But assuming it won't, at least take it easy in the fluff classes."

Largely inspired by my experiences with Carter and then reaffirmed by conversations I had with university faculty, I decided to pursue a career in behavioral sciences. It's going to mean a lot of school, but eventually I want to be trained to help those at-risk for problematic behaviors, and counsel people whose general mentalities err more toward the abnormal.

Carter lucked out by finding me, but if some other girl had crossed his path, I don't know where either of them might have ended up.

Years down the road, I'll be Dr. Ellis, and I'll be able to help people with their problems while doing something that interests me, too. It's the perfect career for me, and with Carter's dad paying for my undergrad study, I won't be afraid of any potential debt I might incur pursuing my PH.D. either. Plus, Lucis is on the same path, and he has already told me I could work as a TA while I'm doing my grad work.

I can't hold back a little sigh. There's plenty of day-to-day stuff I could stress over, but ultimately, so much is going right in my life, and I would rather focus on that.

Giving me a light squeeze, Carter asks, "What's that sigh for?"

"I'm just happy. Everything is so perfect right now. Even this snow," I add, holding my hand out to catch a few crystal flakes on my cashmere glove. Peering up at him with a smile, I tell him, "I love our life."

"So do I."

Carter opens the heavy black door for me when we get to the upscale steakhouse where we're having dinner. One of his friends owns the place, so we have a standing reservation. There are black, leather-upholstered seats lining each wall of the entrance cove, both of them completely full of people. Carter puts a hand at the small of my back and walks straight to the hostess stand.

"Reservation for two. Carter Mahoney."

The hostess looks up, her gaze nearly as sharp as her jawline until she sees Carter, then her face softens into a little smile. Disinterestedly, she flicks a glance at me. I flash her a smile that she doesn't bother returning, then she consults her list, doesn't find what she's looking for, and looks back at him. "What time were you supposed to be here?"

"Whenever I show up," he states, a touch arrogantly, given her dismissal of me. "Other list, sweetheart."

Her posture is already astounding, but she stiffens at his tone. Flipping that list, she consults a much shorter list behind it. "Ah, there it is." Covering the exclusive list back up, she grabs two menus and leaves her hostess stand. "If you'll just follow me, Mr. Mahoney."

The hostess walks us through the crowded restaurant, past the bar dotted with well-dressed women and men in suits, or at least dress shirts and ties if they've taken their jackets off. I'm not sure if there's an actual dress code here, or just an unspoken understanding that it's not civilized to show up in jeans if you're going to spend this much on a steak.

The reserved seats are the ones you never have to wait for, and also the best seats in the place. We're escorted up a floor and led back to a private corner, removed from the noise and chatter that filled the dining room downstairs. The hostess waits for us to take our seats, then she hands us our menus and removes the additional place settings. She comes back to light the candle on the table between us and fill our water goblets, then she tells us our server will be over in just a few moments.

We look over the menu for a few minutes, but I usually get the same thing. There are no prices on the menu, thank goodness, because I know from accidentally seeing the bill last time we stopped in for drinks and dessert, they would make me lose my appetite. This place has my favorite dessert in the city, though. An incredible slice of chocolate cake. That's it, just chocolate cake, but I don't know what is *done* to the cake. Obviously, it is dipped in sin and sprinkled with ecstasy, because it is the loveliest thing my taste buds have ever come into contact with.

My mouth waters just thinking about it. Our waitress finally comes our way, but she's carrying a tray and we haven't ordered yet. I glance around, but there are no other diners in our little nook, so she must be bringing it to us.

Smiling, she puts the tray down in front of us. It's a tray of caviar with two glasses of champagne.

"Oh, we didn't order…"

The waitress is already nodding. "On the house."

Carter smirks, unrolling his napkin full of utensils. "He saw us."

I sigh, much less amused. "He's here."

The waitress stifles a knowing smile, then asks, "Did you two need a minute to look over the menu, or…?"

"Nope, we're all set," Carter tells her, then proceeds to order our food.

Once the waitress is gone, I eye the caviar, but only reach for the champagne. "If he's gonna send over free food, he should skip the foreplay and send me cake."

Amused, Carter assures me, "You'll get your cake after we eat."

"I'll take pre-dinner cake *and* cake for dessert. There's never enough cake. I would like cake in a house, I would like cake with a mouse. I would like cake here or there. I would like cake anywhere."

"No more Dr. Seuss bedtime stories for you," Carter tells me.

I shake my head. "I have to train my brain to stop memorizing everything my eyeballs skate across more than once."

I'm not a big fan of caviar at all, but I'm so hungry, I eat a little of it while we're waiting for our food. Other than popcorn at study group, I haven't eaten anything all day, so the single glass of champagne makes me a little loopy.

I process everything more slowly when I'm tipsy, so it takes until a moment after the scent of expensive cologne and bad decisions wafts my way, then I sense trouble standing behind me.

I tip my head back gracelessly and tip backward in my chair, my back pressing into the knuckles of the man standing there with a firm grip on my chair.

His blue eyes gleam with amusement as he looks down at me. "Hello, Zoey."

"You sent over strong champagne," I say accusingly.

"I sent over *Cristal*. You're a lightweight."

"I think it's extra strength champagne," I tell him argumentatively.

"With your discerning palate, I'm shocked Zagat hasn't recruited you yet," he deadpans. Dismissing me, he looks across the table at Carter. "You sure you want to bother with food? I think you have her in an ideal state already. Just clear out of here and head home. Your job is done."

"I'm not leaving until I've eaten my weight in chocolate cake," I state, holding onto the edge of the table so I can sit back up.

"How about one piece?" he suggests, openly looking down at my breasts, then letting his gaze drift over the rest of my body. "Hate to see you lose that lovely shape."

"Ugh. I hate you."

He grins, utterly pleased with himself, then turns his attention to Carter. They bullshit for a few minutes, and I zone out, thinking about all the presents I still have to wrap.

Now that Chloe lives with us, we essentially have a child, so Christmas is a pretty big deal. This being her first Christmas with us on top of it, I went way overboard on presents in a bid to make the change easier. The presents are mostly stashed in the unused cabinets under the marble counter in my walk-in closet. Chloe never goes in there, so it was the only feasible hiding spot.

I need to get bows. I have lots of wrapping paper and glittery nametags, but no bows. I pull out my phone to order some bows, but before I can shop, I see a message from Lucis.

"Study group is tedious without you."

I'm not sober enough to guard my phone from potential misinterpretations, and my awkwardly slower reflexes do not help me tilt it away quickly enough when Carter's stupid asshole friend leans down and asks, "Who is Lucis, and why does he miss you so much?"

"Have you ever heard of privacy?" I ask him.

"Have you ever considered not being a cocktease?" he shoots back.

My eyes widen in disbelief. "I am not a cocktease."

"He sends you unmitigated longing completely unprovoked, then?" he questions, arching a golden eyebrow.

"That is not what that message was. You're twisting it up to cause trouble."

"I'm not trying to cause any trouble. Just pointing out that this guy wants to fuck you on the off-chance Carter didn't already know."

"See," Carter says, nodding smugly and leaning across the table. "Give me that fucking thing. I have some words for Lucis."

I cradle the phone protectively, then sneak it back into my purse before anyone can humiliate me. "Absolutely not. He's the TA in my psych class and he doesn't wanna fuck me." Before either of them can disagree, I add, "And even if he *does*, it doesn't matter. I am happily on the inside of a committed relationship. You can't honestly think I'm goin' anywhere."

"I don't, but I don't like him sending you texts like that. It's disrespectful." Carter's hand is still out, waiting for the phone. "Hand it over."

I shake my head. "No. All he said was that study group was boring without me, it's nothing scandalous."

"Oh, yeah? That's funny; according to you, Max and Cadence are the main sources of study group entertainment. But it's boring without you there?"

Asshole Face doesn't help, offering, "Must not be able to stroke his cock to thoughts of either of them."

Glaring up at him, I ask, "Don't you have actual work to do?"

"Nah," he says, grabbing a chair from a nearby table and pulling it up to ours. "I can join you, if you'd like?"

"I wouldn't like," I inform him. "I wouldn't like at all."

Shaking his head, Carter grabs his champagne glass and takes a drink. "I don't like Lucis," he informs me.

"He doesn't like you either."

"Well, of course not, I get to fuck you and he only gets to dream about it," Carter replies. "I wouldn't expect him to like me."

Smiling faintly, I shake my head. I know he's not really as worked up about Lucis as he pretends to be, he just likes the drama. He likes the surge of jealousy, the friction and the play fighting. Then when he gets me home, he'll throw me down on the bed, devour me, and fuck me with the kind of sensual violence Lucis never would.

One of the many reasons he knows he doesn't have to worry about Lucis or anybody else.

Still, Carter likes his games, and I don't mind playing them. I especially won't mind later, when he's punishing me with his body, and I feel freer and sexier for it.

My blood warms with the mental images of what he'll do to me in bed later, and suddenly I *am* ready to forego the cake—and the food—to go home now. Can't do that, so instead, I reach back into my purse and draw out my phone. Lacking any attempt at stealth, I start typing out a text.

I feel Carter's eyes on me, then my body responds like it's been hit by a jolt of electricity when his voice drops low and he asks, "Who are you texting?"

I look up at him innocently. "Who do you think?"

A hint of pleasure glistens in his eyes right before he narrows them at me. "Delete the message and put the phone away."

"Or what?"

Carter cocks an eyebrow at me, then he reaches into his pocket. The vibrator comes to life inside me and I jump, startled. Taking a shallow breath, I shift, trying to get my bearings, but it's difficult not to squirm noticeably as the little bullet stimulates the most sensitive part of my body.

I don't know if there's no low setting on this thing or he just ramped it up to punish me, but I'm having the hardest time sitting still. Even my breathing is hard to control already, my body wanting to respond naturally to the pleasure triggered by the vibration.

I clench and unclench my hands, struggling to hold in helpless noises that are just begging to escape my throat. His friend is watching me, his blue eyes narrowed with suspicion. I'll die if he figures out what Carter just did, but I'm not being as subtle as I'd like to be, either.

Casting my boyfriend a pleading gaze across the table, I silently beg him to turn it off.

Carter cocks a dark eyebrow, silently challenging me to obey him or endure the consequences.

I close my eyes, attempting to summon every unsexy thought I can muster, but pleasure moves through me in waves and it's a physical challenge to hold it in.

This is torture.

Jittery and barely able to keep my shit together, I tap my screen, erase the message I was going to send, and flash Carter the screen as proof.

"There, it's gone," I snap, a little breathless.

"Good girl," he says, more than mildly amused.

Every muscle in my body taut with the effort of holding back an orgasm, I wait for him to reach into his pocket and turn it off, but damn him, he reaches for his champagne and takes a slow sip instead.

My eyes widen in betrayed disbelief, then narrow as I glare at him. "Carter…"

"Yes, princess?" he asks, as if innocent.

"Aren't you forgetting something?"

Pretending to consider, he rubs his chin. "Hm, I don't think so."

If we were at home, the bullet vibrator probably wouldn't be so potent, but the knowledge that we're in public and his friend is standing right here, watching Carter toy with me…

Fuck, I'm going to come. I don't want anyone to notice, but I squeeze the edge of the table and close my eyes as the pressure builds and builds, as I approach—

Just before I get there, he turns it off.

I groan and let out a breath of frustration, sinking back in my chair and glaring at Carter.

His hand comes out of his pocket, and he smirks at me across the table. "Something wrong, baby?"

I could growl, I'm so irritated. Uncaring of how it looks, I push back my chair, storm over to Carter's side of the table, and grab him by the arm. He doesn't stop me as I literally drag him out of his chair, in front of his friend, and toward the bathroom.

"Don't you want to grab your purse?" he asks, letting me drag him.

"Fuck my purse," I snap, picking up the pace as my insides clench around nothing, desperate to be filled.

We barely make it inside the bathroom. It doesn't even offer the privacy of a single stall restroom, it's a whole row of stalls that anyone could be inside or come in to use, but I don't care. I close my eyes as he takes control, roughly grabbing my arms and backing me up against the wall. Fire ignites low in my belly at the familiar signal that it's go-time.

"Kiss me," I say breathlessly, half demand, half plea.

He leans in close, pressing his body against mine, making me feel the enticing heat rolling off his well-sculpted body. "Now, princess, is that how you ask?"

I'm too turned on to play resistance games, so I don't. "Please."

Just like that, his mouth is covering mine, my body weakening as my mind is assaulted by an explosion of pleasure. Our tongues tangle for a few seconds, then he wrestles mine into submission, bringing a hand up to palm my breast through the fabric. I gasp into his mouth, my body so sensitive already from the pleasure he ignited inside me back at the table.

"Please, Carter, I need you," I tell him, digging my fingers into his back, trying to pull him closer.

Carter bends his head to kiss my neck, sending yet another frenzy of pleasure coursing through me. As he works magic on my neck, he reaches between my legs, slides a finger inside me, and removes the bullet, catching my moans against his mouth.

He slips the small toy into the pocket of his slacks, then goes to drag my panties down. I free up a hand and reach down to help, to try to push the damn things off faster, causing Carter to chuckle.

"Someone's eager."

"You're so mean," I tell him. "Do you know how close I was?"

Grinning evilly as he gets my panties off, he says, "Yes."

He shoves my panties into the same pocket. I get the feeling he's not going to give them back, but I don't care. I have no need for panties, only for him. I look down, as eager as he accused me of being, as he unbuttons his pants and frees his cock from the dastardly constraints of his clothing.

Yes, yes, yes, that's what I want.

Carter's hand slides down my side, then he braces both hands under my butt and lifts me. I wrap my legs around him and don't even attempt to hold back a moan, throwing my head back as he swiftly pushes himself inside me. Knowing I'm already warmed up, he only gives me a few seconds to adjust to the invasion, then he picks up a steady pace, withdrawing and thrusting mercilessly, just the way we both like.

"Look at me," he demands, since my head is still tipped back, my eyes closed.

I hold on to his broad shoulders for strength and coax my

eyes open, bringing my gaze back to his. His brown eyes are so beautiful, so intense as he pulls back then thrusts forward, angling his hips and forcing his cock even deeper inside me. I moan again, my head falling back. It's too hard to keep it upright, but I try. I bring my gaze back to him and hold it there, hissing through my teeth as he pounds me again and again and again.

"Tell me you love me," he demands.

That's a no-brainer. I can barely open my mouth fast enough for the words to tumble out. "I love you. I love you so much."

Even though he knows that already, I can see that my vehemence satisfies him. To reward me, he crushes his lips against mine, tangling one hand in my hair and cradling my head in his large hand. His kiss is as unrelenting as his thrusts and every bit as mind-melting. My brain ceases to function as he fucks me against this wall, my senses of right and wrong, of modesty, of basic human decency falling away like unnecessary baggage. The door could fly open right now and I would still beg him to keep going.

For this, I don't have to beg. Not tonight. He slams into me until I can't take it anymore, until I'm crying out his name in pleasure and finally flying over the edge into ecstasy.

My body is boneless as I come back down. My head is even harder to hold up now, so I let it fall forward against his shoulder. Carter's eyes are closed too, one hand braced on the bathroom wall like he needs it to help him remain on his feet, but he's still supporting all of my weight, too, so he must not.

"Fuck," he mutters, then presses a kiss to the side of my face.

Sighing blissfully, I offer him a loopy smile. "I don't know about you, but I feel much better."

Carter chuckles, pulling me in for a hug. Once we've both come back down, he eases me down, but doesn't let go until I'm steady with both feet on the floor.

I tug my dress down, then cast a glance toward the thankfully empty bathroom stalls. "I should probably clean up."

"Nope. You keep my cum inside you and get your disobedient little ass back to the table."

I slide him a stern look, but he ruins it completely by

smacking me hard on the ass and making me jump. "Can I at least have my panties back?" I request.

"No."

"I figured as much," I mutter.

When we return to the table, his friend has left and the waitress hasn't yet returned. Thankfully, we are alone in this corner, so my purse remains on the floor where I left it and my phone is still on the table. Not that anyone who can afford to eat here is likely to steal purses, I guess, but it was still irresponsible to leave my belongings and run to the bathroom for a quickie.

Worth it, though. Even if someone had run off with my purse, it would have been worth it.

Pleasantly satisfied, I take my seat and sip my expensive champagne. I'm certain I finished my glass already, but someone must have refilled it because now it's a little over half full.

Now that our sexual needs have been met, Carter doesn't pick pretend fights with me over texts from a man incapable of making him feel threatened. Lucis texts me again, but I can't even bring myself to care enough to read it. I'll get to it later... or tomorrow. At some point.

The waitress brings out our steaks and reminds me why I come to this place, even though Carter's friend is such a nuisance and the prices are so high. The steak is so perfectly cooked, so amazingly tender, it practically melts in my mouth as I'm chewing. The whole time I'm eating it, I feel like I'm cloaked in a blissful blanket of all around satisfaction.

By the time my cake comes out, I might as well be walking on sunshine. Usually, Carter and I share a dessert, but he knows when it comes to this cake, I want my own. He orders a slice for both of us, but only takes a few bites of his and then has it boxed up so I can have it tomorrow. He's the best.

I'm still a little buzzed from the champagne and sex when we leave the restaurant. I'm leaning on Carter a little more heavily than I mean to, but I'm getting tired. It's been a long day, and all I want to do is go home and curl up in bed with him.

"Thank you for a lovely date night," I tell him, as we walk back toward Rockefeller Center.

"You're welcome," he says, subtly checking his watch. "We need to pick up the pace a bit."

"Why?" I murmur sleepily. "I'm tired. We should get a cab."

"Because if we don't hurry, we're going to miss the last light show."

"Light show?" I gasp, suddenly realizing why we are heading back toward Rockefeller Center. "Will we make it?"

"Starts in three minutes," he tells me.

I love the Christmas light show at Sak's Fifth Avenue, and Carter knows it. It reminds me of the light show and fireworks at Disney World this past summer when we took Chloe. She was almost too tired to hold her little head up by that point, falling asleep in Carter's lap while we sat on the ground to give our feet a rest. Then the show started, and she rallied the last bit of energy her tiny body could muster. She gazed in awe at the projections on the castle, eagerly watching with magic reflected in her eyes as fireworks lit up the sky above.

At Christmas, we get just a little bit of that here. Chloe loves the light show, too. We've brought her a few times since the season started, but tonight, it's nice that it's just me and Carter.

We make it just in time for the last show to start. There's a smaller crowd of people than there has been when we've come earlier. Carter stands behind me and wraps his arms around my waist, pulling me back against him as we watch the light show. He's still feeling affectionate, rubbing his thumb over my knuckles, then twining our fingers together while he holds me.

I lean my head back against his shoulder, sighing contentedly. "I love you, Carter."

I feel his warm breath on the side of my face as he murmurs, "I love you, too. I have one more early Christmas present for you."

I grin up at the building as I tell him, "If you keep this up, there won't be anything left to put under the tree."

"Then I'll just buy more," he says, simply.

"You're spoilin' me, Carter Mahoney."

"I'm always going to spoil you," he promises. "You deserve to be spoiled."

I reach my hand back to caress his face, but when I do, I

freeze, seeing something on my finger catch the light. I didn't put my gloves on when I left the restaurant so my hands are so cold, I can barely feel them. When I turn my wrist, my wide eyes land on a gorgeous diamond and aquamarine ring that has appeared on my left hand.

"Carter..." I trail off uncertainly, then look back at him.

He turns me around, capturing the hand he sneakily slid the ring on. Holding my gaze, he brings the hand to his lips and kisses my knuckles. Then, still holding onto my hand, he drops to one knee.

I gasp, and so do a few people in the crowd around us. A helpless grin splits my face, happiness welling up inside me like a volcano that's about to explode.

"I'm sure you already know you're the best thing that's ever happened to me. I can't imagine what my life would have been like without you, and even if I could, I wouldn't want to. You're my partner, my best friend, and the only thing in this world I can't afford to lose." He offers me a little smile, knowing the answer even before the words leave his perfect lips. "Zoey Ellis, will you spend the rest of your life with me?"

"Yes, yes, yes, yes, yes, yes, yes," I say rapidly, nodding and grinning. Then, saying to hell with it, I throw my arms around his neck and tackle him.

He manages to stay upright even with me coming down on top of him. He catches my weight in his arms, holding me against his chest and smirking down at me. "You sure?"

I squeeze him harder, then pull back, allowing myself a moment to actually look at and admire this beautiful ring. It's not an ordinary engagement ring; the main stone is pale blue in color —aquamarine, not a diamond. The diamonds are set around the band and in a halo around the main stone. It's the perfect ring for a winter proposal. The perfect ring, period. I've never seen a prettier ring, and I'm not just saying that because this one is for me, from Carter.

Well, maybe I am, but it doesn't matter. I maintain that it's the most beautiful ring in the world, and he's the most wonderful man in the world, and if I get any happier tonight, I will literally explode.

Sighing and winding my arms around his neck again, I lean in and give him a big kiss. There are some responses from the people still gathered around, some chuckles and awws, one person inexplicably recording this on their phone, like the moment belongs to them.

It doesn't matter. They could project this proposal on the building like they did the light show and I wouldn't mind. All that matters is that we found each other, that we make each other happy, that he loves me so much, he wants to marry me.

And I love him, too. I love everything about him, the good, the bad, and the in between. And now I know with an unshakable certainty, we get to spend the rest of our lives together.

That's pretty damn lucky, if you ask me.

THE END

I hope you enjoyed Carter and Zoey's story!

Next, I recommend checking out Hunter and Riley's story, *The Boy on the Bridge*! Their story takes place in the same universe, and you never know—you might even see a familiar face or two. ;)

ALSO BY SAM MARIANO

In this gripping dark romance series, Mia Mitchell's life changes forever when she witnesses a crime and gets sucked into the dark, twisted games of Chicago's notorious Morelli crime family. This series has a little bit of everything: scorching sexual tension, twists and turns around every corner, and an epic journey to happily ever after. Make *Accidental Witness* your next read and find out how the villain gets the girl!

Accidental Witness (Morelli Family, #1)

Amazon: http://amzn.to/2hUyVk2

Amazon UK: My Book

Amazon CA: My Book

Amazon AU: My Book

ALSO BY SAM MARIANO

Contemporary romance standalones

The Boy on the Bridge (second chance bully romance) I recommend reading this one after Untouchable!

Descent (dark billionaire romance)

Resisting Mr. Granville (steamy forbidden romance)

The Imperfections (forbidden romance)

Stitches (MFM ménage romance)

How the Hitman Stole Christmas (steamy, darkly funny, a pinch of mafia)

Mistletoe Kisses (student-teacher romance)

Coming-of-age, contemporary bully duet

Because of You

After You

Forbidden, taboo romance

Irreparable Duet

And the **Coastal Elite** series features a dark hero even crazier than Carter. Meet Dare in ***Even if it Hurts***!

ABOUT THE AUTHOR

Sam Mariano has a soft spot for the bad guys (in fiction, anyway). She loves to write edgy, twisty reads with complicated characters you're left thinking about long after you turn the last page. Her favorite thing about indie publishing is the ability to play by your own rules! If she isn't reading one of the thousands of books on her to-read list, writing her next book, or playing with her adorable kindergartener... actually, that's about all she has time for these days.

Feel free to find Sam on Facebook (Sam Mariano's General Reader Group), Goodreads, Instagram, or her blog—she loves hearing from readers! She's also available on TikTok now @sam-marianobooks, and you can sign up for her totally-not-spammy newsletter HERE

If you have the time and inclination to leave a review, however short or long, she would greatly appreciate it! :)

Made in the USA
Columbia, SC
22 June 2025

59672372R00270